Across the Arno

THE OLTRARNO PASSAGES
BOOK ONE

MICHAEL MANOSCA

Visit the author's website at www.michaelmanosca.com

Across the Arno

The Oltrarno Passages - Book 1

ISBN:

978-1-969915-13-0 (paperback)

978-1-969915-15-4 (electronic)

978-1-969915-14-7 (hardcover)

Library of Congress Control Number: 2026903652

First Edition.

Los Angeles, California, United States of America

"In the middle of the journey of our life, I found myself in a dark wood, for the straight way was lost."

— Dante Alighieri, *Inferno* (14th century, Florentine)

Prologue

THE PHONE CALL that changes everything never announces itself.

Graham was in the kitchen when it came. Tuesday morning. Snow falling outside in that quiet Maine way—steady, unhurried, as if it had all the time in the world.

He'd been about to set up the coffee maker when he caught himself. Simon wouldn't be home for hours yet—the flight, the drive back from Logan, traffic if they hit it wrong. No point in brewing it now. It would just sit there going stale, and Simon would complain about it the way he complained about everything Graham did in the kitchen. *You can write a seven-book series set in Renaissance Florence, but you can't figure out a coffee maker.* Graham always told him that was what husbands were for—to make the coffee, to complain about the coffee, to drink it anyway because it was made with love.

Thirty years of that routine. Thirty years of Simon reaching for a mug Graham had filled.

He set up the timer instead. Programmed it for 5:30, which would give the coffee time to brew before they walked in the door. Simon would drop his bag in the hallway—always the hallway, never the bedroom where it belonged—and make a beeline for the kitchen, and the coffee would be ready. Perfect.

Simon had been gone five days. A conference in London. Some academic thing about Renaissance art restoration that Graham pretended to understand and Simon pretended Graham's pretending was convincing. They'd been doing that dance for three decades—Simon, the scholar, the art historian, the one who could talk for hours about the influence of Florentine banking on Medici patronage; Graham, the writer, the observer, the one who turned Simon's passion into fiction and set it in the streets of the Oltrarno.

That's how the books had started, actually. Simon would come home from a conference or a research trip, eyes bright, talking a mile a minute about some fresco he'd seen or some archive he'd unearthed, and Graham would listen. Really listen. And somewhere in the listening, stories would form. Characters would emerge. A world would build itself in Graham's mind—Renaissance Florence, with its artists and merchants and quiet intrigues—and he'd write.

Simon called himself Graham's muse. Graham called Simon his encyclopedia. They were both right.

He'd be home today. Flight landing at 3:15 at Logan. Graham had checked it twice this morning—on time, no delays, cruising somewhere over the Atlantic at forty thousand feet. He'd leave in about an hour. The drive took nearly two on a good day, longer if traffic decided to be a bastard, and Graham would park in the cell phone lot and wait, the way he always did. Simon would text when he'd landed, text again when he'd cleared customs, and Graham would pull around to the curb. Simon would toss his bag in the back, slide into the passenger seat, and lean over for a kiss—quick, familiar, the kind of kiss that said *I'm home* without needing words—and some Logan Airport traffic cop would already be blowing his whistle at them to move it along. Every single time.

Thirty years, and it still made Graham smile.

He'd already planned dinner. That roast Simon loved—the one that took all afternoon, the one Graham only made for special occasions. Coming home from five days away counted as special. The wine was breathing on the counter. He'd even bought flowers, which Simon would tease him about because Graham buying flowers was roughly as common as Graham voluntarily attending an opera.

Graham stood at the kitchen window and watched the snow accumulate on the bird feeder Simon had installed last spring. They'd spent an entire Saturday arguing about the placement—Simon wanted it where he could see it from his reading chair; Graham wanted it where the squirrels couldn't reach it. Simon won, because Simon usually won, and now Graham filled the damn thing every morning and pretended he didn't enjoy watching the cardinals come.

Eight more hours. Less, really. Simon was already in the air, already on his way home. Graham just had to get through the morning, drive to Boston, wait in the cell phone lot. Easy.

The phone rang.

He almost didn't answer. He was watching the snow, thinking about the chapter he'd promised his editor, thinking about whether he'd remembered to take the roast out of the freezer. He had. He'd checked twice. He was thinking about nothing at all.

He answered.

A woman's voice. Calm. Professional. The kind of calm that comes from training—from saying terrible things to strangers so many times that the words become routine.

"Mr. Tierney? I'm calling from British Airways. I'm afraid there's been a medical emergency on your husband's flight."

Graham's hand tightened on the phone. His eyes went to the window, to the snow, to the bird feeder. As if any of those things could anchor him to the moment before—the moment when Simon was still alive, still coming home, still leaning over for that kiss in the passenger seat.

"A doctor on board administered CPR. They used the portable defibrillator. I'm so sorry, Mr. Tierney."

Sorry. People said that word so easily. Sorry I'm late. Sorry I forgot. Sorry your husband—

"Your husband passed away approximately forty minutes ago. The captain wanted you to be informed before the flight lands."

Passed away. As if Simon had simply stepped out of the room. As if he'd wandered off to find a better view, and Graham only needed to wait for him to wander back.

"The flight is still three and a half hours from Boston. We can have someone meet you at the airport if you'd like, Mr. Tierney. Is there someone who can be with you? Someone we can call?"

Graham said something. He didn't know what. Maybe thank you. Maybe I understand. Maybe nothing at all. The woman kept talking—details, logistics, things he would need to know later—and Graham heard none of it. He was watching the snow fall on the bird feeder Simon had installed. He was looking at the coffee maker he'd programmed for 5:30. He was standing in the kitchen of the home they'd built together, and Simon was forty thousand feet above the Atlantic Ocean, already dead, still in transit.

He set the phone down. Carefully. Gently. As if it might break.

He called Anthony.

Anthony, who had lost Theodore two and a half years ago. Anthony, who understood this particular horror in a way no one else could. Anthony, who had sat in Graham and Simon's living room after the funeral, hollow-eyed and broken, while Simon held his hand and Graham made tea no one drank.

Now it was Graham's turn.

The phone barely rang once. Graham heard himself speaking—words, sounds, something that conveyed the essential information—but his voice seemed to be coming from very far away. Anthony's response was barely audible. A choked sound. A click.

Graham stood in the kitchen. He should do something. Get ready. The airport. He needed to go to the airport. Simon was coming home. He just needed to—

The front door burst open. No knock. Anthony was there, coat half-buttoned, face wet, looking more shattered than Graham felt. Which was strange. Graham didn't feel shattered. Graham didn't feel anything. He was floating somewhere above himself, watching a man who looked like him stand very still in a kitchen while the snow fell outside.

Anthony crossed the room in three steps and wrapped his arms around Graham. Held him. Graham let himself be held, but he didn't cry. Couldn't cry. The tears were somewhere far away, with the rest of his feelings, locked in a box he couldn't access.

"I'll drive," Anthony said. His voice was rough. "Come on. I'll drive."

Graham nodded. That made sense. Someone should drive. He didn't think he could drive. He wasn't sure he could do anything.

They left the house. Graham forgot to turn off the coffee timer. He forgot to put the roast back. He forgot to lock the door. None of it mattered. None of it would ever matter again.

The drive to Logan took forever and no time at all. Graham watched the landscape slide past—snow-covered trees, highway signs, other cars full of other people living other lives—and felt nothing. Anthony kept glancing at him, worried, but didn't speak. There was nothing to say.

At the airport, they parked and walked to the terminal. Inside the doors, a man in a navy British Airways coat stood holding a small placard with Graham's surname written in neat letters. He was young—too young, Graham thought, to be doing this job. To be meeting men whose husbands had died at forty thousand feet.

"Mr. Tierney?" The ambassador's voice was soft. Practiced. "I'm so sorry for your loss. If you'll come with me."

Graham followed. Anthony followed Graham. They were led through a door Graham had never noticed before—a hidden entrance, employee-only—and through a security checkpoint that seemed to want to object but ultimately waved them through. Down a hallway. Into an office that smelled like industrial carpet and grief.

"Your husband's remains—" the ambassador began.

Remains. The word hit Graham like a slap. Remains. As if Simon were leftovers. As if he were something left behind after the important part was gone.

"—will be removed from the aircraft before the other passengers disembark. He'll be taken to our transport facility, and you can meet him there."

Meet him. As if Simon would be waiting. As if Graham could walk into a room and Simon would be there, reaching for his hand, complaining about airplane food, alive.

Graham nodded. Said something appropriate. Thank you. I understand. Whatever words were required.

Anthony's hand found his. Squeezed. Graham squeezed back, but he was still floating, still watching from somewhere far away. This was happening to someone else. This couldn't be happening to him.

Later—hours later, days later, he couldn't say—Graham went home. Anthony drove him. Anthony wanted to stay, but Graham sent him away. He needed to be alone. Needed to stand in the silence and understand that this was real.

The house was dark. He'd forgotten to leave a light on. The coffee maker had brewed at 5:30, right on schedule, and now the pot sat cold and untouched on the counter. The roast was still in the refrigerator. The wine was still breathing. The flowers he'd bought were still in their paper wrapping, waiting to be put in a vase.

Graham didn't cook the roast. Didn't pour out the coffee. Didn't unwrap the flowers.

He just stood in the kitchen, in the dark, in the silence, and looked out the window at the bird feeder Simon had installed. Barely visible now against the snow.

Thirty years. Thirty years of reaching for each other, and now there was no one to reach back.

The world tells you grief gets easier. That time heals. That you'll learn to live with the absence, the way you learn to live with a missing limb—still feeling it there, still reaching for it, but eventually accepting that it's gone.

The world is full of shit.

Eight months later, Graham was still reaching.

Chapter One

THE LINE WAS LONG—LONGER than he'd expected when Graham walked into all the chaos. He normally tried to come here during a quieter time, but he'd finished his Thursday gym session early. His trainer, the man who helped him try and forget the emptiness of his home now that Simon was no longer around, had called in sick. So Graham did a quick routine and decided to drop by Whole Foods on the way home.

At 6:30 at night. What was he thinking?

Graham had joined the gym at the urging of Simon's friends after the world collapsed around him. *Get out of the house.* He spent too much time with the ghosts. He couldn't help that his job literally required him to sit in his home, at the mid-century Danish modern desk he and Simon had designed together—the one in the office with floor-to-ceiling windows that looked over the wooded back of their property just outside Portland. Simon had said the light would give him great joy and help him write stories.

But the stories had disappeared along with Simon.

The gym was supposed to keep him fit, but it was more about keeping his mind from consuming itself. Graham observed everything. That was his job. He wanted to get business cards that simply said "Graham Tierney — Observer." Simon would've loved that.

And there it was again. He couldn't go five minutes without thinking of him.

So—the gym. His trainer. A man slightly older than Graham's fifty-three years, but built like a brick shithouse. Graham always loved throwing in a tidbit of profanity into his stories—nothing gratuitous, but it gave them grit and allowed him to feel a little naughty. Something totally unlike him in person.

His trainer had been assigned to him almost as a gimmie—Graham would be easy, have him do some treadmill and call it a day. But Graham took to the exercises surprisingly well. In fact, his trainer had invited him to join his little crew of bodybuilders. Men who wouldn't normally give the beanpole of a man a second glance, but they'd warmed to Graham. Liked him. Took him under their wings. Taught him a thing or two. Spotting him bench-pressing seventy-five pounds was almost a joke for them, but for Graham, it was serious business, and he was committed. That's what they loved about him. That, and his way with banter. He always had a wit that made them smile.

But tonight, his trainer had the flu. So—calisthenics and some stretches and Graham called it a night.

The Amazon box was more a pain in the ass to return than simply tossing it and ordering another. But he could hear Simon bitch about him being wasteful. It was a sixteen-dollar coffee grinder. And he didn't even drink coffee—hated it, actually. Couldn't stand the smell. But he needed to grind spices for a recipe he was trying to teach himself, something he'd seen Alton Brown make on a rerun. It looked easy watching him do it. But the Amazon delivery guy must have missed that episode, because he'd tossed the package onto the porch with such ferocity that the damn thing arrived dented. Graham could probably still use it, but come on.

So—the chaos of the store. He'd almost forgotten it would be like this. Of course it would. Traffic just to get into the parking lot was beyond hopeless, but he'd persevered and caught a spot just as someone was leaving, probably pissing off someone who'd been circling before him. Just a quick pop in, pop out, easy peasy.

Line.

Long line.

The returns at this store were odd, to say the least. Instead of a customer service counter around back like most stores, this was an older location, built well before Amazon was even a thing. Whole Foods must've been here before they came calling, so the "return desk" was a kiosk counter with a portable wire shelf next to it, positioned up front, just by checkout aisle seven. One was supposed to queue neatly along the plate glass windows flanking the front of the store while shoppers both entered and exited beside them. Additionally, shoppers were checking out, their precious organic, free-range, homegrown whatevers being bagged in recycled hemp totes that proudly carried logos suggesting, passive-aggressively, that they were better shoppers who didn't kill whales with plastic.

Add to this the overhead lights, which hadn't been changed since the Reagan administration, and the endless need for some recorded happy voice to proclaim what discounts and value-driven opportunities awaited throughout the store. Graham wondered why the world felt the need to fill up every goddamn minute with noise. Couldn't people simply shop without added irritations from every speaker?

Graham was behind three others, and the woman at the front was seemingly there to waste everyone's time. Why someone would think an entire cartload of Amazon boxes—all of which needed to be returned simultaneously—was socially acceptable, he didn't know. The poor clerk, who looked like he'd just arrived from high school, seemed overwhelmed. Hell, Graham was overwhelmed just looking at it.

Ahead of him was a guy with dark wavy hair that bobbed around his shoulders, almost permed. He was slightly smaller than Graham—probably five-nine—but seemed to have a broad chest and shoulders. Looked like he worked out. Reminded Graham of a guy at the gym. Nice biceps, although they were concealed under a winter coat. It was cold outside; the first snows had already come, and it was still a week before Thanksgiving.

Thanksgiving. His first without Simon.

Behind him, a woman stepped up with her small son—probably four or five—and she looked like she'd already run a marathon. The boy was asking if they could get dinosaurs for dinner, and Graham only hoped he meant the chicken-shaped nuggets. But actual dinosaurs might be fun too, he thought, and smirked to himself.

Turning back around, the returns lady up front was on her sixth package with five more to go—Graham counted. The guy ahead of him, Mr. Bicep, was wearing what looked like Airpods and shifting his legs. People kept bumping into everyone in line as they attempted to make their way out of the store with carts that felt like Thunderdome.

Finally. *Finally*, the Amazon woman left. The next customer started toward the poor clerk, who looked like he needed a cigarette.

Graham snickered and muttered that perhaps he could collect his social security check after all this time. But the guy in front didn't move forward. He was too busy doom-scrolling on his phone. Graham cleared his throat, as one does in these situations.

Nothing.

Finally, Graham tapped his shoulder, which startled him, and he turned around.

He was a nice-looking fellow. Deep eyes. Something almost olive to his skin, but not quite a tan. He had a look about him that seemed happy—like, always, even when he wasn't. Graham found himself smiling despite himself.

The guy couldn't have been more than twenty-five, if that. Dressed well enough—looked like he worked in an office. Khakis and a button-down with a belt under a red winter coat lined around the hood with fake fur. It reminded Graham of the winter coat he'd had in the seventies when he was a boy.

Graham apologized and pointed to the space ahead, letting out a smartass joke about the Amazon lady finally being finished. He noticed the guy was looking right into his eyes. It made him slightly uncomfortable—like the man was looking right through him.

Then he spoke.

And Graham realized he'd been mistaken. Those weren't Airpods. They were hearing aids. The man wasn't deaf, obviously—otherwise, why the hearing aids? But he definitely had some sort of hearing difficulty, because his voice was... well, politely put, it sounded like someone who couldn't quite hear himself speak. Slightly difficult to understand.

But he seemed nice. Apologizing and laughing at Graham's joke about the Amazon lady. Said he hadn't realized how long he'd been waiting. Graham replied that they'd already celebrated another birthday for him—the kid behind was three when they arrived, and now he was off to college.

The guy laughed. And it was another sign of his hearing difficulties. Graham didn't feel pity for him; the man certainly didn't look like he needed or welcomed it. But Graham could tell. Even in his laugh.

The clerk yelled down the way: "Next!"

Graham knew the man in front wouldn't have heard it. He was looking right at Graham, his back to the returns kiosk.

"You're finally next," Graham smiled and pointed.

The man followed his hand. "Thank you," he returned with a slight nod before spending thirty seconds returning whatever treasure had turned to trash and walking out the door.

Graham followed his progress—that red coat was hard to miss—then heard the kid behind him yell, "Can we go already?" which was Graham's cue to get a move on.

Walking out of the store, the snow had started coming down harder. In this part of Maine, it wasn't as bad as up north, but it was still pretty damn cold, and driving in it was something Graham never enjoyed. Good thing he lived only a few blocks away, which made it convenient on the way home from the gym. Everything was convenient. They'd bought the home for opposing reasons: Simon for its beauty and wooded scenery, Graham for its convenience.

Getting into his car, he had to practically yell at a woman who was nearly blocking him in, her blinker on telling the world *this is going to be my parking spot—fight me if you want*. Time to get the hell out of this madness, he thought.

Pulling up and turning right, the darkness fell as the overhead towers of blue LED lights began to fade. But he noticed a flash of red. That coat. The coat from the deaf guy.

Well, not deaf, his mind corrected him. But he knew what he meant.

The man was sitting in a bus stop, shaking. Coat or not, it was freezing. And he was sitting on a metal bench that looked like snow had overtaken it earlier. His ass must have been stuck to the metal, given the way his body looked as Graham drove past and up to the light.

He felt for anyone out in this weather without a portable heater and shelter. You know—like a warm car.

The light changed. He pulled forward down the block to the next large intersection. It was no longer a road, more like a highway with a stoplight. At the last moment, he got into the right-turn lane, a car flying up and honking because how dare anyone not read his mind and get out of his way. Graham mentally flipped him off and turned, then turned right again into a neighborhood.

He didn't know anyone there. Didn't know the streets. But he was looking to circle back.

It was all happening on autopilot. Graham was fighting with himself.

What are you doing?

Turning back, thank you.

But why? For what?

To help that poor man freezing in the cold.

But why? You don't even know him.

Because... because... I don't know why. But it seems the right thing to do.

Graham pulled up to the bus stop and clicked the button for the passenger window to lower, just as his mind was telling him: *Creep much?*

Okay, he thought to himself. This does look a little creepy. Or like he's picking up a hooker. Not that he ever had. God, he was getting himself flustered.

The guy looked up at him through shivers and chattering teeth, confused. Then he recognized Graham—although they hadn't really met.

"I'm sorry," Graham finally said.

Good move. That's a great line to win friends and influence people. Apologize for being a dumbass right out of the gate.

"I... I felt bad seeing you in the cold. Can I give you a lift?"

The man stood and walked tentatively toward the car, wary. Confused. Graham realized he probably hadn't heard him. Or not well.

He repeated: "I saw you shivering. Do you want a ride?"

Before the man could decline, Graham added: "I know this looks weird —some creepy old man asking if you want a lift. I promise I don't have any candy, nor do I want to know how much."

He gave a halfhearted laugh, hoping the man would find his humor funny. Or at least palatable. Or at least hear him, for that matter. God, this was stupid, he felt. What was he even doing?

The guy leaned down without touching the car and smiled. He had heard.

"And here I was looking forward to some candy."

Graham's breath caught for a moment. Humor. The guy was playing back. Oh. Okay. This would be okay.

Then his brain kicked in again. *What if* he's *the one to look out for, huh? What if* he's *the creep?*

Oh, shut the hell up, he told himself. He's freezing.

"Can I give you a ride somewhere? I hate to see anyone cold like this."

"Uh... well... it's like twenty minutes away. I can take the bus. I don't mind."

"No, it's no trouble. I don't have anywhere to be. I was just going home."

"You sure?"

"No, I'm not sure. I'm positive."

The guy smiled. "You're an interesting fella."

"What are you, from the 1940s?"

Now, Graham meant it as a joke. But what the man thought he was hearing was disdain for his voice, which he knew wasn't great. His hearing loss had blessed him before he'd exited the womb, although his folks hadn't known until he was nearly two. He could hear some things—low bass sounds mostly—and if he watched your lips and caught your mannerisms, he'd generally figure things out. But he had difficulty vocalizing words so they sounded "normal."

And he knew it.

But this guy was making fun of him? Was that it?

Graham saw his look and appeared mortified. "No—I meant your phrases sounded... You know what, I'm sorry. I didn't mean that the way it sounded."

The way it sounded? His brain kicked him in the nuts. *What the hell sort of hole are you digging?*

"Sorry... I'm... I'm a dumbass. Your voice is fine. I was trying to make a joke. It wasn't very good."

"Or a joke," the man said.

"Touché. You're right. I apologize."

The man's smile returned. "You sure you don't mind?"

Graham was eating humble pie, and it needed something more than sour. "Yes... I haven't ever..." He flustered.

But the car door was already opening, and the man sat down, pulling it shut and lowering his hood, fake fur and all. His hair spilled out and he smiled.

"Thank you for taking me. I've never come over this way before."

"Yeah? You just wanted to return your Amazon out this way for a change of pace?"

The man laughed. Really laughed. And Graham's smile returned.

"No—I work just up the way."

"Really? Where?"

"LL Bean."

"Oh? What do you do?"

"I'm in accounting. Boring."

"Oh no—I'm terribly fascinated by accounts receivable. In fact, I'm writing a book all about general ledgers."

The man laughed again. "You're quite the smartass, you know?"

"I take pride in that."

"What do *you* do?"

"I write. Little hobby."

"Really? Anything I'd know?"

"Probably not. I'm not much. So, where am I dropping you off—without any candy?"

The man smiled. He liked this guy. Something seemed trustworthy. Easy. He gave Graham the directions as they pulled away from the curb, just before an actual bus came and honked at Graham for not being part of Greater Portland Metro.

"By the way," the man said, "my name is Eli."

"Graham."

"Like the cracker?"

Graham had to snicker. It wasn't like he hadn't heard that growing up, but the way it came out of Eli's mouth was precious. "Yes. Like the cracker."

They volleyed back and forth as Graham navigated through the evening traffic. Eli didn't understand Graham sometimes in the darkened car, as much as he tried to look at Graham's face while driving, but they got along well. Eli turned out to be Graham's match in snark and banter, his timing more impeccable than Graham's—and that was saying something. Simon used to quip that Graham could hold his own in the National Smartass of the Year finals.

"So you take the bus everywhere?" Graham asked as they turned onto a main road heading toward Portland.

"Pretty much. Don't have a car."

"By choice or...?"

"By budget." Eli shrugged, though Graham caught a flicker of something underneath the casual gesture. "I'm trying to save up. Buy a place of my own eventually. Nothing fancy—just something small. A little house, maybe. Somewhere that's *mine,* you know?"

Graham nodded. He understood that. The wanting of a place that was yours.

"My roommates are great," Eli continued, "but they've... got their own lives. I think they'll be moving out soon, anyway and then I'll need to figure out what's next. So every dollar I don't spend on a car payment or insurance or gas is a dollar closer to a down payment."

"That's smart. Disciplined."

"That's one word for it." Eli grinned. "My mother calls it 'stubborn as a mule.' My father just shakes his head and asks if I need money, which I don't. I mean—I do. But not from them. I want to do this myself."

"Nothing wrong with that."

"Try telling my mother."

Graham laughed. "Mothers are like that. Mine was convinced I'd starve to death if she didn't send care packages well into my thirties."

"Did you? Starve?"

"Nearly. Turns out I'm a disaster in the kitchen. My hus—" Graham stopped. The word caught in his throat. He hadn't said it out loud in months. Hadn't needed to. Everyone who knew him already knew. "My husband was the cook," he finished quietly. "I just showed up and ate."

Eli was quiet for a moment. Graham could feel him looking, assessing. But there was no pity in it. No awkward sympathy. Just acknowledgment.

"Was?" Eli asked gently.

"He passed. Earlier this year. March."

"I'm sorry."

"Thank you." Graham kept his eyes on the road. "It's... it's been a while now. I'm fine."

He wasn't fine. They both knew it. But Eli didn't push, and Graham was grateful.

"Well," Eli said after a moment, "if you ever need someone to not cook with, I'm also terrible at it. We could burn things together."

Graham surprised himself by laughing. A real laugh—the kind that came from somewhere genuine, not the polite sounds he'd been making for months when people tried to cheer him up.

"I might take you up on that."

Pulling up to a less-than-stellar neighborhood, Graham stopped in front of an older apartment building. The kind of place that was clean but tired, doing its best with what it had.

"This is me," Eli said, unbuckling his seatbelt. "Thank you, Mr. Cracker—I mean, Graham. I really do appreciate the ride."

Graham smiled. He liked the fellow. "It's been my pleasure. But the first one's free. I charge after."

"Oh—Uber Black?"

"No, I'm more high-class. I actually have vodka in my complimentary water bottles."

Eli laughed. "I'll have to request you specifically next time."

"Well—" Graham hesitated. This was probably odd. Probably overstepping. But something made him say it anyway. "Here. Let me give you my number. In case you ever need a ride again. Or someone to burn dinner with."

Eli looked surprised. Then pleased. "Really?"

"Really. It's 207-585-0147."

Eli pulled out his phone—an older model, Graham noticed, well-worn but functional—and tapped in the number. A moment later, Graham felt his own phone buzz in his pocket.

"There," Eli said. "Now you have mine too. That was me saying hi."

"Very efficient."

"I try not to abuse the privilege."

"Please. Abuse away. I'm an old man with nothing but time."

"You're not old."

"I'm fifty-three."

Eli looked at him. Really looked. "No, you're not."

"I assure you, I am."

"There's no way you're fifty-three. I thought maybe... I don't know. Thirty-eight? Forty at most?"

"Fifty-three." Graham held up his hand as if taking an oath. "I have the birth certificate to prove the first and last time I touched a vagina."

Eli burst out laughing—a real, full laugh that filled the car. "Oh my God."

"It's true. Documented and everything."

"You're insane."

"Seasoned *and* insane. I'm a catch."

"Clearly." Eli was still grinning, shaking his head. "Fifty-three. Unbelievable. Whatever you're doing, keep doing it."

"Clean living and spite."

"That tracks, actually."

"You're very strange, Eli."

"Thank you. I take pride in that." Eli opened the door, letting in a rush of cold air. "Good night, Graham. And seriously—thank you. For the ride. For the company. For not being a serial killer."

"The night is young."

Eli laughed again—that slightly off-kilter laugh that Graham was beginning to find endearing—and climbed out of the car.

"If I ever have more Amazon returns, I'll be sure to head to your Whole Foods again," Eli said, leaning down to look through the open door.

"Be prepared. The Amazon lady might still be there."

Graham pulled away as Eli waved goodbye, watching in his rearview mirror until the red coat disappeared into the apartment building.

He found himself wondering what *that* had been all about. He never did anything like that—gave his number to strangers, offered rides, made jokes about burning dinner together. God, Simon would kill him if—

Simon.

He almost felt guilty for enjoying the twenty minutes in the car. But Simon would hate that for him. Simon would want him to talk to people, make friends, stop rattling around in that empty house like a ghost haunting his own life.

Go make a friend, he could almost hear Simon saying. *One who makes you laugh. God knows you need it.*

Graham smiled, just a little, and turned toward home.

Still, it was nice. Having a conversation that wasn't about grief or casseroles or "how are you holding up." Having someone who didn't know the Before, who only knew him as a man in a Whole Foods line making bad jokes.

It was nice to be seen as something other than a widower.

Even if only for twenty minutes.

GRAHAM BARELY WALKED in the door from the garage, pulling off the beanie that Simon always said made him look like he was twelve but kept his head warm, when his phone buzzed. Sitting on the mudroom bench, he tugged off his boots—the kind with fur along the edges, not unlike what Eli had on his coat, he realized—and fished his phone out of his pocket.

Speaking of which.

Man! I just had the craziest Uber driver! Had vodka in the water bottles and kept stalking the bus stop! Can you imagine?

Graham smiled and leaned back against the stack of coats and jackets still hanging on the wall. Most needed to be put away for winter, but some were still Simon's, and this had become an unofficial memorial he couldn't find the willpower to touch.

Gotta watch out for those Uber drivers! Especially the ones stalking customers around Whole Foods.

Yeah? Well, at least he had a 5-star rating. But I dunno...

5-star, huh? What did you give him?

Oh, 5 stars. But...

But?

He didn't have snacks. And you know what that means?

Graham snickered, biting his tongue slightly as he saw where this was going.

No, what?

We could've been hit with a sudden blizzard and stuck with nothing to go with the vodka. Imagine? We might have starved to death!

Graham imagined Eli swooning at the thought and giggled. He felt like he was twelve.

Just think of the children!

Right?!

Well, we can't have that, can we?

Dinner?

Can't have you starving to death with nothing but vodka hidden in water bottles to survive. Tomorrow?

The message indicator spun, then stopped. Graham waited.

Perhaps he was being too forward. This was fun, and it might be nice to have dinner with someone who wasn't worried about "how he was holding up" or reminding him that "Simon would have been proud." But maybe Eli was just being playful. Maybe Graham came across like he was trying to pick him up.

He was never good at these things. He really wasn't.

Simon used to accuse him of being oblivious to guys checking him out, and Graham couldn't argue. Had no clue. Likewise, if he came across as flirty, he didn't know. For Graham, he just enjoyed the banter. Two people having fun together didn't signal romantic interest in his mind. But what did he know? Now that he thought about it, he probably was being too much—

Sorry, I was being too...

But his phone buzzed before he could finish. Eli had responded.

Sure! But I'll need to schedule an Uber to meet you. I don't have a car, remember.

He let out a sigh and deleted his half-typed apology before retyping:

Funny! I'm on call tomorrow night. And I hope to keep my 5-star rating.

Graham, you don't need to drive me around. I can meet you somewhere if you want.

Eli's break from their banter gave Graham pause. It really wasn't any trouble—it was welcome, actually. It gave him an excuse to get out of the house, somewhere beyond the bubble of his neighborhood.

I know you can, but your place is on the way to one of my go-to's by the harbor. 7? Is that enough time to get home from work and clean up?

Clean up? I don't work in the mud.

No? I thought you said you were a mud wrestler.

Oh, I forgot. Tomorrow I'm just an accountant. Saturdays I'm in the mud.

See! I do pay attention!

<sigh> Fine. 7pm. I'll wear my best outfit.

Leisure suit?

With ruffles. Just for you!

You're the best.

And you're loopy. But I love it. So—7pm tomorrow. I'll be the one outside with hearing aids.

I'll have the snacks ready.

Bye, Goofy.

Bye, Donald.

Donald?

Aren't we doing Disney characters?

Go to bed.

Night.

Graham set his phone down beside him and looked over at the cupboards lining the mudroom wall.

Was this a date?

No. He didn't think so. Nor did he want one. But it was fun to think he was going to have dinner with someone tomorrow night. Friday nights tended to be the most difficult. Even though he worked from home, Friday evening signified the start of the weekend.

And weekends had always involved going out somewhere with Simon. He'd insisted they get out of the house at least once a week, if not more. And by Friday, if Simon was home from his work trips, he would organize something. Anything.

But now Friday nights were quiet. Graham would often turn on Netflix and let it play—not watching, not caring—but it was something for noise. Something Simon might have done. Many a night, he'd walk through the house looking for something, anything, to do with himself. But all paths led back to Simon. Some closet that needed organizing would be filled with bits and bobs from some trip or another *with Simon*. Setting out the Halloween decorations meant confronting Simon's quirky touches. Changing from summer to winter linens reminded him this had been Simon's domain — before Simon, Graham didn't even know there was such a thing as summer versus winter sheets.

The absolute worst was not finding anything to do and ending up standing in front of their bedroom door, looking in. He usually held it together, but this—this was the single most difficult path, and one he purposely avoided at night. He'd barrel through on his way to brush his teeth and head straight to bed. Flash through and get to sleep so he didn't have to confront the ghosts of Simon.

But tomorrow—Friday—he was going out. To that little place he hadn't been to since...

Simon.

"I hope you like Italian food," Graham said slowly, trying not to overdo it. The lighting was low, and he wanted Eli to be able to understand him even if he couldn't see his lips as clearly as he'd like.

Eli gave an "uh oh" look, his eyes widening, teeth gritting slightly.

Graham nearly fainted. He hadn't told Eli where he was taking him—hadn't even thought of it, to be honest. This place was so memorable for him. But Eli hated Italian? Oh god.

"I *love* Italian!"

Graham's heart popped back into his chest.

"Especially Beefaroni and—"

"You know, I can take you back to wait in line at Whole Foods."

"Oh please! No! Not behind the Amazon lady! I'll be good!" Eli feigned fear dramatically—*over*-dramatically—causing Graham to laugh.

"Good boy."

"What am I? A dog?"

"Woof."

"You're so goofy." Eli laughed and reached for his water glass. "I take it you come here often?"

Graham's laughter faded. Eli noticed the change.

"I haven't been since..."

Eli became quiet. He'd told himself before Graham picked him up to be careful about what he said. Graham hadn't shared much, but Eli knew his husband was gone. And he now realized this was one of *those* places—memory spaces—where Simon probably still lived.

"Graham?"

"Sorry—I'm... sorry. I didn't realize how..." He paused. "It's been months since..."

Eli just let him be. Gave him an "I'm here" look and held tight.

"Simon used to take me here sometimes. It hasn't changed in probably twenty years."

Eli nodded. Listening.

"I'm sorry—this is not..." Graham collected himself. "We're here to have a nice dinner, so let's have a nice dinner."

Eli smiled.

Graham ordered the toasted ravioli and some crusty bread—just to have something at the table.

The waiter had difficulty understanding Eli, and Graham worried whether he should intervene and order for him. He wanted to help but didn't want Eli to think he was parenting or taking over.

After the waiter left, Eli looked slightly exasperated and gave Graham a "see what I deal with" look.

"Sorry about that."

"It's okay. I... sometimes I wish I could just write things down so people could understand. I hate it when they keep asking me to repeat over and over. It's humiliating."

Graham nodded. He couldn't understand the feeling firsthand, but he empathized with it.

"If you don't mind me asking, have you thought about sign language?"

Eli bit his lip and gave a small smile. "Sign."

Of course he had. Many, many times. But his folks had wanted him to get along in the world without needing others to learn his language. And more practically, they hadn't had the means to send him to a specialty school. Back when he was growing up, programs like that weren't exactly plentiful, and the idea of being sent away to some school had scared the hell out of him. Besides, he could hear some. Not a lot. But enough, he felt. And as long as he did his best to watch people and try to figure out what they were going to say ahead of time, more often than not, he got along okay.

The problem had always been his voice. He'd had so many lessons and trainers at school. And he did pretty well, but he knew it would never sound like a hearing person's. Not exactly. And it wasn't like he was blind or had something visible where people would immediately know. Aside from his hearing aids, you wouldn't know he had an issue. Until he had to speak. Then you might think he had some sort of problem—until it hit you: *he can't hear very well.* Or the opposite—people would assume he was completely deaf, no hearing whatsoever, and they'd do all sorts of silly things to try to communicate. When all they had to do was simply speak. Not loudly. Not shouting. Not mumbling either. Just treat him normally. That's all he wanted.

Graham listened. Nodded when appropriate. Really felt the frustration Eli carried.

It was Eli's turn to apologize, even though he didn't need to. "Sorry—I don't mean to shit on everyone. It's... well... I'm fine. Sorry."

"No, it's okay. No need to apologize. It's helpful that I know how you feel."

They both took a drink and looked around the room before Graham paused and met Eli's eyes.

"Boy, aren't we just the life of the party? I mean, I'm breaking down over my late husband and you're just trying to get the damn waiter to understand you." He gave a hesitant laugh.

Eli smiled.

Graham raised his water glass in a toast. "To the best damn Friday night dinner fifteen dollars can buy!"

Eli laughed and clinked his glass against Graham's. "Wow! You're a big spender!"

"Nothing but the best, Eli. Nothing but the best."

Dinner went much better after that. The food was good. The company better.

Eli was curious about Simon but hesitant to push. Graham could tell it came from a good place and began telling him how they'd met in college. What their life had been like "back in the olden days."

Eli laughed.

How they'd bought their home together. Simon's career.

"You said you're a writer?"

"Yeah. Just a few books. No big deal."

"Sounds like fun. I love reading."

"Yeah? Well, we need more of you. Most people can't read more than thirty seconds on a Facebook post or whatever."

"Facebook? That's for, like, old people."

"Oh, I'm not on social media."

"Any?"

"Nope."

"Not even Insta—"

"Not even that."

"Wow."

"What?"

"I mean... I don't think I use it much, but... you don't even watch stupid cat videos online?"

"Not a one. I'm a cat-video virgin."

"What? That can't be. Here, I need to show you—" Eli started to retrieve his phone, but Graham waved him off.

"Nope. I feel like I'm much better off not knowing anything about it."

Eli shrugged. "You're probably right. I feel like shit after spending an hour scrolling. I keep thinking there'll be something interesting if I just scroll to the good stuff."

"And there's no good stuff, right?"

Eli blushed, like he'd been caught.

"I thought so."

"Well, if you don't scroll through mindless crap, what do you do then?"

"Well, I write for work, so I don't really do that for fun..."

"You don't think it's fun?"

"I do—I love it—but it's work, you know?"

Eli nodded. He understood. Or thought he might.

Graham told him about his trainer and the bodybuilding buddies who'd adopted him. About his little gang of misfits he occasionally went to dinner with—Anthony and Jason and the whole group.

"They sound like fun."

"They are. But they've also been too worried about me, especially since..."

Graham paused.

"Simon," Eli said.

Not as a question. He'd helped Graham finish the phrase for the second time tonight.

"Yes." Graham recovered. "I know they mean well. But sometimes I don't want to deal with it, you know?"

"I think I do."

"What about you? Is there a Mr. Eli?"

"My dad?"

"Oh, god no! I meant... is there someone special in your life?"

"Oh—" Eli felt foolish. "No. No one who's anything."

"Nobody?"

Eli wasn't sure how much he should share. They were barely twenty-four hours into knowing each other. But Graham seemed so kind, and Eli felt like he could say anything and it would be okay.

"I've tried. But no one wants to date someone like me. Or..."

"Or?"

"They just want a hookup and then they're gone."

Graham shook his head. He'd never gone home with anyone other than Simon. His whole life. And even if sometimes he'd gotten bored with their sex life, or things weren't exactly rosy from time to time, it had never occurred to him to even think about being with someone else. But he didn't want to judge—even though he couldn't help himself.

"I never understood hookups."

"Yeah?"

He explained about Simon being his first. And only.

"Wow. That's, like, super rare, I'm pretty sure."

"Yeah? You think?"

"Graham, most guys I know are on Grindr and—"

"What's Grindr?"

Eli nearly spit out his water.

Graham smiled. Once again, he was so naive.

"Well, it's a dating app. Well... not really. It's a... well..."

Graham looked confused.

"To be candid, Graham, it's a hookup app."

"Hookup app?"

"Yeah. To, like... you know... hook up."

He still looked confused. Eli widened his eyes and tilted his head. *Get it?*

No. He didn't. "You mean like a blind date or something?"

"Graham?"

"Yeah?"

"It's where guys meet to fuck."

"Oh! *OH*. Oh... *that*."

Eli nearly laughed himself off his seat. Diners at the next table looked their way.

"C'mon, Graham. Surely you knew guys *did that*, right?"

"Well, yeah, but I just... well, I never thought of..."

"Of course you haven't, Graham. It's one of the things that makes you charming."

"You think I'm charming?"

"Well, yeah. In a Graham sort of way."

"What's *that* supposed to mean?" He was smiling. This was kind of fun.

"Oh, I don't know. You're different."

"Bad?"

"No. Just... you're not like the guys I've dated."

"Well, we're not dating." Graham said it simply, as a point of fact. But something about it took Eli aback, and Graham noticed.

"Sorry, I mean—"

"I know what you meant. No, we're not dating. I... well..."

"I mean, Eli—I could practically be your dad."

"No, you couldn't."

"Of course I could. I'm fifty-three."

"I know. And you still don't look it. But my dad... I couldn't imagine you being my dad."

"Why? Is he—"

"I love my dad. He's a good man. He and my mom have been good parents. But they don't get me. Let's just call it that."

Graham observed something deeper surrounding that statement and decided it was best to move on.

"Well, the point being, I'm like an old fuddy-duddy."

Eli laughed. "Only when you use those words." He leaned forward slightly. "You know what you are, Graham?"

"What? Tell me."

"You're a really nice man. And if you were my age, I'd try to pick you up."

"Really?" Graham seemed incredulous.

"Of course I would."

"Why?"

"Why? Because you're a really nice man. And you're good-looking..."

Graham let out a *pssst* and reached for his glass. He wasn't good at taking compliments.

"...and you've got quite a wit, and you tell the worst jokes—"

"What?! I do not! My jokes are fantastic!"

"Fantastically *bad*!"

Graham clutched his heart as if the dagger had gone in, but his smile betrayed him. Eli latched onto it.

"You *know* it's true!"

"I'm deducting your Uber rating by a star!" Graham teased.

"You can't. I take the bus, remember?" Eli laughed.

They went on telling more about themselves. Their histories. Eli's dreams of having a place of his own. What Graham planned to do with his future. The holidays coming up. All of it. Jokes sprinkled throughout, seriousness when it came time to split the bill—Graham wanted to treat; Eli insisted they go Dutch.

And then the ride home.

Graham pulled up to Eli's building and put the car in park, keeping the engine running for the heater.

"I had a great night, Graham. Thank you for taking me out."

"I hope that means you'll rate the ride five stars."

"Only if I can take you somewhere next time."

"Next time?"

"Of course. What are you doing next week?"

"It's Thanksgiving, remember?"

"Oh, I forgot," Eli said.

"Do you go up to visit your folks?"

"They want me to. A few cousins and my uncle will be there. All shouting because they think that's how I hear. And Mom will ask if I've found the right girl yet, and..."

"They don't know?"

"They know. They just don't want to know. If you know what I mean."

"I know."

"Great, then everyone knows!" Eli seized the opportunity to turn it into a joke, deflecting the pain. "What about you?"

"Oh, the gang wants me to come over to Anthony's. They're all going to put on a 'Let's Be There for Graham' show since it'll be my first Thanksgiving since..."

"Simon."

Eli had helped him finish the phrase again.

Graham could only nod.

"Sounds..."

"Awful," Graham finished for him.

They both sat looking out at the darkness, the car headlights illuminating the snowflakes as they fell onto the old apartment building's roof.

"I have an idea," Eli said, perking up. "We could volunteer at the shelter downtown. You know? Help with Thanksgiving meals. I volunteered there once before—not for Thanksgiving, but our office had a volunteer day last summer, and it was actually really nice."

"You want to wash dishes and serve food for Thanksgiving?"

"Well, we'd already be doing that, right? Only this way, it'd be with people we *want* to be with..."

"Not family."

"Exactly!"

Graham smiled. "Okay. I suppose there are plenty of people who need it more than me."

"Or me."

"Fine. Let's do it. I'll tell Anthony."

"And I'll tell my mom."

"They're going to complain, you know," Graham said.

"You mean bitch."

Graham laughed. The way Eli's voice shaped the word made it almost adorable.

"Yes. Bitch."

Eli smiled.

"I'm in."

"Me too."

"Well—I'll see you. Drive safe, Graham. Thanks again."

"Anytime. I had fun. We'll chat about Thursday beforehand, okay?"

"It's a date."

Graham pulled away and thought about Eli's words. *It's a date.*

Only it wasn't. It was just dinner. Or it would be—volunteering. With Eli. A really nice guy. Who'd told him that if he were younger, he'd be all over him.

That surprised him.

And made him smile.

Chapter Three

THE GREEN BEANS had gone cold an hour ago, but people kept coming.

Graham stood behind the serving line, metal spoon in hand, placing a scoop onto each plate as it slid past. Beside him, Eli was on roll duty—one per plate, sometimes two if someone asked nicely or looked like they needed it. They'd been at it since ten that morning, and Graham's lower back was starting to protest in ways it hadn't since his last ill-advised attempt at yard work.

But he didn't mind. That was the strange thing. He didn't mind at all.

The shelter was loud—voices echoing off the cinderblock walls, folding chairs scraping against linoleum, children running between tables while their parents called after them. It was chaos, but the good kind. The kind that meant people were fed, warm, together. Graham found himself smiling at strangers, wishing them a happy Thanksgiving, meaning it in a way he hadn't expected to mean anything today.

Eli caught his eye and grinned, holding up a roll like a trophy. Graham shook his head and laughed. They'd developed a rhythm over the past few hours—no words needed, just the easy coordination of two people who'd figured out how to work alongside each other.

"You two," the volunteer coordinator said, appearing at Graham's elbow. She was a sturdy woman in her sixties named Marjorie, with a clipboard and the air of someone who had seen everything and was surprised by nothing. "Line's thinning out. Go get yourselves some dinner."

"We're fine," Graham started, but Marjorie was already shooing them away from the serving station.

"Everyone eats. That's the rule. Go on—through the line like everyone else. Tom and Beth will cover."

Graham set down his spoon and untied his apron. Eli did the same, and they made their way around to the front of the line, grabbing trays and joining the queue.

It felt different from this side. Graham had expected to feel like a volunteer playing at being served—a tourist in someone else's hardship. But the woman behind the counter just smiled and asked if he wanted dark meat or white, same as she'd asked everyone else. The man ladling gravy didn't know or care that Graham had been scooping green beans ten minutes ago. He was just another person in line, hungry, grateful, part of the community that had gathered here tonight.

Eli nudged him as they reached the end of the line. "Pie?"

"Obviously."

They each took a slice of pumpkin pie and carried their trays into the dining hall, scanning for an empty table. Most were full—families clustered together, elderly couples eating in silence, young men sitting alone with their heads down. Graham spotted two empty seats at the far end of a long table and nodded toward them.

They sat. The food was better than Graham had expected—the turkey moist, the stuffing well-seasoned, the green beans (his green beans, he thought with some pride) perfectly adequate. Eli was already halfway through his roll before Graham had even unfolded his napkin.

"Hungry?"

"Starving," Eli said. "I forgot to eat breakfast."

"How do you forget to eat breakfast?"

"I was nervous."

"About what?"

Eli shrugged, suddenly interested in his mashed potatoes. "I don't know. Today. Being here. Doing something different."

Graham understood. He'd been nervous too—had woken up at five in the morning and lain in bed for an hour, staring at the ceiling, thinking about all the Thanksgivings before this one. Simon in the kitchen, wearing that ridiculous apron with the turkey on it. The smell of sage and butter. The sound of Simon humming while he cooked.

He'd gotten up at six and gone to the gym, just to have something to do with his body. Then he'd picked up Eli at nine, and they'd driven to the shelter in comfortable silence, and now here they were. Eating turkey with strangers. Not alone.

"This was a good idea," Graham said.

Eli looked up. "Yeah?"

"Yeah. Thank you. For suggesting it."

Eli smiled—that open, genuine smile that Graham was starting to recognize. "Thank you for saying yes."

. . .

They were halfway through their pie when the family sat down.

A woman first—mid-thirties, maybe, though she looked older. Worn in a way that suggested life had been hard and wasn't getting easier. Behind her, a teenage boy, maybe thirteen or fourteen, with the guarded expression of someone who'd learned not to expect much. And finally, a little girl, eight or so, with pigtails and a gap-toothed smile that hadn't yet learned to be guarded about anything.

They settled at the far end of the table, the mother helping the little girl into her seat, the boy sitting down heavily and staring at his plate like it had personally offended him.

Graham glanced at Eli, who'd noticed them too. They both looked away, giving the family space, returning to their own conversation.

But the little girl had other ideas.

"Mommy," she said, loudly enough to carry, "that man talks funny."

Graham saw Eli freeze, his fork halfway to his mouth.

"Lucy!" The mother's face flushed. "That's not polite. We don't say things like that."

"But he *does*—"

"Lucy. Enough."

Eli set down his fork. Graham watched him take a breath, watched him make a decision. Then Eli turned toward the little girl and smiled.

"You're right," he said. "I do talk funny. Do you want to know why?"

Lucy's eyes went wide. Her mother looked mortified, already opening her mouth to apologize, but Eli waved her off gently.

"It's okay," he said to the mother. "Really." He turned back to Lucy. "I can't hear very well. See these?" He pointed to his hearing aids. "These help me hear a little bit, but not everything. And because I can't hear very well, my voice sounds different. Make sense?"

Lucy nodded slowly, fascinated. "Can I see?"

"Lucy—" her mother started.

"It's fine," Eli said. He tilted his head so Lucy could get a better look at the small device tucked behind his ear. "Pretty cool, right?"

"It's like a tiny computer," Lucy said.

"Exactly like a tiny computer. For my ear."

Lucy seemed satisfied with this explanation. She turned back to her plate, and her mother mouthed *thank you* at Eli, still looking embarrassed but grateful.

The teenage boy was watching now too, though he was trying to pretend he wasn't. Graham caught his eye and smiled. The boy looked away.

"I'm Graham," Graham said, keeping his voice warm, not pushing. "This is Eli."

"Susan," the mother said. "And this is Levi and Lucy."

"Nice to meet you all. Happy Thanksgiving."

"Happy Thanksgiving," Susan said quietly.

The conversation could have ended there. Should have, maybe. But Graham found himself not wanting it to.

"First time here?" he asked.

Susan nodded, not quite meeting his eyes. "We heard about it from... someone. Thought we'd check it out."

"The food's good," Graham said. "Eli and I were serving earlier. I can personally vouch for the green beans."

That got a small smile from Susan. "They were good."

"I made the rolls," Eli said. "Well, I put them on the plates. Someone else made them."

Lucy giggled. "You didn't *make* them."

"I made them appear on your plate. That's basically the same thing."

"No it's not!"

"Are you sure? It sounds the same to me."

Lucy was laughing now, delighted by this strange man with the funny voice who was willing to be silly with her. Eli grinned, clearly enjoying himself.

"So," Susan said, relaxing slightly, "what do you two do? When you're not serving green beans and putting rolls on plates?"

"I work at LL Bean," Eli said. "Accounting. Very boring."

"Oh, that's interesting. I've always liked that store."

Lucy tugged at Eli's sleeve. "Can I get more pie?"

"Lucy," Susan said tiredly, "you've had enough. Don't bother the nice man."

"It's no trouble," Eli said. "I was thinking about getting more myself. What do you say, Lucy? Want to come with me?"

Lucy was already sliding off her chair. "Yes!"

"You don't have to—" Susan started.

But Eli was already standing, offering his hand to Lucy. "We'll be right back. Come on, partner."

Lucy grabbed his hand and they headed toward the serving line, Lucy chattering away about something Graham couldn't hear. Eli bent down to listen, nodding seriously at whatever she was saying.

Graham watched them go, then turned back to the table.

"And what about you?" Susan asked. "You said you two—what do you do?"

"I'm a writer," Graham said.

Susan's eyebrows rose. "Really? Anything we'd know?"

"Probably not. Just a few books. Historical fiction, mostly. Set in Florence."

The shift in Levi was immediate. His head came up. His eyes focused on Graham with sudden intensity.

"Like *The Oltrarno*?"

Graham blinked. "I... yes, actually. That's my series."

"No way." Levi's guarded expression had vanished, replaced by something raw and eager. "You write *The Oltrarno*? Seriously?"

"Seriously."

"Oh my god." Levi looked like he might fall off his chair. "Those are my favorite books. I get them from the library when we—" He stopped abruptly, glancing at his mother. Something passed between them. "I just... I read a lot," he finished quietly.

"I'm glad you enjoy them," Graham said carefully, not acknowledging the stumble. "Which one's your favorite?"

"The first one," Levi said immediately. His enthusiasm was returning, the guarded teenager giving way to something younger, more open. "I love how Marco finally gets into the academy and meets Alessandro, and they're so different but they just *get* each other, you know? And the way they..." He paused, a flush creeping up his neck. "The way they become friends. It's really good."

Graham watched him. Levi knew. He understood what the book was really about—two boys falling in love in Renaissance Florence, finding each other against all odds. But he couldn't say it. Not here, not in front of his mother, maybe not anywhere yet. He was holding that knowledge close, a secret thing, precious and fragile.

"That's one of my favorites too," Graham said. "Marco and Alessandro were based on people I knew. A long time ago."

"Really?" Levi's eyes were shining. "That's so cool."

Susan was watching her son with something like wonder. "I didn't know you liked those books so much, honey."

"They're really good, Mom. You should read them."

"Maybe I will." Susan smiled—pleased that her son was animated for the first time all evening, though she clearly had no sense of the books' significance or the man sitting across from her. To her, it was just nice. A writer. How about that.

Across the dining hall, Eli was heading back from the serving line with Lucy skipping beside him. He was balancing five styrofoam plates in a precarious stack, his arms extended, his chin holding the top plate in place while Lucy tried to "help" by pushing against his leg.

Susan half-stood. "Oh—he's going to drop those."

Levi started to rise too, but Susan waved him back. "Stay—I'll go. I should get Lucy anyway before she knocks the poor man over."

She hurried across the dining hall, reaching Eli just as the top plate began to slide.

Graham and Levi were alone.

The noise of the shelter continued around them—chairs scraping, voices echoing, the clatter of the kitchen—but at their end of the table, it was quiet.

"Is he your boyfriend?" Levi asked, his voice low.

Graham looked at him. "No. He's a friend. A new friend, actually. We just met a few days ago."

Levi nodded, processing this. Graham could see the questions behind his eyes—questions he probably couldn't ask, not yet, maybe not for years. But he was asking them. That was something.

"Keep reading," Graham said softly. "The books, I mean. There's more to Marco and Alessandro's story."

Levi's face flickered—surprise, then something like gratitude. He understood what Graham was really saying.

Susan was heading back now, Lucy in tow, Eli beside her with the plates safely redistributed between them.

"Eli got us all more pie!" Lucy announced, returning to the table in triumph.

Eli was behind her, balancing five styrofoam plates precariously. Graham jumped up to help, steadying the wobbling stack and distributing slices around the table.

"I shouldn't," Susan murmured, but she took a bite anyway and closed her eyes briefly. "Okay, that's good."

Levi was already halfway through his slice, his earlier wariness completely gone. Lucy was showing Eli a drawing she'd made on her paper placemat—a house with a big sun and what might have been a dog or possibly a horse.

"That's beautiful," Eli said, leaning in to look. "Is that your house?"

"It's the house I want," Lucy said matter-of-factly. "With a yard. And a dog."

"What kind of dog?"

"A big one. Named Biscuit."

"Biscuit is an excellent name for a dog."

Graham watched them—Eli patient and present, Lucy basking in the attention, Susan looking at her daughter with an expression that was equal parts love and heartbreak. Whatever their story was, whatever had brought them to this shelter on Thanksgiving night, it wasn't an easy one.

The volunteer coordinator appeared at their table. "How's everyone doing? Enjoying the meal?"

"It's wonderful," Susan said. "Thank you so much for having us."

"You're always welcome. Always." Marjorie turned to Graham and Eli. "I hate to steal these two away, but we could use some help with the dishes."

"Work never ends," Graham said, standing.

Susan smiled. "Thank you both. For spending time with us."

"Thank you *Uncle Eli*!" Lucy launched herself at Eli, wrapping her arms around him in a fierce hug. Graham saw Eli's face—the surprise, the emotion, the way he had to blink rapidly to keep from crying.

"You're welcome, Lucy," Eli managed. "You take care of that pie, okay?"

"I will!"

Lucy released Eli and ran around the table to Graham, throwing her arms around his waist. "Thank you, Graham!"

"You're very welcome, sweetheart."

Levi had retreated back into himself, the guarded teenager returning. But when Graham looked at him, something passed between them. An understanding. A recognition.

Levi stood and moved toward Graham, offering an awkward half-hug, the kind teenage boys give when they're not sure what they're doing. Graham pulled him in properly, wrapping his arms around the kid and holding on for a moment longer than necessary.

He felt Levi melt into it. Felt the tension leave his shoulders. Felt him hold on like he needed this more than he knew how to say.

"Take care of yourself, Levi," Graham said quietly. "Keep reading."

"I will."

They shook Susan's hand. They turned to go. Graham made it three steps before he stopped.

"Hold on."

He hurried over to Marjorie. "Do you have a scrap of paper? And a pen?"

She produced both from somewhere in her clipboard. Graham scribbled quickly—his name, his email, then, after a moment's hesitation, his phone number. He walked back to the table and handed the paper to Levi.

"This is my contact information," he said, looking at Susan as he said it. "I hope you'll keep in touch. And if you ever need anything—anything at all—please reach out."

Susan's chin lifted slightly. Pride, Graham recognized. The thing that kept you going when everything else was falling apart.

"We're fine," she said. "But thank you."

"Of course. But I mean it. I'm always around."

Levi was staring at the paper like it was something precious. He folded it carefully and put it in his pocket.

"Thank you," he said. "For... thank you."

"Come on, Eli," Graham said, tilting his head toward the kitchen. "Showtime."

Eli caught Levi's small laugh as Susan motioned for Lucy to sit back down. As they made their way to the kitchen, neither Graham nor Eli said anything, but they both understood: this little family was staying put until the very last moment.

The dishes seemed endless.

Graham's hands were pruned and wrinkled, his back aching, his feet sore. Eli was at the next sink, scrubbing a massive pot with the kind of determination usually reserved for mortal combat. They'd been at it for over an hour, and they'd barely made a dent.

Through the kitchen's pass-through window, Graham could see the dining hall slowly emptying. Volunteers were wiping down tables, stacking chairs. Most of the guests had bundled up and headed out into the cold. But a few lingered—an elderly man nursing a cup of coffee, a young woman reading a paperback in the corner.

And at the far table, Susan and her children. Still there. Lucy had her head down on her arms, half-asleep. Levi was staring at nothing. Susan sat very still, watching the door like she was dreading walking through it.

He knew why they were staying. The shelter was warm. Whatever waited for them outside—a car, a motel, a relative's couch—wasn't.

"I think this pot is winning," Eli said, pulling Graham's attention back.

"Don't let it sense weakness. They can smell fear."

Eli laughed and attacked the pot with renewed vigor.

Marjorie's voice came over the PA system: "We'll be closing up in about fifteen minutes, folks. Thank you all for coming. Stay warm out there."

Graham glanced back through the window. Susan was standing now, helping Lucy into her coat. Levi was pulling on a hat, his movements slow, reluctant. Graham forced himself to look away. Back to the dishes. Nothing he could do.

He lost himself in the rhythm of scrubbing for a few more minutes—rinse, scrub, stack, repeat—until someone tapped his shoulder.

"You've got visitors."

He turned, nudging Eli to look.

It was Levi and Lucy, standing at the edge of the kitchen with Susan behind them. Bundled up now, ready to face the cold. They must have detoured on their way out.

"We wanted to say goodbye," Lucy said. "For real this time."

Graham dried his hands and walked over, Eli following. The family stood there—three people he'd met only hours ago but who already felt like more than strangers.

He wanted to ask if they had somewhere to go. If they had a car. A home. Anything. He wanted to offer money, a place to stay, some solution to whatever problem had brought them here. But he could see Susan's spine, straight and proud, and he knew that asking would only hurt her.

So he just smiled and said, "It was wonderful to meet you all. Happy Thanksgiving."

"Happy Thanksgiving," Susan said. "And thank you. For everything."

"Take care of each other."

Susan nodded. She put a hand on each of her children's shoulders and guided them toward the door. Levi looked back one more time, his hand pressed against the pocket where he'd put Graham's phone number.

Then they were gone.

By the time they finished cleaning up, it was 9:30.

Graham looked at his watch and blinked. "We've been here almost ten hours."

"Seriously?" Eli stretched, his back popping audibly. "It didn't feel like it."

"I know."

They said goodbye to Marjorie, who hugged them both and made them promise to come back. They walked out into the cold night air, their breath fogging in front of them, the parking lot nearly empty now.

The drive to Eli's apartment was quiet. Neither of them had the energy for banter, and that was fine. Graham found himself appreciating the silence—the comfortable kind, the kind that meant you didn't need to fill every moment with words. The kind that came from knowing each other, even if that knowing was only a few days old.

He pulled up to Eli's building and put the car in park.

"What do you think is going to happen to that family?" Eli asked, staring out the windshield. "I worry about Lucy. And her brother."

"And their mother," Graham added. He knew what Eli was feeling because he was feeling it too. "I don't know what to do to help them. We don't even know that they need help, right?"

Eli turned to look at him, and Graham could read his expression clearly now. *Come on. We both know.*

"Levi seemed excited once he knew you were an author," Eli said.

Graham felt his face warm. "Oh. Well. That."

"I thought you said no one would know your stuff."

"It's nothing, really."

"I'd like to read some sometime."

"I'm not really that good, you know. Seriously."

"Well..." Graham paused. It was late. They were both exhausted. His better judgment was probably already asleep. "You want to come over tomorrow? Just for lunch or something. No funny business, mister." He made a joke of it. Eli smiled.

"Unless you're shopping for Black Friday or something."

"Oh god, no!" Eli's voice pitched higher with horror. "I couldn't imagine that level of hell!"

Graham chuckled. "What?"

"What?" Eli was smiling, confused.

"You really sound like..."

"Like what?"

"Like you're going to start calling me 'gurl' and flip your hair."

Eli burst into laughter, playfully slapping Graham's arm.

"I am *not* that gay!"

Graham raised a single eyebrow.

Eli laughed again, another arm slap. "Fine—*GURL!*" He snapped his fingers for emphasis.

It was the funniest damn thing Graham had seen or heard in forever. The way Eli's voice shaped the word made it absolutely perfect.

"Okay, Princess—how about I pick you up at—"

"That's *Ms.* Princess to you!" Eli laughed.

"Fine. *Ms.* Princess—"

"You don't need to keep driving me, Graham. I can get to your place."

"How? You don't even know where I live."

Eli paused.

"True."

"How about this—I give you a lift tomorrow, that way you know where it is, and next time you can take an Uber."

"Next time? There's going to be a next time?"

"Well, I hope so. Unless you graduate to Your Majesty the *Queen* and us commoners are beneath a visit."

Eli shrieked with delight. "*Queen!* Oh, I like the sound of royalty."

Graham laughed—a real, full laugh, the kind that came from somewhere deep. He'd been doing that more these past few days.

"Goodnight, Eli."

"Goodnight, Graham."

Eli climbed out of the car, then leaned back in. "Thank you. For today. For everything."

"Thank you for suggesting it."

"See you tomorrow. Gurl."

"Goodnight, Your Majesty."

Eli closed the door, still laughing, and headed into his building. Graham watched until he was safely inside, then pulled away from the curb.

The drive home was quiet. But it was a different kind of quiet now—not the heavy silence of an empty house, but the peaceful silence of a full day. A good day. A day spent being useful instead of being pitied.

Simon would have liked Eli, he thought. Would have liked his humor, his kindness, the way he'd taken Lucy's hand without hesitation. Would have liked seeing Graham laugh again.

See? he could almost hear Simon saying. *That wasn't so hard, was it?*

No, Graham thought. It wasn't.

He was still smiling when he pulled into his driveway. The house was dark—he'd forgotten to leave a light on again—but for once, it didn't feel empty.

It just felt like home.

Chapter Four

GRAHAM PULLED up to his home as the garage door opened, revealing a white Volvo parked inside a sparse yet tidy garage. Eli was taking it all in.

He'd come to collect him around 11:30 and made a quick stop to purchase drinks, but abandoned the idea when he saw the grocery parking lot situation. Black Friday was not for the faint of heart.

"You're good with water or beer, right?"

Eli nodded, his eyes never leaving the state of chaos outside the car window. Even if Graham had only dishwater, he'd drink that rather than brave this madness.

Eli had sensed Graham was well off. Not that he showered cash around, but his car was a new-looking BMW and Graham dressed nicely. Not fashionably, exactly—Graham was more "Ralph Lauren meets Helly Hansen"—he seemed polished. That was probably the best word.

But he couldn't believe the home.

Graham hadn't been kidding when he said he lived near some woodlands. It was like a couple of acres. Or at least it felt like it. The house had trees out front, but the woods seemed to devour it from the back. Everything was so tasteful—the snow complemented the home perfectly, a single-story midcentury modern that had obviously been updated because it looked practically brand new.

Seeing the Volvo in the tidy garage—not a stain on the floor, not a box out of place—made Eli's curiosity spill over.

"Two cars?"

Then he realized. A second too late.

But Graham didn't seem fazed. It was still hard knowing Simon wasn't there waiting for them. But it didn't hurt as much thinking about him, especially when Eli asked.

"It's Simon's. Was... Simon's."

Eli remained quiet, admonishing himself to shut the hell up next time. But Graham picked up on it.

"You don't have to walk on pins and needles about Simon. Okay? It's helpful to talk about him sometimes without... well... without people feeling sorry for me."

Eli knew the feeling. Pity was not a party he ever wanted to attend.

"Did Simon design everything?"

"Mostly. Although I came down hard against painting the brick fireplace white."

"He wanted to paint it white?" Eli looked genuinely horrified. "Oh, dear god."

"Right? Thank you!" Graham's face lit up. "Everyone thought *I* was the crazy one. Just wait until you meet Anthony. I want you to tell him that exact sentence and then he can see who was right."

"I'd like to meet him. He sounds nice."

They got out of the car and walked into the mudroom as the garage door closed behind them.

"Anthony's husband passed away a couple of years ago. So..."

"I'm so sorry. That's... I can't imagine."

"Let's hope you don't have to anytime soon."

Eli simply smiled as he stood awaiting instruction from Graham. Shoes off or on? Coats? What was he supposed to do?

Graham looked at him, momentarily forgetting what he was talking about, then got it.

"Oh, just kick your shoes off here. It's mostly wooden floors anyway, but Simon would kill me if..." He paused. "He would've..."

Eli made quick work of squeezing out of his boots and hung his jacket on a hook that already held a couple of windbreakers, a perpetual indentation formed from years of use.

"Come on—let me show you around."

He took him into the kitchen, which doubled as a family room complete with the aforementioned non-whitewashed brick fireplace. The walls on either side were windows looking out to the woods. The kitchen was nothing short of Scandinavian bliss—clean lines, polished woods, metal and glass. It was all so... Graham.

Rounding the corner into the formal living room, Graham mentioned that he was never in here. It was more of the same style—another fireplace, comfortable if more formal-looking chairs surrounding a circular wooden table, a great place to watch the fire and read a book.

The step up to the foyer was stone, and more wood. Down the hall, the first door was a powder room, which Eli took advantage of.

Stepping out, he didn't see Graham, who had wandered naturally into his office next door and—absentmindedly—called out that he was there. Then he realized he was a dumbass and Eli wouldn't have heard him.

Popping back out, he caught Eli's eyes and welcomed him into the space where he spent most of his time.

The desk looked out through a glass wall of windows into the woods, offering a grand view of snowy evergreens and a frozen creek bed down the hillside slope. Eli took it all in without saying a word, touching the desk gingerly like it was an altar.

Then he turned and saw the back wall of bookshelves.

He stepped closer and scanned—loads of books of all sorts. And then he saw it.

The series he'd fallen in love with over the years. *The Oltrarno.*

Eli loved reading. It had been his respite growing up. It didn't require him to hear a damn thing. Or deal with people who didn't understand him. He'd read everything, going through phases: first horror books, but they kept him awake, so he switched to fantasy and dragons. That led to historical fiction and some classics. He made it through Jane Austen and found it good, if a bit much for his taste. Still, he kept exploring.

Somewhere along the way, he'd stumbled across the second book in *The Oltrarno* series and read it, not fully understanding everything at first, but then falling in love. He found a copy of the first, and it all made sense.

It was also the first book he'd ever read with two gay characters his own age. And they were... normal. Real guys—even if they had funny names from olden times. They loved each other. And that was okay. In fact, it worked out in the end.

Eli had never read a book with a gay character who wasn't just a nobody played for laughs, or the guy who died of AIDS, or something tragic. This was different. These characters were normal. And he liked them. No—he loved them. He'd imagined himself in Florence with them, at the academy. It was...

He pulled the first book from the shelf and looked at its cover. He'd only ever read the paperback, but this was leather-bound with colorful engraving and...

Graham's name.

Wait. He realized that in all this time, he'd never known Graham's last name. Nor had Graham ever asked his.

Graham watched as Eli turned, holding the book.

"Pelletier," Eli said.

"What?"

"Pelletier. It's my last name. I don't think I ever told you."

Graham realized he hadn't. He hadn't even noticed. It somehow hadn't seemed important enough. Eli was just Eli.

"Eli Pelletier," Graham said, trying it out. "French?"

"Canadian. Dad's side. Although they don't know anyone there anymore."

"I like it. It suits you."

"And..." Eli asked, somehow knowing the answer but wanting confirmation before he burst. "What's yours?"

"Mine? Oh dear. I can't believe we never told each other our last names. This is so funny."

"Yeah... so?"

"Oh, mine? Tierney. It's a bit of—"

"I KNEW IT!" Eli's face transformed. "Oh my god! You're THE Graham Tierney? This is YOUR book?" He held it up, nearly shaking.

Graham gave the embarrassed smile he always gave when he received compliments like this, or when people treated him like a celebrity, which he firmly believed he was not.

"Yes. I told you I was a writer."

"A writer, yes! But not THE writer of *The Oltrarno*! I can't believe—and you said it wasn't anything! I can't believe you—"

"It's not. They're not. Just something I came up with when Simon—"

"They ARE too, Graham!" Eli's voice cracked with emotion. "Don't you know how many gay boys like me finally saw something of themselves for the first time in these books? Something I could read and my mom wouldn't even give a second thought about, but inside I'd go to bed wondering what happened next? Would they fall in love? Would they live together? Would they be safe? Just like me! These books were incredible!"

Graham could only stand there, humbled. He'd heard versions of this before, but somehow he still saw himself as just a little writer scratching out meaningless books that reminded him of Simon and himself when they were young.

"I... I can't believe you're the one who gave me a lift home last week. Who bus-stalked me!"

"I didn't bus-stalk you!" Graham laughed.

"This is so—"

"Eli!"

"What?"

"Breathe! It's just me. Graham. The same man who tells the best jokes, remember?"

Eli's smile shifted, his former self reappearing with a slight eye roll.

"You mean the *worst* jokes."

"Ahhh... now there's the Eli I know."

They both laughed.

"Graham? Would you..."

"What?"

"Never mind. It's dumb. So—what's for lunch?"

"Nope. You don't get to ask half a question and then change the subject."

"It's dumb. Don't worry about it. Let's go to the kitchen and—"

Graham stood in the doorway, blocking the exit. "What?"

Eli paused. "Promise you won't laugh at me."

"No."

"I hate you, you know that, right?"

"No, you don't."

"Damn it, can't I be right at least once?"

"What is it?"

"Fine." Eli looked down at the book in his hands. "Would you sign a copy for me sometime?"

Graham laughed, having expected something else entirely. Was that all?

"Sure. If it means something to you."

Eli's snark caught back up with him. "Oh, and can you also sign your autograph to this blank check for me while you're at it?"

"Oh, my hearing aid battery just went out. What did you say?"

Eli reached over and slapped Graham's arm, laughing. "You're a bitch, you know that?"

"I love hearing you say that word."

"Bitch?"

Graham chuckled.

"What's so funny about the way I say bitch?"

He couldn't stop laughing, and Eli's repeated use of it only made it more endearing.

"Bitch. Bitch. Bitch," Eli said, grinning as he did it. He knew Graham wasn't making fun of him—he loved seeing Graham laugh. And if all it took was his way of saying a stupid word, he was going to keep doing it.

"Come on," Graham finally managed. "Let's make lunch."

Chapter Five

GRAHAM PULLED up to the nondescript parking lot of an office complex just off the highway from his neighborhood. He'd passed the general area on trips toward Boston, but it had been a while, and he'd never had reason to stop at this place before.

LL Bean's corporate offices were here—not the flagship store up in Freeport, but where the accountants and pencil-pushers worked. Eli's world.

When Eli had suggested dinner and mentioned a place he liked nearby, Graham offered to pick him up after work. No sense in Eli taking the bus in this weather just to double back.

The reason for his trip stood waiting outside—coat and gloves on, a scarf wrapped around his face to shield against the blowing snow. Graham barely recognized him.

"You ready?" Graham asked once Eli was safely in the warm car. Keyword: warm. Eli unwrapped the scarf and let out a breath. "It's freezing!"

"Why were you standing outside? I said I'd be here in fifteen minutes. And—" Graham glanced at the console clock. "It's been twenty-five. Sorry."

"You're buying!"

"Deal. Sorry again, I thought—"

"Just drive. I'll send you the directions."

Eli sent them to Graham's phone. Easier than trying to navigate verbally. Eli didn't mind talking with Graham—in fact, Graham was one of the few people he wasn't self-conscious around. But this was easier. And it gave him time to stop shivering.

. . .

The place was a blip on the road. Graham almost passed it, making a hard right once he spotted the entrance and causing Eli to nearly bang his head on the window.

"Sorry," Graham said for the third time that night.

"You want me to drive home?" Eli teased, checking to ensure all bits of himself were still intact.

"Okay, smartass. We're here, aren't we?"

Eli raised his eyebrows and caught Graham's smile.

Inside, they took a booth. It was a quiet Japanese-wannabe place that really served what Americans thought was authentic—bento boxes with potato salad and grilled pork cutlets, but with ketchup. The food wasn't as good as the ambiance. And by ambiance, Eli meant he could both see and hear without the distraction of nonstop chatter, over-bassed music cranked too high, and a crowd eyeballing your table the moment you sat down.

This place was the opposite. Only two other tables were occupied. No background music. A lamp hung low over their table, illuminating everything, including Graham's face. It also meant they could have a conversation without anyone eavesdropping.

"What's good?" Graham asked, studying the laminated menu bound on a ring.

"I usually have the teriyaki chicken and rice." Eli paused. "With onion rings."

Graham's eyes rose over the plastic menu. Eli gave him a "so sue me" look and shrugged.

Orders placed, Eli kickstarted the conversation by reaching into his backpack and pulling out a well-worn paperback.

He slid it across the table toward Graham, a pen alongside it, his face smug.

Graham noticed it was the first book of his series. And Eli hadn't lied—the book had been read. And reread. Often, from the looks of it.

"So?"

Graham smiled. Eli had been serious about wanting it signed. Book signings were something Graham didn't enjoy. Avoided, actually. Simon used to get after him about it. *You owe it to your fans*, he'd say. *What fans?* Graham would shoot back.

But when he did sign something, it pleased him more if it was well-used, like a comfortable sweater. Not just a trophy for a signature—something that demonstrated the reader had actually gotten something from it.

He opened the cover and looked at Eli for a moment, thinking. Then he began to write, angling the book so Eli couldn't see. When he finished, he closed it and pushed it to the side, setting the pen on top.

Eli reached for his book, but Graham caught his hand.

"Not until later. When you're home."

Eli looked at him like Graham had just told him he could see Santa but couldn't open his presents. He smirked, dismissing the order and reaching for the book again.

Graham grabbed it, laughing, and laid it on the seat beside him.

Eli looked like someone had taken his puppy away. Then he stuck out his tongue, just like the proper seven-year-old he apparently was.

Graham snickered. "Glad to be the adult at this table."

Eli laughed and relaxed back into the booth. "Fine."

They sat for a moment before Graham remembered.

"Angie and Sonya are throwing their HanukkahChristmaKwanzika party this Sunday at their place. They asked me to drag you along. You up for it?"

"Me? They know me?"

"Of course. Anthony knows you, which means everyone does. That girl can't keep a secret to save his life."

Eli laughed, picturing it.

"It's early this year—planning anything closer to Christmas is just foolhardy."

"Foolhardy? What are you? Grandpa? Eli grinned.

"Fine. Folks got shit to do. Better?"

"Much."

"It starts at six, which means we need to be there at five-thirty."

"I thought it was fashionably late."

"Not with us old folk." Graham paused. "Oh, and it's potluck, so..."

"I'm not a very good cook."

"Which is why I'm stopping by Whole Foods beforehand to pick up something from both of us."

"You're going to get pissed at the parking lot, you know that, right?"

"I'll be okay. As long as I mentally prepare myself."

"And Amazon lady might be there," Eli teased.

"Now *that* might break my spirit."

"Don't worry. I'll save my returns for another day."

"I'll pick you up after. No sense dragging you through that mess. Besides, it's right by the house. And Angie and Sonya's is up north anyway."

Eli got reflective. "Do I need to wear anything?"

"Well, clothes might work. They're good people, but you showing up naked might be a little awkward."

Eli slapped at his hand across the table. "Now who's the smartass?"

Graham laughed.

The food arrived in all its "fake Japanese" glory, and they began to eat.

. . .

"Graham?"

"Yeah?" He was trying to balance a piece of chicken between two cheap wooden chopsticks, the kind you break apart.

"You said you met Simon in college."

Graham paused slightly, then continued chewing. "Mmhmm. I was a freshman."

"Did you... date before?"

He smiled, his eyes taking on a faraway quality, like he was calling up old memories. "I told you—I've only ever been with Simon."

Eli nodded. "But did you, like, date anyone? Before Simon, I mean."

"No."

"Really?"

"No. I was too scared, initially."

"Not even a crush?"

Graham's eyes lit up, as if he'd been transported back to the mid-eighties.

"In seventh grade... no, I can't..." He laughed, embarrassed.

"No—tell me. What?"

"No, it's too embarrassing."

"No fair! What happened in seventh grade? Come on." Eli picked at a battered green bean, waiting.

"There was this kid—Jason Reynolds. He was..." Graham set down his chopsticks and gazed off, as if watching a rerun play on the wall behind Eli.

"What? Cute?"

"Beyond. I was in love. Or what I thought was love."

Eli could only imagine Graham at thirteen. In love.

"He sat two desks away from me in English, and every day I'd get there early just to watch him walk in. He..." Graham trailed off.

Eli noticed Graham speaking differently than he had before. Transformed somehow into a nerdy, bookish, sweet kid sitting at a desk in seventh-grade English, falling in love with a boy named Jason.

"So did you ask him out?"

"Oh, god no!" Graham laughed. "I could never do that. I was..."

"What?"

"I wasn't sure how to. Or even if he was..."

"Gay?"

Graham nodded.

"So what did you do?"

"Just admired. Sometimes he'd talk to me, and I'd get all flustered. My heart would race, and then..."

"What?" Eli's smile couldn't be contained.

"I'd go home and dream about kissing him."

"Aww, that's so sweet, Graham. I never thought of you like that."

Graham looked away, shy, recalling his youth. Then his expression shifted to a slight frown.

"What?"

"Nothing. It's... nothing." Graham picked up his chopsticks to resume eating.

"Graham—something's wrong. What is it?"

"Just... remembering high school."

Eli noticed the air cooling around them. He wanted to know but didn't want to push Graham down a dark path. Something had happened, he could tell.

Graham seemed preoccupied with his thoughts. Eli began pushing his food around, unsure how to change the subject, when Graham continued.

"I was too scared about being gay all through high school. Although one boy my senior year sort of came out to me. And..."

Eli stopped playing with his food and leaned closer, listening, watching Graham's lips.

"We were at my house. He'd come over a couple of times after school. Stayed the night twice. I liked him, but I didn't know if he... you know. Liked me."

Eli nodded. He imagined the two of them.

"Anyway, he was over one Friday night, and it was late. My folks were in bed, I thought. And we were laughing and doing—I don't remember what. But my door wasn't closed all the way. And then..." Graham paused, his face lighting up slightly. "He leaned in and started to kiss me."

Everything went silent for a beat. Graham nearly closed his eyes, reliving the moment. Eli tilted his head, watching this man across from him become his younger self—his first kiss.

But the nostalgia vanished. Graham's voice dropped lower, which made it harder for Eli to hear. He didn't want to be rude and interrupt, but he was having difficulty matching what he was seeing with the little he could make out.

Gently, almost without thinking, Eli touched Graham's hand, startling him enough to look up.

"Sorry—I can't hear you, Graham."

Graham apologized, took a breath, and started again.

"My father had been walking down the hall. He saw the two of us through the crack in the door. He slammed it open—startled us before we even touched lips."

Graham's voice steadied, but something in his eyes had gone distant.

"He was disgusted. Angry. Not himself. I'd always thought my father was a kind man. Didn't speak much. But apparently not if his son was about to be kissed by another boy."

Eli listened, barely breathing.

"The other boy was mortified. Scared. He said we weren't doing anything—just play-pretending. He started to cry. My father yelled. Loudly. I'd never heard him like that. His face was red, like he'd been drinking or was so angry his cheeks had frozen."

Graham paused.

"The boy grabbed his bag and ran past my dad, out the door. I don't know where he went. I just stood there, staring at the space where he'd been, and then at my father. Who was only getting started."

Eli's chest tightened.

"He told me I 'knew better.' That I was 'supposed to do what you're supposed to do.' That 'ain't nothing better than the comfort of a good woman.' That 'no son of his was going to hell' with all those 'perverts and child-molesting bastards.'"

Graham's voice had gone flat, reciting words he'd clearly never forgotten.

"Something in me caught fire. Something painful. Crushing. And whatever small amount of energy I had just... doubled. Tripled. Boiled up until it exploded out of me. I yelled back at him."

Eli sat frozen.

"I said, 'Okay, Dad—I know, I know!' He told me not to talk to him in that tone. I asked, 'What tone, *Dad*?' He said he ought to smack it out of me. Raised his hand." Graham's voice wavered. "I flinched. But my anger doubled. I said, 'What? You going to smack the gay out of me?'"

Graham touched his cheek, unconsciously, as if feeling the memory.

"He asked what I'd said. I told him. 'I'm gay, Dad.' He told me not to use that word in his house. So I said it again. 'Gay. I'm gay, Dad. Always have been. You've just never noticed.'"

Eli's hand had risen to cover his mouth.

"He said no son of his was 'that.' I said, 'Gay?' And then—"

Graham stopped. His hand was still on his cheek.

"He hit me. Hard enough to knock me down. I fell and hit my head on my desk chair."

Eli gasped audibly.

They sat in silence. Graham staring into space, touching his face. Eli unsure what to say or do.

"Graham?" Eli finally asked. "Are you okay?"

Graham paused, then returned to the present and looked at Eli. He apologized.

"Why are you apologizing?" Eli's voice cracked. "I can't believe your dad hit you."

Graham shook his head and didn't respond. He didn't know why he'd told that story. The only other person who knew was Simon.

"What happened?" Eli didn't know what to ask, but clearly something more had.

Graham let out a breath. He looked at the table, then remembered he needed to let Eli see his face. It was difficult, but he made himself look up.

"I woke up in the hospital."

Eli let out a sharper gasp than before. "Oh my god, Graham."

"It's okay. I'm fine. That was a long time ago."

"But still—what did he do to you? Did you have any damage? Did you break anything?" The questions tumbled out, many of which Graham had asked himself over the years. Truth was, he'd been unconscious and didn't know much beyond what his mother told him later. But she'd glossed over most of it. So he hadn't been sure of the details until he came to.

He explained what little he knew.

His mother had come running when she heard the arguing. She found her son lying awkwardly on the floor, his head turned wrong, unconscious. His father was seething with anger but hadn't fully registered the state of his boy. His mother screamed at him to call for help. His father said Graham was just being dramatic. Told him to wake up.

The ambulance came. They took Graham away in a head restraint.

He was lucky—just a concussion, no brain bleeding. The blow would have snapped the base of his skull if his head had been rotated a few inches further. As it was, he had a three-inch fracture that would heal. If you pressed your finger to the right spot, you could still feel the line where the two halves had fused back together.

His memory of that time was fuzzy. But within a week, aside from some headaches, he was back to normal.

Normal, that is, except that he went to stay with his aunt until he finished high school.

He never spoke to his father again.

Eli was dumbfounded. Saddened. His heart fell ten stories for Graham, imagining him finishing his senior year away from his family.

"It turned out okay," Graham said quietly. "I got scholarships. Accepted to Columbia. Moved there that summer to take early classes, stayed in the dorms." He tried to smile. "I met Simon during orientation. And... well. The rest is history."

Eli was stunned. What do you say? Nothing. There was nothing he could think of. His heart just wanted to do something—anything—that could convey the profound sense of loss and vulnerability that a younger Graham must have felt back then. Before Eli was even born.

He was no longer hungry. The mood had shifted entirely.

Graham sensed it too, and apologized again.

Eli stopped him. "Please don't. I'm beyond honored that you felt you could tell me that. Especially if Simon was the only other person who knew."

. . .

Graham thought about telling Simon.

It had been between freshman and sophomore year, when Graham wasn't going home for summer. He'd had to explain why. And it had nearly killed Simon. He wanted to hop a train to Maine and beat the shit out of that old man.

But time had already done the deed. Graham's father died of a heart attack early that winter. Graham didn't go to the funeral. Wasn't invited. His mother let him know, but didn't say more than the bare facts. She never gave her opinion of Graham—of who he was, of what had happened—but his sister knew. She wanted to help. She just didn't know how.

To this day, it wasn't talked about.

Even when Simon passed away, she'd been caring. She'd showed up for the funeral. She'd wanted to help her brother through his grief. But she didn't quite know what to do. Graham loved her, and she'd always treated Simon like family. But there was an unspoken distance. And it seemed to have started that night his father caught him.

Almost.

Chapter Six

THE HANNUKAHCHRISTMAKWANZIKA PARTY was an annual tradition—for at least five years now. Angie and Sonya had lamented that it always seemed haphazard who was coming to what or which invitation was open to whom around the holidays, so they took it upon themselves to set the tradition once and for all: the first Sunday of December, before the chaos of the season made scheduling impossible. Whoever showed, showed. No pressure. No fussing with invites. No anxiety over what to wear, who to buy for, or any of that business.

Potluck. Bring what you want. Including booze. They would supply the Christmas ham, and if you didn't like ham, then bring whatever the hell you wanted because that's what you got otherwise. That and a sugar pie Sonya made annually because it reminded her of her nan.

It was Simon who had coined "HannukahChristmaKwanzika" in one of his better moments, assisted by half a bottle of Merlot one night over dinner when the tradition was born. *Why not celebrate everything?* he'd said, and everyone agreed. If their little ragtag group was welcome to all, then by god let it be "welcome to all." T-shirts with the name imprinted were suggested, but nothing ever came of it.

What did come of it was the kind of ease that any of their little dinners provided. The food, activities, or even location were really incidental. The idea that there was an anchor for them to have, especially at that time of year, was what really mattered.

And now their little group was expanding by one.

. . .

Eli ran out to the BMW as the snow fell hard, piling onto the hood faster than the heat of the engine could melt it.

"You survived?"

Graham's knuckles looked white from gripping the wheel too tight, but otherwise he seemed unscathed. "Let's just say, next time I volunteer to go to Whole Foods on a Sunday afternoon before Christmas, please shoot me and put me out of my misery."

"I told you so."

"Aren't you supposed to say that you're *not* going to say 'I told you so'?"

"Nope. Told you so. Told you so." Eli sang it like a little kid, his voice making it even more endearing.

"You're lucky I'm a nice guy, otherwise I'd dump your ass on the side of the road."

"Dump me? Never. I'm the entertainment."

They made their way slowly through the near white-out conditions, heading north toward Angie and Sonya's. Graham filled Eli in on the hosts—how he'd been introduced to them by Anthony. Angie looked like Mrs. Santa Claus with her white hair and wire-rimmed glasses, while Sonya retained her long brunette hair, now greying, and was the "take charge, go-getter" of the two. They'd been together since forever, as far as he knew, although they both had grandchildren.

Eli looked at him inquisitively.

"I gather they were both married well before my time and somehow found each other. I don't ask."

Anthony would be there, of course.

"What's his deal?"

Graham explained how Anthony had lost his husband Theodore a couple of years ago. It was tough—for everyone. First in their group to deal with something like that. He seemed to be doing well now, lived just down the way from Graham. He and Theodore used to come over for dinner often with Simon and him. The thought of Anthony made Graham laugh.

"What?"

"Just wait until you get him and Angie together."

"Why?"

"Just wait."

Eli snickered.

Then there were Jason and Thomas—both Graham's age, living a little farther away than everyone else. They'd built a new home a couple of years back, beautiful place. They'd been hoping to have somewhere to retire one day, and this was it.

"Are they retired?"

"Oh, god no. I don't think they ever could. Jason is too busy saving the world with some political thing or another, while Thomas, when he isn't being some sort of tax accountant, teaches swimming at the Y."

"Hey, I'm an accountant."

"Good. You and Thomas can talk then. I can never understand half the things he says. Sounds boring to me."

"Hey!"

"I stand by my words."

Eli smirked.

"Oh, and then there's Brett. Poor Brett." Graham laughed as he strained to see through the windshield. The snow wasn't relenting, but they were almost there.

"What about him?"

"He's fine. The token straight man. Drinks beer. Watches football or whatever sport thing that is."

"You are so gay!"

"What? I can't help it if I don't understand what those sports ball competitions are all about."

"Sports ball?" Eli laughed again.

"Yeah, where they throw the field goal or some such."

"I happen to like football!" Eli protested, though his laugh gave him away.

"Well then, Brett will have an ally. Poor Brett doesn't have anyone who understands or gives a damn about the 'latest game' or 'scores.'" Graham perked up, remembering. "Oh! Then there's his wife, Donna."

"Yeah? What about her?"

"There are no words."

Eli looked at him funny.

"Seriously. She's someone who just needs to be met, is all."

Eli looked a little nervous.

"She's a sweetheart—don't be worried. But let's just say she commands the room."

"How do she and Brett know everyone, given they're..."

"Straight?" Graham smiled. "It's not just the gay boys and girls club, you know."

Eli shrugged.

"Brett and Thomas work together, and—"

"Accounting?" Eli said hopefully.

"Oh god. We've got three in our group now!" Graham bemoaned, but Eli nearly bounced in his seat. "You're all going to take over the table conversation talking about Roth conversions and depreciation schedules and—"

"It'll be so much fun!"

"Good thing we're here. I need fresh air!"

• • •

They pulled up to a rather homey but comfortable 1940s bungalow that looked like Santa's elves had been loaned out to decorate. Even amid the snow and blowing wind, everything was lit up festively—a plastic Santa and reindeer, angels glowing beside the front door, multiple snowmen aglow from incandescent bulbs inside, wreaths with twinkle lights on each window, and best of all: a seven-foot-tall snow angel in white, gold, and blue, tied down with stakes so she wouldn't fly off in the wind.

Eli was mesmerized.

Graham took one look at him and knew he'd turned twelve all over again. It did that to everyone. "Come on. It's freezing," he said, certain Eli hadn't heard him—his face was still turned to take everything in as they stood by the trunk collecting their Whole Foods contribution to the potluck.

Bringing Eli back from his winter wonderland gaze, Graham loaded his arms with a box and slammed the trunk shut.

Angie greeted them at the door, both stomping their feet to shake off the snow while she ushered them inside out of the weather. Sonya appeared and collected the grocery bag from Graham while Angie helped Eli with the box, allowing them to shake off their coats and adjust to the steaming heat that fogged up Graham's glasses and was already drying out Eli's lips.

Graham began walking toward the kitchen, where the activity seemed to be happening, when Angie's voice stopped him.

"Graham!"

"What?" He turned and saw Eli standing there looking like he should say something.

"Oh—I'm not used to these social things." He gestured between them. "This is Eli. Eli, these are the old broads."

Angie slapped at his arm while Sonya took Eli by the elbow, telling him not to pay attention to that dreadful old man.

Eli laughed and caught Graham's eye, noticing how everyone seemed to enjoy this playful banter.

"Oh—" Graham turned back before forgetting. "Eli's a little hard of hearing, so make sure you let him see your face." He started to turn away, then stopped, looking at Eli. "If you can keep your eyes on them that long."

Eli looked mortified, but Sonya just pulled him along. "Don't pay any attention to him, Eli. Santa brought a lump of coal in his stocking this year."

"To warm the cold recesses of his dark heart," Eli added.

Sonya slapped Eli's arm as she ushered him through. What was she going to do with these two?

. . .

The rest of the gang stood around the kitchen island. This may have been an older home, but the inside was completely updated, and Eli noticed how charming everything seemed—decorations placed here and there as if children were coming to see their grandma's holiday treasures. Which, he thought, perhaps they were.

"Graham!" the group shouted, some raising their glasses in a toast.

Angie positioned herself in front of Eli and addressed the room. "Since this old man can't be trusted to do proper introductions, this is Eli."

"Eli!" the gang echoed, raising their glasses again, smiling. He couldn't help but smile back as Sonya let go of his arm and took her place by the sink—obviously the caretaker-of-everyone for the night. She pressed a glass of something into his hand just as a man with a small white beard made his way over.

"I'm Anthony, but I'm sure Graham has told you about me already."

Before Eli could respond, Angie stepped next to Anthony. "We're also a pretty good Mr. and Mrs. Santa Claus, don't you think?"

Eli stopped, then realized—give them red suits and they would be. His eyes widened, and he felt like he was meeting celebrities. "Oh my god, you would!"

It was the first time anyone had heard Eli speak. The "Clauses" smiled warmly, both clearly prepared by whatever Graham had gently told them beforehand.

"Eli, let me introduce you to the others, since I know Graham won't." Angie shot him a look. Graham had already been caught stealing an olive from the charcuterie board and gave a "who, me?" expression.

She started properly with Anthony, then moved to Jason and Thomas.

"Graham said you're an accountant like me."

"Did he?" Thomas replied, eyebrows raised.

Eli hesitated — had he gotten it wrong? Maybe Graham had said something else and he'd misread it.

But Thomas was smiling. "Oh, I am. I'm just surprised Graham even remembered."

Eli laughed, noticing how everyone seemed to give Graham shit—but in a playful way.

Graham loved it, actually. It meant they weren't trying to "be there for him." It felt like old times.

"And this is Brett."

"Hey, Eli. I'm the token."

Eli cocked his head. "Token?"

"Token straight man." Brett laughed. "I like sports, unlike the rest of this heathen crew."

Eli let out a barrel laugh, remembering his conversation with Graham in the car. "I actually like football."

Brett's face lit up. "Really? Wow! Thank god! There's finally *one of you* I can talk to about something other than Broadway shows and celebrity gossip!"

"I'm not really into that stuff myself," Eli said, commiserating. "Who's your team? Let me guess... Patriots?"

Brett became animated. "Hell no! I'm from New York. Jets all the way, baby!"

"Jets?" Eli got into it. "They suck! Pats or nothing!"

"Them's fightin' words."

"Oh, good lord! You didn't tell us he's one of *them*, Graham!" Jason called over, watching Brett and Eli talk sports.

Graham shrugged. "All of us can't be refined."

Eli hadn't heard their exchange, but Brett sure did. "What do you mean, refined? Eli and I know a good thing when we see it."

Thomas grabbed Eli's arm and spoke directly to him. "Don't worry, darling. They're just jealous of your ability to actually speak 'Brett.'"

Eli laughed while Brett mocked offense, then smiled.

"Speaking of which," Thomas added, "where's that tornado of yours?"

"She had to pick up Niles," Brett said. "She'll be here."

Eli realized they were speaking of Brett's wife. He couldn't remember her name from Graham's briefing, but he did remember Graham being cagey about her.

He didn't need to wait long to understand why.

Everyone's attention turned toward the front of the house. Eli could only hear some sort of commotion, but realized that must be her entrance.

Of course it was. Not bothering with the doorbell, she swooped in with a "Honeys! I'm home!" and flowed proudly into the kitchen, her scarf and coat somehow coming off as if she were a whisper of air breaking free. Her son, Niles, was left to close the door and keep up, collecting her things as she deposited them in his arms.

She headed straight for Eli across the room, and he didn't know what hit him.

"So, you must be the mysterious Eli we've all heard about." She extended her hand.

He didn't know whether to kiss it or shake it.

Brett leaned in and whispered something, forgetting Eli couldn't hear him.

"Darling," his wife admonished, "I don't think he quite heard you. Care to share with everyone? Louder?"

Eli turned to see Brett blushing.

"Eli—" She touched his hand to get his attention. "My husband here was trying to tell you how *wonderful* it is to have you in our little band of misfits. Right, darling?"

"Of course, sweetheart."

Graham laughed. Angie smiled. Sonya shook her head and handed Donna a champagne flute—full.

"Lay off the kid, Donna," Jason said, but she kept her gaze on Eli.

"So Graham tells us you've gotten to know each other better." She turned over her shoulder. "Right, Graham?"

He shrugged and went back to picking at the charcuterie.

"We haven't been able to get Graham out of the house since—"

Everyone gave her a death stare.

Graham didn't seem to have heard. Or cared.

"What? It's true. Seems Eli here has single-handedly been able to bring our little Graham back to life."

Anthony walked over and took Eli's arm, guiding him to the other side of the kitchen. "Forgive her, Eli. She knows not what she does."

The others snickered while Eli tried to figure out if this was still playful or if something else was happening.

Anthony steered him toward a shy-looking young man—a mini version of Brett, but with Donna's eyes and hair. Lanky, tallish, still in his winter coat, khakis, boots, and a button-down flannel. Eli thought he looked like a Portland bookworm.

"This here is Donna and Brett's offspring," Anthony said, which made the young man shrink even further into himself. "Niles, this is Eli. Graham's friend."

The way Anthony said "friend" made it seem as if there were hidden meaning—which there wasn't. Niles didn't look him in the eye, just mumbled something that might have been hello. Eli couldn't tell.

"Nice to meet you, Niles." Eli said it a bit louder than Niles was probably expecting. The young man looked up, curious, before catching Eli's eye and returning to his usual quiet stance.

"Niles is shy, but he's a good guy." Anthony winked at him, and Niles smiled. He liked Anthony—Anthony was always nice to him, treating him like the real Santa Claus would.

Sonya appeared with champagne flutes for both Eli and Niles just as Donna announced a toast to their newest little misfit.

Graham smiled, wanting the group to have time with Eli, but made his way over.

"To Eli!" Everyone toasted and clinked. Eli drank, smiled a little embarrassed, and turned to find Graham beside him.

"So, welcome to the little club."

"Thanks." Eli blushed.

Graham noticed Niles hovering behind them, as if trying to become one with the wall. Typical Niles. He motioned for him to join, and after a moment's hesitation, Niles took two steps forward—never making eye contact.

"Niles is in college," Graham offered, more to make conversation than anything. He always tried to include Niles. Not that anyone treated him poorly, but Graham had watched him grow up and always felt he needed to be a bit more on the kid's side during these gatherings. Simon used to tease Graham about being Niles's second daddy when the boy was little.

"Where do you go to school?" Eli asked.

Niles mumbled something, and Graham started to speak up. "Niles, Eli is a bit hard—"

But Eli interrupted him. While he appreciated Graham trying to help, it was his story to tell.

"I'm hard of hearing, Niles."

Niles looked up, intrigued by Eli's voice.

"So it's easier if I can see your lips to understand you."

Niles nodded, realizing the awkwardness of his usual head-down posture.

Eli smiled. "So, where do you go to school?"

"USM."

"That's cool. Like it?"

"Yeah. It's okay."

"Are you staying in the dorms, or..."

"I'm still at home. Easier." He added "you know" to sound more normal.

Eli nodded. "I understand. What year are you?"

"Senior. Graduating in May."

Eli noticed that Niles's responses were clipped—answers to a quiz, almost.

"Cool. Declared a major?"

"I'm going to be an electrical engineer. But I also like robotics too."

"Wow. You must be very smart."

Niles blushed—he always did when people said that, which was often.

"Have you built any robots, or are you—"

"I've got two finished, and I'm working on a humanoid one right now, and it's really cool because I've programmed it to—" Niles stopped, hearing himself. "I mean... it's pretty cool."

Eli smiled. He could tell Niles relaxed when speaking about something that interested him.

"That sounds amazing. Maybe you can show me sometime?"

Niles blushed again. No one had ever seemed genuinely interested in his projects—usually it was just polite chit-chat. Everyone here was older, and he knew they were just trying to be nice. But Eli seemed different.

"Really?"

"Sure! I love that stuff."

"What do you do?" Niles asked tentatively.

"Me? I'm an accountant. Boring stuff."

"Hey now!" Thomas had overheard and made his way over, placing an arm around Graham's shoulders. "Us accountants rule the world, you know. Without us, all these poor slobs wouldn't know how much money they have!"

"Or waste!" Eli added.

"Or waste!" Thomas agreed.

"Oh, good lord." Graham sighed, smiling. "Niles, get ready to fall asleep."

Niles giggled.

"What's the problem, Graham?" Thomas pressed. "The real excitement is in ledgers, right, Eli?"

Eli grinned. "I think I'm staying out of this one."

"Good boy," Graham teased.

"You could run for office, Eli." Thomas laughed.

"Niles, want to go look at the decorations?" Eli asked, spotting his escape.

Niles looked like Eli had been speaking to someone else entirely.

Eli raised his eyebrows—*Let's leave these two before they rope us into more old-folk talk.* Niles smiled and gave a slight nod.

Graham saw what Eli was doing, and it warmed his heart.

"Niles can't save you all the time, Eli," Thomas called after them.

Eli just took Niles by the shoulder, and they wandered into the living room.

Angie and Sonya must have spent days decorating. Every branch of the tree held tightly wired lights of all colors, garland, popcorn strings, and more ornaments than anyone could count—not a hole anywhere. Eli studied the animated ornaments: tiny lit-up Christmas scenes, dancing snowmen, a Santa popping up and down a chimney, and a clever ice skating rink with tiny figures gliding around.

Niles lingered near that one too. He'd always loved these moving diorama ornaments—they'd sparked his interest in how things worked. He supposed they still did.

Eli pointed toward the far end of the room, where a complete winter village scene sprawled across a table. Lit up with moving cars, carolers, a snowball fight on the edge, and a Christmas carnival up top—complete with ice skaters, a Ferris wheel, and penguins sliding down an ice slide.

Eli was delighted. It felt like being in a toy store.

Niles stood next to him and began to mumble something, then realized his mistake. He tapped lightly at Eli's shoulder, and when Eli turned, Niles felt suddenly nervous under his full attention.

"I... I..."

Eli gave him a look of encouragement.

"I helped build this with them. A couple of weeks ago."

"You did this?"

Niles looked down and nodded.

"Wow! This is incredible, Niles. How did you get the skaters to move like that?"

Niles lit up, explaining about the magnets and how underneath the table was a whole electromechanical world he'd developed to make everything run.

"Here. Look." He knelt down on the carpet, and Eli followed.

They spent the next ten minutes examining the underside of the village rather than the village itself, but Eli didn't mind. It was fascinating, and Niles was clearly in his element—animated, articulate, a completely different person when talking about something he loved.

"Boys? What are you doing?" Jason had knelt down and stuck his head under the table alongside them.

"Niles is showing me all his work."

"You did this?" Jason seemed genuinely surprised.

Niles nodded as the three of them stood, Jason stretching his back with a groan while Eli laughed inwardly at the old-man stretch.

"Honey—come look at Niles's handiwork!" Jason called toward the kitchen.

Everyone wandered in to see, gushing and complimenting. Several mentioned how it reminded them of growing up.

"Back in the olden days?" Eli teased.

"Yes, Eli," Anthony shot back. "Back when we rode horses to school!"

Graham laughed, enjoying how Eli had found his footing. Even Niles seemed more present—almost comfortable.

Sonya interrupted the fun. "Time for supper!" She ushered everyone toward the dining room, a space a little too small for all of them, but they made it work.

"Grab a plate in the kitchen and make your way here. No assigned seats, so..."

"Service is so hard to find," Donna lamented.

"Tell me about it!" Sonya agreed, and everyone laughed—even Donna, who secretly loved the whole evening.

"Okay, who brought the three-bean dip as a main?" Thomas called out.

Everyone looked around. Graham's hand went up slowly.

"It's all they had."

"Really, Eli? You couldn't have taught him better?"

Eli threw his hands up. "I said I'd help, but he went on his own!"

Graham laughed along with everyone, but something flickered behind his eyes. Simon was the one who would have gotten those things right. But he wasn't here. Graham thought about him for a moment, and Anthony caught the shift, coming over to usher him along in line. No words. Just knowing.

Eli sat down next to Niles, and both began eating without waiting for everyone else.

"Hungry?" Angie admonished them mildly.

Niles immediately set down his fork, but Eli just grinned. "Starving!"

It made Niles laugh, and he picked his fork back up.

The night progressed in the same easy way—tiny arguments over whose pumpkin pie was better (Jason and Thomas versus Anthony, all store-bought), debate over where Donna's perfume came from (Sonya thought it was "okay," but Angie hinted that Santa might like to bring it this year), speculation about how much snow would fall before Christmas. The usual banter of old friends.

Plates were thrown away ("Nothing but the best paper for this crowd!" Sonya had declared), the table cleared, and a mild poker game got going. Eli and Niles sat out, watching.

"I've got no poker face," Eli admitted.

Thomas winked. "All the more reason to join."

Everyone lost to Anthony, who looked like he didn't know how to play. That Santa face was good for bluffing.

Graham caught Eli's eye and nodded—time to head out. The roads had already been bad coming; who knew what they'd be like now.

Hugs and kisses all around. Laments about leaving so soon. Donna made Eli promise to take her out to lunch sometime, and Thomas teased that she meant it—*he'd* be taking *her* out. They laughed. Donna smiled. She knew.

Niles offered his hand, but Eli pulled him into a hug like everyone else. He felt Niles stiffen, then slowly relax. When Eli let go, he smiled.

Angie mothered over Eli as he put on his coat and gloves, pulling his hat down over his curly hair like his own mother would, making sure his coat was properly buttoned. Eli enjoyed the fuss, even as Graham tried to wave her off.

"Let him be, Angie! You're suffocating him!"

A dash through the snow. Eli helped Graham clear the windshield, and off they went, the heater straining to warm up.

"So, there's the gang." Graham exhaled as he pulled away.

"I like them."

"They're a good bunch."

"And I feel for Niles."

Graham nodded, eyes on the snowy road. "He's a special kid."

"He's not a kid, Graham."

"Guy? Better?"

"I think he just needs a friend or two."

"His mom's been hoping for that for years. Simon used to—" Graham paused, took a breath. "Simon used to say that he suspected Niles..."

"Of what?"

Graham glanced at Eli, then back at the road. "Of being an Olympic champion. What do you think?"

Eli got it and laughed.

"You know, you're kind of a bitch sometimes."

Graham giggled—there was that endearing way Eli said the word.

"Bitch! Bitch! Bitch!" Eli spat at him, laughing.

Chapter Seven

THE SNOW WAS ALREADY FALLING when Eli stepped off the bus.

Not the gentle kind that drifted down like confetti—this was the serious stuff, the kind that meant business. The wind had picked up too, cutting through his coat and finding every gap between his scarf and collar. The weather app on his phone had been screaming warnings all day: 8-10 inches expected, temperatures dropping below zero overnight, stay home if you can.

But Eli needed milk. And bread. And something for dinner that wasn't the sad remainder of last week's leftover pasta.

The Hannaford parking lot was chaos—cars circling for spots, shopping carts abandoned in snowdrifts, everyone with the same idea at the same time. Eli pulled his hood tighter and made his way toward the entrance, head down against the wind.

Inside was barely better. The aisles were packed, half the shelves already stripped of essentials. Eli grabbed a basket and navigated through the crowd, collecting what he needed: milk, bread, eggs, a frozen pizza, some apples. Nothing fancy. Just enough to ride out the storm.

He found a checkout line that looked marginally shorter than the others and settled in to wait, scrolling through his phone. Graham had texted earlier—something about hoping Eli had enough supplies, an offer to bring anything he needed. Eli had assured him he was fine. He was always fine.

The line crept forward. Eli looked up occasionally, people-watching to pass the time. A woman gesturing emphatically at her husband, pointing at the three gallons of milk in their cart—he could imagine the argument.

A teenager slumped behind his mother, radiating the particular misery of being dragged along. An elderly man squinting at his receipt, lips moving as he checked each line.

The noise in the store was a wall of sound—registers beeping, carts rattling, voices blending into an indistinguishable hum. Eli couldn't make out any of it. Just movement and chaos and the slow shuffle forward.

And then—a flash of movement. A small figure darting between shoppers, heading straight toward him.

"UNCLE ELI!"

He felt more than heard it—the high pitch cutting through, the shape of his name on her lips. Before he could process what was happening, something collided with his legs. He looked down.

Lucy.

She was grinning up at him, her face flushed with cold, her too-thin coat dusted with snow that hadn't quite melted yet. She was talking rapidly, bouncing with excitement, her face turned up and then away and then up again—impossible to follow.

Eli knelt down to her level, gently turning her face toward his.

"Slow down, sweetheart. Look at me so I can understand you."

Lucy took a breath, visibly trying to calm herself. She pointed across the store. "Levi's over there! We're getting food!"

Eli followed her gesture. Two registers over, he could see a familiar figure—tall for his age, hunched over a small collection of items on the conveyor belt. Levi. His back was to them, and even from here, Eli could see the tension in his shoulders.

"Come on," Eli said, taking Lucy's hand. "Let's go say hi."

He stepped out of line, abandoning his place without a second thought, and made his way toward Levi with Lucy practically skipping beside him.

As they got closer, Eli saw what was happening.

Levi was at the register, but he wasn't checking out. He was pulling items off the belt—a loaf of bread, a jar of peanut butter, a package of cheese, some crackers—and setting them aside. His lips were moving, counting silently. The cashier's mouth was moving too, impatient. Behind Levi, a woman with a full cart kept checking her watch.

Levi hadn't seen them yet. He was too focused on the math—the impossible math of making not-enough stretch.

Lucy tugged free and ran to him, pulling at his coat.

Eli watched Levi look down, confused, then register his sister. His head came up, scanning—and found Eli instead.

The expression on his face was something Eli recognized. He'd worn it himself, once or twice. The particular shame of being caught in a moment you'd do anything to hide.

Levi said something—Eli caught the shape of his name, maybe "what are you doing here"—but the noise swallowed the rest. Eli stepped closer.

"Hey, Levi."

The people nearby glanced over at the sound of his voice—that familiar quick look, the slight surprise, the polite looking-away. Eli was used to it. Had been his whole life.

Levi's face flushed deeper. He gestured at the line behind him, said something apologetic to the woman waiting, and stepped out of the queue. He gathered the items he'd set aside—the things he'd been putting back—and moved toward Eli, Lucy trailing behind.

They found a spot near the end of an aisle, away from the worst of the crowd.

"Where's your mom?" Eli asked.

Levi's eyes dropped. His lips moved, but Eli shook his head slightly—*I need to see you*—and Levi looked up, tried again.

"She had... an appointment. She's picking us up later."

An appointment. In this weather. Eli didn't push.

He looked at the items Levi was clutching. Bread. Peanut butter. Cheese. Crackers. A couple of apples. Basic stuff.

"What do you need?" Eli asked.

Levi shook his head. "We're fine. I just—I miscounted. I need to put some back."

"Levi."

The boy stopped.

"What do you need?"

Levi's jaw tightened. He glanced at Lucy, who was watching them both with wide eyes, not quite following the conversation but sensing its weight.

"All of it," Levi said quietly. "But I don't have enough."

Eli nodded. He looked toward the registers—the lines had grown longer in the few minutes they'd been talking.

"Come on," he said. "We'll get back in line. I've got some things too."

They found a queue and waited. Lucy stood between them, holding Levi's hand, looking up at Eli with curiosity. He smiled at her, but he could see she was having trouble understanding him when he spoke—the noise, the chaos, her angle. Levi bent down and repeated things for her, translating Eli into something she could follow.

When they were a few people from the front, Eli knelt down to Lucy's level.

"Lucy. Can you do me a favor?"

She looked at Levi, uncertain. He nodded, encouraging her.

Eli pulled out his wallet and counted out some bills. He pressed them into her small hand.

"When we get up there, I need you to pay for the groceries. Give this to the cashier. Can you do that?"

Lucy's eyes went wide. She looked at the money, then at Levi. "Can I really?"

Levi's face was tight, but he knelt down beside Eli. "It's okay, Luce. You can do it. Just hand her the money when she tells you the number."

She clutched the money like it was treasure.

When they reached the register, Eli loaded everything onto the belt—Levi's items, his own items, all of it. The cashier scanned without comment, announced the total. Lucy stepped forward importantly and handed over the bills.

The change came back: four dollars and some coins. Eli took it from the cashier and handed it to Lucy.

"Put this in your pocket," he said, making sure she was looking at him. "Keep it safe for me. Don't lose it."

She shoved the money into her coat, patting it to make sure it was secure. Levi watched, his throat moving as he swallowed.

"Thank you," he said, barely loud enough for Eli to catch.

"Come on. Let's get out of here."

The wind hit them like a wall the moment they stepped outside.

Eli gasped, pulling his scarf up over his nose. The snow was coming down harder now, visibility already dropping. The parking lot had become a slow-motion disaster of spinning wheels and cars barely moving.

"Hold on," Eli said, setting the bags down just inside the vestibule.

He pulled out his phone and texted Graham:

Found Levi and Lucy at Hannaford on Forest Ave. Their mom not with them. Storm is bad.

He looked up at the two kids. Lucy was shivering despite her excitement. Her coat was thin—not meant for weather like this. Levi was trying not to show that he was freezing, but his jaw was tight and his hands were shoved deep in his pockets. His coat wasn't much better.

"How were you getting home?" Eli asked.

Levi's lips moved. *Bus.*

"Me too. Next one's not for about twenty minutes." Eli rubbed his arms. "I'm freezing. And I didn't have lunch—I'm starving."

He looked across the parking lot. Through the swirling snow, he could see the golden arches of a McDonald's on the other side of the shopping center.

"Would you two keep me company?" He pointed toward it. "We could warm up while we wait."

Lucy's face transformed. "McDonald's?"

Levi hesitated. Eli could see the calculation—the pride, the not wanting to accept more. But Lucy was shivering, and the wind was brutal, and twenty minutes out here could be dangerous.

"We don't have—" Levi started.

"I just need somewhere warm to sit," Eli said quickly. "You'd be doing me a favor. I hate waiting alone."

Levi glanced at Lucy, who was practically vibrating with hope.

"Okay," he said. "We'll wait with you."

Eli grabbed the grocery bags in one hand and Lucy's hand in the other. They walked across the parking lot, heads bowed against the wind, Levi trailing behind. Eli positioned himself to block the worst of it from Lucy without being obvious about it.

Inside McDonald's, he texted Graham again:

At McDonald's across parking lot. Keeping them warm.

His phone buzzed almost immediately:

On my way.

The warmth was a relief. Eli guided them to a booth near the back and brushed the snow from Lucy's coat, then his own. Lucy had stopped shivering, at least.

"Levi, save our spot?" Eli gestured toward the booth. "Lucy, come help me order."

Levi nodded, sliding into the booth while Eli walked Lucy to the counter. She reached on her toes, pointing at pictures.

"What do you want?" Eli asked, kneeling so she could see his face.

"Happy Meal! With the toy!"

"You got it."

He ordered—a Happy Meal for Lucy, a twenty-piece nugget with large fries, drinks. More than he needed. That was the point.

When they returned to the booth, Eli set the tray down and slid in across from Levi.

"I think I over-ordered." He pushed the nuggets and fries toward the center of the table. "Help me out?"

Levi looked at the food but didn't move. Lucy was already tearing into her Happy Meal, pulling out the toy first—priorities—then shoving fries into her mouth.

Eli picked up a nugget and ate it. Casual. Like it was nothing.

Levi watched. His jaw tightened.

Eli reached for a fry. Ate that too. Kept his attention on Lucy, who was showing him the toy—some small plastic figure he couldn't identify.

Out of the corner of his eye, he saw Levi's hand move. Slowly. Almost reluctantly. It hovered over the fries, then retreated.

Eli said something to Lucy about her toy. She laughed.

Levi's hand moved again. This time it landed—one fry, lifted quickly to his mouth. Then another. Then a nugget.

And then he was eating. Really eating. The mechanical, steady pace of someone who hadn't had enough in too long.

Eli noticed. But he kept his eyes on Lucy, giving Levi the space to take what he needed without having to ask for it.

Graham arrived about fifteen minutes later, stomping snow off his boots and scanning the restaurant until he spotted them. His face broke into a smile that looked entirely genuine—and entirely surprised.

"Well! Look at this!"

Lucy's head snapped up. "Graham!"

"Hello, Miss Lucy." He made his way to their booth. "What a coincidence. Mind if I join you?"

"We're sharing nuggets!" Lucy announced.

"Are you? Lucky me—I stopped in for a quick bite. Didn't feel like braving the grocery store chaos in this weather." Graham slid in next to Eli. "Figured I'd grab something fast and head home before the roads get worse."

Levi was watching Graham carefully, then glanced at Eli. Something flickered in his expression—suspicion, maybe, or the beginning of understanding.

Eli gave him nothing. Just reached for another nugget.

Graham glanced around the restaurant, then back at the table. "Well, I'm starving. Anyone want anything while I'm up there?"

"We're good," Eli said.

Graham slid back out of the booth and made his way to the counter — making a show of being unable to decide, leaning over the menu board, asking the cashier questions no grown man needed answered. He came back with a tray loaded with more than one person could eat and pushed the extra burger toward Levi.

"My eyes are always bigger than my stomach. Help me out here. I hate wasting food."

Levi took it without protest. He was tired. Eli could see it—the particular exhaustion of holding everything together for too long.

When the food was mostly gone, Graham checked his watch.

"I should probably get going before the roads get any worse." He looked at Eli. "You need a lift? I'm headed your direction anyway."

Eli hesitated—just long enough to make it seem natural. "I was going to take the bus, but... especially in this weather. If you're sure it's not out of your way."

"Of course not." Graham turned to Levi. "What about you two? Can I drop you somewhere?"

Levi tensed. "The bus is fine. Our mom is picking us up at the library."

"The library! Perfect—I've been meaning to stop by anyway." Graham was already standing, gathering trash onto the tray. "I'll drop you right at the door. No sense waiting for a bus in this mess."

Levi looked at Lucy, then at Eli, then back at Graham. The offer was there, easy, no pressure. Just a ride. Just getting out of the cold.

"Okay," he said quietly. "Thank you."

"Wonderful." Graham stood and looked at Eli. "Would you help Lucy wash her hands and use the bathroom before we head out? It's going to be a slow drive."

Eli nodded and slid out of the booth. "Come on, sweetheart. Quick stop before we go."

Lucy hopped down and took his hand. Eli walked her toward the back of the restaurant. He waited in the hallway outside the women's room, leaning against the wall, giving Graham time alone with Levi.

From across the restaurant, Eli couldn't hear what they were saying. But he watched.

Graham had moved to sit across from Levi now, leaning forward slightly, his voice low. He wasn't stern—his face was kind, open. He was asking something. Levi shook his head at first. Graham said something else, patient, unhurried.

Levi's shoulders dropped. He stared at the table, his mouth moving. Graham listened without interrupting. Levi talked for a while—longer than Eli expected. His hands gestured occasionally, then fell still. He looked up at Graham, and even from across the room, Eli could see the fear in his face. The vulnerability of someone who'd been carrying a secret too heavy for his shoulders.

Graham nodded. Said something quiet. Reached across the table and put his hand over Levi's for just a moment.

Levi's face crumpled. He pressed the heels of his hands against his eyes, his shoulders shaking once, twice. Graham didn't make a fuss, didn't draw attention. Just sat there, solid and present, while the boy across from him finally let himself crack.

Eli understood now. Graham had asked where they were really going. And Levi, exhausted and overwhelmed and faced with someone who seemed genuinely safe, had told him.

Lucy emerged from the bathroom, wiping her hands on her coat.

"Did you wash them?" Eli asked.

She nodded proudly.

"Good girl. Let's go."

When they returned, Levi was composed again—or at least wearing a reasonable imitation of composure. His eyes were red-rimmed, his jaw set. Graham was leaning back, relaxed, as if they'd just been discussing the weather.

"Ready?" Graham asked brightly. "Let's go before we need a dogsled to get home."

The library was only a few blocks away, but the drive took ten minutes. Graham's windshield wipers worked overtime against the snow. Eli sat in the front. Levi and Lucy were in the back, quiet except for Lucy's occasional commentary about how everything looked like a snow globe.

When they pulled up, a figure was hurrying up the front steps—Susan, her coat pulled tight, head down against the wind.

"There's your mom," Graham said.

Levi was out of the car almost before it stopped, Lucy scrambling after him. Eli and Graham followed more slowly, gathering the grocery bags from the trunk.

Inside, Susan was already hugging her children, relief evident on her face. She looked up as Graham and Eli approached—and her expression shifted through surprise, confusion, wariness.

"Mr.... Graham?" She straightened, one hand still on Levi's shoulder. "What are you—"

"We ran into each other at McDonald's," Graham said easily. "Complete coincidence. I was grabbing dinner, and there they were. Small world."

Susan's eyes moved to Eli, then to the grocery bags.

"Eli helped us," Lucy announced. "I paid for everything!"

Susan's face tightened almost imperceptibly. She looked at Levi. Something passed between them—mother and son, a whole conversation in a glance.

"That was very kind," Susan said carefully. "Thank you."

Lucy tugged at her mother's coat. "Mommy, can I go to the books? The ones with Clifford?"

Susan hesitated, glancing toward the children's section.

"Why don't you both show Eli your favorite spots?" Graham suggested. "Levi, I bet you know this place pretty well. And Lucy, I bet Eli would love to see the Clifford books."

Lucy's face lit up. "Come on, Uncle Eli!" She grabbed his hand and started pulling.

Eli let himself be led, but not before catching Graham's eye. *I've got this*, Graham's expression said. *Go.*

Levi followed them toward the stacks, glancing back once at his mother before disappearing into the children's section.

They found Lucy's usual spot. She immediately pulled a picture book from a low shelf and plopped down on the carpet, patting the space beside her.

"Read with me, Uncle Eli?"

Eli sat down cross-legged, and Lucy climbed into his lap, settling against his chest with the book open in front of them. She began "reading"—pointing at pictures, telling the story in her own words. Eli couldn't hear most of it, but he watched her small finger trace across the pages, nodding when she looked up at him for confirmation.

Levi sat nearby, thumbing through a Highlights magazine for kids—the only thing within reach—but his eyes kept drifting across the library to where Graham and his mother sat in a corner, away from everyone else.

Graham had pulled two chairs together, angled toward each other but giving Susan a view of her children across the room. He could see Levi watching them, trying to pretend he wasn't.

Susan sat stiffly, arms crossed, her body angled slightly away. Waiting. Braced for whatever was coming.

Graham didn't push. He settled into his chair and looked around the library—the tall windows, the old wooden shelves, the particular quiet that libraries held.

"Simon used to drag me to places like this all the time," he said. "Libraries. Museums. Galleries. Anywhere with books or art, really. I used to complain, but..." He smiled. "I think that's where I got the bug to start writing, actually. All those places he took me."

Susan glanced at him, uncertain. This wasn't what she'd expected.

"Simon?"

"My husband." Graham's smile softened. "We met in a library, actually. At Columbia, many years ago. I was pretending to study. He saw right through me."

Susan blinked. Husband. The word landed differently than she'd expected. Graham was... she hadn't realized. He didn't look—well, he didn't look like anything, really. He just looked like Graham. A nice man with kind eyes who wrote books her son loved. She'd never met anyone who spoke so openly about having a husband. It wasn't bad, just... different. And somehow, the surprise of it made her forget her anxiety for a moment.

"He must be really something," she said.

"He was."

Susan caught the word. "Was?"

"He passed away last March."

The air between them shifted. Graham's voice had gone quieter, and Susan saw something flicker across his face—grief, still raw despite the months. He blinked a few times, looked toward the window.

"I'm sorry," Susan said. And she meant it—she could hear the ache in his voice, recognized it as something she knew too well herself. "That's... I'm so sorry."

"Thank you." Graham cleared his throat. "Thirty years. Met him when I was barely older than your son. He was this brilliant art historian who could talk for hours about Renaissance frescoes, and I was just this kid from nowhere who didn't know anything about anything." He laughed softly, but his eyes were bright. "He dragged me all over the world. Florence, Paris, Vienna. Every museum, every gallery. I complained the whole time, but..." He stopped, swallowed hard.

Susan watched him struggle to compose himself. This wasn't a performance—he was genuinely moved, caught off guard by his own grief. And something in her softened. Here was this man who must have everything —a beautiful house, a successful career, friends who loved him—and he was still broken by loss. Just like her.

"He sounds wonderful," she said quietly.

He loved this place. I can picture him right over there, tucked into some corner with a stack of books, completely oblivious to the time.

Susan almost smiled. She looked toward the children's section, where Eli sat on the floor with Lucy in his lap, both of them bent over a picture book. Levi was nearby, pretending to read a magazine, watching her.

"After Simon died," Graham said, his voice steadier now, "I didn't know what to do with myself. We'd been together so long. I didn't know how to be just... me. I stopped going places. Stopped seeing people. Just rattled around in that big empty house, waiting for something that was never coming back."

Susan's eyes had gone distant. Graham could see her drifting somewhere else—her own memories, her own loss.

"My friends kept showing up anyway," Graham continued. "Wouldn't take no for an answer. Kept dragging me out, making me eat, making me talk. I hated it at first. Thought I was fine on my own." He shook his head. "I wasn't fine. I was drowning. I just couldn't see it."

He looked toward the children's section again. Eli was nodding seriously at something Lucy was telling him, her small finger pointing at pictures in the book.

Eli was one of those people," Graham said. "We met by accident a few weeks ago. I don't even know how to explain it — he just showed up. And kept showing up.

Susan followed his gaze. Watched Eli brush a strand of hair from Lucy's face as she turned a page. The gentleness of it. The patience.

"I'm not telling you this to make you feel sorry for me," Graham said gently. "I'm telling you because I know what it looks like when someone's carrying more than they should have to. And I know how hard it is to let anyone help."

Susan's eyes snapped to his. For a moment, he saw the fear there—the fear of being seen, of being known, of having the careful walls she'd built come tumbling down.

I don't know what's going on," Graham said. "And you don't have to tell me. But I've got eyes, Susan. And that boy over there is carrying more than he should be.

Susan's chin trembled. She pressed her lips together, looked away.

"I have a house," Graham said. Then he stopped. Rubbed his face. "Okay, I'm going to say something, and I need you to hear the whole thing before you decide I'm either a serial killer or a rich guy with a savior complex. Because I promise you I'm neither. I'm just a tired old man with too many empty rooms who doesn't want two kids sleeping in a car tonight."

Susan went very still.

"Since Simon's been gone, that house has gotten even bigger and even emptier." He said it plainly — not for sympathy, just as fact. "The roads are getting worse. Below zero tonight, wind chill even worse. I'm asking you to follow me home, let the kids sleep somewhere warm, ride out the storm. That's it. Tomorrow morning, you leave whenever you want. No questions. No strings."

Susan's jaw was tight. She wasn't looking at him.

"And I know how this sounds. A stranger offering his house to a woman and her children." He paused. "It'll just be me — Eli's got his own place. You can lock the guest room door. Call anyone you want, give them my address, my phone number. Whatever you need to feel safe."

Susan shook her head. "I can't just — we can't just—"

"Sure you can." Graham leaned back in his chair. "One night, Susan. Nobody's solving anything tonight. We're just getting through the storm."

Susan was crying now — silent tears sliding down her cheeks. She swiped at them angrily, embarrassed.

"I don't even know you," she whispered. "Why would you—"

"Because I almost didn't make it." The words came out quieter than he intended. He glanced toward Eli, still patient on the floor with Lucy. "After Simon died, I was done. Finished. And people like Eli — people I didn't ask for, people I didn't think I needed — they wouldn't let me disappear." He looked back at Susan. "If they hadn't done that, I don't know where I'd be right now. So. That's why."

Susan followed his gaze to the children's section. Watched Eli help Lucy turn a page, nodding as she chattered about something he probably couldn't hear. Watched Levi pretending not to watch them, the Highlights magazine forgotten in his lap.

"Just for tonight," she said finally. The words almost didn't make it out.

"Just for tonight," Graham agreed. "And tomorrow, we'll see. No promises, no expectations. Just... one night of not having to worry."

Susan nodded slowly. She wiped her face with her sleeve, took a shaky breath.

"Okay," she said. "Okay."

Graham stood and walked to the front desk, returning a moment later with a few tissues. He handed them to her, positioning himself to block the children's view.

When she was ready, she stood. Graham offered a small smile.

"Shall we?"

They walked over to the children's section together. Lucy looked up from her book, beaming.

"Mommy! Uncle Eli is reading with me!"

"I see that, baby." Susan's voice was steady now, only slightly rough around the edges. "That's very nice of him."

Eli looked up, meeting Graham's eyes. Graham gave a small nod.

"Susan tells me the roads are practically impassable," Graham announced, his voice warm and easy. "I've insisted you all stay with me tonight—I've got plenty of room, and we can ride this storm out together. How does that sound?"

Lucy scrambled out of Eli's lap. "Stay with you? At your *house*?"

"If that's okay with you, Miss Lucy."

"Is it big? Does it have a fireplace?" Her face lit up even brighter. "Do I get my own bedroom?"

The room went quiet. Graham looked at her — this little girl, snow still melting in her hair, asking for the most basic thing in the world like it was Christmas morning.

"You sure do," he said.

Susan pressed her hand to her mouth.

He glanced at Susan and saw her eyes filling again, but she was smiling this time. Levi was looking at his sister like she'd said something profound, and maybe she had.

Eli had only caught bits of the exchange, but he could see the shift in the room — the way the tension had broken, the way everyone was breathing again.

Graham reached down and offered Eli a hand up. "We should get going before the roads get any worse."

Eli took his hand and stood, brushing off his jeans. Lucy was already tugging at Susan's coat, chattering about what her bedroom might look like.

They gathered coats and bags and headed out into the storm. The snow was coming down even harder now, the wind whipping it into swirling patterns under the streetlights. Susan's old sedan was parked at the curb, already accumulating a fresh layer of white.

Levi hesitated at the door, then looked at his mother. "Can I ride with Graham and Eli?"

Susan looked at Graham.

"Of course," Graham said. "He can keep me company. You just follow right behind us, okay?"

Susan studied her son for a moment — then nodded. "Don't let me lose you in this mess."

"Wouldn't dream of it," Graham said.

The drive was slow.

Graham's BMW crept through the snow, headlights barely cutting through the white. Susan's sedan followed at a careful distance, a dim glow in the rearview mirror.

Eli sat in the passenger seat. Levi was in the back, silent, staring out the window at the snow.

No one spoke. The only sound was the hum of the heater and the rhythmic swish of the wipers.

They dropped Eli at his apartment first. Graham pulled to the curb and Eli grabbed his grocery bags from the trunk. Levi was already out of the car, taking a bag from Eli's hands before he could protest, and the two of them walked to the front door of the building.

Graham watched from the car. Eli said something to Levi — Graham couldn't hear it, but he saw Levi nod. Then Eli pulled him into a hug. Levi stiffened at first, the way he had at the shelter — that rigid posture of a kid who'd been holding himself together so long he'd forgotten how to let anyone in. But he didn't pull away. His shoulders dropped, and for a moment he held on, like he needed it more than he wanted to admit.

It reminded Graham of Thanksgiving. That same boy, same tension, same slow release.

Eli let go, said something else with a smile, and disappeared inside. Levi stood there for a second, then jogged back through the snow and climbed into the front seat.

Graham pulled away from the curb. Susan's headlights appeared in the rearview mirror, right behind them.

"He's a good guy," Graham said.

Levi nodded, his eyes still on Eli's building as it shrank behind them.

Twenty minutes to cover what should have been ten. But they made it. Graham pulled into his driveway, the garage door rising to welcome them, and Susan pulled in behind.

As Graham put the car in park, Levi's voice came from the passenger seat.

Quiet. Almost too soft to hear.

"Thank you."

He wasn't looking at Graham. He was still staring out the window, at the snow, at the house rising before them. His favorite author's house. The man who wrote the books that had saved him in the library when everything else was falling apart. And now he was here. Going to stay here. All of it unreal.

He didn't know how much weight he'd been carrying until this moment — the moment someone else reached under it and helped lift.

Chapter Eight

LEVI WOKE BEFORE FIVE.

He didn't need to check a clock—his body just knew. It had learned to know, these past months. Five o'clock meant the garbage truck would come rumbling down the street behind the warehouse where they parked. Five o'clock meant he needed to be awake, alert, ready to make sure no one bothered them. Ready to slip out quietly, find a spot behind the dumpsters to pee, have a few minutes to himself before Lucy stirred and needed something and his mother woke with that look on her face—the one she thought she hid, the one that said *another day, another impossible day*.

But he wasn't in the car.

He was in a bed. Sort of. A chaise lounge, long enough for his growing frame, soft in a way that felt almost wrong. Across the room, in the large guest bed, his mother and Lucy slept tangled together. Lucy's arm was flung across their mother's chest. Susan's face, even in sleep, looked exhausted.

Graham had offered Levi his own room. *I've got plenty,* he'd said. *Take your pick.* But Levi couldn't do it. Couldn't be that far from them. It felt wrong to be separated, even by a hallway. So he'd taken the chaise, and he'd watched them fall asleep, and he'd lain awake for a long time listening to the wind howl outside and the house creak and settle around them.

Now he was awake again. And he couldn't fall back asleep.

He slipped out from under the blanket—soft, thick, the kind of blanket that probably cost more than a month of groceries—and crept toward the door. His socks made no sound on the hardwood floor. He eased the door open, glanced back once at his mother and sister still sleeping, and stepped into the hallway.

The house was dark, but not entirely.

Moonlight poured through a row of floor-to-ceiling windows that lined the hallway to his left, illuminating everything in pale blue-white. Snow had piled up outside overnight—more than Levi had ever seen, drifts reaching halfway up the glass. The storm had done its work.

He walked slowly, drawn toward the light. Along the opposite wall hung framed drawings and paintings—some sketches, some full color, all of them looking like they belonged in a museum. Levi squinted at them in the reflected glow. They reminded him of something. The illustrations in Graham's books, maybe. The ones he'd studied for hours in the library, tracing the lines with his eyes, imagining himself inside them.

He wondered if these were the originals. If Graham had drawn them himself, or if someone else had, and Graham had kept them because they mattered.

At the end of the hallway, a doorway opened to the left. Wood, elegant, simple. Levi hesitated, then peered inside.

More windows. The same floor-to-ceiling glass, the same view of snow and moonlight and the dark shapes of trees beyond. And in the center of the room, positioned to face that view, a massive wooden desk.

Levi stepped inside without meaning to. His feet carried him forward before his brain could object.

The desk was neat. Tidy. An old typewriter sat to one side—Levi knew what those were, had seen them in movies, though he'd never touched one. To the right, a corkboard was covered with notecards, each one pinned carefully, each one covered in handwriting he couldn't quite read in the darkness. Ideas for stories, maybe. Scraps of dialogue. Character names.

He turned and saw the wall behind him.

Bookshelves. Floor to ceiling, taller than him, stuffed with books of every size and color. Two chairs sat nearby, nicer than anything in any library he'd ever been to. Leather, maybe. The kind of chairs that invited you to sink in and never leave.

Levi stepped closer to the shelves, squinting in the moonlight, scanning the spines. History. Art. Travel. Fiction. And then—

There.

The Oltrarno.

Not the battered paperbacks from the library, held together with tape and hope. These were hardcovers. Leather-bound, from the looks of them. Gold lettering on the spines. Beautiful in a way that made Levi's chest ache.

He reached out, then stopped himself. He was already intruding. Already somewhere he shouldn't be, touching things that weren't his, wanting things he had no right to want.

But he could just look. Just for a second. He'd be careful.

His fingers brushed the spine of the first book. The leather was smooth, cool. He started to pull it from the shelf—

"Couldn't sleep?"

Levi jumped so hard he nearly knocked the book to the floor. He caught it awkwardly, clutching it to his chest, and spun around to find Graham standing in the doorway.

"I'm sorry," Levi whispered. The words came out too fast, tumbling over each other. "I didn't mean to—I wasn't trying to—I'll go back to—"

"Levi." Graham's voice was calm. Quiet. "It's okay."

"I shouldn't have—"

"You're not disturbing anything." Graham stepped into the room, and Levi noticed he was already dressed—or maybe he'd never undressed. A sweater, soft pants, socks. Like he'd been awake for a while. "I'm an early riser. Simon used to hate me for it."

Levi didn't know what to say. He stood frozen by the bookshelf, the leather-bound book still pressed against his chest like a shield, caught between wanting to flee and wanting to sink into the floor and disappear entirely.

Graham studied him for a moment. Then he held up one finger—*wait*—and crossed to a small lamp that sat on the table between the two chairs. He clicked it on.

Warm yellow light filled the space. Not bright—just enough to see by, just enough to make the room feel like a sanctuary instead of a crime scene. Graham gestured to one of the chairs.

"Sit."

Levi sat, the leather-bound book still clutched in his hands. He perched on the edge of the cushion, back straight, holding it like evidence of a crime. Waiting to be spoken to. Waiting to find out how much trouble he was in.

But Graham didn't lecture him. Didn't ask what he was doing. Instead, he moved to a large file cabinet in the corner and began sorting through folders, muttering something Levi couldn't hear.

Levi watched, confused. What was he looking for?

Graham pulled out a folder—large, overstuffed, papers threatening to spill from every edge—and closed the drawer. He carried it back to the chairs and paused, looking at the book Levi was still gripping.

"Here," Graham said, holding out his hand. "Trade you."

Levi hesitated, then surrendered the leather-bound book. Graham took it gently, set it on the side table, and sat down in the chair beside Levi. He leaned forward so the lamplight fell across the folder's surface.

"I want to show you something," Graham said.

He opened the folder.

Inside was chaos. Yellow legal-pad paper, covered edge to edge with handwriting. Notes in margins. Lines crossed out, rewritten, crossed out again. Arrows pointing from one paragraph to another. Pages that looked like they'd been crumpled and smoothed flat again. Everything old, slightly creased, the paper gone soft with age.

Levi's eyes widened.

Graham lifted the folder and set it gently in Levi's lap. Then he sat back in his chair and said nothing.

Levi looked at him. "Can I...?"

Graham nodded.

Levi looked down. His hands were trembling. He hadn't noticed until now—hadn't noticed that his legs were bouncing either, jittering up and down until the folder started to slide. He caught it, stilled himself, and forced his eyes to focus on the first page.

At the top, in Graham's handwriting, a title had been written and then scratched out with heavy black lines:

FLORENCE BY LINE

And beneath it, in different handwriting—bolder, more confident—two words in large letters:

THE OLTRARNO

Levi stopped breathing.

"Florence by Line was my idea," Graham said quietly. "A play on words. Drawing, you know. Simon hated it. Said it was too clever by half. He's the one who suggested Oltrarno. He knew the area—he'd studied there, walked those streets. He said the title had always been there, waiting. Like Michelangelo and his David. It wasn't about creating something new. It was about uncovering what already existed."

Levi couldn't speak. He was staring at the crossed-out title, at the bold letters beneath it, at the pages and pages of handwritten words that followed.

This was it. The actual manuscript. The real one. Graham's handwriting on paper he'd touched, words he'd written before Levi was even born.

"Take your time," Graham said. He rose from the chair, his knees cracking softly. "Look through it. All of it, if you want. I'll be in the kitchen when you're ready for breakfast."

He moved toward the door, then paused.

"Levi?"

Levi looked up, eyes wet.

"I'm glad you found it," Graham said. And then he was gone.

• • •

Levi sat alone in the lamplight, the folder heavy in his lap.

He turned the first page.

The bells wouldn't stop.

Marco heard them before he saw the city. He'd been walking for three days—sleeping in barns, once under an olive tree that had more bugs than shade. His feet were wrecked. His clothes smelled like sweat and hay. Everything he owned was in the bag over his shoulder: one extra shirt, a piece of charcoal worn down to almost nothing, and a stack of drawings his mother swore were good enough to change his life.

She'd been crying when she said it. Marco still didn't know if that made it more true or less.

Levi remembered this. The opening paragraph. He'd read it so many times he could almost recite it from memory. But seeing it here, in Graham's handwriting, with words crossed out and rewritten, with notes in the margins—

He traced his finger along a crossed-out line. The original had read: *His mother had promised they were good enough.* Graham had scratched it out and written above it: *His mother swore they were good enough to change his life.*

Such a small change. But it mattered. Levi could feel why it mattered.

He turned the page.

He was sixteen. He had nowhere else to go.

The road went up a hill, and then there it was. Florence. The city the merchant had described in that greasy voice of his—right up until Marco ran from his wagon in the middle of the night, leaving behind his "apprenticeship" and whatever else the merchant had planned to take from him.

The merchant hadn't lied about the city, at least. The dome of the cathedral rose over the rooftops, huge and impossible, more beautiful than any drawing could ever be. Marco had seen sketches of it. The sketches were lies. Nothing on paper could capture what he was looking at—the dome, the towers, the river cutting through the valley like a silver ribbon.

The city was alive. He could feel it from here, humming with energy, pulling at something inside his chest.

He stood there way too long, just staring. Some farmer with a cart of cabbages had to steer around him, muttering about dumb country boys with their mouths hanging open.

Marco barely noticed.

. . .

Levi smiled despite himself. He remembered that line—*dumb country boys with their mouths hanging open*. He'd read it in the library and thought: *that's me. That's exactly me.*

He'd felt like Marco then. A dumb country boy from nowhere, standing at the edge of something huge and impossible, wondering if he had any right to want it.

He turned another page.

The bells sounded sad, he realized. Not like celebration. Like mourning.

Something had happened. Something big.

He started walking faster.

The next section described Marco arriving at the city gates. The chaos. The guards. The questions he couldn't answer.

"Where are you from?"

"Greve, signore. The Chianti hills."

"What business in Florence?"

Marco's answer—the one he'd rehearsed for three days, the one that sounded ridiculous even to him:

"I'm looking for L'Accademia dell'Oltrarno, signore. I want to study there."

Levi paused. His throat was tight.

He remembered reading this part for the first time. Sitting in the back corner of the library, Lucy asleep in the chair beside him, his mother somewhere in the stacks pretending to look for job listings. He'd read Marco's words and thought: *that's crazy. That's the craziest thing I've ever heard. Walking three days to a city you've never seen, with nothing but some drawings, hoping someone will let you in.*

And then he'd thought: *but what else was he supposed to do?*

What else was any of them supposed to do?

The guard laughed. Not mean, exactly. Just tired.

"The Academy," he said. "You have papers? A letter? A patron?"

"I have drawings, signore."

"Drawings." The guard said it like it was a joke. "And who sent you to Florence with drawings?"

"My mother, signore."

Levi's vision blurred. He wiped his eyes with the back of his hand.

His mother had sent him to the grocery store yesterday with not enough money and a list of things they needed. She'd looked at him the way Marco's mother must have looked at Marco—desperate, hopeful, terrified. Knowing she was asking too much. Knowing there was no other choice.

He turned the page.

The guard shook his head, but he wasn't being cruel.

"Boy, Lorenzo de' Medici died four days ago. The whole city is holding its breath. You picked a hell of a time to show up with drawings from your mother."

Lorenzo. Dead. Marco had heard that name whispered like a prayer in every village between here and Greve. Lorenzo the Magnificent. The prince who wasn't a prince. The man who made Florence the center of the world.

"I didn't know, signore."

"No. I don't imagine news travels fast to the Chianti hills." The guard stepped aside. "Cross the bridge. Keep walking until you reach the Oltrarno. Ask anyone for the Academy."

"Thank you, signore."

"Don't thank me yet." The guard was already turning away. "Good luck, boy. You'll need it."

Good luck. You'll need it.

Two people had said that to Marco in the same day. Levi remembered thinking that was a bad sign, the first time he read it. Remembered wondering if Marco would make it, if the story would have a happy ending, if—

He'd needed it to have a happy ending. Needed it more than he could explain.

He turned another page, and another. Marco entering the city. The chaos of the streets. The smells and sounds and overwhelming crush of people. Marco keeping his hand on his bag, remembering the merchant's hands in the dark, learning that a boy alone was prey.

Best to be invisible. Best to be quick.

Levi knew about being invisible. Knew about being quick. Knew about keeping your head down and not making eye contact and hoping no one noticed you were there.

. . .

The bridge was packed with shops—goldsmiths, jewelers, stuff that cost more than Marco's mother would earn in her whole life. He didn't look too close. Looking at things you couldn't have only made you want them more.

Levi almost laughed. He'd learned that lesson too. Don't look at the Happy Meals other kids were eating. Don't look at the winter coats in store windows. Don't look at houses with warm lights glowing inside.

Don't look. Don't want. Don't hope.

Except he did. He couldn't help it.

The Oltrarno was different. Quieter. More workshops than palaces. The smell changed—sawdust, paint, hot metal from a blacksmith's forge.

Marco passed a man carving a wooden angel in a doorway, hands moving like it was easy, like he'd been doing it forever.

"Excuse me, signore. L'Accademia dell'Oltrarno—do you know where it is?"

The carver looked up. Kind eyes. Wrinkled at the corners.

"New to the city?"

"Yes, signore."

"You and half the boys in Tuscany." But he said it nice enough. "Two streets down, turn left at the fountain with the lion. Big wooden doors."

"Thank you, signore."

"Don't mention it." The carver went back to his angel. "Good luck. You'll need it."

Third time. Three people saying the same thing.

Marco didn't know if that was a sign or a curse.

Levi turned the page. The paper was soft under his fingers, worn smooth by time. He imagined Graham sitting at this desk, years ago, writing these words. Crossing things out. Starting over. Finding Marco's voice one sentence at a time.

The doors of L'Accademia dell'Oltrarno were huge. Twice Marco's height, dark wood carved with saints and angels and Christ and the Virgin. They were also closed.

Marco stood in front of them, his hand raised to knock, his courage completely gone.

What the hell was he doing here?

. . .

Levi's breath caught. That line—*What the hell was he doing here?*—hadn't been in the published book. He looked at the manuscript. Graham had originally written: *What was he doing here?* And then, in the margin, scrawled an addition: *the hell.*

Two words. They changed everything. Made Marco feel real. Made him feel like a kid, scared and uncertain, not some character in a story.

Levi understood why Graham had added them.

He was a bastard from the hills. Son of a nobleman who'd never spoken his name and a seamstress who'd been kicked out of her village for being young and pretty when the wrong man noticed. He had a bag of drawings his mother thought were good, but what did she know? She'd never been to Florence. Never seen what real artists could do.

He should turn around. Find work in a stable, a kitchen, anywhere that would take him. Accept his place and stop reaching for things that weren't meant for boys like him.

Levi read that paragraph three times.

Stop reaching for things that weren't meant for boys like him.

He knew that feeling. Knew it like he knew his own heartbeat. The voice that said: *you don't belong here. You're not supposed to want this. Stay small. Stay invisible. Stop hoping.*

But Marco hadn't listened to that voice.

But his mother's face rose in his mind. The tears. The fierce grip of her hands on his shoulders.

You have a gift, Marco. God gave it to you for a reason. Don't let anyone tell you otherwise. Don't let anyone take it from you.

He knocked.

Levi's hands were shaking again. He didn't try to stop them.

The sound echoed. Nothing happened. He knocked again, harder.

A small door opened inside the bigger door. An old man's face appeared—bald, suspicious, looking at Marco like he was a stray dog.

"We're closed. Come back in a week."

"Please, signore—I walked three days from Greve. I just want someone to look at my drawings. If someone could just—"

"A week." The old man wasn't budging. "We're in mourning for Lorenzo. No new students until—"

"Beppe." A voice from inside. Young. Used to being listened to. "Who is it?"

The old man turned. "No one, signore. Just a boy from the country."

Footsteps. The small door opened wider. The old man was pushed aside—gently but firmly.

And Marco saw him.

Levi held his breath.

He knew what was coming. Had read it a hundred times. But here, in Graham's handwriting, it felt different. New. Like he was meeting Alessandro for the first time all over again.

The young man in the doorway was maybe a year older than Marco—seventeen, he guessed. He was dressed simply but well: white linen shirt under a leather apron splattered with paint. He'd been working when he came to the door. His dark hair fell across his forehead like he'd been running his hands through it.

But it was his eyes Marco couldn't stop staring at. Light brown, almost golden. Like honey held up to the sun.

He looked at Marco. Not past him. Not through him. At him. Like Marco was worth the effort of seeing.

No one had ever looked at Marco like that in his life.

Levi wiped his eyes again. The tears wouldn't stop.

He remembered sitting in the library, reading this part for the first time. Remembered his heart pounding, his face flushing, something opening up inside him that he hadn't known was closed.

Like Marco was worth the effort of seeing.

That was all he'd ever wanted. To be seen. To be worth seeing.

"You walked three days," the young man said. It wasn't a question.

"Yes, signore."

"From where?"

"Greve, signore. In the Chianti hills."

"And you want to show someone your drawings."

"Yes, signore."

The young man studied him. Marco felt his face go hot but didn't look away. He'd walked three days. He'd escaped a merchant who wanted things Marco would never give. He'd slept under an olive tree with bugs crawling on him. He'd earned the right to stand here, dirt and blisters and all.

Something shifted in the young man's expression. Not quite a smile. But something that recognized what it was seeing.

"My name is Alessandro Rinaldi," he said. "Come inside."

Levi closed his eyes.

He was back at the library. Behind the building, kneeling on the cold pavement, pretending he'd dropped something so no one would see him crying. Weeping into his hands because a boy in a book had found someone who saw him. Who let him inside.

He'd wanted that so badly. Had needed it so badly. Those two words — *Come inside* — had undone him completely.

He'd hoped, sitting there on the pavement, that someday someone would say those words to him. Would look at him the way Alessandro looked at Marco. Would see him, really see him, and not turn away.

He'd known it was stupid. Knew it was just a book. Just a story someone made up.

But now he was sitting in that someone's office. Holding the actual pages. The very words, in the very handwriting, that had made him believe—even for a moment—that things could get better.

And last night, Graham had said: *You could follow me home. Let the kids sleep somewhere warm.*

Come inside.

Levi closed the folder carefully, pressing the pages flat, making sure nothing would fall out. He held it against his chest for a moment, like it was something precious. Something sacred.

Then he stood, wiped his face with his sleeve, and walked toward the kitchen.

Graham was sitting at the island, a mug of hot cocoa in his hands, looking out the windows at the snow. A second mug sat waiting on the counter, steam still rising. The sky was just starting to lighten—deep blue fading to gray at the edges, the first hint of sunrise still an hour away.

He turned when he heard Levi's footsteps.

"Hey," he said softly.

Levi stood in the doorway, the folder still clutched to his chest. He opened his mouth to say something—thank you, or I'm sorry, or I don't know why I'm crying—but nothing came out.

Graham just nodded. Like he understood. Like he'd known all along.

He gestured to the waiting mug. "Made you some. Careful—it's hot."

Levi crossed to the island and sat, setting the folder carefully on the counter in front of him. He wrapped his hands around the warm mug and watched the snow turn pink as the sun began to rise.

Chapter Nine

THE PHONE RANG AT HALF past eight.

Angie was elbow-deep in biscuit dough—her domain, her kitchen, her rules—when it rang, so Sonya answered. She'd been put to work fetching ingredients from the pantry, which was about as far into the cooking process as Angie ever let her get. They'd established that boundary back in the Reagan administration.

Sonya listened, offering the occasional "uh huh" and "oh my" and "well, I'll be," while Angie kept her eyes on the dough. You didn't interrupt a phone call. You waited until the other person was good and ready to share.

The phone clicked back into its cradle.

"Well?" Angie asked without looking up.

"That was Graham."

"Figured as much."

Sonya pulled out a chair and sat at the kitchen table. That meant it was serious. Sonya didn't sit unless there was something worth sitting for.

Angie wiped her hands on her apron and turned around. "What's he gone and done now?"

"You remember that family Graham and Eli mentioned at the party? Woman with two kids?"

Angie remembered. Graham had brought it up briefly—something about meeting them at the Thanksgiving shelter, how the boy had recognized his books.

"They been living in their car," Sonya said.

Angie's hands stilled on the apron.

"Eli found 'em at the grocery store yesterday," Sonya continued. "In the storm. Kids didn't have enough money for food. Long story short—"

She paused. Sonya never told a story short in her life, but Graham had given her the condensed version, and Angie appreciated that.

"—Graham's got 'em staying at his place now. The mama's proud, he says. Don't want no charity. But she ain't got nowhere to go."

Angie nodded slowly. "Those poor babies."

Sonya was already untying her apron—well, the dish towel she'd tucked into her waistband, since Angie would never let her wear an actual apron.

"She needs to come here," Sonya said.

Angie smiled. "I was gonna suggest the same thing."

"'Course you were."

Angie untied her apron. "Did you tell Graham we'd be down shortly?"

Sonya gave her a look—the kind that said *you've known me how long?*

Angie answered her own question. "Of course you did."

Sonya was already reaching for her coat.

Graham had "let" Susan make pancakes for breakfast.

She'd insisted, and he was no cook himself, so he'd stepped aside and let her take over the kitchen. Besides, it seemed to help her—gave her something to do with her hands, something to contribute. He wasn't about to take that away from her.

He made no mention of "what now" or "let's talk about your future." Felt best to simply let the day unfold. Sometimes, he'd learned through experience, things had a way of working out if you just stepped aside.

Levi had moved from the kitchen to the living room after their early morning hot cocoa, the manuscript folder clutched to his chest. He'd barely looked up since, completely lost in the pages Graham had shared with him.

Lucy, meanwhile, was "helping Mommy." Graham had found a small pan and spatula for her to "cook" with, though he'd suggested it might be best if she cooked while seated at the table. The stove was for Mommy only.

""I'm making a pancake for Santa!" Lucy announced, stirring air in her empty pan.

"Is that so?" Graham leaned against the counter, watching Susan flip the real pancakes with practiced ease. "What kind does Santa like?"

"Chocolate chip!"

"Ah. Very sophisticated taste." He almost added something about Christmas being just a few weeks away, but stopped himself. He wasn't sure what kind of Christmas they had to look forward to.

"Breakfast is ready," Susan called toward the living room. "Levi!"

A groan from the other room. Susan crossed her arms and waited. After a long moment, Levi appeared in the doorway, the manuscript folder still clutched to his chest like he couldn't bear to set it down.

"Leave that and come eat," Susan said.

He looked like she'd asked him to abandon a child. But the look on her face left no room for negotiation, so he set the folder carefully on the counter and slid into a chair at the table.

They ate together—Susan serving, Lucy chattering about her imaginary pancake, Levi shoveling food into his mouth with one eye on the manuscript folder, Graham genuinely enjoying every bite.

"These are wonderful," he said, and meant it.

Susan's face flushed with pride. "It's nothing. Just pancakes."

"Best pancakes I've had in years."

"I helped!" Lucy announced.

"And it shows. Very professional."

Levi was already pushing back from the table, reaching for the folder.

"Where do you think you're going?" Susan asked.

"I just want to—"

"You just ate breakfast in four minutes flat. You can wait."

Graham hid a smile. The boy was utterly absorbed. He'd never watched someone read his work like that before—like it was oxygen, like they couldn't survive without it. Whatever those words had done for Levi in the past, they were still doing it now.

Simon would have told him to be proud of himself. Would have nodded toward Levi and said something like, "See? You're not completely useless after all." And then he'd have followed it up with some snarky comment about not getting too big for his britches.

Graham smiled, thinking of him. It still hurt, knowing he was gone. But at least now he could smile instead of cry.

The doorbell rang.

Actually, it didn't so much ring as announce itself briefly before the door swung open. Angie and Sonya had stopped waiting for Graham to answer sometime after Simon died. They'd just started walking in, afraid he'd be too lost in his grief to hear the bell.

"Hello?" Angie's voice came from the front hall. "Graham? We're here!"

Lucy looked up from her plate. Through the kitchen doorway, she could see Angie stepping into the living room—red winter coat with white fur trim, white hair perfectly styled, round grandmotherly face, wire-rimmed glasses perched on her nose.

Lucy's fork clattered to the table.

"MRS. SANTA CLAUS!"

She was off her chair and running before anyone could stop her, nearly knocking Levi over in her rush to get to the living room. Susan half-rose from her seat, startled, unsure what was happening.

"It's okay," Graham said, touching her arm. "They're friends."

Angie had already knelt down to Lucy's level, arms open wide. Lucy crashed into her like a small hurricane, wrapping her arms around Angie's neck and holding on tight.

"Mrs. Claus! You came to see me!"

"Of course I did, sweetheart." Angie's voice was warm as fresh cookies. "I heard there was a very special little girl here."

Graham watched Lucy wrapped around Angie, her face alight with pure wonder. Mrs. Claus. The girl had no doubt in her mind. An idea struck him. He slipped out while everyone was focused on the reunion and slipped down the hall.

In his bedroom, he dialed Anthony's number.

"What's up?"

"How fast can you get here in the Santa costume?"

A pause. Then: "Give me five minutes."

Graham smiled and hung up.

By the time he returned to the kitchen, Sonya had already introduced herself to Susan—firm handshake, direct eye contact, the kind of confidence that came from decades of not taking shit from anyone. Susan looked slightly overwhelmed but also... intrigued. Like she was meeting someone she recognized, even though they'd never met.

"—and Angie here loves to cook," Sonya was saying. "Me, I ain't allowed in the kitchen 'cept to fetch things. Ain't that right, Ang?"

"That's right." Angie had guided Lucy back to the table and was helping her into her seat. "Sonya's many things, but a cook isn't one of them."

"I resemble that remark."

Susan laughed—a real laugh, surprised out of her. Graham saw Sonya clock it, file it away.

"Can I get y'all something?" Susan asked, already moving toward the stove. "There's pancake batter left. And I can make coffee—"

"Oh, bless you," Angie said. "Graham's completely uncivilized when it comes to coffee. Simon was our last hope for him."

"Wouldn't say no to a pancake neither," Sonya added, settling into a chair at the table. "Worked up an appetite drivin' through all that snow."

Susan remembered Graham's conversation in the library last night. Simon. His husband. She was starting to see the network of friends he'd mentioned come to life.

Levi was hovering near the table, the manuscript folder clutched in his hands again.

"Can I go back to reading?" he asked his mother.

Susan shot him a look. "We have company."

""Oh, let him go," Angie said, waving a hand. "It's not often you see a boy his age excited about reading. My grandsons just want to watch videos on their phones."

Susan hesitated, then nodded. "Fine. But don't go far."

Levi was gone before she finished the sentence, retreating to his chair by the fireplace.

Angie watched him go. "What's he reading that has him so absorbed?"

"The original manuscript," Graham said. "For the first Oltrarno book. All my notes and chicken scratch."

Angie's eyebrows rose. "You don't show that to anyone."

"I know." Graham glanced toward the living room, where Levi was already lost in the pages again. "Seemed like he needed it."

Angie and Sonya exchanged a look. Graham couldn't quite read it, but it seemed to contain an entire conversation.

Susan set mugs of coffee in front of them, then hesitated, unsure where to sit, what to do with herself. Before anyone could say anything, a thunderous knock came at the front door.

It swung open.

And Lucy screamed. The second time this morning.

"SANTA!"

Anthony stood in the doorway, red jacket buttoned up, red Santa hat perched on his head, black boots stomping snow onto the floor. His white beard had been hastily fluffed, and his cheeks were pink from the cold.

"HO HO HO!" His voice boomed through the house. "Has anyone seen Mrs. Claus? I seem to have lost my reindeer in last night's storm!"

Lucy was already out of her chair, running full speed toward him. Susan stood frozen by the table, utterly bewildered. Levi appeared in the living room doorway, manuscript forgotten, looking completely lost.

Angie rose from her chair, smoothing her red coat, and walked into the living room. "There you are!" she said, her voice shifting into something warmer, grander. "I've been waiting for you, dear. Did you check the back yard? I thought I saw Rudolph out there earlier."

Anthony scooped Lucy up in his arms. "Is that so? Well, we'd better go look for them! What do you say, little one? Want to help Santa find his reindeer?"

Lucy nodded so hard Graham thought her head might fall off.

"I'll need my best helpers," Anthony continued, looking around the room. His eyes landed on Levi. "You there! Young man! You look like excellent reindeer-finding material."

Levi's face cycled through confusion and reluctant amusement. "I... what?"

"Come on!" Lucy was already squirming in Anthony's arms, reaching for her brother. "Levi, come on! We have to find Rudolph!"

Susan found her voice. "Levi, go with your sister."

"But—"

"Go." Her voice was gentle but firm. "Help them find the reindeer."

Levi looked at Graham, who gave him a small nod. *Go along with it.*

The boy sighed and went to get his coat.

"I'll supervise," Graham announced. "Make sure no one gets lost in the snow."

"That makes you the head elf," Anthony said solemnly.

"I've always aspired to middle management."

Angie walked Lucy to the back door, helping her into her coat, playing the part of Mrs. Claus to perfection. But at the threshold, she knelt down and gave Lucy one more hug.

"You go find those reindeer, sweetheart. I'll be right here when you get back."

Lucy beamed and ran out into the snow after Anthony and Levi. Graham followed, giving Angie a wink as he passed.

The back door closed, and suddenly the house was quiet.

Angie returned to the kitchen, where Susan stood at the window, watching her children trudge through the snow after a man in a Santa suit.

"Well," Susan said after a moment. "That was... unexpected."

"Graham does love a production." Angie settled back into her chair. "Come sit with us, dear."

Susan hesitated, then sat.

Sonya didn't waste time on small talk.

"Hope you don't mind me bein' direct," she said, "though you probably will. I'm Andover stock—up in the western part of the state. Don't know how to be nothin' but plain-spoken."

Susan's chin lifted slightly. "I'm from Rumford, originally."

Sonya's eyes sharpened. "That so? Then you know what I mean. There's a particular kind of woman comes from that part of the state."

Susan nodded slowly.

"Good." Sonya leaned forward, elbows on the table. "Then I'll get right to it. Graham called us this mornin'. Said you was havin' a tough go of things. Didn't say what, didn't say how, didn't give us no details that wasn't his to give. Just said you might need some help."

Susan's jaw tightened.

"Now, us women," Sonya continued, "we don't like men gettin' into our business. We know how to take care of our own, thank you very much. Am I right?"

Susan blinked. That wasn't what she'd expected.

"I know it took nearly all my life and blood to get where I am today," Sonya said. "I'm blessed to have Angie and my children and the grandkids runnin' around. And that's all I need. I suspect you might feel somethin' similar."

Susan didn't trust herself to speak. She nodded.

"Here's what else I know." Sonya's voice dropped, rougher now. "I know what men from out that way are like. They want you when you're young and pretty, and then the minute you're knocked up—" She slammed her hands together, making Susan jump. "They disappear faster than any stain laundry soap could get out. Am I right?"

Susan's throat was tight. "You're not wrong."

"'Course I ain't." Sonya sat back. "My no-good piece of shit husband—pardon my French, Angie—"

"Pardoned," Angie murmured.

"—decided some cocktail waitress over in Augusta was more 'his thing.'" Sonya made air quotes with her fingers. "Left me with three babies and a busted-up RV with bald tires and no gas money to get nowhere. I lived in that thing for eight months. Eight months, with three kids under five. You know what that's like?"

Susan's eyes were burning. "I know."

"Figured you might." Sonya's voice softened, just a touch. "So here's what I'm thinkin'. You come stay with us. I been remodelin' the back house—used to be a barn, really, but it's all fixed up now. Two bedrooms, full kitchen, everythin' you need. You can do laundry in the main house, and Angie loves to cook—"

"It's true," Angie said. "I really do."

"This ain't charity," Sonya said firmly. "You hear me? You owe us rent. Two-fifty a month. But not 'til you're on your feet."

Susan opened her mouth to object, but Sonya kept going.

"And I run a printin' shop up the road. Nothin' fancy, but it's mine. Well, ours." She glanced at Angie. "Had to fire that no-good Bobby's ass last week for showin' up drunk again. I don't take that kinda bullshit from nobody. You drink?"

"No," Susan managed.

"Good. I don't mind a beer with a steak dinner, but not on the job. You want work, I got work. Eight to four, Monday through Friday. Pays decent. Enough to cover rent and then some."

Angie leaned in, her voice gentle. "And I can watch the children after school. Or before, if you need. Whatever helps."

Susan's head was spinning. This was happening too fast. She needed to think, needed to—

"I know I'm bargin' in here," Sonya said, her voice softer now. "Barkin' orders, tellin' you how it's gonna be. But honey—" She reached across the table and took Susan's hand. Her grip was rough, calloused, the hands of a woman who'd worked hard her whole life. "I been where you are. I know what it's like to try to hold it all together when everythin's fallin' apart. And I'll be damned if I let another woman from our part of the state go through that alone when I got the means to help."

Susan couldn't speak. Tears were sliding down her cheeks.

"This ain't charity," Sonya repeated. "This is one workin' woman helpin' another. The way it's supposed to be. The way it was before all these city folk decided they knew better than us how to live our lives."

Susan wiped her face with the back of her hand. "I don't know what to say."

"Don't say nothin' yet. Just think about it. Talk to your kids. See how you feel." Sonya squeezed her hand once, then let go. "But know this: you got a place to go. A job waitin'. People who give a damn. That's more than I had when I was in your shoes."

Through the window, Susan could see Lucy running through the snow, laughing, chasing after Anthony's red coat. Levi was beside her, not quite running but not holding back either, something like a real smile on his face. Graham was bringing up the rear, playing the part of the bumbling head elf.

"Your kids are good kids," Angie said softly. "Anyone can see that. You done right by them."

Susan's shoulders shook. She pressed her hands to her face, trying to hold it together, but she couldn't. For months—God, had it been months?—she'd been the strong one. The one who kept going. The one who didn't cry, didn't break down, didn't let the kids see how scared she was.

But here, in this kitchen, with these two women who didn't pity her, didn't judge her, just saw her—

She broke.

Angie was there in an instant, arms around her, holding her the way you'd hold a child who'd finally stopped pretending to be brave. Susan buried her face in Angie's shoulder and sobbed—ugly, gasping sobs that she'd been holding back for longer than she could remember.

Sonya sat quietly, giving her space, her own eyes suspiciously bright.

"It's all right," Angie murmured, stroking Susan's hair. "You're all right now. We've got you."

Outside, Lucy's laughter rang across the snow. Inside, Susan cried in the arms of a woman who smelled like cookies and loved like a grandmother and asked for nothing in return except the chance to help.

The grown-up little girl who'd been trying so hard, for so long, finally let herself be held.

By Mrs. Claus.

Chapter Ten

GRAHAM'S NEPHEW Michael had visited many times before—usually during the summer when school let out and his mother needed a break from his particular brand of teenage energy. Those visits had been full of trips to the coast, hikes through the woods behind the house, and late nights watching old movies with Uncle Simon, who always fell asleep twenty minutes in but insisted he was "just resting his eyes."

But when Uncle Simon died, his mother thought it best Michael stay home. Give Graham space, she'd said. He's got so much to handle—the estate, the house, all of Simon's things. The last thing he needs is a teenager underfoot.

She thought she was doing Graham a favor.

She was wrong.

Michael knew it. He'd heard it in his uncle's voice during their phone calls—that hollow quality, the way Graham would say he was "fine" in a tone that meant anything but. Michael had tried to convince his mother to let him go that summer, but Becca was firm. Maybe next year, she'd said. When things have settled.

But things hadn't settled. Not for Graham. And not for Michael either.

The past six months had been strange for him. He'd always been the happy-go-lucky kid—the one who came in from the rain soaked to the bone but grinning, who looked up with cookie crumbs all over his shirt while swearing he hadn't touched the last one, who found joy in everything and spread it around like confetti. His mother used to say he was born smiling.

But something had shifted after Uncle Simon died. Michael became quieter, more withdrawn. He'd sit in his room for hours, not on his phone, not playing games—just sitting. Thinking. His mother assumed he was grieving, and maybe part of him was. He'd loved Uncle Simon. Everyone had.

But that wasn't all of it. That wasn't even most of it.

There was something else. Something Michael couldn't name, couldn't look at directly. Something that had been growing inside him for longer than he wanted to admit, and Uncle Simon's death had somehow cracked it open, made it impossible to ignore.

He didn't know what to do with it. He didn't know who to tell.

"So he said nothing. And the silence made him withdrawn, distant. His friends at school thought he was being dramatic. His mother thought it was still about Simon."

Finally, in early December, Michael pushed back.

"I want to go see Uncle Graham for Christmas."

His mother hesitated. "Honey, I don't know if that's a good idea. He's still—"

"He's alone, Mom. He's going to be alone on Christmas."

That had gotten her. Becca couldn't imagine her big brother sitting in that house by himself, staring at whatever tree he'd managed to put up—if he'd even bothered.

"Let me call him," she said. "We'll see."

The call lasted nearly an hour.

Graham had protested at first—he didn't want to be a burden, didn't want Becca to feel obligated. But she heard what Michael had heard: the loneliness underneath the words. The hollow places where Simon used to be.

"He wants to come," Becca said. "And honestly, Graham, I think he needs it too. He's been... different. Since Simon passed. Quiet in a way that worries me. I can't put my finger on it."

Graham was quiet for a moment. "He's seventeen, Bec. That's a hard age even without losing someone."

"I know. But this feels like more than that. Like he's working something out that he can't tell me about." Her voice tightened. "You two always had something special. Maybe being there with you would help."

"We did," Graham admitted. And they had—Michael had always gravitated toward Graham and Simon during visits, staying up late to talk about books and movies, asking questions about their life together with the unfiltered curiosity of a child who didn't yet know such questions might be considered impolite.

"So let's plan on the 26th," Becca said. "Flights should be easier, and I want him here for Christmas morning."

She hadn't even finished the sentence before Michael's voice came from the doorway. He'd been hovering nearby.

"Mom. The 26th? That's—"

"Michael Allen, I am on the phone with your uncle—"

"But that's *after* Christmas. He's going to be alone."

"Michael—"

"What's the point of me going if he's already spent Christmas by himself?"

Becca closed her eyes. She could picture it clearly: Graham in that big quiet house, no tree, no decorations, just the ghost of every Christmas Simon had made bright.

"Becca?" Graham's voice came through the phone. "Everything okay?"

"Hold on." She covered the receiver and looked at her son. He stood in the doorway with his arms crossed, jaw set in that stubborn way that reminded her so much of Graham. Of herself, if she was honest.

"I want you here for Christmas," she said. "With the family."

"Uncle Graham *is* family."

"That's not what I meant."

"Then what did you mean?"

She didn't have an answer. Or rather, she had too many—that she wanted to hold onto him, that Christmas morning without her son felt wrong, that some part of her sensed he was slipping away and she didn't know how to stop it.

Michael didn't push further. Didn't plead. He just stood there, waiting, and somehow that was worse. The old Michael would have argued, cajoled, turned on the charm. This Michael just watched her with those guarded eyes, like he'd already learned not to expect too much.

When had that happened?

"Let me call you back," she said into the phone, and hung up before Graham could respond.

The negotiation that followed wasn't really a negotiation. Michael stayed quiet, answering her questions about flights and logistics but offering nothing else. No arguments. No persuasion. Just patience—the kind that felt less like maturity and more like resignation.

It broke something in her.

Every instinct she had screamed to keep him close. To fill the house with family and noise and distraction, to wrap Christmas around him like a shield. But underneath that instinct was something quieter. A whisper she didn't want to hear.

Let him go.

She didn't understand it. Didn't like it. But she'd learned, over seventeen years of motherhood, that sometimes the thing your child needed most was the thing that terrified you.

She picked up her phone and texted Graham.

Would the 22nd work? Michael is practically ready to hitchhike your way. Rather get him there before Christmas Eve flights and traffic.

The reply came a minute later.

Are you okay with that?

No. But I'll get there. Just make sure he's safe. And you FaceTime me Christmas Eve. I mean it.

Promise.

I MEAN it, Graham.

I know you do. He'll be safe. And Bec... thank you.

She stared at the screen, then looked up at Michael. He was still standing in the doorway, still waiting, his expression carefully neutral.

"December 22nd," she said. "Through New Year's."

Something flickered across his face—relief, maybe, or hope—but it was gone before she could name it.

"Thanks, Mom."

"You call me when you land. And you listen to your uncle. And if you need anything — *anything* — you pick up the phone."

"I will."

He didn't hug her. The old Michael would have. This one just nodded and retreated to his room, and Becca stood alone in the kitchen wondering when her son had learned to hold himself so carefully apart.

Let him go.

She was trying. God help her, she was trying.

Graham stared at the phone for a while after the last text. Then he looked around.

No tree. No decorations. No lights. Simon would have had the place transformed by now — garlands on the mantle, candles in every window, that ridiculous inflatable snowman he'd insisted on putting in the front yard every year despite Graham's protests.

Michael was coming. His nephew was going to walk into a house that looked like nobody lived in it.

Graham looked at the bare walls, the empty mantle, the corner where a tree should be. He wasn't Simon. Didn't have his touch, his vision for how things should look. Simon was the one who made Christmas happen; Graham had just followed instructions and hauled boxes.

He should do something about it. He knew that.
He turned off the lamp and went to bed.

The next morning, Graham sent Eli a message:

My nephew is coming Thursday

Nephew?

Baby sister's son. Michael. Was supposed to come last summer but..

He didn't want to get into it over text.

Interested in helping?

How old?

Who?

Santa Who you think?

Smartass M is 17 I think I'm old

You are

Hey!

Time?

Flight's at 4

So 10?

What?

$100 it's delayed

I don't gamble

Did with me

Graham muttered something about him being a bitch, but smiled.

Fine.

You're good

I try

Coming or not?

Yes Does he know about me?

No.

I'll dress in clown suit then

Maybe I should ask Anthony

I'll be good

Fine.

Mostly

He's going to love you

Too young

Not what I meant.

I did

Say goodbye Eli

I just did

What??

Said goodbye out loud You told me to

Bye

The flight was delayed.

"You owe me a hundred dollars," Eli said, settling into the hard plastic bench beside Graham.

"Like hell I do."

"We bet. It's delayed. I win."

"That wasn't a real bet."

"You said 'fine.' That's binding."

"In what court?"

"The court of Eli." He stretched his legs out. "I accept Venmo."

Graham muttered something uncharitable. The arrivals board had already updated twice—first to five-fifteen, now to six-forty-five. The terminal was packed, every bench claimed, travelers sprawled across the floor near charging stations. They'd been lucky to snag two seats together.

"I'm getting coffee," Eli announced, standing. "Want anything, Grumpy McGrump?"

"Get off my lawn."

Eli laughed and disappeared into the crowd toward the small café near security.

Graham settled back against the uncomfortable bench and checked his phone. No messages from Becca, which meant Michael's connecting flight had probably gone fine. He looked up at the board again. Six-forty-five. The kid had been traveling since noon.

Eli returned a few minutes later with something that looked more like dessert than coffee—whipped cream, caramel drizzle, the works.

"He's going to be exhausted," Graham said. "Poor kid's been in the air all day."

"He's seventeen. He'll bounce back."

"I remember seventeen. I would not have bounced back."

Eli laughed. "Fair point."

The board updated again: landed.

Graham stood, suddenly nervous in a way he hadn't expected. He hadn't seen Michael in person since last winter — at Simon's funeral, and neither of them had been in any state to really talk. Before that, it had been two summers ago. Michael had been fifteen then. Gangly, awkward, still more boy than young man.

He wouldn't be that kid anymore.

The doors to the secure area opened, and passengers began streaming out—business travelers with rolling bags, families with crying toddlers, college students heading home for break. Graham scanned the crowd.

And then he saw him.

Michael had grown. He was taller now, nearly Graham's height, with the same mop of dark hair he'd always had but a face that had lost its boyish roundness. He looked tired—dark circles under his eyes, shoulders hunched under his backpack—but when he spotted Graham, something in his expression cracked open.

"Uncle Graham!"

He crossed the distance between them at almost a run, and then he was in Graham's arms, holding on tight, and for a moment he wasn't seventeen at all. He was twelve again, or eight, or five—every age he'd ever been when he'd run to his uncle for a hug.

Graham held him. Didn't say anything. Just held him.

When they finally separated, Michael's eyes were wet, though he was clearly trying to pretend they weren't.

"Hey, kid," Graham said softly.

"Hey." Michael's voice cracked slightly. He cleared his throat. "Sorry. Long flight."

"Nothing to be sorry for."

Michael seemed to notice Eli for the first time—standing a few feet back, giving them space.

"Oh," Michael said. "Hi. Sorry, I didn't—"

"Michael, this is Eli. The friend I told you about."

Eli stepped forward and extended his hand. "Nice to finally meet you. Graham talks about you constantly."

Michael shook his hand, then tilted his head slightly. There was something about Eli's voice—not quite what he'd expected. The cadence was different. Some of the sounds seemed softer, slightly imprecise.

"Nice to meet you too," Michael said, but Eli didn't respond right away. He was looking at Michael's mouth, waiting.

"Sorry," Eli said. "I didn't catch that. You're a mumbler, aren't you?"

"What? No, I—" Michael looked at Graham, confused.

"Eli's hard of hearing," Graham explained. "He needs to see your face when you talk."

"Oh!" Michael's eyes widened. "Oh, sorry. I didn't realize—I mean, you don't—" He stopped, clearly unsure how to finish that sentence without making it worse.

Eli grinned. "I don't what? Sound deaf?"

Michael's face flushed. "I didn't mean—"

"Relax." Eli clapped him on the shoulder. "I get it all the time. People expect me to sound like... I don't know. A robot? Something weird?" He shrugged. "This is just my voice. Has been my whole life. Seems pretty normal to me."

Michael laughed, some of the tension leaving his shoulders. "Yeah. Okay. Sorry. I just—"

"Stop apologizing. We're good." Eli grabbed Michael's backpack from him. "Come on. Your uncle promised me dinner."

"I did?" Graham said.

"Yes. Besides, I'm starving."

"You're always starving."

"Growing boy."

"You're twenty-four."

"Still growing. Vertically. Horizontally. Spiritually."

"That last one's debatable."

"Rude." Eli turned to Michael. "You see what I put up with?"

Michael found himself smiling. "Seems rough."

"It is. He's a tyrant." Eli threw an arm around Michael's shoulder and steered him toward the exit, navigating through the chaos of the arrivals hall. "Come on. Let's get out of here before he makes us pay for parking twice."

Graham followed behind, shaking his head.

Michael glanced back at his uncle, who simply shrugged—a look that said *this is just how he is.* Michael turned back to Eli, who was already asking him about his flight, whether the airline had fed him anything edible, and if he had strong opinions about Mexican food.

These two, Michael thought. They seemed to *click.* Like they'd known each other for years instead of—how long had it been? He wasn't sure. But there was an ease between them. A rhythm.

They ended up at a chain restaurant near the airport—one of those places with oversized menus and televisions on every wall. Not Eli's preference, Graham knew. He'd have chosen somewhere local, somewhere with character. But it was late, Michael was exhausted, and the familiar comfort of American chain dining held a certain appeal for a seventeen-year-old who'd been traveling all day.

"This okay?" Graham asked as they slid into a booth.

"Perfect," Michael said, already scanning the menu. "We have one of these back home."

Eli caught Graham's eye across the table and gave a small shrug. *It's fine.* He picked up his own menu and immediately began searching for something that might pass for authentic Mexican food. Graham suspected he'd be disappointed.

The server came and went. Waters all around, a Coke for Michael, and the promise to return shortly.

Michael hadn't stopped looking around since they sat down—at the other diners, the decorations, the general chaos of a restaurant two days before Christmas. But Graham noticed he kept glancing back at Eli, curiosity written plainly on his face.

"So," Michael said, setting down his menu. "How long have you two known each other?"

"Few weeks," Eli said. "Just before Thanksgiving."

"Feels longer," Graham added.

"That's because you're old. Time moves differently for the elderly."

"I'm going to throw this salt shaker at you."

Michael grinned, watching them. "How'd you meet?"

Graham glanced at Eli.

"Whole Foods," Graham said.

"Amazon return line," Eli added.

"There was a woman ahead of us with about a hundred packages."

"We bonded over our shared suffering."

"It was a long wait."

Michael laughed. "Sounds romantic."

"Oh, I have *zero* interest in the old man over here," Eli said, thumbing toward Graham.

Graham was already nodding along, smiling. "Exactly, we're just—" He stopped. "Wait a minute. I'm a catch!"

"For some fisherman, maybe."

Michael laughed, looking between them.

Graham straightened in his seat with mock indignation. "What this rude, *rude* man over here—" He thumbed back at Eli, who smiled broadly as if proud of himself, which made Michael laugh again. "—means is that there is absolutely no way I'd ever have any interest in someone as uncouth as him."

"Uncouth?" Eli's eyebrows shot up. "What are you, a hundred?"

"It's a perfectly good word."

Eli stuck out his tongue, then winked at Michael.

Michael laughed again. These two were crazy. "Sorry, I didn't mean to—"

But Graham waved him off, still chuckling. "We're good friends, Michael. That's all." His smile softened. "Besides, I'm fine being just myself."

The lightness shifted, just slightly. Michael saw it. Eli saw it too.

Simon. Everyone was thinking of Simon.

The server returned with drinks and took their orders—burger and fries for Michael, quesadilla for Eli (with low expectations), and a club sandwich for Graham. Once she'd gone, Michael turned his attention fully to Eli.

"Can I ask you something?"

"Shoot."

"When did you lose your hearing? Or—wait, is that rude to ask? I don't know the rules."

Graham watched Eli's face, curious how he'd respond. But Eli just shrugged.

"Not rude. I was born with it. Well—born with some. Lost more over time. It's progressive."

"That sucks."

"It is what it is."

"Is it a bitch?"

Graham nearly choked on his water. He'd forgotten how Michael's vocabulary had evolved since he'd last seen him—the shy fifteen-year-old who barely spoke above a whisper around adults had apparently discovered profanity. He wondered if Becca knew. Probably not. She'd always been more of a prude about that sort of thing, though he loved her anyway.

Eli, for his part, didn't bat an eye. "Sometimes. Mostly I'm used to it. The hard part is—" He gestured vaguely at the restaurant around them.

"Places like this. Lots of noise. Hard to hear, hard to read lips when everyone's moving and talking and there's music and—"

"Oh." Michael's face fell. "Sorry. We could've gone somewhere quieter."

"It's fine. I'm adaptable." Eli leaned forward. "Just need you to stop mumbling."

"I'm not mumbling."

"Bullshit!" Eli exaggerated looking down at the table, chin tucked to his chest, muttering nonsense syllables.

Michael laughed.

Eli smiled. "See! Now I can see your lips."

"Oh. Right. Sorry."

"Stop apologizing."

Michael made a conscious effort to look directly at Eli, enunciating carefully. "Is. This. Better."

"Now you sound like a robot."

"You said—"

"Just talk normal. But *at* me." Eli demonstrated, pointing at his own face. "Here. Words go here."

Michael laughed and tried again. This time he made it about halfway through a sentence before instinctively looking down at his napkin.

Eli reached across the table and physically turned Michael's head back toward him.

"Hey!"

"I warned you."

Graham watched them, something warm spreading in his chest. They'd known each other for less than an hour and already they were acting like brothers — teasing, pushing back, finding their footing with each other.

The food arrived. Michael immediately took an enormous bite of his burger and then, still chewing, turned to Eli with a question clearly forming.

Eli held up a hand. "Nope. Can't understand you with a cow in your mouth."

Michael's eyes crinkled with mischief. He chewed slowly, deliberately, maintaining eye contact the entire time.

Eli narrowed his eyes. "You're doing that on purpose."

Michael took another huge bite, still staring.

"Oh, it's like that?" Eli picked up his fork and started tapping it against Michael's plate, making a racket. "I can be annoying too."

Michael nearly choked laughing, bits of burger threatening to escape. Graham handed him a napkin and shook his head.

"Children," he muttered. "I'm dining with children."

They settled into a rhythm after that—Michael asking questions, Eli answering and lobbing questions back. What grade was Michael in? Junior. Did he play sports? Used to play soccer, quit last year. Why? Didn't feel like it anymore. Fair enough. What did Eli do? Worked at L.L. Bean. Was that boring? Sometimes. Did he like it? It paid the bills. What did he actually want to do?

Eli paused at that one. "Still figuring it out."

"You're twenty-four."

"And?"

"Shouldn't you know by now?"

Eli laughed. "Kid, I'll let you in on a secret. Nobody knows what they're doing. We're all just pretending."

Michael seemed to consider this. "That's kind of terrifying."

"Also kind of freeing. Means you don't have to have it all figured out either."

Graham watched the exchange quietly, content to observe. He was learning things about both of them—seeing sides of Eli he hadn't encountered before, watching Michael test boundaries he'd never tested with Graham. It was good. Strange, but good.

Then Eli circled back.

"So earlier—what made you think I was gay, anyway?"

The question landed differently than Michael expected. Eli's posture had changed—shoulders squared, chin lifted, something almost challenging in his eyes.

"I—I mean—" Michael glanced at Graham. "I just assumed because Uncle Graham is, and you two seem close, and—" His face was reddening. "Oh god, I'm sorry. I wasn't trying to assume. I didn't mean anything by it."

Eli held the serious expression for another beat.

Then he broke.

"Gurl, I *got* you!"

The camp came out of nowhere—a complete shift in energy, voice, posture. Eli was laughing, one hand pressed to his chest dramatically, and Michael sat there with his mouth hanging open.

"Your *face*," Eli wheezed. "Oh my god, your face."

"That's—you can't just—" Michael sputtered.

"I absofuckinglutely did!"

Michael had never heard something like that—laughing, but trying to stay cool. Eli didn't give a shit who heard or even cared. Graham just kept eating, hiding a smile. Michael could fend for himself. Besides, he'd rarely seen this side of Eli—not in public, not so openly. Eli usually kept that part of himself more contained, more careful. But something about Michael had drawn it out. Permission, maybe. Safety.

Michael still had his mouth hanging open. Eli reached across the table and pushed his chin up, closing it.

"Flies," Eli said. "You'll catch flies."

Michael swatted his hand away, but he was fighting a smile now. "You're mean."

"I'm hilarious. Ask anyone."

"Uncle Graham?"

"He's a menace," Graham said. "But yes. Also hilarious."

Michael shook his head, stuffing more burger in his mouth. He was chewing—deliberately, pointedly, staring at Eli—when Eli lobbed the next question.

"So do you have a boyfriend?"

It was asked casually. Easily. The same tone someone might use to ask what grade are you in or do you like sports.

Michael stopped chewing.

The shift was subtle but immediate—a stillness in his shoulders, a careful blankness settling over his face. Graham saw it. He was pretty sure Eli saw it too.

"No," Michael said. His voice was flatter now. Guarded. "I don't."

Eli shrugged. "Oh well."

He went back to his quesadilla, and just like that, the question was dropped. No follow-up. No probing. Just acceptance and a return to normalcy.

But Michael had gone quiet. The rapid-fire questions stopped. He focused on his food, on the television mounted in the corner, on anything that wasn't the two men across from him.

Graham let the silence sit for a moment. Then something occurred to him.

"Oh—I forgot to tell you. Susan."

Eli looked up. "What about her?"

"Well, after that night—when you ran into Levi and Lucy at the grocery—Angie and Sonya came over the next day."

"Yeah?"

"I wasn't part of the conversation, but something happened. Susan and the kids—they've moved into the little house behind Angie and Sonya's place."

"Wait, really?"

"And apparently Sonya's putting Susan to work at the printing shop." Graham smiled. "So. Good news."

"That's amazing." Eli's whole face softened. "How's my favorite girl?"

Michael's eyebrows raised.

Eli caught it immediately. "Jealous?"

Michael shrugged, feigning disinterest—slipping back into that brother banter from earlier.

Eli rolled his eyes overtly. "She's *five*."

Michael didn't miss a beat. "You like 'em young?"

Graham nearly choked on his sandwich. Eli looked at Michael like he'd just met his master.

"Touché, Monsieur Michel."

Michael smiled, clearly proud of himself.

"Anyway," Graham said, "you'll never guess what Levi found when they stayed over at the house that night."

"What?" Eli said, stuffing his face with a quesadilla and opening his mouth wide to gross out Michael — who retaliated by showing off a mouthful of half-chewed burger. They were both seven, apparently.

"As I was *saying*—" Graham tried again.

Eli pivoted, grinning. "He found your private collection of—"

"Don't you dare finish that sentence." Graham cut him off.

Michael nearly spit out his food. Eli looked innocent as an angel, fake-polishing a pretend halo above his head.

"He's my *nephew*, for god's sake," Graham said, shaking his head.

"So? He's seventeen! I guarantee he's got his own collection by now!" Eli shot back, then smiled at Michael.

Michael turned bright red.

"See!" Eli pointed. "He does! Look at that face!"

"You're such a child."

Michael was still laughing, still red.

"*Anywayyyy*," Graham dragged the word out, attempting to regain some semblance of order. "Levi found my original manuscript files for the book."

"Which one?"

"The first."

"No way." Eli leaned forward. "Where?"

"In my office."

"You *let* him?"

"I gave them to him, actually. But he found the copies I have in the bookcase first."

"You gave *the book* to him, but not *me*?"

"I didn't *give* him the book. It's not even a book—it's my papers and such."

"Same difference."

Michael chimed in. "How can something be the same *and* different?"

Eli looked at him like he'd grown horns.

"What?" Michael asked, smiling. Clearly back.

"*Anyway*—" There were a lot of "anyways" in this conversation, or what was passing for one. Eli turned back to Graham. "What did Levi do? When you gave it to him?"

Graham paused, remembering. "It was like he was transported. I think he's like Marco, you know?"

Eli nodded slowly. "I could see that."

Michael didn't know who Marco was, or Levi, or any of this. But he was witness to something. A shift in the air. A weight to the words that told him this mattered—whatever *this* was.

Eli glanced at Michael, then did a double-take. "Wait. You know what we're talking about, right?"

Michael shook his head.

Eli stared at Graham. "You never told him?"

"It never came up."

"It never—" Eli looked back at Michael, incredulous. "Your uncle is a famous author and it *never came up*?"

Michael glanced between them, confused. "I mean, I knew he wrote stuff. But I didn't know it was, like, a big deal."

"A big deal," Eli repeated flatly. "Graham. Your nephew doesn't know about Oltrarno."

"Clearly."

"This is a crime."

Graham held up his hands. "He was always more interested in video games when he visited. I wasn't going to force my own books on him."

"Still a crime." Eli turned to Michael, something evangelical lighting up his face. "Okay. So. Your uncle wrote this series set in Renaissance Florence—"

"Maybe save it for tomorrow?" Graham interrupted. "It's a long story, and we should probably get this one home before he falls asleep in his burger."

Michael protested weakly, but he was flagging—the travel finally catching up with him. Eli conceded, but not without pointing a finger at Michael.

"Tomorrow. You're getting the full story."

"Okay, okay."

Graham flagged down the server for the check. But Eli wasn't done.

"Actually—" A lightbulb seemed to go off behind his eyes. "Graham. What if we invited Levi over tomorrow? He could meet Michael, finish reading the manuscript, and—" He turned to Michael. "Maybe we could decorate? Your uncle's house is criminally bare."

Michael perked up immediately. "Wait, really?" He turned to Graham. "You haven't decorated yet? Not even a tree?"

Graham shrugged, studying his coffee. "Haven't gotten around to it."

Eli gave him a look. He knew better.

"It's fine," Graham said. "It's just a house."

"It's *Christmas*," Michael said, as if Graham had just suggested the earth was flat.

"We could help. Me and Michael. And if Levi comes—that's four people. We could knock it out."

Graham looked at his nephew—at the hope that had crept back into his expression. He thought about Lucy, living next door to Angie and Sonya. She'd thought Anthony was the real Santa. He wondered if she'd asked yet why Mrs. Claus didn't live at the North Pole. Had her own wife instead.

This would be her first real Christmas in a while, he suspected. Maybe Levi's too.

Something in him cracked open. The way ice cracks in spring, making room for water to flow again.

"Okay," he said. "Let's do it."

Michael's face broke into a grin—wide and bright, the kind Graham remembered from summers past.

"But you'll both have to help me," Graham added. "Simon... he was the one with the plan. I just followed orders."

Eli nodded, his expression softening. "We'll do him proud."

"Don't be so sure." Graham signaled for the check. "There's a lot."

THE NEXT MORNING, Graham called Susan.

"He's been asking every five minutes," she said, and Graham could hear the smile in her voice. "I think he'd walk there if I let him."

"Tell him I'll pick him up around ten. I need to swing by and get Eli on the way back."

"That works. Lucy's a little sore she can't come along, but Angie's got something cooked up for her."

"Mrs. Claus duties?"

Susan laughed. "They're gonna decorate Lucy's own little tree and make a gingerbread house. She's beside herself."

"Sounds perfect."

"Thanks for including him. He's been a whole different kid since we moved in here, and I reckon a good bit of that's on account of you. Boy won't stop talking about that manuscript of yours."

"He's welcome anytime. I mean that."

"I know you do." A pause. "That's what makes it different."

After he hung up, Graham found Michael in the kitchen, already dressed and eating cereal.

"You're up early."

"Couldn't sleep." Michael shrugged. "Excited, I guess."

"Want to come with me? I'm picking up Levi, then Eli."

Michael's spoon paused halfway to his mouth. "The kid you were talking about? The one reading your book?"

"That's him."

"Sure." Michael took another bite, chewing thoughtfully. "What's he like?"

Graham considered the question. What was Levi like? He thought about the boy sitting in his office, utterly absorbed in a manuscript. The careful way he held the pages. The look on his face when he'd realized Graham was the author.

"He's... quiet. But not shy, exactly. More like he's watching everything. Taking it all in." Graham leaned against the counter. "He's had a hard time. His family. But he doesn't make a big deal of it."

Michael nodded slowly. "Okay."

"You'll like him."

"You keep saying that."

"Because it's true."

They pulled up to Angie and Sonya's place a little after ten. In daylight, the decorations Graham had seen at the party told a different story — the plastic Santa looked sun-bleached and slightly drunk, leaning hard to one side from the wind, and the snow angel had developed a lean of her own. But the candy cane stakes still lined the walkway like little soldiers, and someone had added a hand-painted sign on the front door that read "Lucy's Workshop" in glitter and crayon.

Graham smiled. That had Angie written all over it.

Behind the main house sat the old barn Sonya had renovated—now a small home with smoke curling from its chimney and curtains in the windows.

"That's where they live now?" Michael asked.

"Just moved in last week."

"It's cute."

Graham honked lightly. A moment later, Levi emerged, pulling on a coat that was at least a size too small—the sleeves stopping well above his wrists. His hair was getting long, falling into his eyes, and he kept pushing it back as he walked toward the car.

Halfway across the yard, Levi slowed. He'd spotted Michael in the passenger seat. His steps became more hesitant, his expression shifting from eager to uncertain.

Graham rolled down his window. "Levi—this is my nephew Michael. He's visiting from Tennessee. Hop in."

Levi nodded, his earlier enthusiasm dampened. He climbed into the back seat quietly.

"Hi," Michael said, turning around.

"Hi." Levi's voice was guarded.

An awkward silence settled over the car.

Graham pulled back onto the road. "Michael's going to help us decorate today."

"Okay." Levi was looking out the window now, his shoulders tense.

Graham glanced at Michael beside him and gave a small shrug. Give it time.

They pulled up to Eli's apartment—the same tired building Graham remembered from that first ride home.

"Michael, why don't you pop in the back before Eli comes down?"

Michael climbed out and opened the back door, sliding in next to Levi. The two of them sat there awkwardly while Graham texted Eli.

A moment later, Eli bounded out of the building and slid into the passenger seat.

He turned around immediately. "Levi! Good to see you again." He grinned. "Graham told me Lucy's convinced Anthony is the real Santa?"

Levi relaxed slightly. A familiar face. "Yeah. She won't stop talking about it."

"Smart kid." Eli's eyes moved over Levi's face, then he tilted his head. "Hey—I never noticed before. Your eyes are different colors."

Levi blinked. "What?"

"Your eyes. One's blue, one's kind of green. That's cool."

Michael leaned forward, looking more closely. Eli was right—Levi's left eye was blue-green, while his right was solid blue. How had he missed that?

"Oh." Levi's hand drifted toward his face self-consciously. "Yeah. It's just... a thing."

"A cool thing," Eli said firmly. "Own it."

Levi didn't respond, but something in his posture loosened slightly.

"Also," Eli added, "you need a haircut."

"Eli," Graham warned.

"What? He does. I'm just saying."

Levi almost smiled. Almost.

"Alright," Graham said. "Let's go see how bad this is going to be."

The boxes were worse than Eli had imagined.

Graham had warned them, but warnings didn't quite capture the reality of the basement: stacks upon stacks of plastic bins, each labeled in Simon's neat handwriting. *Outdoor Lights - Icicle. Outdoor Lights - Colored. Tree Ornaments - Vintage. Tree Ornaments - Modern. Garland - Mantle. Garland - Staircase.*

"There's no staircase," Eli said.

"We used to live in a different house."

"And you kept the staircase garland?"

"Simon kept everything."

Michael was already pulling bins off shelves. "This is insane. This is like... professional-level Christmas."

"Simon didn't do anything halfway." Graham's voice was soft. "I told you—he had the vision. I just followed orders."

Levi stood near the back, taking it all in. His eyes moved from bin to bin, reading Simon's labels.

"Okay," Eli announced, clapping his hands. "Here's the plan. Graham—you and I are going to get a tree."

"Now?"

"Yes, now. It's December 23rd. If we wait any longer, we'll end up with a Charlie Brown situation." He turned to Michael and Levi. "You two—start bringing boxes up. Get the lights sorted. We'll be back in an hour."

Michael saluted. "Yes, sir."

"I like him," Eli said to Graham. "He takes direction well."

"Don't get used to it."

Graham hesitated, looking at Levi. The boy was still standing near the back, his too-small coat hanging off his thin frame.

"Levi—you okay to stay and help Michael?"

Levi nodded. "Yeah. I'm good."

"Okay. We'll be back soon."

Graham followed Eli up the stairs, but paused at the top to look back. Michael was already chattering at Levi about something—which box to grab first, probably—and Levi was listening with that quiet watchfulness Graham had noticed before.

They'd be fine.

He hoped.

The tree lot was picked over, as expected.

"This one's not bad," Eli said, circling a Douglas fir that was missing branches on one side.

"It's half a tree."

"We put the bad side against the wall."

"Simon would have a stroke."

"Simon's not here." Eli said it gently, without judgment. "And I think he'd rather you have half a tree than no tree at all."

Graham stood there for a moment, the cold biting at his cheeks. Around them, other families wandered the lot—kids running between rows, parents debating heights and fullness, the smell of pine and wood smoke filling the air.

"You're right," he said finally. "Let's get the half-tree."

"That's the spirit."

They paid, and with some twine thrown in from the tree lot, managed to strap it to the roof of the BMW. Neither really knew what they were doing, but they made it work.

Graham drove slowly, checking the rearview mirror every few seconds to make sure the tree hadn't escaped.

"So," Eli said. "Levi."

"What about him?"

"He needs a haircut."

Graham laughed. "You mentioned."

"And a new coat. And probably new everything."

"I know."

"Are you going to do something about it?"

Graham was quiet for a moment. "I've been thinking about Santa."

"Santa?"

"Lucy thinks Anthony is the real Santa. And she lives next door to 'Mrs. Claus' now." Graham smiled slightly. "I figure Santa might need to make a delivery this year."

Eli nodded slowly. "That's a good idea."

"I just don't want to embarrass them. Susan's proud. She doesn't want charity."

"It's not charity. It's Christmas." Eli looked out the window. "There's a difference."

"Precisely. That's why you and I are depending on *Santa* to deliver those things, right?"

Eli understood.

Back at the house, chaos had erupted.

Graham pulled into the driveway and stopped short. Michael was sprinting across the front yard, a tangle of Christmas lights wrapped around his shoulders like a cape. Behind him, Levi was giving chase—actually running, actually laughing—with a handful of snow already forming in his bare hands.

Michael looked back, saw Levi gaining, and promptly tripped over his own feet. He went down hard, disappearing into a snowbank with a muffled yelp.

Levi skidded to a stop, then doubled over laughing.

Eli raised an eyebrow at Graham.

"Well," Eli said. "They're getting along."

They got out of the car just as Michael emerged from the snowbank, sputtering and covered in white. He spotted them and immediately pointed at Levi.

"He started it!"

"I did not!" Levi was still laughing—actually laughing, his whole face transformed by it. "You threw tinsel at my head!"

"It was a joke!"

"So was the snow!"

Graham watched Levi's face, the way his smile made him look younger, lighter. It was infectious, that smile—a rare treat, the kind of thing that made you want to see it again. Michael had noticed too, Graham could tell. He was staring at Levi with something like wonder.

"Children," Graham said mildly. "I leave you alone for one hour—"

Eli was already bending down, scooping snow into his hands.

"Eli," Graham warned. "Don't you dare—"

The snowball hit him square in the chest.

For a split second, nobody moved. Michael's eyes went wide. Levi looked like he was trying to decide whether to run or hide.

Graham looked down at the snow splattered across his coat. Looked up at Eli, who was grinning like an idiot.

"Oh," Graham said quietly. "It's like that."

He reached down.

What followed was thirty seconds of absolute chaos—snowballs flying in every direction, alliances forming and breaking in real-time. Graham and Levi against Michael and Eli. Then Eli against everyone. Then somehow Michael and Levi ganging up on both adults until Graham held up his hands in surrender.

"Truce! Truce! I'm too old for this!"

"You're not old," Eli said, breathless and grinning.

"I'm fifty-three and my back is screaming."

Michael was lying in the snow, making what might have been a snow angel or might have been a cry for help. Levi stood over him, still holding a snowball, looking more relaxed than Graham had ever seen him.

"That was fun," Levi said quietly. Almost surprised by it.

"Yeah." Michael grinned up at him. "It was."

Inside, Graham made cocoa while the others stomped snow off their boots in the mudroom.

"Alright," he said, handing out mugs. "Eli and I need to get the tree set up. You two—lights. Sort them, test them, throw out anything that doesn't work."

"How do we test them?" Michael asked.

"Plug them in."

"Revolutionary."

"Don't be a smartass."

"Too late," Eli said. "It's genetic."

"Come on," Eli said, heading for the garage. "Let's wrestle this half-tree inside before it freezes to the car."

. . .

With Graham and Eli occupied with the tree, Michael and Levi settled into the living room with boxes of lights spread around them.

The silence was different now. Less awkward. More... waiting.

"So," Michael said, untangling a strand of white lights. "You're fifteen?"

"Almost sixteen. February."

"I just turned seventeen. In November."

"November? When?"

"Wednesday before Thanksgiving."

Levi looked at him. "You're a Thanksgiving baby?"

"That's what my mom says. She was thankful I finally came out and gave her a rest." Michael grinned. "Apparently I kicked a lot."

"No way!" Levi laughed.

"Way. She brings it up every year."

Levi shook his head, still smiling.

Michael tried again. "You go to school around here?"

"Not yet. We just moved. Mom says maybe after New Year's, once things settle."

"That sucks. Starting mid-year, I mean."

Levi shrugged. "I'm used to it."

Something about the way he said it made Michael pause. "You've moved a lot?"

"Enough."

Michael let that sit, focusing on the lights for a moment. Testing a strand. It worked. He set it aside and grabbed another.

"I've never moved," he said. "Same house my whole life. Same school, same friends, same everything."

"That sounds nice."

"It's boring."

Levi looked at him. "Boring isn't bad."

Michael didn't have a response to that.

They worked in silence for a few minutes. Michael kept glancing at Levi—at his too-long hair, his thin frame, those striking mismatched eyes. There was something about him. Something that made Michael want to keep talking, even though he wasn't sure what to say.

"Do you have brothers or sisters?" Michael asked.

"A sister. Lucy. She's five."

"I have a younger sister too. Erin. She's fourteen." Michael made a face. "She's annoying."

Levi almost smiled. "Lucy's not annoying. She's just... little. She doesn't understand everything."

"Understand what?"

The question hung in the air. Levi's hands stilled on the lights.

"Just... stuff," he said finally. "Life stuff."

Michael nodded like he understood, even though he wasn't sure he did. There was weight in Levi's voice. History. The kind of thing you didn't push at.

"What about your parents?" Michael asked, then immediately wished he hadn't. "Sorry—you don't have to—"

"It's fine." Levi's voice was flat. "My mom's great. She works really hard. My dad's not around."

"Oh."

"It's fine," Levi said again, like saying it twice made it true.

Michael thought about his own parents—his mom who worried too much and his dad who worked too much and how neither of them seemed to understand him lately, but they were there. They were always there.

"My uncle Graham and Uncle Simon basically raised me during summers," Michael offered. "I mean, not raised. But I spent a lot of time here. Simon was..." He trailed off.

"I'm sorry about Simon," Levi said quietly. "Graham talks about him sometimes. You can tell he really loved him."

"Yeah." Michael swallowed. "He did."

Another silence. But this one felt different. Shared.

"Do you have a girlfriend?" Michael asked, then immediately felt stupid. Why had he asked that?

Levi's expression flickered. "No. Too much other stuff going on."

"Yeah. Same." Michael focused intently on the lights in his hands. "I mean, not the same stuff. Just... I don't know. I'm figuring things out."

Levi glanced at him. Something passed between them—a recognition, maybe. Or just the understanding that some things were hard to say out loud.

"Yeah," Levi said. "Me too."

The garage door rumbled.

"That's them," Michael said, standing. "Come on—let's help with the tree."

They headed for the mudroom, but Levi paused as they passed Graham's office. Through the open door, he could see the desk, the windows looking out into the woods, and there—sitting exactly where he'd left it—the manuscript.

His manuscript. Graham's manuscript. The one he hadn't finished.

"You coming?" Michael called from down the hall.

"Yeah." Levi tore his eyes away. "Coming."

The tree was, as predicted, a disaster.

"It's leaning," Michael said.

"It's not leaning," Eli insisted. "It's... characterful."

"It's leaning to the left."

"That's its good side."

Graham stood back, arms crossed, watching Eli and Michael wrestle with the trunk while Levi steadied the top from a stepladder. The half-tree looked even more half in the living room than it had at the lot, but there was something endearing about it. Something real.

"Simon would have sent it back," Graham said.

"Simon's not here to judge," Eli grunted, tightening something at the base. "And if he is, he can haunt someone else's tree."

Levi laughed—a surprised, genuine sound. Michael glanced at Graham, worried the joke had gone too far, but his uncle just smiled and rolled his eyes.

"Okay," Eli said, stepping back. "Let go. Slowly."

Levi released his hold. The tree stayed upright. Mostly.

"Good enough," Graham declared. "Let's decorate before it changes its mind."

They worked through the afternoon, box by box.

Graham had forgotten how much there was. Garland for the mantle. Stockings—his and Simon's, which Graham hung without comment. It would have felt strange to hang just one. Candles for the windows. A ceramic nativity set that had belonged to Simon's grandmother. Ornaments sorted by color, by era, by sentiment.

Levi handled everything with care, as if each piece might break. He read the labels on boxes before opening them, studied ornaments before placing them, asked permission before touching anything that looked old or fragile.

Halfway through the tree, he paused with an ornament in his hand—a small glass replica of the Florence skyline, the Duomo rising in miniature.

"This is beautiful," he said quietly.

Graham looked over. "Simon and I picked that up in Florence. Years ago."

Levi's head snapped toward him. "You've been there? To Florence?"

"Several times."

"To the Academy?"

Graham smiled. "The Accademia? Yes. We saw the David."

Levi's eyes went wide. "What was it like?"

"Crowded. Overwhelming. Smaller than you'd expect from pictures, but also... bigger, somehow. More real." Graham paused, remembering. Simon's hand in his. The hush of the gallery. The way the marble seemed to breathe. "It's one of those things you have to see in person to understand."

Levi was still holding the ornament, staring at it like it contained a secret.

Eli appeared at his shoulder. "The Academy scene is one of my favorites in the book. When Marco sees the David for the first time and realizes—"

"—that beauty can be carved out of something broken," Levi finished. "That someone saw the potential in a flawed piece of marble and made it into something eternal."

They grinned at each other, that instant recognition of shared obsession.

"And Alessandro watching Marco's face," Eli added. "Realizing he's falling in love with someone who sees the world differently than anyone he's ever met."

"That part wrecked me," Levi said. "The way Graham wrote it—you could feel Alessandro's whole world shifting."

Michael stood a few feet away, an ornament dangling forgotten from his fingers. He had no idea what they were talking about.

Eli caught his expression and stopped. "Oh wait—you still don't know what we're talking about, do you?"

"Not a clue."

"Right." Eli turned to Graham. "Your nephew still hasn't read your books. This is a travesty that needs to be corrected immediately."

"So correct it," Graham said mildly, hanging a silver bell on a high branch.

"You should tell him. It's your story."

"Why? You two seem to know it better than me."

Eli looked at Levi. Levi looked at Eli. Some silent agreement passed between them.

"Fine," Eli said. "We'll do it. But you're filling in the parts we get wrong."

"I wouldn't dream of interrupting."

They kept decorating as they talked, but the ornaments became secondary. Background. The real work was the story.

Eli started. "Okay, so. Renaissance Florence. Late 1400s. There's this boy, Marco—"

"He's poor," Levi jumped in. "Like, really poor. His father died when he was young, and his mother takes in washing to survive. But Marco has this gift. He can draw. He can paint. He sees things other people don't see."

"And his mother—she knows he's special. So she scrapes together what little they have and sends him off to Florence. Walking. Alone. Just this kid with nothing but hope and talent."

Levi nodded, picking up the thread. "But when he gets there, everything's falling apart. Lorenzo de' Medici just died—he's the guy who basically runs the whole city—and nobody knows what's going to happen. The Academy might close. There are no spots for new students. The ones already there don't even know if they'll be allowed to stay."

Eli was watching Levi now, not adding to the story so much as witnessing it. There was something in the way Levi spoke—an urgency, a tenderness—that made it clear this story didn't just live in his head. It lived somewhere deeper.

"Marco almost gets turned away," Levi continued, his voice softening. "He's got nothing. No money, no connections, no letters of introduction. Just himself. And he's standing there, about to lose everything before it even starts, when this other boy steps in."

Levi had stopped decorating entirely. So had Michael. Eli noticed that Levi wasn't really telling the story to the room anymore—he was telling it to Michael. Just Michael. As if the rest of them had faded into the background.

"Alessandro," Levi said. "He's maybe a year older than Marco. Rich family, all the right connections. The kind of boy who's never had to fight for anything in his life. But there's something about Marco that catches his attention. He takes Marco in as his assistant. Gives him a place to sleep. A chance."

Michael was very still.

"And they become friends," Levi said. "Real friends. Alessandro teaches Marco how to navigate the politics, the social rules, all the stuff Marco never learned. And Marco—Marco shows Alessandro how to actually *see* things. How to feel them. Alessandro's been surrounded by art his whole life, but he's never really looked at it. Not the way Marco does."

Eli leaned against the wall, content to watch. What he was seeing was something he recognized. Marco and Alessandro. Standing right in front of him.

"And somewhere along the way," Levi said quietly, "they fall in love."

The words hung in the air.

"But it's dangerous," Levi continued. "Like, really dangerous. This isn't now—this is Renaissance Florence. If anyone finds out, they're dead. So they have to hide everything. Every glance. Every touch. Every moment alone together."

"So how do people find out?" Michael asked. The words came out quieter than he intended.

Levi looked at him. Those mismatched eyes, steady and serious.

"Marco kisses Alessandro."

The room was very quiet.

Eli let out a soft sigh. "God, that scene. It wrecked me." He pressed a hand to his chest dramatically. "I just want an Alessandro to kiss, you know? Is that too much to ask?"

Levi shook his head slowly. "You've got it wrong."

"What?"

"You're not Marco. You're more like Alessandro." Levi was smiling now. "You're looking for a Marco to kiss you."

Eli's mouth dropped open in mock offense. "Excuse me? I am absolutely a Marco. Scrappy. Underestimated. Hidden depths."

"You're dramatic, well-dressed, and you've never had to walk anywhere."

Michael snorted.

"Okay, first of all—rude." Eli pointed at Levi. "And second of all, if you're so knowledgeable, which one are *you* then?"

The question was teasing. Light. But Levi's smile faded.

"I'm definitely Marco," he said quietly. And then, almost to himself: "And I'd have Alessandro kiss me."

His whole body changed as he said it. The tension he always carried seemed to melt away, his shoulders dropping, his face softening into something almost wistful. Like he'd forgotten anyone else was there. Like he was somewhere else entirely—somewhere better.

Then his eyes found Michael's.

Michael was looking at him with an expression Levi couldn't quite read. Intrigue, yes. But something else too. Something more direct. More focused.

Levi's face flushed. He looked away quickly, fumbling with an ornament.

"I mean—that's just—it's a good book, that's all. The characters are—"

"See!" Eli threw an arm around Levi's shoulders, pulling him in. "Me too! Isn't Marco the best? We're both Marcos. It's decided."

He was grinning, easy and warm, and Levi let out a shaky breath. Eli wasn't making fun. He was bringing Levi into the fold. Making space for him.

Michael watched the two of them. His mind was turning over what he'd just heard.

A gay love story. His uncle had written a gay love story.

But even as he thought it, something pushed back. Why was it a *gay* love story? Wasn't it just a love story? Period?

He looked over at Simon's stocking, hung beside Graham's on the mantle. Then at his uncle, who had remained quiet through all of this. Watching. Listening. He seemed... sad? No—quiet, sure. But more than that. Like he was standing alone when Simon should've been there with him.

That was a love story.

And something else clicked.

. . .

Graham turned back to the mantle, but his mind was elsewhere.

He remembered writing that first book. The tiny apartment he and Simon had shared in the city, barely bigger than a closet. Simon reading pages as Graham finished them, offering suggestions, catching inconsistencies, falling in love with Marco and Alessandro the same way he'd fallen in love with Graham.

Because that's what the story was, underneath the Renaissance setting and the historical details. It was them. Simon—the brilliant scholarship student who'd scraped his way into Columbia with nothing but talent and determination. Graham—the comfortable middle-class kid who'd never wanted for anything but had never felt anything either. Until Simon.

Simon was Marco. Had always been Marco. The one with the rough hands and the fire inside. The one who saw beauty everywhere and made Graham see it too.

And Graham had written it all down, disguised it just enough to be publishable, and watched it take off. Watched readers connect to something he'd thought was too personal to share. Watched young men—boys, really, not much older than Michael or Levi—write to him saying the book had saved their lives. That seeing Marco and Alessandro love each other had made them feel less alone.

He'd kept those letters. Every single one. Simon had insisted.

Now, listening to Levi tell the story — his story, their story — Graham just watched him. Levi's guard was completely down. He wasn't thinking about impressing anyone or protecting himself. He was just sharing something he loved with people he was beginning to trust.

Graham recognized that feeling. That hunger for connection. That fear of being seen and that desperate hope to be seen anyway.

Will anyone ever love me?

He'd asked himself that question at fifteen, sixteen, seventeen. Had asked it in the dark of his childhood bedroom, in the stacks of the library, in every crowded room where he'd felt utterly alone.

Simon had been the answer. Thirty years of the answer.

And now Simon was gone. But the story remained. And somehow, impossibly, it was still finding the people who needed it.

"The manuscript," Levi said suddenly, then caught himself. "I mean—your manuscript. The original one. It's still on your desk. In your office."

Graham blinked, pulled back to the present. "It is."

"I didn't finish it. Before we moved." Levi's voice was careful, uncertain. "I was wondering if... I mean, if it's okay..."

"Levi." Graham waited until the boy looked at him. "This is your home too. You're welcome here anytime. And yes—you can finish the manuscript. Stay as long as you need."

Something flickered across Levi's face. Not quite a smile, but close. Gratitude, maybe. Or relief.

The moment stretched, tender and fragile.

Then Eli's stomach growled. Loudly.

"Oh my god," Eli said, pressing a hand to his abdomen. "When's lunch? I'm dying."

"You're always dying," Graham said.

"I'm a growing boy!"

"You're twenty-four!"

"Still growing!"

Levi laughed. Michael laughed. And just like that, the heaviness lifted.

"Lunch," Graham announced. "Then we finish this."

After lunch—sandwiches, nothing fancy, eaten standing around the kitchen island—they dove back in.

The afternoon passed quickly. Eli strung lights while Michael held the ladder. Levi arranged ornaments with careful precision, spacing them evenly, stepping back every few minutes to check the overall effect. Graham handled the high branches and the outdoor lights, grumbling about the cold but secretly enjoying himself.

By four o'clock, the light outside was already fading. Winter nights came early this far north. But inside, the house was transformed.

Graham stood in the living room doorway and took it in. The tree, for all its lopsidedness, glowed with color. The mantle was draped in garland, the stockings hung in a row. Candles flickered in the windows. The fire crackled softly.

He walked over to the old radio on the bookshelf and turned it on. It took a moment to find a station, but eventually the familiar sounds of Christmas music filled the room—Bing Crosby, Nat King Cole, the classics Simon had loved.

It felt like a memory of days he'd never actually lived. But it was nice. More than nice.

Michael was sprawled on the couch, exhausted but content. Eli was in the armchair, scrolling through his phone. And Levi—

Levi was sitting on the edge of the sofa, very still, just taking it all in.

Graham noticed his socks. With his shoes off, the damage was impossible to miss—worn through at the heels, the fabric so thin his toes were visible. Levi didn't seem to notice, or maybe he was just used to it.

Graham made a mental note. Santa's list was getting longer.

Michael was watching Levi too. Graham caught him looking—not staring, exactly, but watching. Like he was trying to figure something out.

Graham knew that look. Had worn it himself, once upon a time.

Eli glanced up from his phone, caught Graham's eye, and gave an almost imperceptible nod.

He'd noticed too.

"My mom's probably starting to wonder where I am," Levi said eventually. "Could I... call her?"

Graham noticed the hesitation. Then it clicked—Levi probably didn't have a phone. He saw Michael and Eli register the same realization, their expressions shifting slightly before smoothing over.

"Of course." Graham handed him his iPhone.

Levi took it and walked off to the kitchen. He returned a minute later.

"Mom says I should head home soon. She's gonna come get me in—"

"I'll take you," Graham interjected.

"She said she'd be on her way in a bit."

Graham took the phone back and dialed Susan's number again. "Susan? It's Graham. Listen, I've got errands to run anyway—I'll bring him home. No trouble at all." A pause. "Of course. You're welcome." Another pause. "Oh, before I forget—he doesn't know yet, but I was going to offer to pay him to help me shovel the driveway tomorrow. If that's okay with you?"

Levi looked up, surprised.

"Oh, I absolutely will pay him if he wants to. I haven't asked yet. He's not going to work for free." Graham smiled. "Yes, I'm sure. Of course. I'll talk to him now. See you in twenty minutes or so. Bye."

He hung up. Levi didn't wait.

"You want me to—"

"If you're okay helping? Sure."

"Really?" Levi was lighting up.

"Of course. Say..." Graham had no idea what it cost to shovel a driveway. "Twenty dollars?"

He paused, thinking. The driveway was long. And there was a lot of snow.

"Since it's so long and there's all that snow... how about a hundred?"

Levi's mouth dropped. So did Michael's.

"A hundred dollars?" they said in unison.

Graham laughed. Then he got to thinking. Levi couldn't do it alone—it really was a big job. And Graham didn't particularly feel like hauling his own ass out there, not after how he'd felt during the snowball fight earlier.

"Michael, if you want to help Levi..." He turned to Levi. "Assuming you want the job?"

Levi nodded vigorously.

"Well, then. Michael, assuming you want to help—a hundred for you, too."

Eli's hand shot up like he was in school.

"What?" Graham asked, somehow knowing where this was going.

"Me too?" Eli bounced excitedly, causing the boys to giggle.

"Sure. You get five dollars."

"Five bucks?!" Eli's voice went up an octave. "Why do *they* get a hundred and I only get five?"

"Because I know they'll do a good job."

"And I won't?"

"You'll push the shovel once and then stop before breaking a nail."

Michael and Levi burst out laughing. Eli looked down at his nails, as if considering whether Graham might be onto something.

"Well..." he said slowly. "Maybe."

Another laugh from the boys.

"Come on, Levi—let's get you home." Graham grabbed his coat. "Eli, might as well give you a lift on the way."

"Fine. Fine." Eli stood, stretching dramatically. "Use me and then throw me away when the tree is done. I know how you are."

"Wise?"

Eli turned to Michael. "I want you to study your uncle. Then do everything opposite. Okay?"

Michael grinned and exchanged a look with Levi.

"Come on, old man," Graham said to Eli, pulling on his coat.

Levi started to say something to Michael—something about how he'd had fun, how it was nice to meet him—but the words tangled up. Michael looked equally awkward, wanting to say the same but not knowing how.

Graham noticed. "Michael, why don't you come along too? Keep me company on the drive home." He grabbed the keys. "Maybe I'll let you drive back. Something tells me you might want to use the car to drive up that way in the future."

Michael and Levi looked at each other. Something passed between them—surprise, maybe. Or anticipation.

Before either could respond, Eli stepped behind them both, placing a hand on each of their shoulders and pushing them toward the door.

"Come on, Marco and Alessandro."

Chapter Twelve

THE TEXT CAME in just after ten that night, while Graham was sitting in the darkened living room staring at the half-tree.

So what time tomorrow

Susan's dropping Levi around 8. Shoveling.

Cool. I'll help. Gotta leave early tho

Where you off to

Parents. Obligatory Christmas visit. Didn't go for Thanksgiving so I owe them one

How are you getting there

Rent a car

Don't rent a car. Take mine.

Graham

Take the car.

That's your only car

I have Simon's Volvo in the garage.

...

You sure?

I'll be fine. Take the BMW.

Ok. What time you want me there

I'll come get you at 7:15.

I can catch the bus

No. I'll come get you.

I can

Shut up.

Fine. Bitch.

Graham set the phone down on the armrest and leaned back. The half-tree glowed in the corner, its bare side faithfully pressed against the wall. Michael and Levi had done a decent job with the lights, even if half of them were tangled in ways that would have made Simon lose his mind.

Simon's Volvo.

He hadn't driven it since before the funeral. Hadn't even opened the driver's side door. Anthony had moved it into the garage for him back in March because Graham couldn't look at it sitting in the driveway anymore—Simon's car, waiting for someone who was never coming back.

Anthony, being Anthony, hadn't let it sit. He'd come by a few times over the months—never making a fuss about it, never asking permission—to start the engine, run it for a while, take it out for an oil change. Keeping it alive, even if Graham couldn't bring himself to touch it. That was Anthony. Taking care of things that needed taking care of, whether you asked him to or not.

But it needed to be driven. Really driven. Simon would have hated the idea of his Volvo being nursed along like a museum piece. That was the kind of wastefulness Simon couldn't abide.

Graham turned off the lamp and went to bed.

He picked Eli up at seven-fifteen on the dot. Eli climbed in with a travel mug of coffee and a backpack slung over one shoulder.

"Merry Christmas Eve," Eli said. "Or as I like to call it, Christmas: The Prequel."

"Please don't."

"Christmas: The Night Before. Christmas Eve-ning. Christ—"

"I will turn this car around."

They drove to the house in quiet. The roads were mostly empty—plowed but still icy in patches, the kind of morning where the cold had teeth. Graham pulled into the garage and cut the engine.

"Susan's dropping Levi at eight," he said. "Michael's already up."

"Of course he is. Kid's like a puppy."

They went inside. Michael was in the kitchen, dressed and eating toast, looking like he'd been awake for hours. He nodded at Eli, who immediately stole a piece of his toast.

"Hey—"

"Tax," Eli said, taking a bite. "For showing up this early."

By eight, Susan's car pulled up. Levi climbed out bundled in his old coat and waved as his mother backed out of the driveway.

"Ready to earn your keep?" Graham asked from the porch.

Levi nodded, already eyeing the driveway. It was long. And there was a lot of snow.

Graham had unearthed four shovels from the garage—two proper ones and two flat-edged ones that Simon had used for the walkways. He handed them out.

"Alright. Driveway, front walk, path to the mailbox. Whoever finishes first gets bragging rights."

Michael and Levi set to work immediately, attacking the snow with the kind of energy that only comes from being seventeen and wanting to impress someone—though neither would have admitted who. Levi took the driveway's left side, Michael the right, and they fell into an unspoken competition that had them both sweating within ten minutes.

Eli lasted approximately two.

He made a show of shoveling one scoop, examined it critically, shoveled another, then leaned on the handle and watched the boys work.

"I think I pulled something," he announced.

"You shoveled twice," Graham said from the porch, where he'd stationed himself with his tea.

"Exactly. Twice more than I planned." Eli propped the shovel against the railing and held out his hand, palm up. "Five dollars, please."

Graham stared at him. "You can't be serious."

"A deal's a deal. Five dollars for Eli. That was the agreement."

"The agreement was that you'd help."

"I did help. I supervised." He wiggled his fingers. "Pay up."

Graham reached for his wallet. He'd prepared for this—gone to the ATM yesterday specifically. He pulled out the bills: two fives and ten twenties. He peeled off a five and slapped it into Eli's palm.

Eli held it up between two fingers, examining it like a jeweler appraising a diamond. "Thank you. I will treasure this forever."

"I'm sure you will."

Michael and Levi had paused to watch the exchange, leaning on their shovels, grinning.

"Back to work," Graham said. "You two actually earn your money."

They did. It took them the better part of an hour and a half, but by nine-thirty the driveway was clear, the walkways were scraped down to concrete, and both boys were red-faced and breathing hard. Graham called them to the porch and counted out five twenties each.

"A hundred dollars," Levi said, looking at the bills in his hand like they might evaporate.

"You earned it."

"This is... this is a lot."

"It's a long driveway." Graham tucked his wallet back into his pocket. One five-dollar bill left. "Hot chocolate inside. Go."

The boys disappeared into the house. Eli lingered on the porch, the five-dollar bill now folded neatly into his coat pocket.

Graham looked at him. Then past him, toward the garage.

"I need you to do something for me," he said. "And I need you to not fight me on it."

Eli's smile faded. He knew that tone.

"Don't—" Graham held up a hand. "Don't say anything yet. Just listen." He took a breath. "I want you to take Simon's car."

"Graham—"

"I said don't. Not yet." He gripped the porch railing. "The Volvo's been sitting in the garage since March. It needs to be driven. Simon would lose his mind if he knew I'd let his car rot because I couldn't—" He stopped. Started again. "It needs to be driven. And you need a car to get to your parents. So take it."

Eli was quiet for a long moment. "That's not just a car to you."

"I know what it is."

"Then you know I can't just—"

"You can. And you're going to." Graham's voice was steady, but his knuckles were white on the railing. "I can't have this conversation, Eli. Not today. Not right now. I've made up my mind and if you argue with me, I'm going to fall apart, and I'd rather not do that on Christmas Eve in front of two teenagers. So just—" He exhaled. "Just take the keys. Drive it. Bring it back. That's all I'm asking."

Eli studied him. Then he nodded slowly.

"Okay."

"Okay."

"Where are the keys?"

"Hook by the garage door. The one with the leather fob."

Eli went inside. Graham heard him moving through the house, heard the door to the garage open. A minute later came the sound of the engine turning over—rough at first, coughing, but catching. Settling into a low, familiar hum that Graham felt in his chest like a second heartbeat.

The garage door opened. The Volvo backed out slowly. White, just like Simon had wanted. Not flashy. Understated. The kind of car that said *I have good taste but I don't need you to know it.*

Eli pulled up alongside the porch and rolled down the window.

"I'll pick up Levi on my way back. Be home before dark."

Graham nodded. He didn't trust his voice.

Eli looked at him for a moment longer, then pulled away. Graham watched the Volvo turn onto the street and disappear around the corner, and he stood there on the porch in the cold until he couldn't hear the engine anymore.

When he went back inside, Michael and Levi were at the kitchen table, both hands wrapped around mugs of cocoa. They looked up. Michael didn't say anything about the redness around his uncle's eyes.

"I should probably get home," Levi said, reading the room in that quiet way of his. "Mom said before lunch."

"Right." Graham cleared his throat. "Michael, you want to drive?"

Michael was already grabbing the keys.

The ride to Angie and Sonya's was short and mostly quiet. Graham sat in the passenger seat, watching the houses go by. Michael glanced at him a few times but didn't push. He could feel it — the Volvo, Simon, Christmas Eve, all of it pressing down on his uncle like weather.

When they pulled up, Michael put the car in park and got out. Levi was already halfway to the door when Michael caught up and pulled him into a hug — quick, a little awkward, but real. Levi stiffened for a second, then held on.

"Merry Christmas Eve," Michael said.

"Merry Christmas Eve."

Graham stayed in the passenger seat. He gave Levi a small wave through the window. Levi waved back, then disappeared inside.

Michael climbed back behind the wheel and sat for a moment, both hands on the steering wheel. He looked at Graham.

"So," he said. "We need food. For tonight."

"Michael—"

"We can't just eat cereal on Christmas Eve."

"I've survived on worse."

"Uncle Graham." Michael gave him a look that was pure Becca. "We need a ham. Or something. And pie. And—I don't know—stuff."

Graham almost smiled. "Stuff."

Michael, it turned out, was a cautious but competent driver. He checked his mirrors more than necessary and took turns a little wider than needed, but he was steady. Deliberate. And—Graham noted with genuine surprise—he parallel parked at the grocery store on the first try, sliding into a spot between a pickup truck and a minivan like he'd been doing it for years.

"You're better at that than I am," Graham admitted.

"Mom made me practice in the church parking lot. Every Saturday for a month."

"That sounds like Becca."

The grocery store was predictably chaotic—last-minute shoppers with the panicked look of people who'd forgotten something essential. Graham and Michael moved through the aisles quickly, grabbing what they needed: a precooked ham that looked reasonable enough, a pumpkin pie that was store-bought but respectable, a tub of vanilla ice cream, a bag of rolls, and a can of whipped cream that Michael dropped into the cart with a grin.

"Essential," he said.

"For the pie?"

"For everything."

As they rounded the end of an aisle near the registers, Michael stopped. He reached over to a display of poinsettias—red ones, wrapped in foil, marked down to five dollars—and set one in the cart.

Graham looked at it. "What's that for?"

"Eating." Michael kept walking. "I thought it might make a nice change from cereal."

Graham snorted. The kid had been around Eli too much. He wished Simon could see this—his nephew, dry as dust, pushing a shopping cart on Christmas Eve with a five-dollar poinsettia riding shotgun. Simon would have loved him.

They loaded the bags into the trunk. Michael put the poinsettia on the floor of the back seat so it wouldn't tip. Then he got behind the wheel, pulled out his phone, typed something into Maps, and started driving without a word.

Graham didn't notice at first. He was watching the streets go by—the houses with their lights, the inflatable Santas slowly deflating in front yards, the occasional family loading a car for somewhere warmer. His mind was elsewhere. On the Volvo. On Simon. On Christmas mornings that used to mean something.

He didn't even hit the imaginary brake on the passenger side, which was a first. Michael was driving a little slower than Graham would have, but honestly, it was better than Simon, who'd driven like he was being chased by the law.

It wasn't until Michael pulled into the parking lot that Graham looked up and registered where they were.

"Oh, god."

"What?"

"The mall." Graham stared at the building like it had personally offended him. "You brought me to the mall."

"I need to shop."

"It's Christmas Eve."

"Which is why I need to shop."

"Michael. It's going to be a nightmare in there."

"Probably." Michael was already unbuckling his seatbelt. "Come on."

Graham had never liked malls. Even before Simon died, even before grief made crowds feel like all out war, he'd avoided them. The noise, the fluorescent lighting, the dead-eyed kiosk workers trying to sell you phone cases and hand cream—it was his personal circle of hell. Simon had always done the mall shopping while Graham waited in the car like a dog whose owner had gone into the post office.

But Michael was already walking toward the entrance, and Graham didn't have it in him to sit in a parking lot alone on Christmas Eve. Not today.

Inside was exactly as terrible as he'd expected. Christmas music blaring from every direction. Children screaming. A line for Santa that snaked past the food court. The combined smell of Cinnabon and desperation.

Michael seemed unfazed.

"I need to look at some stuff," he said. "Give me an hour?"

"An hour." Graham said it like Michael had asked him to hold his breath underwater.

"Maybe an hour and a half."

"Michael."

"Just—go get a drink or something. I'll find you."

"What are you shopping for?"

"Christmas gifts."

"Little late, aren't you?"

"Well, I haven't exactly had time to shop. I've been shoveling snow and decorating trees and watching you argue with Eli about everything."

Fair point.

"You don't need to get me anything," Graham said.

"Who says it's for you?"

Graham blinked. "Ouch."

"Need money?"

"You literally just gave me a hundred dollars two hours ago."

"Right."

"Plus I have a little from Mom and Dad." Michael paused. "But I won't say no to more."

Graham rolled his eyes and opened his wallet. One five-dollar bill. He'd forgotten — the boys and Eli had cleaned him out.

"I have five dollars."

"Wow. Big spender."

Graham sighed and pulled out his credit card. "Don't go crazy."

Michael took it with a grin that was slightly too wide.

"Are you sure you aren't Eli's younger brother?"

Michael took that as a compliment and disappeared into the crowd.

Graham stood in the middle of the mall concourse, surrounded by shoppers, holding nothing but his phone and the vague sense that he'd been outmaneuvered by a seventeen-year-old. He looked around. Spotted an Orange Julius. Couldn't believe they were still in business.

He ordered one. Found one of those padded benches near a built-in brick planter that probably hadn't held a living plant since the 90's, sat down and pulled out his phone.

His phone buzzed.

Get me out of here!

That bad?

No just boring. Mom keeps asking if I've met any nice girls

Have you?

I'm keeping the car just for that

Simon barely drove it. At least it's getting used.

How's loverboy? You both miss me?

We're at the mall.

MALL?? ON EVE??

Michael said he needed to buy gifts.

Hope he got me something really nice

He was looking at Spencer's.

BE GOOD!

Levi coming over later?

Yeah. Can you pick him up on your way back?

Already planned on it. Be back by 4ish

Drive safe. And Eli?

?

Thank you. For driving it.

Graham pocketed his phone and sipped his Orange Julius, which tasted exactly the same as it had in 1987. Some things, at least, didn't change.

Michael found him nearly an hour later, carrying two shopping bags that he held close to his body like state secrets.

"Whatcha get?"

"Nunya."

Graham looked at him blankly. "Nunya?"

"Nunya business."

Graham stared at him for a full three seconds before it landed. Michael was already walking toward the exit.

"I'm too old for this," Graham muttered, and followed him out.

The house was quiet when they got back. Michael immediately vanished into his room with the shopping bags and closed the door. Graham put the groceries away, set the poinsettia on the kitchen table, and stood looking at it for longer than a five-dollar plant probably warranted.

He made himself useful. Cleaned the kitchen. Straightened the living room. Adjusted ornaments on the half-tree that didn't need adjusting. Moved Simon's stocking from the mantel to the drawer in the hallway, then moved it back. Left it.

Around four, the crunch of tires on the freshly shoveled driveway. Graham looked out the window. The Volvo pulled in and parked.

Eli got out of the driver's side. Levi climbed out of the passenger seat, looking slightly windblown and carrying a plastic bag.

Graham opened the front door.

"How was it?" he asked Eli.

"Survived. Mom sent cookies." Eli held up a tin. "And guilt. Lots of guilt."

"That's what mothers are for."

"I stopped by Angie and Sonya's to get this one." Eli jerked his thumb at Levi, who was stamping snow off his shoes. "Lucy almost wouldn't let him leave."

"She's making cookies for Santa," Levi said. "She's been at it all afternoon."

"Were they good?" Graham asked.

Eli held up a hand, fingers spread. "I had to taste-test five of them. Quality control. Very important job."

"Five?"

"Well, three. But then she made another batch and I had to make sure those were up to standard too. And then one more for the road, just to be safe."

"How selfless of you."

"I'm basically a hero."

Levi laughed.

"Susan said have him home before ten."

"And Lucy said—" Eli dropped to one knee, hand over his heart, mimicking a solemn vow. "He's gotta be asleep before Santa gets here. I crossed my heart."

"You're going to make a wonderful father someday," Graham said dryly. "Come inside before you freeze."

Inside, Michael's door was still closed. Sounds of rustling and the occasional rip of tape.

Eli walked straight to the door and knocked. "Hey! What are you doing in there?"

"Nothing! Go away!"

"Are you wrapping presents? Let me see!"

"No!"

Eli tried the handle. Locked. He turned to Levi with exaggerated offense. "Can you believe this? Locked out. On Christmas Eve."

Levi shrugged, trying not to laugh.

Eli knocked again. "Levi wants to see too!"

"I really don't—" Levi started.

"No one is seeing anything!" Michael called through the door. "Go away!"

"Fine!" Eli threw his hands up. "I'm stealing your boyfriend, then." He grabbed Levi by the sleeve and pulled him toward the kitchen, leaving Levi's face approximately the color of the poinsettia on the table.

Behind the closed door, Michael's face wasn't much different. He stared at the half-wrapped box in his hands, his heart doing something inconvenient. Eli was just being Eli. Teasing. Being stupid. The way they'd been since they met.

He went back to wrapping.

• • •

In the kitchen, Graham was staring at the ham.

"Shouldn't that be baked?" Eli asked, watching Graham open the microwave.

"I don't know. It says precooked."

"Precooked doesn't mean microwave it like a burrito, Graham."

"It's a ham. How complicated can it be?"

Levi quietly picked up the packaging and read the instructions. "It says to heat in the oven at 325 for about fifteen minutes per pound." He looked at the ham, then at Graham. "This is maybe eight pounds? So about two hours."

Graham looked at the microwave. Then at the oven. Then at Levi.

"Well," he said. "Good thing you're here."

Levi took over with the competence of someone who'd been feeding himself and his family for longer than anyone his age should have. He preheated the oven, found a roasting pan that looked like it hadn't been used since Simon was alive, and got the ham situated. While it heated, he warmed the rolls, found some butter in the fridge, and set everything up so it would all be ready around the same time.

Graham was relegated to setting the table and pouring drinks.

"I feel like I've been demoted in my own kitchen," he said.

"You were never promoted," Eli replied, setting out napkins.

Dinner was better than it had any right to be. The ham was actually good—warm and glazed and surprisingly tender for something that had come in a plastic bag. The rolls were soft. The poinsettia sat in the middle of the table like it had always been there.

They ate without ceremony—no prayer, no formal toast, just four people passing dishes and talking over each other. Eli told them about his mother's interrogation—had he met anyone, was he eating enough, why didn't he call more often—and performed both sides of the conversation with such accuracy that Levi nearly choked on a roll.

Michael asked Levi about Lucy and whether she really believed Anthony was Santa. Levi confirmed that she absolutely did, and that Angie being "Mrs. Claus" only reinforced the theory. The fact that they lived next door to Mrs. Claus was, in Lucy's mind, proof that they had landed exactly where they were supposed to be.

"She's not wrong," Graham said quietly, and no one argued.

Pie came next. Then ice cream—big bowls for the boys, an even bigger bowl for Eli, all of it drowning in whipped cream. Michael sprayed it directly from the can, building a small mountain on Eli's bowl that was structurally unsound.

"That's too much," Graham said.

"There's no such thing as too much whipped cream," Eli said, and took a massive bite that left a streak of white across his nose.

"You have—" Levi pointed at his own nose.

"I know. It's my look." Eli didn't wipe it off. Michael was laughing so hard he had to put his spoon down.

Graham poured himself hot apple cider and settled into his chair by the tree. The half-tree. Their tree. The lights cast a warm glow across the room, catching the ornaments Michael and Levi had hung two days ago—some of Simon's, some ancient ones from the box in the attic, a few that were clearly just balls of tinsel someone had wadded up and stuck on a branch. It was imperfect and lopsided and missing half its branches, and it was the most beautiful tree Graham had ever seen.

Levi noticed the gifts underneath. He didn't say anything—just glanced at them, then away. After a moment, he excused himself quietly and walked to the mudroom where his thin coat was hanging. He reached into the inside pocket and pulled out a few envelopes, holding them close to his chest. He made his way back to the tree while the others were arguing about whether Eli had more whipped cream on his face than in his bowl—Eli maintaining this was by design—and slipped the envelopes underneath, tucking them between the wrapped packages.

Then he saw it. A small tag on one of the boxes. His name. Written in handwriting he didn't recognize.

He stepped back and sat down on the sofa, his heart doing something he wasn't sure he could name.

Graham was the first to speak.

"Before anyone gets too comfortable," he said, setting his cider on the side table, "Santa stopped by earlier. Left a few things before his big run tonight."

Eli looked up, whipped cream still on his nose. "How's Anthony doing?"

Graham gave him a look. "Why don't you make yourself useful and distribute."

"Ooooh." Eli slid off the armchair and onto the floor in front of the tree, rubbing his hands together. "Let's see what I got!"

"That's not—" Graham started. "Fine. Just hand them out."

Eli dove in, pulling packages out with the enthusiasm of someone half his age. He read tags aloud with theatrical flair, sorting them into piles.

"Michael... Michael... Graham... Levi..." He paused, holding up a small flat package. "Ooh, this one's for me." He shook it. "Light. Could be cash. Please be cash."

"Just open it after you've handed everything out," Graham said.

"You're no fun."

Michael had settled onto the sofa next to Levi—close, though not so close that either of them would have to acknowledge it. Graham watched from his chair. The fire wasn't lit—he hadn't built one, hadn't known how, that had been Simon's department too—but the tree lights were enough. The room felt warm anyway.

Eli found a collection of envelopes tucked between the packages—Levi's letters—and started to hand one to Michael, but Levi sat up quickly.

"Wait—those—" Levi's voice was tight. "Can you just... set those aside? Open them later. After."

Eli looked at him, then at the envelopes. He understood something in Levi's expression—the vulnerability of having written something by hand when everyone else had bought something, the fear of it being read aloud, of it not being enough. He set them in their respective piles without comment.

"Moving on," Eli said smoothly. "Who goes first?"

"You do," Michael said. "Obviously."

"Obviously." Eli grabbed the small flat package—Michael's gift—and tore into it. Tissue paper went flying. He pulled out a black T-shirt and held it up, unfolding it.

Across the front, in bright rainbow letters: **WOKE UP GAY AGAIN**.

Eli's face split into the widest grin Graham had ever seen. "Oh my god."

"It's from Spencer's," Michael said quickly. "I wasn't sure if it was too—"

"I love it." Eli held it against his chest, beaming. "I love it so much. This is the greatest gift anyone has ever given me."

"If the shoe fits," Graham said from his chair.

Levi was caught somewhere between amusement, embarrassment, and delight—a complicated cocktail that left him grinning at his own knees. Eli was already pulling it over his head, wearing it over his sweater.

"How do I look?"

"Like a billboard," Graham said.

"A *beautiful* billboard." Eli struck a pose. Michael was watching him with visible relief—he'd been hoping it wasn't too much, but judging by Eli's reaction, it was exactly right.

Then: a Whole Foods gift card from Graham, attached to a small note that simply read: *yuk yuk*.

Eli held it up, grinning. "Yuk yuk," he read aloud.

"Full circle," Graham said, sipping his cider.

Eli laughed — the real one, the one that came out a little too loud and a little uneven, the one Graham had first heard in the returns line of what felt like decades ago. "You're such an old man."

"And yet you got in the car."

"Worst decision of my life." Eli tucked the card into his pocket. "Thank you."

Then the last gift in his pile—the one he'd bought for himself. He pulled the wrapping off a hardcover book, glossy and pristine. A premium edition of *The Oltrarno,* Book One. The spine uncracked. The pages untouched.

He held it up, then looked at Graham. "I believe you know what to do." He produced a pen from somewhere—his pocket, the floor, thin air—and held both out.

Graham took the book and the pen. "What do you want me to write?"

"Just sign it."

"No 'To my dearest Eli, light of my life'?"

"Tempting, but no. Just your name."

Graham opened to the title page and signed his name in that practiced script of someone who'd done this at book signings but hadn't in years. He handed it back.

Eli took it, examined the signature with mock seriousness, then—without ceremony—shoved it back into its box, wadded the tissue paper around it in a way that could only loosely be called wrapping, and placed it in front of Levi.

"What—" Levi started.

"It actually had your name on it." Eli shrugged. "It just wasn't finished yet."

Levi looked at the box. Then at Eli. Then at Graham, who was leaning back in his chair with an expression Eli couldn't quite read—surprise, maybe. Or something warmer.

"Open it," Eli said.

Levi pulled the tissue paper away and lifted the book out. The weight of it. The cover. The title in gold lettering. He opened to the title page and saw Graham's signature.

His hands were shaking. He tried to stop them and couldn't.

Graham leaned forward. "Can I have it back for a second?"

Levi looked up, confused, but extended the book across.

"Pen?" Graham said to Eli.

Eli handed it over, biting his lip to keep from saying anything. He knew. He'd seen Graham's face change the moment he realized where the book was going.

Graham wrote something below his signature—slowly, carefully. Then he closed the book and handed it back to Levi.

"Don't read it now," Graham said. "Wait until tonight. When it's quiet."

Levi nodded, clutching the book to his chest. He wanted to open it immediately. He wanted to read whatever Graham had written right now, in front of everyone, because whatever it said would be real and permanent and *his*. But Graham had asked him to wait. So he waited.

"Okay," Eli said, clearing his throat. "Moving on before I start crying and ruin my new shirt."

. . .

Michael was next.

Eli handed him a small wrapped box with a tag that said *From: Santa's Favorite Elf.*

Michael unwrapped it to find a bar of soap. Irish Spring.

He held it up. "What—"

"To wash your mouth out," Eli said. "Especially after watching you eat a hamburger."

Eli turned to Levi. "Have you seen this man eat? Disgusting."

Michael laughed and flipped him off at the same time.

Eli turned to Levi again, pointing. "See! He's a total perv!"

Levi nearly fell off the sofa laughing. Michael was too, though the tips of his ears were burning. He made a show of threatening to take away Eli's gift.

"No taksies-backsies!" Eli said, and the way it came out—a little too loud, a little too bright, the slight imprecision of someone who'd learned speech by feel rather than sound—made Michael pause. It was endearing. Unguarded.

"Say it again," Michael said, grinning.

Eli turned to Graham. "Your nephew is such a bitch."

Graham laughed. "There's that word."

"Bitch, bitch, bitch," Eli added, for his own amusement.

Levi couldn't breathe. He was laughing so hard no sound was coming out, which only made Michael laugh harder, which only made Eli more pleased with himself.

When the noise died down, Eli handed Michael another package—an envelope, this time.

"From me, again. You're welcome."

Michael opened it. An LL Bean gift card.

"I get a discount," Eli said, looking pleased with himself.

"Wow," Michael said, turning the card over. "Very personal."

"I put a lot of thought into it."

"I can tell."

Michael smiled and tucked the card into his pocket. "Thank you. Seriously."

"You're welcome. Seriously."

Next: a box with a tag that read *Love, Mom and Dad*. Michael paused.

"They sent it out before you flew up," Graham said gently. "It's been in the hall closet."

Michael opened it. Inside: a hoodie and sweatpants set—nice ones, the kind Becca would pick out. He smiled, pulling the hoodie up to check the size. Then he moved the sweatpants aside and froze.

His face went red. Immediately, without warning, full-body red. He shoved the remaining item back under the sweatpants and tried to move on.

"What?" Eli said.

"Nothing."

"What's under there?"

"Nothing. Next gift."

Levi leaned over to look. Michael tilted the box away. Eli was already on his knees, craning his neck.

"C'mon! What is it?"

"It's nothing, it's just—my mom is—it's—"

"Show us!" Eli was relentless.

Graham could only imagine what his sister had included. He sipped his cider and waited.

Michael, accepting that resistance was futile, reached into the box and held up—with the enthusiasm of a man walking to the gallows—a pair of flannel boxers. Covered in Mickey Mouse.

"OH MY GOD," Eli shrieked. "Those are so cute!" He snatched them out of Michael's hands and held them up against himself, modeling. "Too small for me, but..."

Levi was doubled over laughing.

"I can't believe you're modeling my underwear," Michael said, reaching for them.

"What?" Eli held them just out of reach. "Don't want Levi to see your underwear?"

Eli was savoring every second of Michael's mortification. Michael lunged for the boxers. Eli dodged. Levi was watching the whole thing, laughing hard—and somewhere underneath the laughter, a quiet, involuntary thought: he could imagine Michael wearing them.

He pushed that thought down fast and took a bite of melting ice cream.

Michael finally reclaimed the boxers, stuffed them deep into the box, and pointed at Eli. "We are never speaking of this again."

"I make no promises," Eli said.

From Graham: a small, tidy package. Michael tore the paper off and opened the box. Inside, on a small cushion of cotton, sat a single key.

"For the house," Graham said. "You're here so often, you might as well have one."

Michael stared at it. The key was brass, newly cut, nothing special about it at all. It was the most important thing anyone had ever given him.

He got up from the sofa and hugged his uncle. Graham held him for a long moment—longer than either of them expected. When Michael pulled back, his eyes were wet, but he didn't wipe them. He just sat back down, the key closed in his fist.

Levi watched. He liked how everyone here was a hugger. It was still a little awkward for him—the idea that people just *held* each other, freely, without it meaning you were weak or small. But he liked it.

. . .

Levi's turn.

From a flat box, heavier than expected. Levi opened it to find a leather-bound writing tablet—the kind with thick, cream-colored pages—and a pen set. Not cheap pens. Real ones, with weight in the hand, the kind that made you feel like whatever you wrote with them mattered.

"You should try writing something of your own," Graham said. Casual. Like it was nothing. Like he wasn't telling a boy who'd been living in a car weeks ago that his words might be worth putting down.

Levi ran his fingers over the leather. The paper was thick—felt expensive. "I'm not... I don't think I'm good enough to—"

"You're good enough," Michael said. Quiet, but firm.

Levi looked at him. Then at the pen. He picked it up. It felt right in his hand.

"Thank you," he said to Graham. And meant it in ways the words couldn't carry.

From an envelope. Levi opened it to find an LL Bean gift card. He looked at Eli.

"I get a discount," Eli said.

Levi caught Michael's eye.

"Yeah, yeah," Michael said. "Gift card. Very personal."

"I put a lot of thought into it," Eli repeated, grinning.

"He really didn't," Michael said to Levi.

"I really didn't," Eli confirmed.

"Maybe you can get some boots or something?" Eli added, and his voice shifted—just slightly, just enough that only Graham caught it. The humor was still there, but underneath it was something careful. Caring. He moved Levi along, not letting him dwell on the charity of it, the need. Eli knew what it felt like to receive things you couldn't repay. He wasn't going to let Levi sit in that feeling any longer than necessary.

Then the book. The Oltrarno. Already signed. Already inscribed with whatever Graham had added when he'd asked for it back. Levi touched it with his hand, but didn't open it. His fingers pressed into the cover like he could feel the words through the binding.

Last: the big box. The one from Michael.

Michael had gone very still beside him. His leg was bouncing—a nervous habit he'd had since he was twelve—and he'd clasped his hands in his lap to keep them from fidgeting.

"I hope you like it," Michael said. "I wasn't sure about—" He stopped himself, not wanting to spoil it.

Levi pulled the lid off the box. Tissue paper. He pushed it aside and stopped.

A sweater. Navy blue, crew neck, simple—but the kind of simple that wasn't simple at all. The knit was thick, the material soft, the cut clean and refined.

"I hope it fits," Michael said. "I guessed at the size. If it doesn't, you can take it—"

Levi pulled it over his head.

It fit perfectly.

Michael reached over without thinking and tugged the sleeves down where they'd bunched, then fixed the collar where it had folded in. His fingers brushed Levi's neck for half a second, and neither of them moved.

"You look good in it," Michael said.

Levi's face went warm. "Really?"

"Yeah," Eli added from the floor. "Really."

Graham watched from his chair, his cider going cold in his hands. His heart doing something he hadn't felt in a long time.

"There's more," Michael said, pointing back into the box.

Levi found a button-down shirt underneath—casual but a step above anything Levi had ever owned. Light blue, soft cotton.

"You can roll up the sleeves," Michael said, reaching over again to show him, miming the gesture against the folded shirt. "Just wear it untucked with your jeans. It'll look—" He stopped. "I mean, if you want."

Levi hadn't thought much about fashion. About how clothes could make you look like something other than a kid who'd been sleeping in a car. But Michael saw something. Levi didn't know what it was, but he trusted it.

"I can show you when you change later," Michael said, then immediately seemed to hear how that sounded and went slightly pink.

Eli bit his lip. Hard. He wanted to make a joke about Michael wanting to help Levi get changed so badly he could taste it. But he filed it away for later. This wasn't the moment.

"There's one more thing," Michael said.

Levi reached into the box and pulled out a pair of jeans. Good ones. The kind that fit right and lasted.

Michael held his breath. He'd guessed at the size—measured with his eyes during the shoveling that morning, when Levi's old jeans had been soaked with snow and clinging to him in ways that made the sizing easier and other things harder.

Levi stood up and held them to his waist. For one heart-stopping second, Michael thought he was going to try them on right there—the way he'd pulled the sweater on without hesitation—and his pulse did something unhelpful. But Levi just looked down at them, then back at Michael.

"I think they'd fit," he said.

Then he sat back down and—without planning it, without thinking about it—reached over and pulled Michael into a hug.

It wasn't the stiff, quick kind Levi usually gave. It was real. He held on, his face turned into Michael's shoulder, and Michael could feel him shaking—not crying, not quite, but close. The effort of holding back. The weight of being seen by someone who'd looked at him and thought: *you deserve better than what you have.*

"Thank you," Levi whispered. And Michael's arms tightened around him, one hand on the back of his neck, and he didn't say *you're welcome* because it wasn't enough. Nothing was enough.

Eli, watching from the floor, recognized the moment for what it was. And did what he did best.

"I want more ice cream!" he announced, scrambling to his feet. He grabbed Michael's arm and hauled him up. "Come help me."

"Why can't you get it yourself?" Michael said, still looking at Levi.

"Because you need to bring Levi's too."

"I don't need—" Levi started.

"Already ordered for everyone. Let's go." Eli pulled Michael toward the kitchen, bickering about whipped cream and why Eli couldn't be trusted to operate a can without adult supervision.

Levi sat back on the sofa. The box of clothes on his lap. The book at his side, with the gift card tucked inside. He looked across the room at Graham, who seemed to be gazing at something on the mantel.

Levi followed his gaze. Two stockings on the mantel — Graham's, and beside it, Simon's. Both hung during the decorating the day before. Graham's looked lived-in. Simon's hung perfectly still, waiting for someone who would never fill it.

Levi felt so out of place. And so much at home. He was still getting used to it—the idea that he was no longer worried about where he slept at night, that he had friends, that he was sitting in the house of the man who wrote the book that had kept him alive during the worst months of his life. And now here was round two of too much ice cream, Michael plopping down right next to him—right next to him, close enough that their shoulders touched—smiling, handing him a bowl with a mountain of whipped cream on top.

He swallowed all of it down. The ice cream. The gratitude. The overwhelming, terrifying sense that he might actually be allowed to have this.

Graham was next.

Eli reached behind the tree and pulled out a mesh bag. He tossed it underhand into Graham's lap, where it landed with a soft thud that sent a splash of cider over the rim of his mug.

"Jesus—" Graham fumbled the mug, wiping his shirt. "What is this?"

"Oranges."

Graham looked at the bag. Then at Eli. "Oranges."

"My parents used to get them for Christmas. It's an old tradition." Eli shrugged. "Figured folk your age would appreciate it."

"Folk my age."

"The elderly. The distinguished. The AARP-eligible."

"I'm fifty-three."

"Like I said."

Graham held up an orange, examining it as if Eli had handed him a live grenade. "You went to your parents' house and your big takeaway was *oranges.*"

"I also brought back guilt, unsolicited life advice, and a tin of cookies. The oranges were the best of the lot."

"How generous."

"I thought so."

The boys were grinning. Graham set the oranges beside his chair with as much dignity as the situation allowed.

From Michael: a book. Graham turned it over in his hands. *No Cap: A Boomer's Guide to Understanding What the Youth Are Saying*. He opened to a random page.

"'Slay,'" he read aloud. "'To perform exceptionally well or look extraordinarily good. Usage: She slayed that presentation.'" He looked up. "I know what slay means."

"Do you, though?" Michael said.

"I—yes. I teach writing. I know words."

"What about 'rizz'?"

Graham blinked. "What about what?"

"Exactly."

By the time the last gifts were opened and the wrapping paper had been collected—Eli had tried to wear it as a scarf, been told to stop, and compromised by wearing it as a headband—the house had settled into that particular quiet that comes after the noise. The good quiet. The full quiet.

Eli checked his phone. "I should get this one home. Promised Lucy he'd be asleep before Santa arrives, remember?"

Levi stood, still wearing the navy sweater. Michael helped him gather his things — the box of clothes, the writing tablet and pen set stacked on top, the book tucked carefully inside. They carried it all to the door together.

"Merry Christmas," Michael said.

"Merry Christmas." Levi paused, standing in the doorway with the cold air rushing in. He wanted to say something else—something about how this was the best Christmas Eve he'd ever had, how the sweater fit perfectly, how he didn't know what Graham had written in the book but he already knew it would matter. But the words knotted up, the way they always did when something mattered too much to say wrong.

Michael didn't wait for the words. He pulled Levi into his chest, enveloping him in his arms — something he'd been waiting to do all day. Levi stiffened for a second, but this time, he squeezed Michael tight, hoping he could make this moment last a little longer.

"Let's go, kid." Eli jingled the car keys. "Santa's on a schedule."

They drove the Volvo back to Angie and Sonya's in silence. Levi held the book in his lap the whole way.

"Don't stay up all night reading," Eli said as they pulled up.

Levi smiled. "No promises."

"Merry Christmas, Levi."

"Merry Christmas, Eli." He opened the door, then stopped. "Eli?"

"Yeah?"

"Thank you. For the book. And for—" He gestured vaguely at everything. The car. The night. The way Eli always seemed to know when to make a joke and when to shut up.

"Get out of my car," Eli said gently. "Your sister's waiting."

Levi smiled as carried his things to the front door of their home. The lights were on inside Angie and Sonya's main house—warm and golden through the windows—and he could see the shadow of a Christmas tree. He let himself in. Lucy was already asleep on the sofa, one arm draped over Peanut the elephant—a preview of tomorrow's gift, already claimed. Susan was reading by the lamp. She looked up at his sweater, at the book in his arms, at his face, and her eyes went soft.

"Good night?" she asked.

"Yeah." Levi set his things down carefully. "Really good."

The house was quiet now. Just Graham and Michael.

Graham washed the dishes. Michael dried. They didn't talk much, and that was fine. Some silences are companionable, and this was one—the kind where two people are thinking their own thoughts but glad to be thinking them in the same room.

"Thanks for today," Michael said, hanging the dish towel on the oven handle.

"For what?"

"I don't know." Michael shrugged. "Just... everything."

Graham nodded. "Merry Christmas, Michael."

"Merry Christmas, Uncle Graham."

Michael went to his room. Graham turned off the kitchen lights, checked the locks, and stood for a moment in the living room. The half-tree glowed. The poinsettia sat on the table. Simon's stocking hung on the mantel.

He picked up the bag oranges from the side of his chair—the one Eli had lobbed at him—and held it. Turned it in his hands. They looked dimpled and smelled like something he couldn't quite place. His grandmother's kitchen, maybe. Or something older than that.

He set it back down, turned off the tree, and went to bed.

Midnight. The house breathed.

In his room, Graham sat on the edge of the bed and opened Levi's envelope. Notebook paper, folded twice, blue pen. The handwriting was careful—deliberate, the letters formed by someone who wanted to get it right.

Dear Graham,

I don't really know how to write a letter like this. I've started it like four times already.

Thank you for letting me read your manuscript. I'm being really careful with it. I promise.

My mom would probably kill me for saying this but I don't care. Thank you for helping us. You didn't have to and she won't ever say it so I am.

I don't have any money to buy you a real gift. But I will someday. That's a promise.

Merry Christmas, "Uncle" Graham.

– Levi

Graham read it twice. Then folded it along its creases, set it on the nightstand beside the lamp, and turned off the light.

Across town, in his apartment, Eli sat on the edge of his bed—still wearing the T-shirt over his sweater—and opened his envelope. Same notebook paper. Same blue pen. Different voice.

Dear Eli,

First off, you are very funny (...looking. Ha ha.)

Eli smiled.

But seriously, thank you for being so nice to me. And to my mom and Lucy. You're really funny and you make everyone laugh and I think that's important, even when things aren't that funny.

Also thank you for not making a big deal at McDonald's, I know that's weird to say but it's kind of hard for me sometimes when people do stuff for me and you just acted normal about it so thanks.

I hope someday I can buy you McDonald's back. And I will.

But thanks.

—Levi

Eli set the letter on his chest and stared at the ceiling. He wanted to tell Levi that he didn't need to buy him anything. That the only thing Eli would ever want from him was his friendship—this weird, unexpected, necessary friendship with a fifteen-year-old kid who noticed everything and said almost nothing and wrote letters because he couldn't afford gifts.

He folded the letter carefully, put it in the drawer of his nightstand, and turned off the light.

He left the T-shirt on.

Michael read his letter for the sixth time.

He'd showered. Changed into the hoodie his parents had sent—not the Mickey Mouse boxers, which were buried at the bottom of his suitcase where they belonged and where Eli would never find them. The side lamp threw warm shadows across the notebook paper, the blue ink, the careful handwriting.

. . .

Dear Michael,

Sorry I was so shy when we first met. I'm not great with new people. But I'm glad we did meet. I'm glad Graham brought you. And I'm glad you came along that day.

Is it too soon to say I feel like we're almost best friends? I hope not. I feel like it might be too fast but I don't care.

Thanks for helping me beat "Uncle" Eli in the snowball fight. And for helping with the tree. And for... well... not treating me different. I know I'm not... well... good or anything, but I'm happy you are my friend. I hope you are too.

And at the bottom, after a space:

Love,
Levi

Michael could see it. The way the pen had paused there. The slight smudge where a hand had rested too long. Levi had started to write it, stopped, maybe even thought about crossing it out. But he hadn't. He'd left it. Let it stand.

Michael's stomach flipped. Joy, maybe. Or warmth. Or something he didn't have a word for yet—something that was still taking shape, still becoming whatever it was going to be.

He was glad they were friends. More than anyone back home. More than anyone anywhere.

And Michael thought about that. Back *home*. The house in Tennessee.

His room with the posters. His mother's kitchen. It was home, technically. It was where he lived.

But lately—lying in this bed, in this room, in this house that smelled like pine and old books and the faintest trace of someone who used to live here—lately, this felt like home.

He folded the letter along its creases. Set it on the nightstand. Turned off the lamp.

And across town, in the small guesthouse behind Angie and Sonya's place, Levi sat cross-legged on his bed while his mother and Lucy slept in the next room. The lamp was dim—just bright enough to read by. He opened *The Oltrarno,* Book One, to the title page.

Graham's signature. The familiar sweep of it.

And below, written with more care:

To Marco—

The bridge is long. The other side is real.

Keep walking.

Levi read it three times. Then a fourth. Then he closed the book and held it against his chest and pressed his forehead to the cover and breathed.

Marco.

Graham saw it in him. It wasn't just Levi projecting anymore—finding himself in a fictional character because he needed somewhere to exist. Graham had looked at him and said: *You are him. He is you. And the story doesn't end in the middle of the bridge.*

Levi set the book on the small table beside his bed, turned off the lamp, and lay in the dark. The navy sweater was folded on the chair. The writing tablet and pen set were beside the book. The gift card was tucked inside the front cover.

Through the wall, he could hear Lucy's breathing—slow and steady, the rhythm of a child who believed Santa was coming. And maybe he was.

Levi closed his eyes.

For the first time in a very long time, he wasn't afraid of tomorrow.

Chapter Thirteen

LEVI HAD COME DOWNSTAIRS that morning in his new clothes — the jeans Michael had given him, the light blue button-down with the sleeves rolled just the way Michael had shown him, the navy sweater over top. He'd stood in the small bathroom mirror longer than usual, studying himself. He looked... different. Not bad different. Just different.

His mom had looked at him when he'd stepped out.

"Well, those look nice on you, honey. You dress up real nice." She tilted her head. "Get those from Graham?"

"Michael," Levi said, and felt his face warm without knowing why.

Susan studied him for a second. Then she stepped forward, flattened his collar, and pushed the hair out of his eyes. "We need to get you a haircut."

Eli had said the same thing. Levi ducked away from her hand. "Mom. Let's just go."

When they walked into Angie and Sonya's, Angie noticed right away. "Well, look at you," she said, and Levi's ears went red.

Sonya gave him a once-over and nodded. "Sharp."

He wondered if Michael would think he looked nice too.

He pushed that thought down fast. But it stayed.

Christmas morning at Sonya and Angie's was louder than Susan had expected.

Their daughters had arrived the night before — one from Boston, one from New Hampshire — and with them came grandchildren. Three in total: a ten-year-old boy named Marcus who immediately claimed the best spot on the couch, a seven-year-old girl named Destiny who wanted to help with everything, and Claire.

Claire was four, almost five. A little redhead with freckles and a gap-toothed smile who took one look at Lucy and decided they were going to be best friends.

Lucy was equally enchanted. "Mommy," she whispered, tugging at Susan's sleeve. "Mrs. Claus has grandchildren."

Susan bit back a smile. "She does."

"And one of them is *my age*."

"Almost."

Lucy's eyes went wide, processing this information. Then she turned back to Claire, and within minutes they were on the floor together, playing with the dolls Lucy had found under the tree that morning.

Because Santa had come.

When they'd walked over to Angie and Sonya's that morning—Mrs. Claus's house, as Lucy insisted on calling it—there was more under the tree than Susan had expected.

Lucy had squealed at the baby doll—a real one, with closing eyes and a little bottle. There were other toys too: a tea set, some books, a few coloring sets. Nothing outrageous, but real. Comparable to what other children might receive.

Under the tree, there had been gifts with his name on them too. A gift certificate to Foot Locker in a small envelope, with a note in Sonya's handwriting: *Get what you really want. Merry Christmas.* And a winter parka, navy blue and actually warm, with matching gloves.

He'd looked at Susan with an expression she couldn't read. Surprise, maybe. Or something closer to disbelief.

"Santa knew what you needed," she'd said softly.

He'd nodded, not trusting his voice.

Susan thought back to two days before—December 23rd.

Levi had gone to Graham's to help decorate. Lucy had spent the day with Angie, making gingerbread men and decorating a little tree of her own. And Susan had found herself in Sonya's truck, being driven to the mall whether she liked it or not.

"I've only just started working," Susan had protested. "I can't afford—"

"I paid you early." Sonya's tone left no room for argument. "And we got some things for the kids, so don't bitch about it. Already done."

Susan had opened her mouth to insist they were fine, but Sonya had just looked at her.

"You learn quick," Sonya said, "that once I get something in my head, there's no use trying to change it. Save your energy."

So Susan had saved her energy. And her small amount of money.

She'd bought Lucy clothes—essentials she badly needed. Hers were practically falling apart.

For Levi, she'd hesitated. He was getting to that age where he probably wouldn't appreciate his mother buying his socks and underwear. Sonya had agreed.

"Let him pick his own things," she'd said. "He's almost a man. He'll want to feel like one."

But what to get him instead? It couldn't be extravagant—Susan didn't have the money for extravagant, even with Sonya's early payment. In the end, she'd bought him a wallet. Simple, brown leather, grown-up looking. Inside, she'd tucked a twenty-dollar bill and a note: *We'll go shopping together. I love you. —Mom*

Now, sitting in Sonya and Angie's living room with wrapping paper scattered across the floor and the sounds of children playing and adults laughing, Susan felt something she hadn't felt in a long time.

Safe.

She'd met Sonya and Angie's daughters that morning—warm women who'd welcomed her like she belonged there. They'd handed her coffee without asking, made space for her at the table, included her in conversations without making her feel like an outsider.

And under the tree, there had been gifts with her name on them too.

A winter coat — deep green, warm, practical. Susan had looked at Sonya, startled.

"They had a sale," Sonya said with a shrug. "I needed a new one anyway. Grabbed two."

Susan doubted that very much. But she didn't argue. Not with Lucy watching, not with everyone smiling.

"Thank you," she managed.

"Merry Christmas," Sonya said. And then, quieter, leaning in: "There's a present in the guest room for you too. Open it later. When you're alone."

Susan understood. Personal things Sonya had assumed she needed but would never ask for. Things you didn't unwrap in front of a room full of people.

She'd hugged Sonya then, tight and quick, not trusting herself to speak. Sonya had just patted her back.

While Lucy played with Claire on the floor and the adults gathered around the kitchen table for cards and conversation, Levi found himself on the edge of things.

He wasn't unhappy, exactly. The morning had been good — better than good. The parka actually fit. The gloves were warm. The Foot Locker gift certificate meant he could finally get some new tennis shoes — ones without holes in them. And with Eli's LL Bean card, maybe some boots. He'd ask Michael to come along. Michael had the eye for that sort of thing.

But now, with the chaos of the gathering swirling around him, he felt... restless.

He sat in an armchair near the tree, watching without participating. The daughters were nice enough. The grandkids were fine. But Levi didn't know how to insert himself into any of it. He wasn't good at this—the casual socializing, the quick laughter. He never had been.

His mind kept drifting back to last night. The book Eli had given him — his own copy, brand new, waiting to be broken in. Graham's inscription inside. *Keep walking.* The letters. All of it.

And Michael's gifts.

Levi shifted in his chair. The clothes weren't just clothes. Michael had thought about them. Really thought. The right sizes, the right colors, the way he'd said *just wear it untucked with your jeans* like he already knew how it would look. Which meant he'd been paying attention. Looking. Not just glancing the way people glanced at Levi — past him, through him — but actually seeing him.

He knew my style, Levi thought. And then: I didn't even know I had a style.

But Michael got it. Got *him*. Somehow.

That was the part Levi couldn't stop turning over. Not the clothes themselves, but what they meant. That someone had looked at him — really looked — and thought, *yeah, this is who he is.*

He stared out the window at the bright winter sun reflecting off the snow. He wondered what Michael was doing right now.

At Graham's, the morning had been quiet.

Too quiet, Graham thought. They'd done their gifts the night before — the chaos of wrapping paper and Eli's theatrics and Levi's face when he'd opened that box. But now it was just the two of them, hot chocolate and silence, Michael scrolling his phone on the couch.

Graham had been thinking about it since last night. Watching Michael with Levi — the care he'd taken with those gifts, the way he'd known exactly what to get, the way he'd reached over and shown him how to roll the sleeves. The patience in it. The tenderness, really, though Michael would have died before calling it that.

It reminded Graham of someone.

He went to the bedroom and came back with a small box.

"One more," he said.

Michael looked up. "I thought we did gifts last night."

"This one's just from me. For this morning."

Michael opened it. Simon's watch. Not flashy — Simon hadn't been flashy — but beautiful in the way well-made things are. The kind of watch you kept forever.

Michael held it carefully, turning it over in his hands. The weight of it. The face slightly worn from years on Simon's wrist. He ran his thumb across the glass.

He didn't put it on right away. He just held it, looking at it, and Graham could see the boy understanding what he'd been given. Not a watch. A piece of someone.

"Thank you," Michael said finally. He couldn't manage more than that.

Graham just nodded. He didn't trust his own voice much either.

Michael excused himself and went to his room. He was gone for a while. When he came back, the watch was on his wrist. Neither of them mentioned it. They didn't need to.

They made turkey sandwiches for lunch and settled into the kind of aimless afternoon that holidays sometimes become — Michael on the couch with his phone, Graham wandering the house looking for some project to occupy his hands. It was too quiet for two people. The house felt it.

Graham kept thinking about Eli — alone in that tired apartment building, probably eating cereal for Christmas dinner.

He picked up his phone and texted.

Come over. No one should be alone on Christmas.

The reply came a few minutes later.

I'm fine. Don't want you to drive all the way over here.

I insist.

I'll take the bus.

On Christmas?

It runs. I checked.

Graham sighed. Stubborn as ever.

Michael looked up from his phone. "What's wrong?"

"Eli. He's being difficult about coming over."

"Why doesn't he just let you pick him up?"

"Because he's Eli."

Michael was quiet for a moment. Then: "I could drive."

Graham looked at him.

"What? I did fine yesterday."

Graham couldn't argue with that. The roads were clear, the sun was out, and Michael had been itching to get behind the wheel again since the mall.

"Let me text him."

Change of plans. Michael's driving.

A pause. Then:

Should I be concerned?

He parked at Whole Food yesterday without incident.

And survived?

He did.

No, I meant you.

Get dressed. We're leaving in ten.

Should I wear a helmet?

Graham was about to put his phone down when another text came through.

Actually. If Michael's driving anyway, and you're playing navigator... why not swing up and get Levi too? It's only another 10-15 minutes past my place.

Graham smiled. He knew Eli was up to something.

He didn't say anything to Michael. Just handed him the phone.

Michael read the text. His face lit up—bright and eager—and then, just as quickly, shifted into something like embarrassment. Like he'd been caught.

Graham simply asked, "Well?"

Michael opened his mouth. Closed it. Tried again. "I mean... if he wants to... I don't want to, like, bother him or anything. It's Christmas. He's probably busy with his family. I don't want to seem—"

Before he could finish fumbling, Graham casually took the phone back and dialed Angie's number.

She answered on the third ring, the sounds of laughter and conversation spilling through the speaker.

"Merry Christmas, Graham!"

"Merry Christmas, Angie. Sounds like quite a gathering."

"The whole crew's here. Daughters, grandkids, the works. Susan and her kids too."

"Speaking of—is she nearby?"

"Hold on." Graham heard Angie call out, then the phone being passed.

"Graham? Merry Christmas!"

"Merry Christmas, Susan. Listen — we were wondering if Levi might want to join us for a bit this afternoon. Michael's driving us over to pick up Eli, and we thought Levi might like to come along."

"Is Eli alone today?"

"He is."

"Oh, poor thing."

"Exactly. And we thought Levi might have fun hanging out with us boring folks for a little while. If he's free and wants to, of course."

Susan had been sitting at the kitchen table, cards in hand. Now she looked through the doorway into the living room, where Levi sat in the armchair near the tree. He was watching Lucy and Claire play on the floor, but his eyes had that faraway look she recognized. He was somewhere else entirely.

She'd noticed the change in him. The last few days, something had shifted. He seemed lighter. Happier. And Michael — he'd mentioned Michael more than the others.

She got the impression her son was making a friend.

"Levi!" she called out. "Would you like to go over to Graham's for a while? They're planning on driving up this way."

Levi's head snapped toward her. His face lit up like the tree beside him.

Susan didn't need to hear his answer. "He'd like that," she told Graham. "Very much."

Levi was standing at the edge of the driveway when the BMW pulled in.

He was wearing his new parka—the navy blue one from Santa—and his breath fogged in the cold, sunny air. He'd been waiting for maybe five minutes, but it felt longer. He kept telling himself not to get too excited. It was just hanging out. It didn't mean anything.

Then he saw Michael in the driver's seat, and his heart did something stupid.

Graham noticed the new parka right away. Good. The boy needed a proper coat.

Eli had insisted on being navigator and forced Graham to the back seat when they'd picked him up. Graham didn't mind. He could be chauffeured any day.

Now, as Michael parked, Eli threw open the door with theatrical flair.

He stumbled out of the car, fell to his knees on the snowy driveway, and pressed his hands to the ground like a shipwreck survivor reaching land.

"Solid ground!" he gasped. "Thank God! I thought I'd never see it again!"

"It wasn't that bad!" Michael shouted from inside the car.

Graham was shaking his head and laughing in the back seat.

Levi couldn't help it—he was grinning. These people were insane. He loved it.

Eli dusted off his knees and caught Levi heading for the back door. "Nope." He put a hand on Levi's shoulder, steering him toward the front. "You're up here." He opened the passenger door and practically shoved Levi in. "I'll keep the old man company."

Graham muttered something about respect for elders, but he was still laughing.

Levi settled into the front seat beside Michael.

"Hey."

"Hey."

For a moment, neither of them said anything.

"Don't let him fool you," Eli called from the back, buckling in. "He almost took out a mailbox on the way here."

"I did not!"

"It was close."

"It was *fine*."

"Graham, tell him."

"I'm staying out of this," Graham said.

Michael caught Eli's eye in the rearview mirror—and raised his middle finger at him.

Graham nearly doubled over laughing.

"Please," Eli shot back. "You're way too young for me to do *that*."

Michael blushed and glanced at Levi, who was clearly trying very hard not to laugh.

"I can't believe he lets you drive this thing," Levi said, glancing around the BMW.

Michael grabbed his sunglasses from the console and slid them on, tilting his chin up slightly. "I'm kind of a pro."

"A pro?" Eli repeated from the back. "Who do you think you are, Tom Cruise?"

Another middle finger, but this time Eli reached forward and grabbed it, pulling Michael's hand back toward him. Everyone laughed.

"Kids, kids," Graham said, playing peacekeeper. "Michael, put it in reverse and head home. Do you remember the way?"

"Only from Eli's place."

Eli immediately piped up. "See! He has it for me! I knew it!"

Graham slapped at his arm playfully. "Let him be. He's with..." He nodded toward Levi in the front seat.

Eli mouthed the words *his boyfriend* and nodded, smiling broadly.

Graham put a finger to his lips—*keep it down*—but he was smiling too.

"Don't make me pull this car over back there!" Michael yelled, watching them in the rearview mirror.

Levi laughed out loud.

"Yes, sir!" Graham said, and Eli immediately sat up straight, hands folded in his lap, the picture of innocence.

Levi was so happy they'd come. And they'd barely pulled away from the house.

Back at Graham's, Eli made a beeline for the kitchen.

"Alright," he announced, rubbing his hands together. "Let's see what we're working with."

He opened the refrigerator and stared inside. Then he closed it. Opened it again, as if the contents might have changed.

They had not.

"Graham."

"Yes?"

Eli held the door open and gestured inside like a museum guide presenting a disappointing exhibit. "A scrape of potatoes. Half a roll. And —" He reached in and pulled out the pie tin. One slice. "Who leaves a single slice of pie? What kind of person does that? Either eat it or throw it away. This is just sad."

"I was saving it," Graham said.

"For what? A crisis?"

"Maybe."

Eli set the tin on the counter and looked between Graham and Michael. "So. What's the plan for dinner tonight?"

Silence.

"So. No plan."

More silence.

"You're hopeless. Both of you." Eli turned to Levi. "It's you and me. We're the only functioning members of this family."

Levi grinned — wide and real. He liked being on Eli's team.

"Hey," Michael protested. "I'm the one who drove to the grocery yesterday. If it weren't for me, you wouldn't have even had dinner last night."

"That's true," Graham conceded.

"And," Michael continued, building his case, "the ice cream. With extra whipped cream. That was me."

Eli paused. Considered this. "The whipped cream was good."

"It was great."

"It was acceptable." Eli fought a smile. "Fine. You're forgiven." He looked at Graham. "You're still hopeless."

"I've accepted that."

"Good." Eli grabbed his coat. "We're going out. All of us. We're finding real food."

"Out where? What's even open on Christmas?"

"Something's open. Something's always open." Eli grabbed his coat. "Come on."

It took three tries.

The first place—a diner Graham vaguely remembered from years ago—was dark and locked. The second, a pizza place, had a sign in the window: *Closed for the Holiday. See you December 26th!*

But the third—a Chinese buffet on the other side of town—had cars in the parking lot and lights on inside.

"Told you," Eli said, pulling into a spot. He'd taken over driving duties, claiming Michael needed a break. Graham suspected he just liked being in control.

Michael climbed out of the back seat behind Graham—and immediately threw himself to the ground, arms spread wide, pressing his cheek to the cold pavement.

"Solid ground!" he gasped. "Thank God!"

Levi turned away, shoulders shaking with silent laughter.

Graham applauded slowly. "Well played."

Eli laughed. He reached down and grabbed Michael's hand, hauling him to his feet. "Okay, okay. You got me. Now come on — I'm starving."

Inside, the buffet stretched along one wall—steam trays filled with orange chicken, lo mein, fried rice, egg rolls, crab rangoon, and a dozen other things Levi couldn't identify. The restaurant was maybe half full, families and couples scattered across the booths, everyone looking relaxed and unhurried. Christmas lights blinked in the windows. Soft instrumental music played from somewhere overhead.

It was, Levi thought, nothing like any Christmas he'd ever had. But it was nice.

Eli grabbed a plate and began loading it like a man who hadn't eaten in days. Chicken. Beef. Shrimp. Noodles. Rice. More chicken.

Graham watched him pile on a third scoop of lo mein. "What family are you hoarding that for?"

"This is a cry for help, Graham." Eli added an egg roll. "A cry for help."

Levi and Michael followed behind them at the buffet, hanging back slightly.

"They're like an old married couple," Michael said under his breath.

Levi grinned. "I was thinking the same thing."

Up ahead, Eli was now deliberating between two different types of fried rice. Graham said something Levi couldn't hear, and Eli swatted at him.

"Get a move on up there!" Michael called. "Some of us are hungry!"

Graham glanced back, amused. Then he leaned over and said something to Eli.

Eli immediately slowed down. Dramatically. He studied each dish like he was selecting a fine wine, tilting his head, murmuring to himself, taking his sweet time.

Michael groaned. Levi loved it.

When Levi reached the buffet, he took small portions—a little rice, some chicken, a few vegetables. He wasn't used to places like this, wasn't sure what he was allowed to take, didn't want to seem greedy.

Eli appeared at his elbow. "What is that? That's not a plate. That's a sample."

"I'm not that hungry—"

"Nonsense." Eli began adding to Levi's plate. More chicken. More rice. An egg roll. Some noodles. "You're a growing boy. Eat."

Levi laughed, trying to protect his plate, but it was no use. By the time Eli was done, he had twice as much food as he'd started with.

"There," Eli said, satisfied. "Now it's a plate."

They settled into a booth near the window—Levi and Michael across from each other, Graham and Eli on the outside seats. Late lunch or early Christmas dinner, depending on how you looked at it.

The food was good. Not fancy, but warm and filling. Eli went back for seconds, then thirds. Graham nursed a cup of tea and picked at a plate of vegetables. Michael and Levi worked through their food steadily, exchanging glances across the table.

Levi kept catching Michael's eye—quick looks, nothing obvious—and then glancing over to see if Eli or Graham had noticed. But they were too wrapped up in their own conversation, bickering about something Levi couldn't follow. Politics, maybe. Or movies. It was hard to tell.

It felt easy, sitting here. Natural. Like he belonged.

Eli leaned back in the booth, rubbing his belly. "I couldn't eat another thing."

"Really?" Michael raised an eyebrow. "Because you said that twenty minutes ago. Before your third plate."

"That was different. That was strategic eating."

"Strategic."

"You wouldn't understand."

Levi looked over at the buffet line. Then back at Eli.

"There's nothing left to eat anyway," he said, thumbing toward the steam trays. "I think you ate it all."

Everyone turned to look at him.

The quiet boy. The one who watched more than he spoke. And he'd just delivered the best dig of the day.

Michael burst out laughing, pointing at Eli. "He got you! Oh my God, he got you!"

He reached over and tried to rub Eli's belly like a Buddha. Eli swatted his hand away, but he was grinning.

"Okay, okay." Eli nodded at Levi, conceding defeat. "That was good. That was really good." He raised an imaginary glass. "You're one of us now."

Michael was still laughing, eyes bright. He caught Levi's gaze across the table and nodded, agreeing.

Graham reached over and gave Levi's shoulder a small squeeze. "Welcome to the family."

Levi felt something shift in his chest.

Welcome to the family.

He didn't say anything. Couldn't, really. But he smiled — and looked around the table at these people who had, for reasons he still didn't fully understand, decided to include him.

And when his eyes found Michael's again, he thought: *Part of someone.*

But he kept that inside.

Chapter Fourteen

ELI WENT BACK to work the Monday after Christmas.

The office was half-empty—most people had taken the whole week off between the holidays—but Eli didn't mind. It was quiet. He could catch up on things without the usual interruptions, without having to navigate the open floor plan that made lip-reading a constant challenge.

He was deep into a spreadsheet when his phone buzzed.

DONNA

Lunch this week? It's becoming a tradition!

Eli smiled. They'd only had lunch once—that time at the little Italian place where Donna had talked for two hours straight and Eli had laughed until his face hurt. But apparently once was enough for Donna to declare it a tradition.

This week is crazy. Could we do dinner instead?

Even better! Tuesday? Brett's got some work thing, so it'll just be us girls.

Perfect.

I'll pick the place. Somewhere fabulous.

Eli didn't doubt it.

. . .

Tuesday arrived, and Eli took the bus straight from the office to the restaurant Donna had chosen—a cozy bistro near the waterfront that managed to be both elegant and unpretentious. He spotted Donna immediately, holding court at a corner table, her coat draped dramatically over the back of her chair.

But she wasn't alone.

Niles sat across from her, still in his winter coat, looking like he wasn't entirely sure how he'd ended up there.

Donna waved Eli over with the enthusiasm of someone greeting a long-lost friend. "There he is! My favorite accountant!"

"I thought Thomas was your favorite accountant," Eli said, sliding into the seat next to Niles.

"Thomas is my favorite *old* accountant. You're my favorite young one."

"I'll take it." Eli turned to Niles. "Hey. Good to see you again."

Niles looked up briefly, then back down at the menu. "Hey."

"I hope you don't mind," Donna said, not sounding like she cared whether he minded or not. "Since it was dinner, I thought I'd bring my offspring along. He needs to get out more."

"Mom—"

"What? It's true. You spend all your time in that garage with your robots."

Niles looked like he wanted to disappear into the floor.

Eli caught his eye and gave him a small, sympathetic smile. "I think robots are pretty cool, actually."

Niles glanced up, surprised. Then he seemed to remember their conversation at the party—the winter village, the magnets, the way Eli had actually wanted to crawl under the table and see how everything worked.

"Thanks," he said quietly.

Dinner unfolded the way Eli had expected—Donna doing most of the talking, spinning stories about her holiday disasters (the turkey was dry, Brett had somehow set a potholder on fire, her sister-in-law had brought a fruitcake that could double as a doorstop). Eli laughed in all the right places, genuinely entertained by her theatrics.

But he also kept an eye on Niles.

The kid—though he wasn't really a kid, Eli reminded himself; he was a senior in college, probably only a few years younger than Eli himself—sat quietly through most of it, picking at his food, occasionally smiling at his mother's more outrageous stories.

Eli made a point of including him. Asked about his classes. His robots. Whether he'd made any progress on the humanoid project he'd mentioned at the party.

At first, Niles's answers were short. Clipped. The same quiz-style responses Eli remembered from before.

But slowly, something shifted.

Maybe it was the way Eli actually listened—really listened, leaning in slightly so he could read Niles's lips, nodding along, asking follow-up questions that showed he'd been paying attention. Maybe it was that Eli didn't seem to be just making polite conversation.

Whatever it was, Niles started to open up.

He talked about the servo motors he'd been experimenting with. The challenges of getting a humanoid robot to walk naturally. How he'd spent three weeks debugging a single line of code that turned out to have a misplaced semicolon.

"A semicolon?" Eli laughed. "Three weeks for a semicolon?"

"It's always the semicolons," Niles said, and there was a hint of a smile on his face. "They're evil."

"I believe it. Numbers I can handle. Code would make me insane."

"It's not that different, really. Just... logic. Patterns."

"Maybe you can teach me sometime."

Niles looked at him, uncertain whether he was serious.

"I mean it," Eli said. "I'd like to understand what you do."

Donna watched this exchange with sharp eyes, sipping her wine and saying nothing. But Eli could feel her attention on them, cataloging every detail.

By the time dessert arrived—a chocolate lava cake they split three ways—Niles had made two actual jokes. Small ones, almost under his breath, but Eli caught them and laughed, which made Niles duck his head to hide a smile.

Donna noticed. Eli could tell she noticed.

After dinner, they gathered their coats and made their way outside. The night was cold and clear, the kind of crisp winter evening that made your breath visible and your cheeks sting.

"This was fun," Eli said. "I should probably head out though — I need to catch the bus before it gets too late."

"Nonsense," Donna said. "We'll give you a lift."

"You don't have to—"

"I insist." She looped her arm through his. "Besides, it's freezing. You'll catch your death waiting for a bus."

They walked toward Donna's car—a sleek black sedan that probably cost more than Eli's annual salary. Niles trailed behind, hands shoved in his pockets.

But halfway across the parking lot, Donna stopped.

"Oh." She pressed a hand to her temple. "Oh, that's not good."

"What's wrong?" Niles was at her side immediately, concern flickering across his face.

"Just a little headache. Migraine, probably. They come on so suddenly sometimes." She waved her hand dismissively, but her other hand stayed pressed to her head. "Nothing serious. But I don't think I should drive."

Eli studied her. Her performance was good—just the right amount of distress without being over the top. But he'd spent enough time with Donna to recognize when she was putting on a show.

She was up to something.

"Niles, sweetheart," she said, "would you mind terribly driving us home? You can drop me off first, and then take Eli to his place. It's not far, is it, Eli?"

"Not far at all," Eli said slowly.

"Perfect." Donna handed the keys to Niles and climbed into the back seat, leaving Eli to take the passenger side up front.

Niles looked uncertain but did as he was told.

Niles dropped his mom off at their house—a large colonial that glowed warmly in the winter darkness. She kissed him on the cheek, squeezed Eli's hand, and swept inside with a final wave.

"Feel better!" Eli called after her.

She turned and gave him a look—just a flicker, barely a second—that told him she knew exactly what he knew.

Then she was gone.

Niles pulled back onto the road, his hands tight on the steering wheel.

"So," Eli said. "Your mom's pretty great."

"She's... a lot."

Eli laughed. "Yeah. But in a good way."

Niles nodded, eyes on the road. The silence stretched between them—not quite comfortable, not quite awkward. Somewhere in between.

"Turn left up here," Eli said. "Then it's the third building on the right."

Niles followed the directions, pulling into the parking lot of Eli's apartment complex. The building looked even more tired than usual in the harsh glow of the streetlights.

Niles put the car in park but didn't unlock the doors.

Eli didn't move to get out.

"I had fun tonight," Eli said.

Niles glanced at him, then away. "Yeah. Me too."

"You know, you're different than I expected."

"Different how?"

"At the party, you seemed so... I don't know. Closed off. But tonight, when you were talking about your robots—" Eli smiled. "You kind of light up."

Niles's cheeks flushed. "I just... I don't know how to do the whole... talking to people thing. Not like my mom."

"Nobody talks like your mom."

That got a small laugh.

Eli took a breath. This was the moment. He could feel it.

"Would you want to get dinner again sometime?" he asked. "Just the two of us?"

Niles went very still.

Eli watched him—watched the way his jaw tightened, the way his eyes darted toward the steering wheel and then back to the windshield. He could practically see the gears turning in Niles's head, the overthinking that probably plagued him in every social situation.

"Hey," Eli said gently. "I'm going to ask you something, and I want you to answer honestly. Okay?"

Niles nodded, still not looking at him.

"Would dinner be fun? Or is it scary?"

The question hung in the air.

Niles swallowed. "Both," he admitted quietly. "I think... both."

Eli nodded. "That's okay. Both is okay." He shifted slightly in his seat, angling his body toward Niles. "Here's the thing. I know a place that's really quiet. Not a lot of people. Good food, but nothing fancy. I like it because it's easier for me—with my hearing, you know? Loud restaurants are hard."

Niles finally looked at him.

"But I think you might like it too," Eli continued. "It's not overwhelming. We could just... talk. Like tonight. No pressure."

Niles was quiet for a long moment. Eli could see him wrestling with himself—the fear of something new battling against something else. Hope, maybe. Or loneliness.

"Okay," Niles said finally. He could barely get the word out. "I'd like that."

Eli smiled. "Yeah?"

"Yeah."

"Good." Eli unbuckled his seatbelt, then paused. "I don't actually have your number."

Niles blinked, like this hadn't occurred to him either. He pulled out his phone, fumbled with it for a second, and held up the screen.

Eli typed the number in and sent a text. Niles's phone buzzed in his hand.

"Now I do," Eli said. "Tomorrow night work?"

Niles nodded, still looking slightly dazed.

"Great." Eli reached for the door handle, then paused. He turned back to Niles, leaned over, and pressed a gentle kiss to his cheek.

It was quick—barely a second—but Eli felt Niles freeze beneath the touch.

"Thank you for the ride," Eli said. "And for tonight. I had a really good time."

He climbed out of the car, gave a small wave, and headed toward his building without looking back.

Niles sat in the parked car, engine still running, heat blowing softly through the vents.

His cheek tingled where Eli's lips had been.

He couldn't move. Couldn't think. His heart was doing something strange in his chest—racing and stuttering and generally refusing to behave normally.

Had that just happened?

Had Eli just... kissed him?

It was only on the cheek. It didn't mean anything. People kissed each other on the cheek all the time. His mom did it constantly. It was just... a thing. A friendly thing.

But it didn't feel like just a thing.

Niles caught his own reflection in the rearview mirror and was startled by what he saw.

He was smiling.

Not the tight, forced smile he usually managed in social situations. Not the polite smile he gave when people complimented his projects. This was softer. More genuine.

He looked... happy.

Niles had never particularly liked looking at himself in mirrors. He always saw the awkwardness, the way he didn't quite fit. The things that made him different.

But right now, in the dim glow of the streetlight, with that smile still on his face...

He looked nice.

He sat there for another minute, just breathing. Then he put the car in drive and headed home, Eli's question still echoing in his mind.

Would dinner be fun? Or is it scary?

Both, he'd said. And that was true.

But right now, sitting in the warmth of his mother's car with the memory of Eli's kiss still burning on his cheek, the fun part was winning.

After Christmas, Levi came down to Graham's nearly every day. Sometimes Michael drove up to get him—practicing, he said, though Graham suspected the practice was just an excuse. Other times, Susan dropped him off on her way to the print shop—even though it was nearly twenty minutes out of the way.

Graham's manuscript sat untouched on the desk in his office.

He'd noticed, of course. For the week or so before Michael arrived, Levi had been consumed by that manuscript—desperate to finish it, to see the original cuts and edits, to understand how the story had evolved. Graham had told him he was welcome anytime. The manuscript wasn't going anywhere.

But now, when Levi was at the house, he barely glanced toward the office door.

Graham understood. The manuscript would always be there. Michael was leaving in a week.

He watched them from the kitchen window one afternoon—the two of them in the backyard, breath fogging in the cold air, laughing about something Graham couldn't hear. Michael threw a handful of snow at Levi, who ducked and retaliated. Within seconds, they were chasing each other around the half-dead garden, their laughter carrying across the frozen yard.

Graham smiled and turned back to his tea.

He knew what he was seeing. He'd been young once too.

The phone situation, however, was becoming a problem.

Every time Michael wanted to reach Levi, he had to call Angie and Sonya's house and hope someone was there to walk over to the barn and fetch him. Half the time, no one answered. The other half, there was a delay of twenty or thirty minutes while Levi was located and made his way to a phone.

"This is bullshit," Michael muttered on Tuesday afternoon, hanging up after his third attempt. He glanced at Graham. "Sorry. But seriously—it's impossible to reach anyone."

"Not everyone has a phone glued to their hand," Graham said mildly.

"Everyone should. It's basic communication."

Graham didn't disagree. He'd been thinking about it for days—ever since Christmas, really, when he'd noticed how isolated Susan and her kids still were. Susan was working now, but she didn't have a reliable way to reach her children during the day. And Levi, at nearly sixteen, was the only teenager Graham knew who didn't have a phone.

It wasn't right.

After Michael retreated to his room to try calling again, Graham picked up his own phone and dialed Sonya.

She answered on the second ring, the sounds of machinery humming in the background. "Graham. What's going on?"

"Got a minute?"

"Hold on—" The noise faded as she stepped away. "Okay. Shoot."

"The phone situation. With Susan and Levi."

"Yeah." Sonya exhaled. "Been thinking about that myself."

"It's becoming a problem. Michael's been trying to reach Levi all morning. It's like playing telephone tag through three different households."

"I hear you. You know, I never understood people being glued to those damn things all the time. But now that I've got one, I can't imagine not having it."

"Exactly. I want to help, but Susan's proud. I don't want to—"

"I'll get her a phone through the business. Put it on our plan. It's for the damn job, and if she complains, I'll tell her to zip it."

Graham laughed. He loved how Sonya just cut to the heart of things.

"And Levi?" she asked.

"I'll get him a phone. And I want to take the boys shopping — Michael got him a few things for Christmas, but he needs more than one outfit."

"Just be careful. She's come a long way, but there's a line where it stops feeling like help and starts reminding her what she can't do on her own."

"I know. That's why I'm telling you first."

Sonya sighed. Graham could hear it — the weight of a conversation she'd rather not have, but would have anyway. Because it needed doing.

"Christ, Graham. You're gonna owe me for this one."

Later that afternoon, Michael finally got through.

Angie answered, cheerful as always, and promised to send someone to fetch Levi. Ten minutes later, the phone rang.

"Hello?" Levi's voice was eager.

"Levi! Finally." Michael was grinning. Graham could hear it from across the room. "I've been trying to reach you all day."

"Sorry. I was helping Lucy build a snow fort."

Michael's grin softened into something else. "You're a really great guy, you know that?"

Silence on the other end.

Michael could practically feel Levi blushing through the phone. He'd made it awkward. Why had he said that?

"Uh—anyway—" Michael fumbled. "I was actually calling because... I was wondering if you wanted to do something? I could borrow Uncle Graham's car."

A pause. "Like what?"

"I don't know. We'll figure it out. Just... hang out. Get out of the house."

"Yeah." Levi's voice brightened. "Yeah, I'd like that. But I need to ask my mom first. She's at work."

"Okay. Call me when you find out?"

"I will."

"Promise?"

"Promise."

Michael hung up and turned to Graham with an expectant look.

"Yes, you can borrow the car," Graham said before Michael could ask.

"You're the best uncle ever."

"I know."

A half-hour later, the phone rang again.

"She said yes." Levi sounded slightly breathless, like he'd run to make the call. "I can go."

"Awesome. I'll come pick you up. Twenty minutes?"

"Okay." A pause. "Michael?"

"Yeah?"

"Thanks. For uh… wanting to hang out."

Michael's expression softened. "Of course. See you soon."

He hung up and grabbed his coat, already heading for the door.

Graham watched him go. Something about the way Michael moved—the eagerness, the energy—reminded Graham of himself at that age. Before he knew what to call it. Before Simon helped him figure it out.

He smiled and went back to his tea.

Levi was already waiting at the edge of the driveway when Michael pulled in.

He was wearing his new parka, his breath making little clouds in the cold air. When he saw the car, his face broke into a grin that made something flip in Michael's chest.

"Hey," Levi said, sliding into the passenger seat.

"Hey yourself."

They sat there for a moment, the engine idling, heat blowing through the vents.

"So," Michael said. "Where do you want to go?"

Levi shrugged. "I don't know. You're the one who asked."

"Yeah, but you're the one who lives here."

"I just moved here."

"Still. You know it better than I do."

"You bought ice cream two days ago."

"That was for dinner. That's different."

"How is that different?"

Michael opened his mouth. Closed it.

"Thought so," Levi said.

Michael laughed and put the car in drive. "Dairy Queen it is."

. . .

The place was nearly empty—no surprise, given the weather. A bored teenager stood behind the counter, scrolling on her phone until she noticed them walk in.

"What can I get you?"

Michael studied the menu board. "I'll take a chocolate Blizzard. Medium."

"Same," Levi said. Then: "Actually, no. Can I get a vanilla soft serve cone instead?"

Michael turned to stare at him. "Vanilla soft serve? Over a Blizzard?"

"I like soft serve."

"Vanilla?"

"What's wrong with vanilla?"

"It's... vanilla. It's like the most boring flavor ever."

"It's classic."

"It's sacrilege."

Levi laughed, eyes crinkling. "You're very dramatic about ice cream."

"I take my ice cream seriously."

Levi gave him a look, but Michael pretended he didn't see it and smiled in spite of himself.

They paid and found a booth by the window, the plastic seats cold beneath them. Outside, a few cars passed on Route 1, headlights cutting through the gray afternoon.

Michael took a bite of his Blizzard and watched Levi methodically work his way around the soft serve cone, catching the drips before they could escape.

"You've got a system," Michael observed.

"You have to. Otherwise it gets everywhere."

"Spoken like a true vanilla soft serve professional."

"Don't knock it till you try it."

Michael reached over and took the cone right out of Levi's hands.

"What are you—"

Michael took a long, deliberate lick. Considered it. Tilted his head. Took another.

"Hey — that's mine—"

"Not bad," Michael said, handing it back. "Not chocolate. But not bad."

Levi stared at the cone like it had been violated. Then at Michael's face. Then back at the cone.

He slowly resumed eating it, a small smile pulling at the corner of his mouth.

Michael pretended not to notice. But he noticed. He liked this version of Levi—relaxed, playful, willing to give as good as he got. It was different from the quiet, guarded kid he'd first met at the car that day.

"So," Michael said, leaning back in the booth. "Tell me something about yourself."

"Like what?"

"I don't know. Something I don't know yet."

Levi considered this, licking his cone. "I've never been on an airplane."

"Really? Never?"

"Never. We couldn't afford it. And there was never anywhere to go anyway."

Michael thought about all the flights he'd taken—to Maine every summer, to Florida that one time for a family vacation, to visit his grandparents in Arizona. He'd never thought of flying as a luxury. It was just... something you did.

"What about you?" Levi asked. "Tell me something."

Michael hesitated. There were a lot of things he could say. A lot of things he wasn't ready to say.

"I used to play piano," he offered. "When I was a kid. I was pretty good, actually. But I quit in middle school."

"Why?"

"I don't know. It wasn't cool, I guess. My friends were all into sports, and I wanted to fit in." He shrugged. "Stupid reason."

"Do you miss it?"

"Sometimes. Uncle Simon used to play. He tried to get me to pick it back up every summer, but I never did." Michael's voice went quiet. "I wish I had. Now it's too late."

Levi was watching him with those mismatched eyes—steady, attentive. "It's not too late. You could still learn again."

"Maybe."

"You should. It's never too late to do something you love."

Michael looked at him. There was something earnest in Levi's expression, something that made Michael want to believe him.

"Yeah," he said softly. "Maybe you're right."

They finished their ice cream and got back in the car, the heater working overtime to combat the chill they'd invited in.

"I should probably check in with my mom," Levi said. "Let her know I'm okay."

Michael noticed this about Levi—how he always asked permission, always checked in, always seemed attentive to his mom. Becca could be strict, sure, but she'd never required Michael to keep this close a tab on things. At first it had seemed a little much, but now Michael understood it differently. Levi wasn't annoyed by it. He was protective of her. It was kind of nice, actually.

"We could swing by the print shop?" Michael offered.

"If you don't mind."

Michael hadn't even thought to just use his own phone to call. "Let's go."

Then, as he pulled back onto the road: "Hey—you want to come over for dinner tonight? I mean, if your mom says it's okay."

Levi looked at him, surprised. "Really?"

"Yeah. Why not? Uncle Graham won't care." Michael shrugged, trying to sound casual. "We could hang out more. Watch a movie or something."

"I'd have to ask."

"So ask. When we get there."

Levi nodded, but Michael caught the small smile tugging at the corner of his mouth.

Levi directed him through a series of turns until they pulled up in front of a modest building with a hand-painted sign: *Sonya's Print & Press*.

Inside, the shop smelled like ink and paper. Machines hummed in the background—big industrial things that looked complicated and slightly intimidating. Susan stood at a workbench near the back, bent over what looked like some kind of binding contraption. Sonya was beside her, demonstrating something with her hands.

They both looked up when the bell above the door jingled.

"Well, look who it is," Sonya said, a smile breaking across her weathered face. "The wandering boys."

Susan wiped her hands on her apron and came around the workbench. "Levi! I didn't expect to see you."

"Michael wanted to drive around, so we stopped by."

Susan's eyes moved to Michael, then back to Levi. Her son looked relaxed—happy, even. She couldn't remember the last time she'd seen him this at ease around someone his own age.

"What have you two been up to?" she asked.

"We got ice cream," Levi said.

"Ice cream? In this weather?"

"That's what I said," Michael laughed.

"It was his idea," Levi added, pointing at Michael.

"It was not! You suggested Dairy Queen!"

"You agreed!"

Susan watched them bicker, a small smile playing at her lips. Sonya caught her eye and raised an eyebrow. Susan gave a tiny shrug.

"Mom," Levi said, suddenly remembering. "Can I go to Graham and Michael's for dinner tonight?"

Susan hesitated. "Did Graham say that was okay?"

"I can call him right now," Michael offered, pulling out his phone.

Sonya snorted from behind the workbench. "Lord, I hate those damn things. But I gotta admit—times like this, they're useful."

Susan nodded. "Once I get on my feet, it's my next priority. Maybe one for Levi too, now that he's getting older."

Michael had already dialed. "Uncle Graham? Hey — is it okay if Levi comes over for dinner tonight?" A pause. "Yeah. Okay. Cool."

Susan held out her hand. "Let me talk to him."

Michael hesitated, then handed over the phone.

"Graham? It's Susan. I just wanna make sure this is alright. I don't want him wearin' out his welcome."

"He's always welcome, Susan. Anytime. No need to ask."

"I just don't want him in the way when you're tryin' to work. You got your writing and all —"

"Honestly, he and Michael are like two peas in a pod. They keep each other busy. It's good for both of them."

She was quiet for a moment. "Well... alright then."

She handed the phone back to Michael. Looked at Levi, who was trying very hard not to look like he cared about the answer.

"Go on," she said. "But you mind your manners."

Back in the car, Levi was quiet for a moment.

"Thanks," he said finally. "For... all of this."

"For what? Ice cream and a ride?"

"I don't know. Just..." Levi looked out the window. "It's stupid."

"What is?"

"I'm just... different. When you're around." He shook his head quickly. "That sounds weird. Forget it."

Michael's heart was doing something strange. "No, it's... I mean... I get it. I think."

Levi glanced at him. "Yeah?"

"Yeah." Michael kept his eyes on the road. "I'm different too. Or whatever."

Smooth, Michael. Real smooth.

But Levi smiled. "Good different?"

"Yeah." Michael let out a breath he didn't know he'd been holding. "Good different."

Neither of them said anything else for a while. Michael turned up the radio a little, just to fill the silence. But it wasn't awkward. It was the other kind.

The kind where you didn't need to say anything at all.

While Michael drove back to pick up Levi, Graham texted Eli.

Dinner tonight? Michael's bringing Levi over.

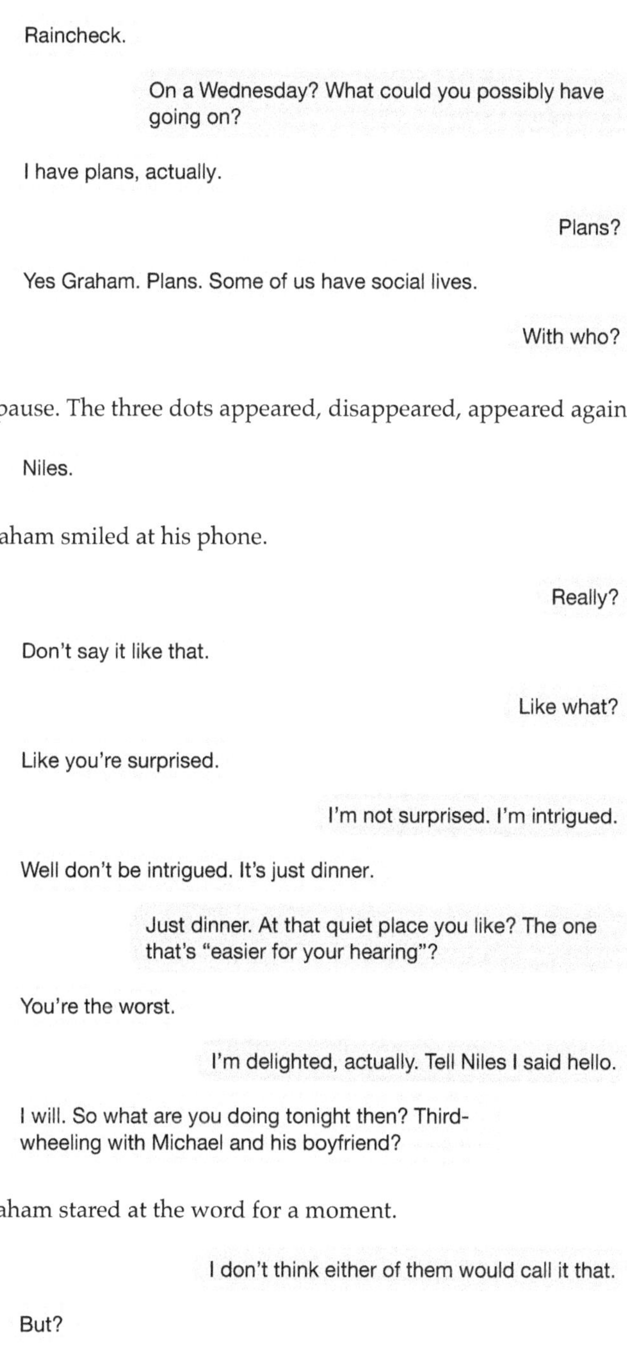

Raincheck.

On a Wednesday? What could you possibly have going on?

I have plans, actually.

Plans?

Yes Graham. Plans. Some of us have social lives.

With who?

A pause. The three dots appeared, disappeared, appeared again.

Niles.

Graham smiled at his phone.

Really?

Don't say it like that.

Like what?

Like you're surprised.

I'm not surprised. I'm intrigued.

Well don't be intrigued. It's just dinner.

Just dinner. At that quiet place you like? The one that's "easier for your hearing"?

You're the worst.

I'm delighted, actually. Tell Niles I said hello.

I will. So what are you doing tonight then? Third-wheeling with Michael and his boyfriend?

Graham stared at the word for a moment.

I don't think either of them would call it that.

But?

But I don't know. Maybe? They haven't told me anything.

Do they even know?

Graham thought about the way Michael looked at Levi. The way Levi lit up whenever Michael walked into a room. The fumbling, the awkwardness, the way neither of them seemed to know what to do with their hands when they were standing close to each other.

I don't think so. Not yet.

I remember that age.

So do I.

Terrifying.

But also kind of wonderful.

Give them time. They'll figure it out.

That's the plan. Just giving them space to be.

You're a good uncle Graham.

I'm trying. Have fun tonight.

Thanks. That means a lot.

Graham set down his phone and stood there for a moment, thinking about all the ways people found each other. The unexpected paths. The quiet moments that turned into quite a bit more.

He remembered his conversation with Sonya. Levi needed more than one outfit. And a phone. The mall would be a nightmare — after-Christmas sales, crowds, the whole circus. But it was the only place he could knock it all out at once.

He took a breath. He could do this.

The front door opened. Michael and Levi tumbled in, mid-debate about whether reading the book or watching the movie was better. Levi was adamant that books were always superior — you got the inner thoughts, the details, the world the way the author intended. Michael countered that movies brought everything to life — the visuals, the music, the actors making it real.

"Change of plans," Graham announced before either could ask him to pick a side. "We're going out for dinner." He said the next word like it was perfectly normal. "The mall."

Michael stared at him.

"There's a Shake Shack. And I want to look at a few things. After-Christmas sales."

"You?"

"Yes."

"Want to go?"

"Uh huh."

"To the mall." This wasn't a question.

"What part of this is difficult to understand?"

"The mall. You. Voluntarily." Michael shook his head. "You called it your 'personal circle of hell' two days ago."

"I don't recall saying that."

"You said it in the parking lot. And then again inside. And then once more at the Orange Julius."

"Michael." Graham held up a hand. "Are you hungry or not?"

Michael looked at Levi, who was watching this exchange with pure delight.

"Starving," Michael said.

"Then let's go." Graham grabbed his keys and ushered them back toward the door.

Chaos.

There was no other word that came to Graham's mind as they entered the Maine Mall, the largest in the state.

He had expected crowds, but this was something else entirely—a post-holiday frenzy of returns, exchanges, and bargain hunters prowling the clearance racks. Music blared from every store. Children screamed. Somewhere, a baby was crying.

"This was a mistake," Graham muttered.

"You suggested it," Michael reminded him.

"I'm aware."

They found the Shake Shack and claimed a table in the corner of the food court. Graham looked at the menu board and wondered if this was what passed for gourmet dining these days. He could only imagine what Eli would say.

But the boys seemed happy. Michael ordered a double burger with cheese fries. Levi got a chicken sandwich and a shake. They ate and talked and laughed, and Graham watched them from across the table, content to be background noise.

After they finished, Graham cleared his throat.

"I want to look around a bit. I need to... buy a sweater."

Michael stared at him. "A sweater?"

"Yes."

"You want to buy a sweater? At the mall?"

"Is that so strange?"

"You hate this place. You literally complained about it the entire drive here."

"I didn't complain. I observed."

"You called it 'consumer purgatory.'"

Graham darted his eyes toward Levi, who was drinking his shake and distracted by the next table over for a moment—some little kid throwing fries at his sister while their exhausted mother tried to intervene.

Michael followed Graham's gaze, thinking his uncle was pointing out the chaos at that table. But when he looked back, Graham was giving him a less subtle look—a widening of the eyes, a slight nod toward Levi. *Help me out here.*

Michael didn't get it.

He looked back at Levi, who still had the straw in his mouth, taking in the antics across the food court. What was his uncle up to?

He turned back to Graham, who now looked like he was silently screaming *do I have to spell it out for you?*

Michael turned back to Levi. The too-short sleeves. The worn jeans. The way he always hung back like he wasn't sure he belonged.

And then it registered.

Graham wasn't here to buy a sweater for himself. He was here to buy clothes for Levi.

Michael had bought Levi an outfit for Christmas — but that was different. He hadn't been thinking about what Levi needed. He'd been thinking about what would look good on him. What he wanted to see Levi wear. That was a different thing entirely, and he wasn't about to examine it too closely.

But looking at Levi now — the rest of his wardrobe, the stuff that wasn't from Michael's box — he saw what Graham saw. Sleeves that didn't reach his wrists. Jeans worn thin at the knees and too short at the ankles. A kid who'd been growing out of everything he owned for months and never said a word about it.

This wasn't about style. Levi needed things. Real things.

And all the shit Michael had been giving Graham about the mall — the teasing, the disbelief, the dramatic recounting of his "personal circle of hell" speech that Levi had been eating up — suddenly landed differently. Graham had sat through every bit of it without breaking. Because this was why they were here.

Graham, with his terrible poker face and complete inability to lie convincingly, was silently pleading with Michael to help him out. And Graham sure as hell wouldn't know what to get a fifteen-year-old, let alone where in the mall to find it.

Michael finally got it.

But it would be really awkward to suddenly thrust Levi into some kind of makeover situation. Graham knew that. And now, so did he.

Michael could do that. He'd have a much better chance at making this believable than his uncle would. Besides, why not? If Graham was offering to pay, why not make it fun for Levi?

And for him, too.

"Okay," Michael said, keeping his voice casual. "Let's look around."

Graham threw a grateful sigh and collected their tray.

They wandered through the mall, Graham pretending to browse while the boys trailed behind. He stopped in front of a clothing store—one of those places that catered to teenagers, all loud music and aggressively casual displays.

"Let's go in here," Graham said.

Levi hung back near the entrance, looking uncomfortable.

Michael caught Graham's eye and gave him a small nod. *I've got this.*

He walked over to a rack and started pulling shirts. "Finally, a decent store. My mom never lets me get what I actually want back home. But Uncle Graham's the cool uncle, so..." He grabbed something off a nearby rack—a garish neon green hoodie with some kind of abstract splatter pattern—and held it up. "What do you think of this?"

Levi blinked. "Me?"

"Yeah, you. I need your opinion. I think this would be perfect for me."

Levi looked at the hoodie. Then at Michael. Then back at the hoodie.

"It's... nice?"

"Nice? Really?" Michael held it up against his chest. "You don't think this screams 'fashion forward'?"

Levi's mouth twitched. "It screams something."

"What's that supposed to mean?"

"It's..." Levi hesitated, then seemed to decide something. "It's hideous."

Michael grinned. "There it is. Okay, so if you're so good at this, what looks good?"

Levi shrank back. "I... I dunno."

But Michael was already reaching for another rack, pulling out a jacket that looked like it had been designed by someone having a fever—orange and purple camouflage with rhinestone accents.

Before he could even get it off the hanger, Levi's hand shot out and swatted it back down.

"Definitely not that."

"No?"

"That's worse than the first one."

"Then what do *you* suggest?"

Levi hesitated for a moment, then slowly turned toward the racks. His eyes moved over the options, finally landing on something that caught his attention. He reached out, touched the fabric, then pulled it off the rack and held it up.

"This is... not bad."

Michael smiled. They were getting somewhere.

Levi was drawn in. He started offering real opinions — this one's too bright, that one's cool, the fit on this looks weird. Before long, he was pulling multiple things off racks, holding them up for Michael to consider.

"You should try some stuff on," Michael said.

"Me? I'm not buying anything."

"So? Try it on anyway. I don't want to go in the fitting room alone. That's weird."

"It's not weird."

"It's weird. Come on."

He shoved a pile of clothes into Levi's arms—jeans, hoodies, a few shirts, a belt—and pushed him toward the fitting rooms.

"I don't get why you want me to—" Levi started.

"C'mon." Michael pushed him forward.

They tried things on for the next twenty minutes. Michael kept passing things over the partition—"Try this one, it's more your style"—until Levi had a small mountain of clothes he'd actually liked. Jeans that fit properly. Hoodies that weren't two sizes too big. Shirts in colors that worked with his eyes.

Michael emerged from his fitting room and grabbed a pack of socks from a nearby display. Threw them on top of Levi's pile. Then another. Then he reached for a pack of boxers.

"Michael—"

"What? I'm sure you could use more underwear."

Levi's face went hot. There was something weirdly personal about Michael thinking about his underwear.

"How would you know?" His voice came out more awkward than he intended.

"Everyone needs underwear. It's a universal truth."

Levi was quiet for a moment. Then, mustering some courage: "What about *you*?"

"Fine." Michael grabbed a couple of packs for himself—one green with stripes, one plain grey. He held them up. "Which ones do you like?"

"On you?" Levi's eyes shot up to meet his.

Michael froze. He'd just been asking which color looked better. But the way Levi said it—*on you*—suddenly made him picture Levi picturing him in...

Heat crept up the back of his neck.

He grabbed the grey ones and tossed the other pack back on the shelf.

"Moving on," he muttered, heading toward the register.

But Levi grabbed his arm. "Wait—I can't afford all this."

"Who said you're paying?"

Levi stared at him. "What?"

But Michael was already walking toward the register, arms full of clothes. Graham appeared out of nowhere—had he been watching the whole time?—and smoothly swiped his credit card before Michael even had to pretend to reach for a wallet.

"Uncles are legally obligated to pay for clothes," Graham said matter-of-factly. "It's in the handbook."

Levi's mouth opened. Closed. "There's no handbook."

"There's absolutely a handbook."

"What handbook?"

""The uncle handbook. Very official. Look it up."

Michael was grinning. Levi looked between them, completely lost.

"I didn't—" Levi shook his head. "I wasn't trying to—this is too much."

"Already paid for." Graham shook the shopping bag lightly. "But there seems to be room in here for a few more things. If you boys wanted to keep looking."

Levi thought he was kidding. But Michael was already heading back into the store.

"Wait—Michael—"

Levi followed, bewildered. "What are you doing?"

"He said we could get more."

"He was joking."

"He wasn't joking. When Uncle Graham offers to buy stuff, you don't argue. Trust me." Michael pulled another shirt off a rack—something colorful that would look good with Levi's mismatched eyes. "This one's cool."

"I don't need—"

"It's not about need. It's about not refusing when the uncle is paying."

Levi laughed. He let Michael lead him through the store, not really intending to get anything else.

And then he saw the jacket.

It was hanging near the back—a simple design, but something about it caught his eye. The cut. The color. He wasn't even sure what drew him to it. He just... liked it.

He reached out and touched the sleeve, then checked the price tag.

His face fell.

"It's okay," he said, already moving away.

"Try it on."

"It's too expensive."

"So? Try it on anyway." Michael grabbed it off the rack. "For shits and giggles."

Levi snorted. "For shits and giggles?"

"That's what I said. Come on."

He practically forced Levi into the jacket, then stepped back to look at him.

Michael's eyes widened. "Dude."

"What?"

"Go look in the mirror."

Levi felt ridiculous, but he walked over to the full-length mirror near the fitting rooms.

And stopped.

He barely recognized himself.

The jacket fit perfectly — like it had been made for him. It made his shoulders look broader, his frame less scrawny. The color brought out something in his eyes, made the blue-green pop against the solid blue.

He looked... good.

Not like a model or anything. But good. Like someone who might actually be worth looking at.

Michael appeared behind him in the mirror. He reached over Levi's shoulders and tugged at the collar, straightening it, adjusting the way it sat against his neck.

"See, that's the thing about a good jacket," Michael was saying, smoothing the fabric across Levi's shoulders, going a mile a minute the way he did when he was focused. "It's all about how it sits right here, and the way the color works with your eyes —"

He brushed a piece of lint off Levi's shoulder and glanced up at the mirror. Something made him pause.

Something in Michael changed. His hands stopped moving. His voice dropped — quieter, slower, like the words were being pulled out of him.

"Levi, you... uh... wow." He swallowed. "You look really... hot."

Levi went still.

No one had ever said anything like that to him. He'd never been someone people noticed — not like that. He'd spent his whole life keeping his head down, staying out of the way, making himself small. He wasn't the kind of person anyone called hot. He wasn't the kind of person anyone called anything.

But lately... something had been shifting. He'd liked the way he looked in those clothes they just tried on. Liked catching himself in the mirror and not hating what he saw. Maybe it was the clothes. Maybe it was just Michael — the way Michael looked at him, the way Michael made him feel like he was… well, something.

And this jacket did look good on him. He could see that. He wasn't sure why, exactly, but it just did.

But Levi knew Michael wasn't talking about the jacket.

He said *he* looked hot. He. Levi. The boy. Well — the guy, he thought now.

He thought about Michael and the way he looked — his jaw, his eyes, the way his hair fell when he leaned forward. How hot *he* looked. But Levi would sooner die than say that out loud. Not the way Michael just had.

Their eyes met in the mirror.

Michael's lips parted — like he was about to say something else. Something bigger. For one second, Levi thought he saw it — the beginning of words that might change everything.

Then Michael's face shifted. The realization of what he'd said caught up to him, and Levi watched it happen in real time — the flash of panic, the scramble to recover, the walls going up.

"You need a haircut," Michael said, deflecting.

The moment folded in on itself. Levi felt the loss of it — whatever had almost been there, almost been said — but he understood. He was too chicken to say a word himself. But he wanted to. God, he wanted to.

He reached up and swiped the hair out of his eyes. "Okay, okay. Fine. Everyone keeps telling me. I don't even know where."

"We'll ask Eli."

"Won't your uncle know a place?"

"Graham?" Michael looked at him. "He can barely spell *style*."

Levi laughed — real and sudden, the tension cracking just enough to breathe again.

Michael started helping him out of the jacket, sliding it off his shoulders carefully and draping it over his arm like they were actually going to buy it.

"It's too expensive," Levi said reaching for it.

Michael grabbed it out of his hands.

"Michael—"

But Michael was already walking away. He snagged another pair of jeans—Levi's size, a style Levi had said he liked—and another shirt, and another pack of boxers for good measure. Then he marched back to the register where Graham was still standing, bags from the first purchase at his feet.

Michael handed everything over. Graham paid without a word. Handed the new bags to Michael, who handed them to Levi.

"What just happened?" Levi asked.

"What?"

"The clothes. The jacket. What—"

Michael shrugged. "They look good on you."

"But—"

"Don't overthink it."

They walked out of the store, Levi clutching the bags like he wasn't sure they were real.

. . .

Graham stopped in front of the Apple store.

"I need to run in here for a minute."

Michael nodded like this was totally normal. Levi stood near the front, still dazed from the clothing ambush.

Graham was inside for maybe ten minutes. When he emerged, he was carrying a small bag.

"Levi, help me out, will you?" He pulled out a box—a new iPhone—and handed it to Levi. "I need to make sure this works. Can you text Michael and see if he gets it?"

Levi blinked. "Uh... okay."

He opened the box carefully, like it might bite him. The phone was sleek and new—nothing like the ancient hand-me-downs he'd occasionally used in the past.

"I don't really know how—"

"Here." Michael stepped close—very close—looking over Levi's shoulder. "I'll show you."

Levi was suddenly very aware of Michael's warmth beside him. His breath. The way his arm brushed against Levi's as he reached over to tap the screen.

"Just type in my number," Michael said. "Then find the emoji keyboard—here—and send whatever."

Levi's fingers fumbled over the screen. He found a couple of emojis—a waving hand, a smiley face—and pressed send.

Michael's phone buzzed. He pulled it out, looked at the screen, and typed something back.

Levi felt the phone vibrate in his hand. He looked down.

A single red heart.

He looked up at Michael, who was still standing right there, close enough that their noses almost touched. Michael gave him a small wink.

Levi's face went hot.

"Does it seem to be working okay?" Graham asked.

Levi nodded, not trusting his voice.

"Good. Can you try one more number for me? Just to make sure everything's working."

Graham recited his number. Levi entered it without thinking — he was the helper, doing what he'd been asked to do. He typed "testing" and hit send.

A moment later, Graham's phone buzzed in his pocket.

Michael's eyes went wide. He looked at Graham. Graham didn't look back.

Graham pulled out his phone, typed something, and slipped it back into his pocket.

Levi's phone buzzed. He looked down at the screen.

testing

Add me to your address book.

He looked up, confused. "Add what?"

"That number. The one you just texted."

"I don't get it."

Michael couldn't help it — he was grinning now, watching this unfold. He stepped behind Levi, reaching around him to take the phone, practically hugging him from behind. "Here — let me show you."

He tapped the number, opened a new contact, and typed *Uncle Graham* in the name field. Hit save.

Levi's head — and his heart — were too busy processing the warmth of Michael pressed against his back, Michael's arms around him, Michael's hands over his. He hadn't really looked at the screen.

Michael stepped back. Levi blinked. Read it.

testing

UNCLE GRAHAM.

Add me to your address book.

"Why would you..." He looked up at Graham.

"You need my number if you're going to text me, right?" Graham said.

Levi looked at Michael, still confused. Michael was all smiles.

"Me?" Levi said. "Text?"

"Yeah. From your new phone."

Levi stepped back. "No." He looked at the phone in his hand. Back at Graham. Back at Michael. "For real? No..."

Graham nodded. "It's all yours."

"I can't—this is too much. This is way too much."

"It's already done."

"But—"

"Levi." Graham's voice was gentle. "Let people do nice things for you. Okay?"

Levi looked down at the phone in his hands. Then at the bags of clothes. Then at Michael, who was just smiling at him.

"Merry Christmas, Levi," Michael said, and stepped forward to hug him.

Levi stood frozen for a second, the phone clutched in one hand, the other hanging at his side. Michael's arms were around him, warm and solid.

And something broke.

Levi's face crumpled. He tried to hold it together—tried to keep the emotions down where they belonged—but they came anyway. His eyes burned. His throat closed up. A sound escaped him that he didn't recognize.

"Hey—" Michael pulled back, alarmed. "Are you okay?"

Levi couldn't answer. He was crying now—really crying, tears streaming down his face, his whole body shaking with the effort of trying to stop.

"Levi—"

"I'm sorry—" The words came out broken. "I'm sorry, I don't know why I'm—"

Michael didn't hesitate. He pulled Levi back into the hug, tighter this time, and held on.

Graham stepped forward and put a hand on Levi's shoulder.

Levi grabbed onto Michael like he was the only solid thing in the world. He buried his face in Michael's shoulder and let it all come out—everything he'd been holding since Graham first found him at Thanksgiving, probably longer. The fear. The uncertainty. The loneliness of being invisible, of never quite belonging anywhere.

It wasn't the phone. It wasn't the clothes. It wasn't even the kindness, though that was part of it.

It was that people gave a shit about him.

Cared.

Welcomed him to the family.

He was crying in the middle of the Maine Mall, surrounded by shopping bags and strangers and a new phone he didn't deserve, held by a boy he barely knew but somehow felt like he'd known forever.

No one stared. Or if they did, Levi didn't notice.

It was just Michael and Levi. And Graham, standing there beside them, helping them learn how to be.

Chapter Fifteen

MICHAEL PULLED up to Levi's around two in the afternoon.

The drive had become familiar now—the winding roads, the snow-covered fields, the way the trees thinned out and then thickened again as you moved north. He'd made this trip half a dozen times since Christmas, sometimes with Graham, sometimes alone. Today was alone.

He liked driving. Liked the quiet of it, the way the car became a small world unto itself. And he liked where the driving led.

Levi was waiting on the porch, bundled in his new parka, breath fogging in the cold air. He raised a hand when he saw the car, and something in Michael's chest did that thing it kept doing lately. That flip. That warmth.

He parked and climbed out, shoving his hands in his pockets against the cold.

"Hey," Levi said.

"Hey yourself."

They stood there for a moment, grinning at each other like idiots. Michael was aware of how stupid they probably looked—two teenage boys just standing in the cold, smiling—but he didn't care.

"You want to come in?" Levi asked. "It's freezing out here."

"Yeah. Okay."

Michael followed him inside.

The barn house was small but cozy. Angie and Sonya had renovated a year ago, turning what had once been storage into a proper living space. The main room served as kitchen, dining, and living area all in one, with a wood stove in the corner throwing off heat. A hallway led to the bedrooms in the back.

Susan was at work. Lucy was with Angie for the afternoon, helping bake cookies or whatever it was they did together. The house was quiet.

"You want something to drink?" Levi asked. "We have... water. And more water. I think there's some juice."

"I'm good."

Levi nodded. He seemed slightly nervous, which was strange. They'd hung out plenty of times by now. But something about being here—in Levi's space, just the two of them—felt different.

"You want to see my room?" Levi asked, then immediately looked like he regretted it. "I mean—it's not much. But it's... mine, I guess."

"Yeah. Show me."

Levi's room was small. Really small. Barely bigger than a closet, with a single window that looked out at the snow-covered yard. A narrow bed was pushed against one wall, neatly made. A small dresser—secondhand, by the look of it—held a few folded clothes. The new clothes from the mall, Michael noticed. Levi had actually put them away properly.

There was nothing on the walls. No posters, no photos, no decorations of any kind. Just bare wood and white paint.

"Told you it wasn't much," Levi said. He was standing in the doorway, arms crossed, like he was bracing for judgment.

"It's yours," Michael said. "That's what matters, right?"

Levi's shoulders relaxed slightly. "Yeah. I guess."

Michael sat down on the edge of the bed — there was nowhere else to sit — and looked around. On the dresser, he noticed a single book. He recognized the cover immediately — the gold lettering, the bridge, the Renaissance cityscape in soft golds and browns.

"That's the one Eli gave you on Christmas Eve."

Levi nodded.

Michael picked it up, turning it over in his hands. He'd seen copies at Graham's house, of course. Had meant to crack one open at some point. But between everything, there hadn't exactly been time.

He opened the cover without thinking. Graham's signature on the title page — that practiced script Michael had seen on stacks of author copies at the house. And below it, in smaller, more careful handwriting:

To Marco—

The bridge is long. The other side is real.

Keep walking.

Michael stared at it. Marco. Not Levi. Graham had called him Marco.

He looked up. Levi had gone quiet, watching him with something shy in his expression — like Michael was seeing something private. Something that mattered more than Levi knew how to say.

"He wrote that for you," Michael said.

Levi nodded again. His eyes dropped.

Michael didn't fully understand it — not yet, not without having read the books. But he understood enough. His uncle saw something in Levi. Something worth naming. Something worth writing down in careful handwriting inside a book he'd spent years of his life creating.

He closed the book gently and set it back on the dresser.

He liked that Levi had it. Liked that it connected them — his uncle and this kid next to him. Like it was something they could all share.

Levi sat on the bed next to him. Close, but not too close.

"So," Levi said quietly. "When's your flight?"

Michael's stomach tightened. He'd been avoiding thinking about it. "Sunday. Eight in the morning."

"Early."

"Yeah."

"That sucks."

"Yeah."

Michael picked at a loose thread on Levi's comforter.

"I'll probably sleep the whole flight," he said. "Won't even notice."

"Probably."

"And it's not like Nashville is that far. I mean, it's far. But it's not like... across the ocean or anything."

"Right."

"And we can text now. Like, actually text. Not that whole calling-Angie's-house thing."

"Right." Levi's voice was quieter now.

Michael looked at him. Levi was staring at the floor, his jaw tight.

"Hey," Michael said. "It's not—I mean—"

He didn't know how to finish. What was he supposed to say? *I'll miss you? I don't want to leave? These past two weeks have been the best of my life and I don't know what I'm going to do when I'm back in Tennessee and you're here and everything is just... normal again?*

He couldn't say any of that. The words were too big. Too much.

So instead, he nudged Levi's shoulder with his own and said: "At least you'll finally have time to finish all that book stuff of Uncle Graham's. The manuscript, right? You never finished it."

Levi looked up. "The manuscript. Yeah."

"See? Something to look forward to."

It was a weak attempt at lightness, and they both knew it. But Levi seemed to grab onto it anyway.

"You still don't even know most of the story," Levi said.

"So tell me."

Levi hesitated. "Really?"

"Yeah, really." Michael shrugged. "I mean, you obviously love this stuff. So what's the big deal? Tell me."

Something shifted in Levi's expression. The sadness about Michael leaving was still there, underneath. But now there was something else too. That spark Michael had seen when Levi talked about the manuscript, about the edits and cuts, about the story feeling "alive."

"Okay," Levi said. "But it's long. And I might not tell it as good as the book does."

"That's fine."

"And you have to actually pay attention. No falling asleep."

"I won't fall asleep."

"You better not."

Levi pulled his legs up onto the bed, sitting cross-legged. Michael did the same, so they were facing each other. The bed was small enough that their knees almost touched.

"Okay," Levi said again. He took a breath. "So. You know about Marco coming to Florence. His mom dying, the scholarship being gone, Alessandro taking him in as a valet."

"Yeah."

"And you know about the bath? When Alessandro watches him?"

Michael raised an eyebrow. "The bath?"

"It's not—it's not *like* that. I mean, it kind of is, but it's also... it's about Marco being seen. For the first time. Being seen as someone worth looking at." Levi's cheeks had gone slightly pink. "Anyway. That's where we were. Marco's first night in the apartment. He falls asleep listening to Alessandro breathe through the wall."

Michael nodded, even though he'd missed most of this context. "Okay."

"So what happens next," Levi said, his voice settling into the rhythm of storytelling, "is that a few weeks pass..."

* * *

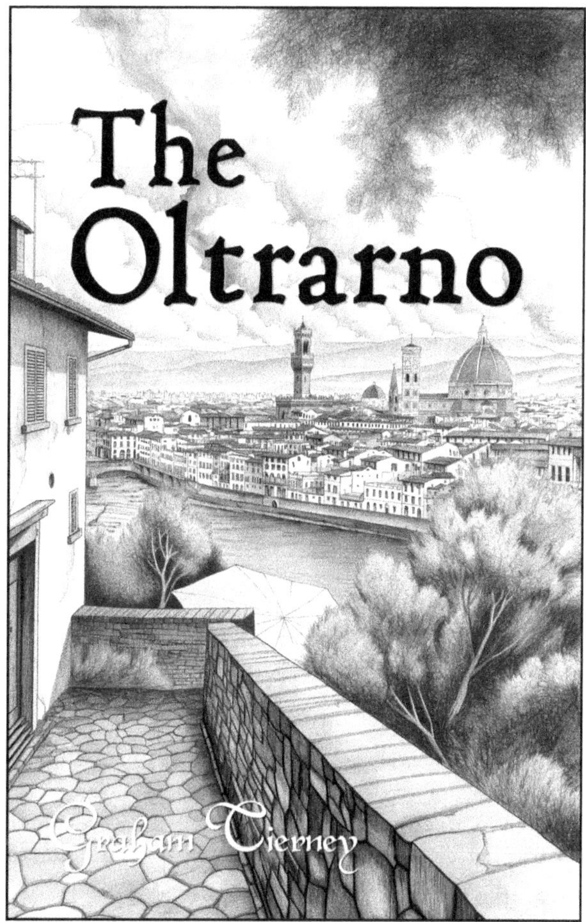

THE OLTRARNO

Marco learned the rhythms of Alessandro's life—the way he rose early and worked until the light failed, the way he forgot to eat when a painting consumed him, the way he sometimes stood at his window for long stretches, staring at the city below as if searching for something he'd lost.

Marco learned his duties too. Preparing the studio each morning: grinding pigments, stretching canvas, arranging brushes in the order Alessandro preferred. Laying out his clothes. Drawing his bath. Attending to whatever small tasks the day required.

Keeping the apartments tidy was easy — Alessandro owned remarkably little for the son of a nobleman. A modest wardrobe, his art supplies, a few books. Whatever palace his family occupied elsewhere, Alessandro had brought almost nothing of it here. Whether by choice or principle, Marco couldn't tell — but the simplicity of it surprised him.

It wasn't hard work. But it was intimate work.

Marco had never been so close to another person's daily existence. He knew now that Alessandro hummed while he painted—fragments of songs Marco didn't recognize. He knew that Alessandro took his wine watered, his bread torn rather than sliced, his candles trimmed to precisely the same height. He knew the sound of Alessandro's footsteps, the rhythm of his breathing, the particular sigh he made when a brush-stroke went wrong.

And Alessandro, in turn, was learning Marco.

Florence grew more unsettled by the day.

Piero de' Medici had proven himself unequal to his father's legacy. The city whispered of conspiracies, of French armies massing in the north, of a friar named Savonarola whose sermons drew crowds that spilled from the cathedral into the streets. The Academy's patrons grew cautious with their coin. Several students had already left, returning to families who could no longer afford the risk of keeping sons in a city that might soon burn.

But inside Alessandro's apartments, the world outside felt distant. A rumor. A story happening to someone else.

Marco spent his evenings drawing.

Alessandro had given him proper materials—good paper, quality charcoal, even a set of red and black chalks that Marco handled like holy relics. He worked at a small table near the window while Alessandro painted or read or simply sat by the fire, and sometimes hours passed without either of them speaking. It wasn't uncomfortable. In fact, it was something else. Something Marco had never experienced before.

Companionship, perhaps. Though that word felt too small.

"Your clothes don't fit."

Marco looked up from his drawing. Alessandro was watching him from across the room, a book open in his lap, though he clearly hadn't been reading.

"I'm sorry?"

"Your clothes." Alessandro gestured vaguely. "The ones I gave you. They're too large. They hang on you."

Marco looked down at himself. It was true—the borrowed garments had been meant for a student with broader shoulders, a fuller frame. Marco had cinched the breeches with a belt and rolled the sleeves of the shirt, but he still swam in them.

"They're fine," Marco said. "They're more than fine. They're better than anything I've ever—"

"They don't fit," Alessandro repeated. "I'll have new ones made."

"You don't have to do that."

"I know I don't have to."

Marco felt heat rise to his face. "I can't repay you. For any of this. The clothes, the materials, the—"

"Did I ask for repayment?"

"No, but—"

"Then stop." Alessandro's voice was firm but not unkind. "You're my valet. You represent me. If your clothes don't fit, it reflects poorly on my household." He paused, and something shifted in his expression. Softened. "Besides. You deserve clothes that fit. Everyone does."

Marco didn't know what to say. He looked back down at his drawing—a study of hands, Alessandro's hands, though he'd never admit that—and tried to ignore the tightness in his chest.

"The tailor will come tomorrow," Alessandro said. "Don't argue with him about the measurements. Just let him do his work."

"All right."

"And Marco?"

Marco looked up.

"Accept things gracefully. It's a skill worth learning."

The tailor came. He measured Marco with brisk efficiency, asked no questions, and left with promises of garments within the week.

When they arrived—three shirts, two pairs of breeches, a doublet in deep green that brought out something in Marco's eyes—Marco tried them on in his small alcove while Alessandro waited in the main room.

"Well?" Alessandro called through the curtain. "Do they fit?"

Marco looked at himself in the small hand mirror Alessandro had lent him. The clothes fit perfectly. More than that—they made him look like someone. Someone real. Someone who belonged in this world of art and beauty and dreams.

"Yes," he managed. "They fit."

"Let me see."

Marco pushed aside the curtain and stepped into the main room.

Alessandro was standing by the window, afternoon light falling across his face. When he saw Marco, he went very still.

"Well?" Marco asked, suddenly self-conscious. "Is it—do I look—"

"You look..." Alessandro stopped. Swallowed. "You look fine. Good. The tailor did good work."

But he didn't look away. And Marco felt something pass between them—something neither of them could name.

"Thank you," Marco said quietly. "For the clothes. For everything."

Alessandro nodded once, sharply, and turned back to the window. "Get back to your duties. The studio needs sweeping."

Marco went. But he felt Alessandro's eyes on him as he walked away.

The days grew shorter. December settled over Florence like a gray blanket, and the city prepared for Christmas despite its troubles—or perhaps because of them. Even in dark times, people needed light.

Alessandro worked on a new commission—a portrait of a merchant's daughter, pretty but unremarkable, destined to hang in some dining hall where no one would truly see it. He complained about it constantly, muttering about how commerce was strangling art, how he'd rather paint beggars and saints than simpering girls in borrowed jewelry.

Marco listened and said nothing. He'd learned that Alessandro didn't want solutions to his complaints. He wanted a witness.

"Hand me the ochre," Alessandro said one afternoon, not looking away from the canvas. "No—the other one. The warmer tone."

Marco found the right pot and brought it to him. Alessandro took it, their fingers brushing in the transfer. He didn't seem to notice. Marco noticed.

He always noticed now.

It had crept up on him—this awareness of Alessandro. The way light caught his hair. The line of his jaw when he concentrated. The particular shade of brown his eyes became in firelight. Marco found himself cataloging these details the way he cataloged details for his drawings, storing them away for later examination.

It was dangerous. He knew it was dangerous. Whatever he was feeling—whatever name it might have—was not something he could speak aloud. Not here, not anywhere. Men had been killed for less.

But knowing a thing was dangerous didn't make it stop.

"You're distracted tonight."

Marco startled. He'd been sitting at his usual table, a half-finished drawing before him, but his charcoal had gone still in his hand. He didn't know how long he'd been staring at nothing.

"Sorry," he said. "I was just—"

"Thinking." Alessandro rose from his chair by the fire and crossed the room. He stopped behind Marco, looking down at the drawing. "What is this?"

It was a study of the courtyard fountain. Or it had been, before Marco's mind wandered. Now it was just shapes. Suggestions of something that might become art, if he could focus long enough to finish it.

"Nothing," Marco said. "It's not very good."

"Don't do that."

"Do what?"

"Dismiss your own work." Alessandro's voice was quiet but firm. "False modesty is still false. If it's not finished, say it's not finished. But don't call it 'nothing.'"

Marco felt his face heat. "It's not finished."

"Better." Alessandro was still standing behind him. Close. Too close. Marco could feel the warmth of him, could smell the linseed oil and pigment that clung to his clothes.

"Your line work has improved," Alessandro said. "Here, especially." He reached over Marco's shoulder and pointed to a section of the drawing—the curve of the fountain's basin. His arm brushed against Marco's shoulder as he did.

Marco forgot how to breathe.

"You're learning to trust your eye," Alessandro continued. "To put down what you see, not what you think you should see. That's the hardest lesson. Most artists never learn it."

"I have a good teacher," Marco managed.

Alessandro was quiet for a moment. His hand was still extended, hovering near the drawing. Near Marco.

"You have talent," Alessandro said finally. "I merely... provide opportunities for it to grow."

He withdrew his hand. Stepped back. The warmth disappeared, and Marco felt its absence dearly.

"Keep working," Alessandro said, his voice slightly rougher than before. "I'm going to bed."

Marco listened to his footsteps cross the room, heard the creak of the bedchamber door, the soft sounds of Alessandro preparing to sleep.

He sat at his table for a long time, the drawing forgotten, his heart beating so hard he was certain Alessandro could hear it through the wall.

It happened on a Tuesday.

Marco would remember that detail later—how ordinary the day had been, how nothing about it suggested that everything was about to change. He'd woken early, prepared the studio, laid out Alessandro's clothes. Alessandro had worked on the merchant's daughter portrait until midday, complained about her nose, and abandoned the canvas in favor of a walk through the city.

"Come with me," he'd said, and Marco had come.

They walked through the Oltrarno, past workshops and churches and crumbling palazzos, saying little. Alessandro pointed out details occasionally—a particularly fine carved doorway, a fresco visible through an open window—but mostly they simply walked. Side by side. Close enough that their shoulders sometimes brushed.

When they returned to the apartments, the light was failing. Alessandro lit candles while Marco built up the fire. They moved around each other with practiced ease, two bodies that had learned each other's rhymes.

"I should work on the portrait," Alessandro said, but he made no move toward the studio. Instead, he stood by the fire, staring into the flames.

"You hate that portrait," Marco said.

"I do."

"Then why work on it tonight?"

Alessandro turned to look at him. The firelight caught his face, casting half of it in shadow. "What would you have me do instead?"

It was an innocent question. It should have been an innocent question. But something in Alessandro's voice—or maybe something in Marco's own treacherous heart—made it feel like more.

"I don't know," Marco said. "Rest. Read. You've been working too hard."

"Have I?"

"You always do."

Alessandro smiled—a small, private thing. "And you've been here long enough to know my habits."

"A few weeks."

"It feels longer."

Marco's heart stuttered. "Does it?"

"Yes." Alessandro took a step toward him. "It feels like you've always been here. Like the apartment was waiting for you to arrive."

"That's—" Marco's voice caught. "That's a strange thing to say."

"Is it?" Another step. They were close now. Very close. "I've been thinking strange things lately. Since you came."

Marco should step back. Should make some excuse, retreat to his alcove, put distance between them before something happened that couldn't be undone.

He didn't move.

"Marco." Alessandro's voice was barely above a whisper. "Do you know what you are to me?"

"Your valet."

"Yes. And?"

"I don't—" Marco's breath was coming too fast. "I don't know what you want me to say."

"The truth. Whatever that is."

The fire crackled. Somewhere outside, a dog barked. The world continued on, indifferent to the two of them standing in this small room, balanced on the edge of something vast.

"I think about you," Marco said. The words came out before he could stop them. "All the time. When I'm drawing, when I'm working, when I'm trying to sleep. I think about—" He stopped, terrified of what he'd already admitted.

"What do you think about?"

"You. Your hands. Your voice. The way you—" Marco closed his eyes. "I shouldn't be saying this."

"Why not?"

"Because it's wrong. Because men don't—because we can't—"

"Marco." Alessandro's hand touched his face. Gentle. Barely there. "Look at me."

Marco opened his eyes.

Alessandro was right there. Inches away. His expression was raw in a way Marco had never seen—open and terrified and wanting.

"I've been fighting this," Alessandro said quietly. "Since the day I saw you at the gate. Telling myself it was charity. Kindness. Patronage of talent. Telling myself anything except the truth."

"What truth?"

Alessandro's thumb traced Marco's cheekbone. "That I wanted you. That I still want you. That I've wanted you every moment of every day since you walked into my life."

Marco couldn't speak. Couldn't move. Could barely breathe.

"If you want me to stop," Alessandro said, "tell me now. I'll step back. We'll never speak of this again. Things will go on as they were."

The silence stretched between them. A heartbeat. Two.

"And if I don't want you to stop?" Marco whispered.

Alessandro's answer wasn't in words.

He leaned in—slowly, giving Marco time to pull away—and pressed his lips to Marco's.

It was gentle. Brief. Barely more than a brush of warmth. But it sent lightning through Marco's entire body, and when Alessandro pulled back, Marco found himself leaning forward, chasing the contact.

Alessandro's eyes searched his face. "Marco—"

Marco kissed him.

He didn't know where the courage came from. One moment he was standing there trembling, and the next his hands were fisted in Alessandro's doublet and his mouth was pressed desperately against Alessandro's and nothing else in the world existed.

Alessandro made a sound—surprise, relief, hunger—and then his arms were around Marco, pulling him closer, and they were kissing like the world was ending, like this was the only moment that had ever mattered, like everything in both their lives had been leading to exactly this.

When they finally broke apart, both of them were breathing hard. Alessandro's forehead rested against Marco's. His hands were shaking where they gripped Marco's shoulders.

"I didn't mean—" Alessandro started.

"Don't." Marco's voice was steadier than he felt. "Don't apologize. Don't take it back."

"I wasn't going to." Alessandro pulled back enough to look at him. His eyes were bright, almost feverish. "I was going to say—I didn't mean to fall in love with you. But I did. I have. And I don't know what to do about it."

Marco stared at him. "Love?"

"What else would you call it?"

Marco thought about the weeks he'd spent learning Alessandro's world. The way his chest tightened every time Alessandro entered a room. The drawings he'd made in secret, trying to capture something he couldn't name.

"Love," he repeated. Testing the word. Finding it fit.

Alessandro's smile was like sunrise. "Is that—are you saying—"

"I'm saying I think about you all the time. I'm saying when you touch me I forget how to breathe. I'm saying I didn't know what any of this meant until right now, but—" Marco took Alessandro's face in his hands. "But yes. Love. That's what I'd call it."

They stood there in the firelight, foreheads touching, hearts pounding, the world outside forgotten.

Everything was different now.

Everything.

* * *

Levi's voice trailed off.

He'd been sitting cross-legged on the bed, hands moving as he talked, eyes bright with the story. But now he'd gone still. His gaze dropped to the comforter between them.

"And then..." he started. Stopped. "I mean, that's basically... that's where it gets..."

Michael waited.

Levi picked at a thread on the comforter. The same thread Michael had been picking at earlier. "They kiss," he said quietly. "That's what happens. Marco and Alessandro. They finally..."

He didn't finish the sentence.

The room felt smaller than it had before. The bed felt smaller. Michael was suddenly very aware of how close their knees were. How easy it would be to reach out and touch Levi's hand.

"So," Michael said. His voice came out strange. "They kiss."

"Yeah."

"And then what?"

Levi shrugged, still not looking up. "I mean, that's just... it's a book, you know? It's not..." He waved a hand vaguely. "It's just a story."

But it wasn't just a story. They both knew it.

Michael thought about Marco—a boy with nothing, showing up somewhere new, being seen for the first time. Being given clothes that actually fit. Being told he was worth something.

He thought about Alessandro — fighting what he felt, telling himself it was charity, kindness, anything but the truth. Sitting a little closer. Letting his hand linger a little longer.

He thought about himself. About Levi. About the past two weeks.

To Marco — The bridge is long. The other side is real. Keep walking.

Marco. Graham had called him Marco. The boy who fell in love with Alessandro.

The room was so quiet Michael could hear Levi breathing. Could hear the wind pressing against the window. Could hear his own pulse in his ears. The space between them had gone electric — charged with something neither of them was naming.

Levi had stopped talking. His hands were still in his lap, his eyes down, his cheeks flushed. He looked like he was waiting for something. Or afraid of it.

Michael didn't realize he was leaning closer until his fingers brushed Levi's.

Levi went still.

Not pulling away. Not moving. Just — still. Like the slightest shift might shatter whatever this was.

Then Levi looked up. Right at him. Right into him. Those mismatched eyes — one blue, one green — wide and certain in a way that contradicted every nervous thing about the rest of him.

Michael leaned in.

So did Levi.

He began to close his eyes.

The front door banged open.

"Levi! Levi, are you home? We saw Graham's car!"

Lucy's voice — bright, loud, unmistakable — followed by the sound of small boots stomping down the hallway. Angie's voice behind her, warm and unhurried.

Michael and Levi shot apart. Both on their feet before they'd consciously decided to stand. Levi's face was crimson. Michael's heart was hammering so hard he could feel it in his teeth.

They looked at each other for one wild, breathless second.

Then Lucy burst through the bedroom door.

"Uncle Mike! You're here!" She launched herself at Michael's legs.

No one had ever called him that. He hated being called Mike — always had. But Lucy, with her arms wrapped around his knees and her face tilted up like he was the most exciting thing that had happened all day — he'd make an exception.

"Hey, Lucy." His voice came out almost normal.

Levi looked like he'd been caught doing something. His hands were fidgeting at his sides, his eyes darting between Michael and his sister, trying to figure out where to land.

"Wanna play a game with me?" Lucy tugged at Michael's hand. "Please? Angie has games."

Michael glanced at Levi. Levi was still frozen.

"Only if your brother plays with us," Michael said.

"Okay!" Lucy spun toward Levi. "Levi, come on!"

Angie appeared in the doorway, smiling. "Why don't y'all come over to the house? I'll make a snack and we can set up at the dining table."

"Okay," Michael said. "Meet you over there. Let me get my stuff."

It was an excuse, and he was pretty sure Angie knew it. She scooped Lucy up and backed out of the room, pulling the door closed behind her. But not before she gave them both a look — unhurried, knowing — that said *take your time.*

The door clicked shut.

Michael looked at Levi. Levi didn't say a word. His lips parted slightly, like he wanted to speak but couldn't find the way in.

"So," Michael said. "Will you, uh... tell me more about the story sometime? Like... like before?"

Like before. Like just now. Like whatever that was before Lucy came in.

Levi's breath caught. "Uh — yeah. Sure."

"Only if you want."

"I want." It came out too fast, too loud. Levi blinked and steadied himself. "I mean... yeah. I'd like that."

Michael smiled. He knew. And he knew Levi knew.

"C'mon." Michael threw his arm around Levi's shoulders and pulled him in — a squeeze, gentle and warm, like it was the most natural thing in the world. "Let's go let Lucy beat us at whatever we're playing."

They walked out together, Michael's arm still draped over Levi's shoulders. Levi didn't say anything about the game. Didn't care what it was.

He just didn't want Michael to let go.

Chapter Sixteen

ELI WAS READY BY SIX.

He'd changed clothes three times, which was ridiculous. It was just a New Year's Eve party. The same people he'd met at the HanukkahChristmaKwanzika party. Nothing to be nervous about.

Except Niles was picking him up. And they were arriving together. And everyone would notice.

Eli looked at himself in the bathroom mirror one more time. The blue sweater—Graham had been right about that. Dark jeans. His good boots, the ones without the scuff marks. He'd even attempted to do something with his hair, though his curls had their own opinions about that.

His phone buzzed.

Here

Eli grabbed his coat and headed downstairs.

Niles was waiting in his mother's car, engine running, heat blasting. He looked nervous too—hands tight on the steering wheel, eyes fixed straight ahead.

Eli climbed into the passenger seat. "Hey."

"Hey."

Neither of them moved. The car idled in the parking lot of Eli's apartment complex, going nowhere.

"So," Eli said. "Ready?"

Niles nodded. But he still didn't put the car in drive.

"Niles?"

"Yeah. Sorry. I just—" He took a breath. Let it out. "Can we... can we wait a minute? Before we go?"

"Sure."

Eli settled back in his seat. He didn't ask why. Didn't push. Just waited.

The heater hummed. Outside, the last light of the afternoon was fading into evening. Someone walked past the car, bundled against the cold, and disappeared into the building.

"There's something I need to tell you," Niles said.

His voice was quiet. Strained. Like the words were being pulled out of him against his will.

Eli turned slightly so he could see Niles's face. So Niles could see his, if he looked. "Okay."

"It's... I've never told anyone this. Outside my family, I mean. My parents know. But I've never..."

He trailed off. His hands flexed on the steering wheel.

Eli waited.

"I have..." Niles stopped. Started again. "When I was a kid, I was... they diagnosed me with..."

Another stop. His jaw tightened. Eli could see the frustration building —Niles fighting with himself, with the words that wouldn't come out right.

Everything in Eli wanted to help. To say *it's okay, take your time* or *you don't have to tell me* or *whatever it is, I'm sure it's fine*. To fill the silence with something, anything, to ease the obvious pain Niles was in.

But he didn't.

He knew what it was like to have people try to help. To have them finish his sentences when he paused to lipread, to have them speak louder and slower like he was stupid rather than deaf, to have them carry the conversation because they assumed he couldn't. They meant well. They always meant well. But it didn't feel like help. It felt like being erased.

So Eli said nothing. He just sat there, present, letting Niles find his own way through.

A minute passed. Maybe two.

"Autism," Niles finally said. The word came out quiet. Practiced, almost — like he'd said it to himself a thousand times but never out loud to someone else. "I'm on the spectrum. That's the clinical term. My parents always said 'high-functioning,' which is..." He exhaled. "It's what people say when they want it to sound like it doesn't count."

He paused. His jaw worked.

"But it counts."

He paused, choosing his words. Eli continued to listen, giving him time.

"I just... I have trouble with people. I don't always know what's happening in a conversation. Like, someone will say something and everyone laughs and I don't know why. Or someone's mad at me and I had no idea — I thought things were fine. I thought I was doing everything right."

He gripped the steering wheel tighter.

"I practice. That's the thing people don't know. I rehearse conversations before I have them. I watch how other people stand, how close they get, when they look away. I've memorized most of it. But it's like... performing a song from sheet music while everyone else just hears it in their head. I can get the notes right, mostly. But they can tell it's not the same."

His voice cracked.

"And the worst part is when I try really hard — when I think I've finally figured it out — and someone still looks at me like... like something's off. Like I almost pass, but not quite."

He stopped. His breathing was uneven. He still hadn't looked at Eli.

"My parents decided when I was little that it was no one's business. That I was fine, basically. That I could pass. And I can, mostly. But it's exhausting pretending to be normal all the time. Watching everyone else and trying to figure out what I'm supposed to do. And people can tell anyway. They can tell something's off about me, even if they don't know what. They've always been able to tell."

Silence again. The heater hummed.

"I don't know why I'm telling you this," Niles said quietly. "I've never told anyone. But I thought... if we're going to... if this is..."

He couldn't seem to finish the sentence.

Eli reached over and put his hand on Niles's arm. Gently. Not gripping, just resting there.

Niles finally looked at him.

"Thank you for telling me," Eli said.

Niles blinked. "That's it?"

"What do you mean?"

"I just told you I'm... that there's something wrong with me. And you're just going to say *thank you*?"

"There's nothing wrong with you."

"But I just said—"

"I heard what you said." Eli squeezed his arm lightly. "You said your brain works different. That's not *wrong*. It's just different."

Niles stared at him. His eyes were bright, like he was fighting back something he didn't want to show.

"I have trouble hearing," Eli said. "You know that. But do you know what that actually means? It means I miss half of what people say. It means I have to watch mouths instead of eyes, which makes people uncomfortable. It means parties are exhausting because there's too much noise and I can't follow conversations. It means people treat me like I'm slow, or stupid, or someone to be avoided."

He paused. "My brain works different too. And I've spent my whole life trying to seem normal. It's exhausting. Like you said."

Niles was quiet, listening.

"So when you tell me there's something *wrong* with you," Eli continued, "I don't hear that. I hear that you understand what it's like to have to work twice as hard just to exist in a world that wasn't built for you."

A tear slipped down Niles's cheek. He wiped it away quickly, almost angrily.

"I don't need you to be normal," Eli said. "I just need you to be you."

Niles let out a breath—shaky, uneven. "You mean that?"

"Yeah. I mean that."

They sat there for a long moment. The parking lot was dark now, the streetlights flickering on. They were going to be late to the party. Eli didn't care.

"I've never..." Niles started. Stopped. Tried again. "No one's ever said anything like that to me before."

"Then everyone else has been missing out."

Niles laughed — half a sob, half disbelief. "That's... that's a weird thing to say."

"I'm a weird guy. We've established this."

Another laugh. Niles wiped his eyes and took a shaky breath.

Eli reached over and took his hand. Niles stiffened for just a second, then relaxed. His fingers intertwined with Eli's.

The car idled. The heater hummed. Niles didn't move to put the car in drive.

Not yet.

The party was already in full swing when Susan arrived with Lucy and Levi at seven.

Thomas and Jason's house glowed with warmth—every window lit, music drifting out into the cold night air, the sounds of laughter and conversation spilling onto the porch. Susan hesitated at the door, Lucy's hand in hers, Levi hovering behind them both.

"You sure this is okay?" she asked. "Us coming?"

Angie had driven with them, Sonya following in their truck. Now Angie put a hand on Susan's back and guided her forward. "For the hundredth time, yes. You're family now. Get used to it."

The door opened before they could knock. Thomas stood there in a ridiculous glittery hat, a glass of champagne in one hand.

"The gang's all here!" He swept them inside with exaggerated grandeur. "Come in, come in. There's food, there's drinks, there's—" He spotted Lucy and immediately dropped to one knee. "And who is this princess?"

Lucy giggled and hid behind Susan's leg.

"This is Lucy," Susan said. "And Levi. My kids."

"Well, Lucy and Levi, welcome to our humble abode." Thomas stood and gestured dramatically at the crowded living room. "Make yourselves at home. The fancy cheese is on the left, the cheap cheese is on the right, and if anyone tells you they can taste the difference, they're lying."

Lucy giggled again. Levi managed a small smile.

And then Michael appeared.

He pushed through the crowd, his face breaking into a grin the moment he saw them. "You came!"

"We came," Levi said. He was trying to play it cool, but the corners of his mouth kept twitching upward.

"I didn't think—I mean, I hoped, but—" Michael was practically bouncing. "This is great. This is really great."

Susan watched the two of them — her son and this boy from Tennessee who couldn't stop grinning at him — and she knew.

She wasn't sure when she'd figured it out. Maybe she'd known for a while and just hadn't let herself think about it. But watching them now — the way Levi leaned toward Michael without realizing it, the way Michael's whole face changed when Levi walked into a room — there was no pretending it was just friendship.

She wondered if they'd said anything to each other. If they even knew what they were. Looking at them, she doubted it. They were too careful. Too close and too careful, all at the same time.

The past few years hadn't left much room for thinking about things like this. She'd been too busy keeping them alive — keeping them safe, keeping them fed, keeping Levi and Lucy from knowing how bad it really was. But this was here now, and she wanted to get it right. Her son deserved that.

The problem was she had no idea how.

She'd grown up in a world that didn't talk about these things. She wanted to believe it was just because people didn't know better — but she knew that wasn't true. The world could be cruel. Had been cruel. She'd seen it, heard it, grown up around it. And the thought of any of that touching her son made her stomach tighten.

Maybe Graham would know. He'd been through it himself — lived it, lost a husband, came out the other side. Or Eli. Eli seemed to know how to talk about anything.

She'd figure out how to ask. She wasn't sure when or who or what she'd even say. But she could tell. Just looking at the two of them, standing there in the middle of this loud, happy room like nobody else existed.

She could tell.

"Why don't you boys go find something to eat," she said. "Lucy and I will be fine."

Levi hesitated. "You sure?"

"Go." She shooed him with her hand. "Have fun."

Michael grabbed Levi's arm and pulled him toward the food table, already talking a mile a minute about something Susan couldn't hear over the noise of the party.

Angie appeared at her elbow. "He's a good kid. Michael."

"He seems like it."

"Graham's raised him right. Well—helped raise him. The summers, you know."

Susan nodded. She didn't know the full story, but she'd gathered pieces. Graham and his husband, Simon. The nephew who came every summer. The loss that hung over everything like a shadow.

"Come on," Angie said, steering her toward the kitchen. "Let me introduce you to everyone. And get this little one some juice."

By eight-thirty, Lucy was fading.

She'd held on valiantly—charming everyone she met, eating her weight in cheese and crackers, playing some complicated game with a balloon that Jason had blown up for her. But now she was curled up on the couch, her head in Susan's lap, eyes drooping.

"I think we need to head out," Susan said quietly to Angie. "She's done."

"Of course. I'll come with you—"

"No, no. You stay. Enjoy the party." Susan stroked Lucy's hair. "I've got the car. We'll be fine."

But before Angie could respond, Sonya appeared. She took one look at Lucy and shook her head.

"Kid's out."

"I know. I was just telling Angie—"

"You need to get her home. That's fine." Sonya glanced across the room to where Levi and Michael were standing by the window, deep in conversation. "But there's no reason the boy has to leave too."

Susan followed her gaze. Levi was laughing at something Michael had said, his whole face lit up in a way she rarely saw. When Michael leaned closer to say something else, Levi's cheeks went pink.

"He's having a good time," Sonya observed.

"He is."

"Angie and I aren't staying past midnight anyway. Too old for this shit." She said it matter-of-factly, without complaint. "We'll bring him home when we leave. Watch the ball drop, then head out. He'll be back by twelve-thirty at the latest."

Susan hesitated. She didn't like leaving Levi. Didn't like the idea of being apart from him on New Year's Eve, even for a few hours. But then she looked at him again — at the way he kept glancing at Michael — and something in her gave.

"You're sure it's not a bother?"

"Susan." Sonya's voice was firm. "Let the kid have this."

Susan took a breath. "Okay. Yes. Thank you."

"Go tell him."

Levi's face fell when Susan approached.

"Already?" He looked at Lucy, asleep in Susan's arms now, and his shoulders slumped. "I guess... yeah. Okay."

"Actually," Susan said, "Sonya offered to bring you home later. After midnight. If you want to stay."

Levi stared at her. "Really?"

"Really."

"But—are you sure? I can come home with you. It's fine. I don't need to—"

"Levi." Susan shifted Lucy's weight on her hip. "Stay. Have fun. It's New Year's Eve."

The hope that broke across his face was almost painful to see. He looked at Michael, then back at Susan. "You're sure?"

"I'm sure. Just stay out of trouble."

Levi grinned. "Mom. We're the youngest people here by decades."

"I resemble that!" Jason called from across the room, having overheard.

They laughed. Susan pulled Levi into a hug, Lucy still balanced on her hip.

"Happy New Year, baby. A little early."

"Happy New Year, Mom."

Then she turned to Michael. He looked a little unsure when she opened her arm to him, but he stepped into the hug just fine. It was the first time she'd hugged him.

Levi watched, something softening in his expression. His mom wasn't usually this huggy. But seeing her welcome Michael like that—it made something in his chest relax.

Susan gave the boys one last smile and made her way toward the door, Lucy heavy in her arms.

She glanced back once. Levi and Michael were standing together, shoulders almost touching, both of them grinning like they'd just been given the best gift in the world.

Maybe they had.

• • •

They sat in the parking lot for a while after Niles's confession. Neither of them in a hurry to move.

Finally, Eli squeezed Niles's hand. "Hey. You hungry?"

Niles looked at him, surprised by the shift. "I... yeah. I guess."

"Let's get dinner before the party. Recharge our batteries."

"But we're already late."

"So we'll be later." Eli shrugged. "It's New Year's Eve. No one's going to notice."

Niles hesitated. Eli could see him turning it over in his mind—the lateness, the disruption to whatever plan he'd had, the anxiety of walking into a crowded party after everyone else had already arrived.

"It'll help," Eli said gently. "Trust me. A little quiet time before all that chaos."

Niles nodded slowly. "Okay. Where?"

Eli grinned. "I know a place."

The restaurant from their first date was open.

Eli had been winging it, honestly. New Year's Eve, no reservation—he'd half-expected to strike out everywhere. But the little place with the dim lighting and the quiet corners had a table available, tucked in the back, away from the modest crowd.

Niles relaxed the moment they sat down. The routine of it, Eli realized. This was a known quantity now. There was comfort in its familiarity.

When the server came, Niles ordered the same dish he'd had before. Same drink too. Eli noticed, and something clicked into place—another piece of the puzzle that was Niles.

Eli couldn't stay quiet for long. He never could.

"You know," he said between bites, "for a deaf guy, I really can't shut up."

Niles smiled—a real one. "I noticed."

"It's a problem. Ask anyone."

"I don't mind."

Eli grinned and took another bite. Then he set down his fork.

"Hey. I meant to say—thanks. For trusting me. Earlier."

Niles looked up. "For what?"

"For coming out to me."

Niles's eyes went wide.

"I mean—" Eli caught himself. "About your... brain." He hesitated. "Is it okay to say that? The word? I wasn't sure if you'd want me to, especially..." He gestured vaguely at the restaurant around them.

Niles understood. "I prefer to keep it to myself, I guess."

"Okay."

"I don't really know why. I just..." Niles looked down at his plate. "I don't want people to feel sorry for me. Or treat me like I'm dumb."

"Makes sense."

"Thanks for asking, though."

"Of course."

"No one ever does." Niles picked at his food. "Most people just nod. Or change the subject. Or they dance around it with all these... euphemisms. And I can't ever figure out what they're actually trying to say."

Eli nodded.

"But with you..." Niles trailed off.

"With me?"

"You're just direct. You say what you mean. You ask what you want to know." He shrugged. "It's easier."

Eli smiled. "I'm glad."

They ate in silence for a moment. Then Niles spoke again, quieter this time—but angled so Eli could read his lips.

"Funny, though. 'Coming out.'" He almost whispered it. "That phrase means so many things now, I guess."

Eli tilted his head. "What do you mean?"

"Like... tonight. In the car. That was me coming out to you. About the..." He tapped the side of his head. "But there's also the other kind. The... you know."

Eli waited.

"I've never actually come out," Niles said. "Not officially. Not to anyone."

"Not even your parents?"

"They know, I think. They've probably known forever." He shrugged. "But we've never talked about it. I've never said the words."

"Do you want to?"

Niles considered this. "I don't know. Maybe it doesn't matter anyway."

"It's not about obvious. It's about you. What you want."

Niles was quiet. His fingers had found the napkin again, folding and unfolding.

"Are we..." He stopped. Started again. "I mean, is this..." He gestured vaguely between them. "What is this?"

Eli didn't answer right away. He could see Niles's brain working—racing, probably. Trying to calculate the right response, the right words, the safest path through the conversation.

"Hey," Eli said gently. "Slow down."

Niles looked at him.

"You're trying to figure out what I want you to say. I can see it." Eli smiled. "Stop. Just tell me what you feel."

Niles opened his mouth. Closed it. His hands were working the napkin again.

"Hey." Eli stilled his hands. "Just answer one question. Do you want to be with me?"

The silence stretched. Niles's hands trembled slightly under Eli's.

"Yes," he said finally. Almost a whisper.

"Okay."

"But I don't —" His voice was barely holding. "I'm not easy, Eli."

"I know."

"And I don't want you to find that out later and wish you hadn't —"

"Niles. I want to be with you too."

Niles stared at him. "You do?"

"Yeah."

"... why?"

Eli laughed — not unkindly. "Because I like you. The actual you."

Niles looked down at their hands. He was quiet for a long time.

"I don't have to try so hard with you," he said. "That's never... I've never had that."

Eli gently reached over and nudged Niles's chin up.

Niles's face flushed. "Sorry. I forgot."

"Don't be sorry. Start over?"

Niles was quiet for a long moment. Then he exhaled.

"I don't have to work so hard. With you. That's never happened before."

Eli didn't say anything right away. He just looked at Niles — and wanted to keep looking. Wanted to keep finding whatever was underneath all that careful stillness.

"So," Eli said, squeezing Niles's hands. "We're together."

"We're together," Niles repeated. A small smile crept onto his face. "Okay."

"Okay."

"What do we do now?"

"Well," Eli leaned back, "first, you're going to finish those dumplings because I'm not letting good food go to waste. Then —" He grinned. "We go to this party and hold hands in front of everyone."

The color drained from Niles's face.

"In front of everyone?"

"Yeah."

Niles pulled his hands back. Not away from Eli — into his own lap, where he could grip them together. His breathing had changed.

"Eli, I can't — that's —" He shook his head. "This is just us. No one's looking. But a room full of people, and my mom, and —"

"Hey." Eli leaned in closer, his eyes steady on Niles's. "I'm not going to drag you in there. That's not what this is."

Niles looked at him.

"But I want you to think about something. Your mom. When she sees us walk in. Together."

"She'll lose her mind."

"She'll be happy, Niles. Like, ugly-cry happy."

Niles almost smiled. Almost. "That's what I'm afraid of."

"Fair." Eli tilted his head. "What about this — we walk in. I hold your hand. If it's too much, you squeeze once and I let go. No questions. No big deal. We just... become two guys standing next to each other."

"You'd do that?"

"Of course I'd do that."

"And you wouldn't be... disappointed?"

"In you?" Eli looked at him like the question didn't make sense. "Niles. You're sitting here holding my hand in a restaurant. You know how big that is?"

"It's terrifying," Niles said quietly. "Even here. Even with no one looking. I keep thinking someone's going to see."

"I know."

"It's not that I don't want to. I just —" He stared at their hands. "It's like every part of me wants to, and every part of me wants to pull away at the same time."

"I know," Eli said again. Not pushing. Just there.

"One squeeze," Niles said, almost to himself. "And you let go."

"That's the deal."

Niles was quiet for a long moment. Then he exhaled — shaky, but real. "Okay."

"Okay." Eli picked up a dumpling with his fingers and held it out. "Now eat. You're going to need your strength for my terrible dancing later."

"You dance?"

"Horribly. It's one of my best qualities."

Niles laughed — barely more than a breath, but his eyes softened. And something in his shoulders released.

They finished eating slowly, talking about small things — Niles's robots, Eli's job, the ridiculousness of New Year's resolutions. By the time they paid the check, it was past nine.

"We should go," Eli said. "Your mom's going to send a search party."

Niles groaned. "She's probably already called three times."

"Then let's not make it four."

They walked out into the cold night. Eli reached for Niles's hand.

He felt the tension immediately — Niles's fingers tightening, his whole body going rigid for a second. But he didn't pull away. He held on.

Eli didn't say anything about it. Didn't draw attention to it. He just held Niles's hand and let him be tense. That's who Niles was. And Eli suspected it's who Niles would always be — the guy who had to fight himself a little every time, and did it anyway.

"Ready?" Eli asked.

"No."

"Good. Me neither."

They got in the car and drove toward the party, hands intertwined on the center console. Niles's grip never loosened. He didn't let go once.

They arrived at the party around nine-thirty.

Eli walked in first, unwinding his scarf with one hand. His other hand was holding Niles's.

The room shifted. Michael noticed. So did everyone else.

Donna, who had been mid-sentence with Angie, went still. Her eyes dropped to their hands. Then back up to her son's face.

She crossed the room in three quick strides.

She went straight to Niles. Took his face in both hands and kissed his cheek. "There you are. I was about to call."

"Sorry, Mom."

"I'm glad you came, sweetheart."

Then she turned to Eli and pulled him into a hug. "And you. Thank you for getting him here."

"Getting him here? Donna, he drove. I was just the hostage."

Donna laughed and swatted his arm. "You know what I mean."

Behind Eli, Niles ducked his head — but not fast enough to hide the smile. Donna caught it. And that was worth more to her than anything either of them could have said.

"We grabbed dinner first," Eli said. "Sorry we're late. Someone needed to read the entire menu twice before ordering."

Niles made a sound — half protest, half laugh. "It was a long menu."

"It was two pages."

"There were a lot of options."

Eli caught the laugh — small as it was — and filed it away. Every time Niles loosened up, even a little, it made Eli want to keep going. Keep pushing just enough to crack him open.

Donna looked between them. "I thought you were just giving him a ride."

"Plans changed." Eli shrugged. "I told him if he was going to kidnap me in his mother's car, the least he could do was feed me first."

Donna's mouth opened. Before she could respond, Niles spoke up from behind Eli.

"He ordered two appetizers and a dessert. I think I know who kidnapped who."

Donna pressed her lips together, her eyes bright. She looked at her son like she was seeing something new.

Eli spun around and stared at Niles, delighted. "Did you just — was that a joke?"

Niles's ears went red. He looked genuinely unsure if it had worked.

"Well," she said, her voice slightly thick. "I'm glad you're here. Both of you."

She drifted back toward Angie, but not before catching Eli's eye. She mouthed something — *thank you* — and Eli nodded.

The hugs had broken them apart. Eli was about to reach for Niles again when he felt it — a tentative hand finding his. Shaky. Deliberate.

He looked down. Niles's fingers were threading through his, slowly, like each one cost him something.

Eli didn't squeeze. Didn't react. Just let Niles hold on.

A few minutes later, Donna pulled Eli aside near the kitchen doorway.

"I need to tell you something," she said, her voice low.

"Okay."

"Brett and I have wondered about Niles for years. Whether he might be... you know." She waved her hand vaguely. "But he never said anything, never showed interest in anyone, and we didn't want to push. We figured if there was something to tell, he'd tell us when he was ready."

Eli nodded, listening.

Seeing my dear boy with you this evening, Eli... You have no idea how much that means to me.

"I know," Eli said quietly.

"Do you really?" She wasn't challenging him. But Eli could feel the mother underneath the elegance and charm. The one who'd been watching over Niles his entire life.

"Donna, I know how difficult it is for him just to be here. We talked about it earlier. Niles is..." He paused, searching for the right words. "Niles is Niles. And I promise you, I will be good to him. As much as he'll let me."

Donna studied him for a long moment. Eli wasn't joking. No playful banter, no deflection. He was serious. She could see it — the untarnished kindness he carried underneath all the humor and the noise. She hadn't expected this for her son. But she could not think of a better man to trust him with.

"Take care of him," she whispered. "Please."

Eli smiled, and the warmth crept back into his face. "I think he's taking care of me."

When she pulled back, she was smiling through tears. "Okay. Enough of that." She dabbed at her eyes. "Go. Be with him. He's probably panicking that I stole you away."

Eli laughed and went to find Niles.

He found him by the food table, methodically arranging crackers on a small plate. Michael and Levi were already approaching.

"Hey, Niles," Michael said. "It's been a while."

Niles nodded, tense. "Yeah. Since..." He didn't finish.

"This is Levi." Michael gestured. "He's a friend. From here."

Levi extended his hand to shake, but Eli grabbed it first as he walked their way.

"Nice to meet you," Eli said, pumping Levi's hand enthusiastically. "Have you tried the shrimp cocktail? It's incredible."

Levi pulled his hand back, laughing, and swatted at Eli's arm. "You're ridiculous."

Niles laughed too—a small, surprised sound. The relief on his face was visible—handshakes with strangers were hard for him. The touch, the eye contact, the pressure of knowing how long to hold on. Eli had seen it coming and intercepted without making it a thing.

Levi caught the quick look Eli gave him. Understood. Said nothing.

The tension had broken before it could build.

Levi turned to Niles. "Hey—have you seen the back patio?"

Niles blinked. "The what?"

"It's like a second-story deck out there. And the moon's almost full tonight." Levi shrugged. "It's quiet. You wanna see?"

Niles looked at Eli, something uncertain in his eyes. Like he suddenly needed permission.

"Go," Eli said. "We'll be right there. Just gonna grab some drinks."

Niles hesitated. Levi was new—a stranger, really. But the door was right there, just off the kitchen. And something about Levi felt... safe. Calm.

"Okay," Niles said quietly.

Levi led the way, and the two of them disappeared through the back door.

Michael turned to Eli. "Niles?" He raised an eyebrow.

Eli gave it right back. "Levi?" He raised his own eyebrow.

Two could play at this game.

Michael's face flushed, and he looked away. "I was just—"

"And since you asked," Eli said, "yes. We're together."

Michael looked back at him. The embarrassment faded, replaced by something warmer. "Really?"

"Really."

"Well—" Michael smiled. "I'm happy for you. Both of you."

"Thanks."

They moved toward the drinks table, grabbing cups and pouring sodas for Levi and Niles.

"So," Eli said casually, "are you and Levi..."

Michael nearly dropped the cup.

He caught it, but soda sloshed over the rim onto his hand. He set it down quickly, but his hands were shaking.

"I don't—what—" He wiped his hand on his jeans. "We're not—I mean—"

"Ahh." Eli nodded slowly. "Haven't talked yet."

"There's nothing to talk about. We're just friends. He's just—I'm not—"

"Michael." Eli's voice was gentle. "It's okay. It's your business, not mine."

Michael stared at the cups, unable to meet Eli's eyes.

"But for what it's worth?" Eli picked up the two sodas he'd poured. "Levi's cute. And he's a catch." He paused. "Believe in yourself."

He walked away toward the back door, leaving Michael standing there, heart pounding.

Believe in yourself.

What did that even mean? What was Eli saying? Was it that obvious? Could everyone see it? Could *Levi* see it?

Michael's mind was racing. But there was no time to think—Eli was already outside, and Levi and Niles were waiting.

He grabbed both cups with unsteady hands and followed.

Graham found Anthony by the fireplace, nursing a glass of something amber.

"Quite a night," Anthony said, not looking away from the room.

Graham followed his gaze. Across the living room, Eli and Niles had returned from the back porch with Michael and Levi — all four of them flushed from the cold, rubbing their hands, Levi still shivering slightly. They clustered near the window now — Eli talking animatedly, Niles angled toward him like Eli was the only fixed point in a room full of noise. Michael and Levi existed in their own orbit — and as Graham watched, Michael's hand came up to Levi's back, rubbing slow circles between his shoulder blades to warm him up. Casual. Unconscious. Like he didn't even know he was doing it.

Anthony glanced at Graham. Graham glanced back.

Neither of them said a word.

"Quite a night," Graham agreed.

"Niles and Eli." Anthony shook his head slowly. "Didn't see that coming."

"Didn't you?"

Anthony considered. "Maybe I did. Eli has a way of drawing people out. And Niles..." He took a sip of his drink. "That boy's been waiting a long time for someone to understand him."

Graham watched Eli lean in to say something to Niles, watched Niles's face relax into something close to a smile. "They're good together."

"They are." Anthony turned slightly, his eyes finding the other pair. "And those two?"

Michael was laughing at something Levi had said. As Graham watched, Levi reached up to brush something off Michael's shoulder—a nothing gesture, barely a touch—and Michael went still for just a second. Just long enough.

"And those two?" Anthony's eyes found the other pair.

Graham watched Michael's hand return to Levi's back. Watched Levi lean into it without thinking.

He didn't answer. Didn't need to. Anthony had been there once too.

They stood in silence, watching. Donna had cornered Brett near the kitchen, gesturing toward Niles and Eli with barely contained joy. Thomas was refilling drinks. Jason was trying to get everyone's attention for some kind of toast, but no one was listening.

They stood in silence for a while, watching. Two old friends who didn't need to say what they were both thinking.

"Michael's leaving Sunday," Graham said.

Anthony nodded. He didn't need to ask what Graham meant by it.

Graham watched Michael lean in to hear something Levi was saying. Watched the way Michael's whole body oriented toward Levi, like a plant toward sunlight. Watched Levi's hands move as he talked, expressive in a way he never was with anyone else.

"Michael's leaving Sunday," Graham said.

Anthony nodded. He didn't need to ask what Graham meant by it.

They stood together, watching. Eli and Niles by the window. Michael and Levi in their own quiet orbit. Donna dabbing at her eyes. The whole messy, loving, chaotic room.

There was a time when Graham would have needed to talk about it — would have needed to name what he was seeing, what he was feeling, what he was afraid of. But that time had passed. He and Anthony had buried husbands. Had survived the worst thing either of them could imagine. Had come out the other side into whatever this was — not whole, maybe, but still here.

Some things didn't need words anymore.

Across the room, Michael said something that made Levi throw his head back and laugh. The sound carried over the noise of the party — bright and unguarded and young.

Anthony put a hand on Graham's shoulder. Graham put his hand over it.

They stayed like that for a while.

"Ten minutes to midnight!" Thomas called out, turning up the volume on the TV.

The room shifted, everyone gravitating toward the living room where the screen showed Times Square—a sea of people, confetti already swirling, the famous ball glittering at the top of its pole.

Michael found himself next to Levi on the couch. They'd barely been apart all night, but now, with midnight approaching, the closeness felt different. Charged.

"You ever been to Times Square for this?" Levi asked.

"No. Have you?"

Levi laughed. "Right. Because my family had money for trips to New York."

"Sorry. Stupid question."

"It's fine." Levi bumped his knee against Michael's. "I've never even been to New York. Never been anywhere, really. Until here."

Michael wanted to say something—something about how Levi should come visit him in Tennessee, how they could go places together, how this didn't have to end just because he was getting on a plane in thirty-six hours.

But the words stuck in his throat.

"Five minutes!" someone shouted.

Eli and Niles had found a spot near the window, slightly apart from the crowd. Eli had his arm around Niles's waist, and Niles was leaning into him—not stiff, not pulling away, just... there. Present. It was the most relaxed Michael had ever seen him.

Graham stood by the fireplace with Anthony, both of them holding drinks they weren't really drinking. Donna had positioned herself where she could see both the TV and Niles, dabbing at her eyes every few minutes. Brett stood beside her, his hand on her back, looking proud in that quiet way dads sometimes did.

Angie and Sonya were near the kitchen doorway. Sonya caught Michael's eye and gave him a nod—*we'll be leaving soon after*. He nodded back. Levi would be going with them.

This was almost over.

"Two minutes!"

The room buzzed with anticipation. Jason was handing out noisemakers. Thomas was pouring champagne into plastic flutes, passing them around. Someone pressed one into Michael's hand, and he took it without thinking.

Levi didn't have one. Michael looked around, spotted another flute on the side table, and grabbed it for him.

"Here."

"Thanks." Levi's fingers brushed his as he took it.

Michael's heart was pounding. This was ridiculous. It was just New Year's Eve. Just a countdown. Just a moment that happened every year, everywhere, to everyone.

But it didn't feel like just anything.

"One minute!"

On the TV, the ball began its descent. The crowd in Times Square roared. In the living room, everyone started gathering closer, forming a loose circle around the screen.

Michael was hyper-aware of Levi beside him. The warmth of him. The way he smelled—something uniquely Levi that Michael couldn't name but would remember. The way his pinky finger was almost touching Michael's on the couch cushion between them.

Just move your hand, Michael thought. *Just take his hand. It's midnight. People do that at midnight.*

But he couldn't.

"Thirty seconds!"

Eli pulled Niles closer. Donna reached for Brett's hand. Thomas and Jason were already wrapped around each other, swaying slightly.

Graham stood alone by the fireplace, his eyes on the TV but seeing something else. Someone else.

"Ten! Nine! Eight!"

The room joined in, voices rising.

"Seven! Six! Five!"

Michael's hand twitched toward Levi's.

"Four! Three! Two!"

Levi's pinky brushed against his. Intentional. Barely there. But unmistakable.

"One! Happy New Year!"

The room erupted. Noisemakers blared. Champagne flutes clinked. On the TV, confetti exploded over Times Square.

Eli turned to Niles.

"Happy New Year," he said. And kissed him.

It was brief. Soft. Barely more than a press of lips. But it was real, and it was in front of everyone, and Niles went completely rigid.

For a second, Eli thought he'd gotten it wrong — pushed too far, too fast, misread everything. Then Niles's hand came up and gripped Eli's arm. Not pushing away. Holding on. Like the room had tilted and Eli was the only solid thing in it.

When Eli pulled back, Niles's eyes were wide. His face was flushed. He looked like he'd forgotten how to breathe.

"You okay?" Eli asked.

Niles nodded. Didn't speak. Couldn't, probably.

Across the room, Donna had both hands pressed to her mouth. Brett put his arm around her and quietly handed her a napkin.

Other couples kissed and hugged and wished each other well. Anthony embraced Graham, holding on for a long moment before letting go.

And Michael and Levi sat on the couch, pinkies still touching, not looking at each other.

The room erupted around them. Noisemakers blared. Champagne flutes clinked. Confetti fell from somewhere — Thomas had rigged something to the ceiling fan, apparently. People were hugging, kissing, shouting over each other. Jason grabbed Thomas and dipped him like they were in a movie. Donna had Brett's face in both hands. Angie kissed Sonya on the forehead.

Someone clapped Michael on the back — Anthony, grinning, saying something about the new year. Then Donna was there, kissing both their cheeks, smelling like champagne and perfume. "Happy New Year, boys." Angie followed, then Thomas, then someone Michael didn't even recognize.

Through all of it, Levi sat beside him. Close. Still.

And then the crowd moved on, and it was just the two of them again.

Michael looked at Levi.

The room was chaos. No one was watching. No one would notice.

He leaned over and kissed Levi on the cheek.

"Happy New Year," he mumbled, the words barely forming because his mouth had forgotten how to work. His heart was slamming so hard he could feel it in his fingertips. He wanted to pull back — needed to pull back in case he'd gotten it completely wrong — but he also wanted to stay right there, to turn Levi's face toward his and kiss him for real. He'd never kissed anyone. Not like that. Not anyone other than his mom and dad when he was little. And yet every nerve in his body was screaming at him to close the distance, to take Levi's face in his hands and just —

But he didn't know how. Didn't know if he was allowed. Didn't know anything except that the kiss on Levi's cheek had felt like something. But it wasn't — it wasn't what he wanted. Well, it was. But he wanted different.

Levi was frozen beside him.

He thought he'd said "Happy New Year" back but he wasn't sure the words actually came out. His cheek burned where Michael's lips had been. He looked away — shy, embarrassed, no — he wasn't embarrassed. He wasn't sure what he was. He just couldn't get his heart to slow down long enough to lean over and return it. To press his lips to Michael's cheek the way Michael had just done. The way everyone else in the room was doing like it was nothing.

It wasn't nothing.

Michael started spiraling. Did he go too far? Was that stupid? Of course it was stupid. Everyone kisses everyone on New Year's. It didn't mean anything. Except it did. And now Levi wasn't looking at him. Why wasn't Levi looking at him? Because it was weird. Because Michael had made it weird. Because —

Why am I this stupid?

Levi saw it. The shift. Michael pulling away, retreating into himself, the light dimming behind his eyes. And without thinking — without planning or considering or weighing a single consequence — Levi reached over and grabbed Michael's hand.

He'd only meant to pull Michael back. To make him look his way. To stop whatever was happening behind Michael's eyes.

But Michael's hand was in his. And time seemed to take a breath.

Michael looked down. At their fingers. At the way Levi's hand wrapped around his, holding on.

Oh my god. His hand.

Levi followed Michael's gaze and realized what he'd done. He hadn't meant to — not consciously. It had just happened. And now he felt the need to let go, to pull away before Michael —

But Michael was holding on.

Michael looked up. And Levi saw it — the fear dissolving, replaced by something else. Michael's head tilted slightly, and his expression shifted from terrified to... Levi didn't know what. But their eyes locked. And something cut through all the noise, all the chaos, all the feelings — like a current pulling them together, impossible to resist.

"Alright, kid. Time to roll."

Sonya's voice sliced through everything.

Michael shook his head like he was clearing fog. Levi looked up — not registering the voice at first, not registering who she was or where he was or what had just happened.

Sonya tilted her head at him. "You okay there, bud?"

Levi blinked. Shook it off. "Uh — yeah. Sorry."

He stood up, and Michael stood with him. They walked to the door together, weaving through the crowd of people still hugging and laughing and making noise.

At the door, Levi pulled on his coat. Sonya and Angie were distributing hugs at the doorway, saying their goodbyes. For a moment, it was just Michael and Levi, half-hidden by the coats and the chaos.

Levi opened his mouth. "Can we —"

Michael snapped back into place. "Text me in the morning, okay? I'll come get you."

"Okay."

Neither of them knew what for. Neither of them cared. They just wanted to be together.

They stood there, the cold air seeping in through the open door, neither of them moving.

"Levi!" Sonya called from the driveway. "Truck's running. Let's go."

"Coming." But Levi didn't move. He was looking at Michael with something raw in his expression. Something that looked a lot like the thing Michael couldn't say.

Then Levi stepped forward and hugged him.

It wasn't like the hugs they'd shared before — quick, casual, the kind of hug friends gave. This one lingered. Levi's arms wrapped tight around Michael's back, and Michael pulled him close, burying his face in Levi's shoulder, breathing him in.

"Happy New Year, Michael," Levi whispered.

"Happy New Year, Levi."

They held on for another moment. Then Levi let go, turned, and walked down the porch steps toward Sonya's truck.

Michael watched him go. Watched him climb into the passenger seat. Watched the truck pull away, taillights disappearing into the dark.

He stood in the doorway until the cold became unbearable, then stepped back inside and closed the door.

The party was winding down. People were gathering coats, saying goodbyes, making plans for the new year.

Graham appeared at his elbow. "You okay?"

Michael nodded. He didn't trust his voice.

Graham put a hand on his shoulder and squeezed. "Come on. Let's go home."

They said their goodbyes—a kiss on the cheek from Donna, a firm handshake from Anthony. Eli made his way over and pulled Michael into a tight hug. Everyone else was busy with their own goodbyes, so no one noticed when Eli said, "Believe in yourself, Michael."

When he pulled back, Niles gave a small wave from across the room. Michael waved back.

The drive home was quiet. Graham didn't push. Didn't ask questions. Just drove through the dark streets while Michael stared out the window at the new year stretching ahead of him.

Tomorrow was his last full day.

Chapter Seventeen

NEW YEAR'S Day was quiet.

Michael woke late, the house still. Graham was somewhere—probably his study, probably staring at the manuscript he still hadn't touched. The silence felt heavy. Full of all the things that would happen today and couldn't be stopped.

He reached for his phone.

You up?

The response came almost immediately.

Yeah

Want to hang out?

Yeah

Pick you up in an hour

He showered. Got dressed. Stood in front of the mirror for too long, trying to make his hair do something it didn't want to do. Gave up. Went downstairs.

Graham was in the kitchen, tea cup in hand, staring out the window at the snow like it was his usual perch.

"I'm going to pick up Levi," Michael said. "Hang out for a while."

Graham nodded. "Take your time."

"You sure?"

"Michael." Graham turned to look at him. "It's your last day. Spend it however you want."

Michael swallowed. "Okay."

"Just be back for dinner. We'll do something. Order in."

"Okay."

He grabbed the keys and headed for the door.

"Michael."

He turned.

Graham was still standing by the window, tea cup in hand. He looked tired. Sad, maybe. But also something else.

"Have a good day," Graham said quietly.

Michael nodded. He didn't trust his voice.

Susan answered their door not ten seconds after Michael knocked.

"Levi's almost ready," she said, stepping aside to let him in. "You boys have plans?"

"Not really. Just... hanging out."

She studied him for a moment—that look mothers had, the one that saw more than you wanted them to see.

"Well," she said. "Have fun. Text me if you'll be late for dinner."

"We will," Levi said from the hallway, pulling on his coat.

Michael hesitated at the door. Dinner. Graham had said something about ordering in tonight. His last night.

"Actually, would it be okay if Levi stayed for dinner? It's my last —"

He stopped. The word stuck.

Susan looked at him. Then at Levi, who had gone very still by the door.

"Of course, honey," she said quietly. She hugged Levi — longer than usual, Michael noticed — then turned and hugged Michael too, which he hadn't expected.

"Just be careful on the roads. They're still icy."

"I will. I have to pack for my flight in the morning, anyway."

The words were more difficult to say, somehow. Levi looked away.

"Go on, then," Susan said gently. "Both of you."

They walked out into the cold, breath fogging in the air.

"Your mom's cool."

"She's something." But Levi was smiling.

Michael started the car. "So. Where do you want to go?"

Levi shrugged. "I don't know. Where's even open?"

"Good question."

They drove.

. . .

Everything was closed.

The coffee shop—closed. The diner—closed. The pizza place, the sandwich shop, the little café near the bookstore—all closed. New Year's Day, and the whole town had decided to stay home.

"This is ridiculous," Michael muttered, pulling out of yet another empty parking lot.

"Maybe we should just go back to Graham's."

"No." The word came out sharper than Michael intended. "I mean—I want to do something. Go somewhere. Just us."

Levi looked at him. Michael kept his eyes on the road.

"Okay," Levi said quietly.

They drove in silence for a few more minutes. Then Michael spotted it—the Dairy Queen sign, lit up against the gray sky.

"No way," he said.

"Is it open?"

"Only one way to find out."

He pulled into the parking lot. One car sat near the entrance. The lights inside were on.

"Holy shit," Levi said. "It's actually open."

The guy behind the counter looked like he'd rather be anywhere else.

He was maybe twenty-two, twenty-three. Stubble on his jaw, dark circles under his eyes, shoulders slumped in a way that suggested he'd given up on something a long time ago. The name tag on his shirt said "Derek."

"Help you?" Derek asked, not really looking at them.

"You're open," Michael said. "On New Year's Day."

"Yep."

"That's... dedication."

Derek shrugged. "Nowhere else to be."

Michael glanced at Levi. Something had shifted in his face — quiet, careful. The look he got when something hit close.

"We'll take some fries," Levi said. "And two vanilla cones."

Michael raised an eyebrow. "That's it? Vanilla again?"

"I ordered for both of us. You're getting vanilla."

"I didn't agree to that."

"Too bad." Levi turned back to Derek. "Two vanilla cones."

Derek almost smiled. Almost. He rang them up and handed over the receipt.

"Be a few minutes on the fries."

"No rush," Levi said. "We've got time."

They found a booth near the window. The restaurant was empty except for them—red plastic seats, fluorescent lights, the smell of fryer grease and soft-serve. Outside, the sky was the color of dirty cotton.

"This is depressing," Michael said.

"I kind of like it."

"You would."

Levi kicked him under the table. Michael kicked back.

Derek brought the fries and the cones, set them down without a word, and retreated behind the counter. He pulled out his phone and started scrolling, clearly done with human interaction for the day.

"You think he's okay?" Levi asked quietly.

Michael looked at Derek — the slumped shoulders, the hollow eyes. "I don't know. Probably not."

Levi picked at a fry, not eating it. "When things were bad for us, people could tell. They'd just..." He shrugged. "Keep walking. Or stare. Like they wanted to help but didn't know how, so they just — didn't."

He was quiet for a second.

"I don't know what his deal is. But it's not — we don't have to fix anything. Just not pretend someone's invisible." He set the fry down. "That's the worst part. When people act like you're not there."

Michael watched him. Levi was more concerned with some stranger behind a counter than he was with himself. That was the thing. That was what got Michael.

He didn't know all of Levi's story. Levi had told him some. Graham had shared a few things, carefully, like he wasn't sure how much was his to give. But Michael knew enough. Knew it had been bad. Knew Levi and his mom and Lucy had gone through things Michael couldn't really picture, no matter how hard he tried.

And here he was — worried about some random guy pulling a shift alone at the Dairy Queen on New Year's Day.

Michael had always tried to be kind. His mom had drilled that into him since he was little. Be nice. Be respectful. Treat people the way you want to be treated. But this was different. This wasn't politeness. Levi was talking about what it felt like when people looked right through you. When they saw you struggling and just — kept going. Like you weren't worth the effort of stopping.

Michael couldn't relate. Not really. His life wasn't perfect — it sucked sometimes, sure. But he'd always had his friends. His room. His mom and dad. A refrigerator with food in it and a bed that was his and a door he could close. He'd never had to wonder if any of that would disappear.

And none of that seemed to matter as much as the fact that the person sitting across from him knew what it felt like to have none of it.

That hurt. More than Michael expected. He hadn't let himself sit with it before — not like this. He'd heard the facts, processed them the way you process something awful that happened to someone else. Not you. Someone *over there*. Away. But watching Levi feel for this guy — a guy they didn't even know, a guy who might just be picking up an extra shift for all they knew — something about it made the whole thing real in a way it hadn't been before.

Levi knew the look. And Michael could tell.

What's more, what Michael felt sitting there watching Levi worry about someone else's pain — it wasn't the fluttery, nervous thing he'd been trying to figure out for two weeks. It wasn't the racing heart or the sweaty palms or the way his brain short-circuited every time Levi smiled at him. It was quieter than that. Steadier. It was the feeling that if he could take every hard thing Levi had ever been through and carry it himself, he would. Without thinking. Without hesitating. That Levi being okay mattered more to him than whether he himself was okay.

He didn't have a word for it. Or maybe he did, but it was tangled up with all the other words he wasn't ready for yet. So he left it unnamed. Let it sit in his chest, heavy and warm, and didn't try to make it smaller than it was.

"So we're just nice to him," Michael said.

"Yeah. That's all."

"So," Levi said eventually. "Nashville."

"Yeah."

"What's it like?"

Michael shrugged. "It's fine. Hot in the summer. Lots of music everywhere. My school's okay."

"You have friends there?"

"Some. Not like—" He stopped.

"Not like what?"

Not like you, Michael thought. But he couldn't say that.

"Just different," he said instead. "It's different there."

Levi nodded slowly. "You excited to go back?"

"Not really."

The words hung in the air. Levi stared at his ice cream cone, not eating it.

"I'm enrolling in school here," Levi said. "After break. Sonya helped my mom figure out the paperwork."

"That's good."

"Yeah. It's weird, though. Being in one place. Knowing I'll be there for a while."

"Weird how?"

Levi was quiet for a moment. "I don't know. Like... I keep waiting for something to go wrong. For us to have to leave again."

Michael didn't know what to say to that. He tried to imagine it—never knowing if you'd have a place to sleep, never knowing if you'd eat, always waiting for the next disaster. He couldn't.

"You won't have to leave," he said finally. "You're here now. You're staying."

Levi looked at him. "You don't know that."

"I do."

"How?"

"Because Graham won't let it happen. And Sonya and Angie won't let it happen. And—" Michael's voice caught. "And I won't let it happen."

Levi's eyes went bright. He looked away quickly, blinking.

"You're in Tennessee," he said. "What are you going to do from there?"

"I don't know. Something. Anything."

Levi laughed—a broken sound. "You're ridiculous."

"So I've been told." But Michael reached across the table and put his hand on Levi's wrist. "Levi. I'd never let that happen to you again."

The afternoon stretched on. They talked about everything — music, movies, the Oltrarno books, school, the party last night, Eli and Niles.

"They looked happy," Levi said. "At midnight."

"They did."

"When Eli kissed him. That was..." Levi shook his head. "I don't know. Brave, I guess."

"Yeah."

Michael thought about that moment. The way Eli had just turned to Niles and done it — no hesitation, no fear. Like they had been together for years. It wasn't anything crazy. Just a kiss. But it was real, and it was honest, and everyone saw it.

Michael had kissed Levi on the cheek at midnight. And it had nearly short-circuited both of them. But that wasn't the same thing. That was something he could hide behind — just a New Year's thing, just what people do. He'd given himself an out, and he hated that he needed one.

Why couldn't he just —

He thought about his uncle. Graham and Simon, together for decades. Michael had grown up with them, spent summers in their house, never thought twice about it. Simon was just Simon. Graham was just Graham. They were just... them.

He thought about Marcus, his friend at school. Out since freshman year. A few idiots gave him shit, but mostly people didn't care. Marcus had a boyfriend now. They held hands in the hallway. No one said anything.

He thought about his parents. His mom, who'd never said a single negative thing about Graham and Simon. His dad — the "man's man," the guy who watched football and drank beer and did all the things dads were supposed to do — who'd never had a problem with any of it. Who trusted Graham and Simon with his son, every summer, without question.

So why was this so hard?

And then it happened. Not slowly, not in pieces, not the way he'd been circling it for weeks — tiptoeing around the edges, brushing up against it, pulling away. It came all at once, like a wall giving way.

Gay.

He was gay.

That word. It punched like a fist. Not because it was wrong. Because it was true. Because it had always been true, and he'd spent so long running from it that finally stopping felt like slamming into something at full speed.

And for one second — one brief, blinding second — he felt free. Like a door had opened and light was pouring through and he could finally, *finally* breathe.

But the feeling didn't last.

Because the boy sitting across from him — the one who had been through hell and come out the other side still caring about strangers, still worrying about some guy behind a counter instead of himself. The boy who'd gone from flinching at snowballs to throwing them back. Who got so lost in his uncle's stories that his whole face changed. Who carried his little sister on his back and never once complained about any of it. Who had every right to be angry and bitter and closed off and was none of those things. The boy whose wrist Michael had grabbed twenty minutes ago and promised *I'd never let that happen to you again* — that boy was sitting three feet away from him.

And Michael wanted nothing more than to reach across the table and take his hand and say *I'm in love with you.*

And that — *that* — scared the shit out of him more than anything ever had.

More than the word. More than what his friends might think or his parents might say or what it meant for the rest of his life. None of that mattered. What mattered was Levi. What mattered was the possibility — the unbearable, paralyzing possibility — that he could say it and Levi could look at him with confusion, or pity, or worse. That he could crack himself open right here in this Dairy Queen and Levi could say *I don't feel that way.*

That was the fear. Not the label. Not the world.

Levi.

Michael's gaze drifted toward the window. The snow was falling again — light, steady, the kind that didn't seem like much but would cover everything by morning. He stared at it without seeing it. His throat was tight. His eyes were burning and he didn't know when that had started.

He tried to hold it together. Tried to push it all back down, the way he'd been doing for weeks. But the wall was gone now, and everything was flooding in, and he couldn't —

"Michael?"

He didn't hear it.

"Hey. Michael."

Levi watched him from across the table. Michael was somewhere else — his eyes fixed on the snow outside, but not really looking at it. His jaw was tight. And his eyes — Levi could see them going glassy, the edges reddening in a way that had nothing to do with the cold.

Levi almost asked if he was okay. The words were right there, automatic. *You okay?* But he stopped himself. Because he knew — from the shelters, from the car, from every time some well-meaning stranger had looked at his mother and asked that useless question — that asking someone who was clearly not okay if they were okay was the most pointless thing in the world.

So instead, he reached across the table and touched Michael's hand. Lightly. Just his fingertips on Michael's knuckles.

Michael blinked. Came back. Looked down at Levi's fingers, then up at Levi.

Levi could see it now — whatever had been building behind Michael's eyes all afternoon had broken through. He looked terrified. Lost. Like he'd been holding something together with both hands and it had finally slipped.

"I'm here," Levi said quietly. "Whatever it is. I'm here."

Michael opened his mouth. Closed it. His chin trembled — just barely, just enough — and he looked away, ashamed of it.

"I —" His voice cracked. He pressed his lips together hard. Tried again. "I have to tell you something."

Levi waited. He didn't pull his hand away.

"I'm —" Michael stopped. His breath hitched. He was staring at the table between them, at the empty fry basket, at Levi's fingers still resting on his hand. "I'm gay."

The word came out small. Broken. Nothing like the grand revelation it was supposed to be. Nothing like Marcus at school, confident and sure. Nothing like Eli, who wore himself like armor. It was just a boy in a booth, barely holding it together, saying the truest thing he'd ever said.

"And I'm sorry I didn't — I should have told you before. I should have said something. I've known — I think I've known for a while and I just couldn't —" He was spiraling now, the words tumbling out faster than he could organize them. "And I know it's stupid. I know I have it easy compared to — I mean, you've been through actual shit, real shit, and here I am crying in a Dairy Queen because I can't —"

His voice broke.

"I'm sorry. God, I'm so sorry. I just — I don't want this to ruin anything. Between us. I don't want you to think — I just — I'm sorry, I can't stop —"

He pressed the heels of his hands into his eyes. His shoulders were shaking.

Levi sat very still.

He heard everything Michael said. All of it. The word — *gay* — registered somewhere deep, somewhere he'd come back to later, somewhere that meant something enormous for both of them. But he set it aside. Not because it didn't matter. Because something else mattered more right now.

Michael was in pain. Real pain. The kind Levi recognized — the kind that came from carrying something too heavy for too long and finally letting go. He'd seen it in his mother. He'd felt it in himself. He knew what it looked like when someone broke, and he knew that the worst thing you could do was try to fix it. You couldn't fix it. You couldn't take it away or make it smaller or explain it into something manageable.

You could just be there.

No one had taught him this. No book, no therapist, no well-meaning adult. He just knew. The way you know how to breathe, how to reach for something in the dark.

Levi gently took one of Michael's hands and pulled it away from his face. Michael resisted — just for a second — but Levi held on. Wrapped his fingers around Michael's and didn't let go.

Michael looked at him through the blur, his face a mess, his breath uneven.

With his other hand, Levi reached across and wiped a tear from Michael's cheek. Then, slowly, he brushed the hair out of Michael's eyes.

He'd never done that before. Never had the courage. But he wasn't thinking about courage right now. He wasn't thinking about what it meant or what Michael might read into it or what any of it said about him or them or whatever they were. He was thinking about the person in front of him, and how much he wanted that person to know he wasn't alone.

"You don't have to be sorry," Levi said softly. "Not to me. Not ever."

Michael's face crumpled. A sound came out of him — not a word, not quite a sob, something in between — and he gripped Levi's hand like it was the only thing keeping him from going under.

They sat like that.

The fluorescent lights hummed. The soft-serve machine whirred behind the counter. Outside, the snow kept falling, quiet and steady, covering everything.

Derek was somewhere in the back. The parking lot was empty. The sky was getting dark.

And two boys sat across from each other in a booth by the window, hands intertwined over an empty tray, saying nothing. Because there was nothing left to say. Not today. Not yet.

But Levi didn't let go.

And neither did Michael.

Chapter Eighteen

THE OLTRARNO

THE KNOCK CAME BEFORE DAWN.

Marco woke to voices in the corridor—low, urgent, the kind of voices that meant trouble. He lay still in his small room, listening. Alessandro's door opened. Footsteps. More voices, too quiet to make out.

Then silence.

Marco waited. Counted his heartbeats. Finally, he rose and crept to his door, easing it open just enough to see.

Alessandro stood in the main room, still in his nightclothes, reading a letter by candlelight. His face was pale. His hands were shaking.

"Alessandro?"

He looked up. For a moment, his face was unguarded — frightened, even — before the mask returned.

"Go back to bed, Marco."

"What's happened?"

Alessandro didn't answer. He read the letter again, lips moving slightly, as if trying to make the words say something different.

"Alessandro. Please."

A long pause. Then: "My father is ill. There's been... trouble. With the Medici. With everything." He folded the letter carefully, precisely, the way he did everything. "I have to go home."

Marco's chest went cold. "When?"

"Today. There's a coach coming to collect me this afternoon." Alessandro looked around the room—at the paintings on the walls, the brushes in their jars, the half-finished canvas by the window. His whole life, contained in these few rooms. "I have to pack. I have to—"

"I'll come with you."

"No." The word was sharp. Final. Alessandro softened it with a breath. "No, Marco. You need to stay here. The Academy—I'll speak with the maestro before I leave. I'll arrange for you to be taken on as a full pupil. You can remain in these apartments. I'll make sure of it."

"I don't care about the Academy. I don't care about—"

"You have to care." Alessandro crossed the room in three quick strides and took Marco's face in his hands. His palms were cold. His eyes were bright with something he was fighting to contain. "Listen to me. This is your chance. Everything we talked about—everything you came here for. You cannot throw it away for—"

He stopped. Couldn't say the words.

For me.

Marco reached up and covered Alessandro's hands with his own. "How long?"

"I don't know."

"A week? A month?"

"I don't know." Alessandro's voice cracked. He pulled away, turning toward the window so Marco couldn't see his face. "My father's enemies are circling. If Piero falls—and he will fall, everyone knows it—then anyone connected to the Medici will be in danger. My family has been too close for too long. We may have to leave Florence entirely. Go south. Rome, perhaps, or further."

Rome. Further. Words that meant gone. Words that meant *not coming back.*

"You'll come back," Marco said. It wasn't a question. He needed it not to be a question.

Alessandro was quiet for a long moment. When he spoke, the steadiness was gone from his voice.

"I want to. God, Marco, I want to."

But he didn't say *I will.*

The coach arrived midday.

Marco helped carry Alessandro's things—a single trunk, hastily packed. Some clothes. His best brushes. A few small paintings he couldn't bear to leave behind. Everything else would stay. The apartments, the studio, the life he'd built here. All of it suspended, waiting for a return that might never come.

They stood in the courtyard, breath fogging in the cold air. The coachman was loading the trunk. They had minutes. Maybe less.

"I'll write," Alessandro said. "As often as I can."

Marco nodded. His throat was too tight to speak.

"But you have to understand—" Alessandro glanced at the coachman, at the windows above them where anyone might be watching. "The letters may be read. Intercepted. I won't be able to say..."

What I feel. What you mean to me. Any of it.

"I understand," Marco managed.

"I'll write about art. About your work. About the Academy." Alessandro's eyes held Marco's, trying to communicate everything his words couldn't. "If I say something that seems strange—something that doesn't quite fit—"

"I'll understand."

"Will you?"

Marco stepped closer. Close enough that their shoulders almost touched. Close enough that he could smell the familiar scent of linseed oil and soap that clung to Alessandro's clothes.

"I'll understand," he said again. "I'll read between the lines. I'll find you there."

Alessandro's composure cracked. Just for a moment. He reached out and gripped Marco's arm — hard, desperate — and didn't let go.

"Don't forget," he said. "Promise me you won't forget."

"How could I forget?"

The coachman cleared his throat. "Signore. We must go."

Alessandro released Marco's arm. Stepped back. Became, once again, the composed young nobleman the world expected him to be.

"Work hard," he said. His voice was steady now, betraying nothing. "Make the maestro proud. Make me proud."

"I will."

Alessandro climbed into the coach. The door closed. The horses stirred.

And then he was gone.

Marco stood in the courtyard until the sound of hooves faded to nothing. Until the sun passed its peak and began its slow descent toward the hills. Until his fingers went numb from the cold.

Then he went back inside, climbed the stairs to the empty apartments, and stood in the doorway of Alessandro's room.

The bed was unmade. A shirt lay crumpled on the chair—one Alessandro had decided not to pack. The air still smelled like him.

Marco picked up the shirt. Pressed it to his face. Breathed.

He hadn't cried since his mother died. He'd made sure of that — held it in, swallowed it down, refused to give anyone the satisfaction.

He couldn't hold it now.

The weeks that followed were the hardest of Marco's life.

He threw himself into his work. What else was there to do? The maestro had taken him on as a full pupil—Alessandro's final gift—and Marco was determined to prove himself worthy. He arrived at the maestro's studio before dawn and stayed until the light failed. He ground pigments until his arms ached. He sketched until his fingers cramped. He painted like he was trying to outrun something. Canvas after canvas, each one better than the last.

The other students noticed. Some resented him—this country boy who'd risen so quickly, who'd been the favorite of the brilliant Alessandro di Rinaldi. Others admired him. A few even sought his company, inviting him to taverns and gatherings and the kind of social events that Alessandro had always navigated with ease.

Marco declined them all. He wasn't interested in making friends. He wasn't interested in anything except the work—and the letters.

The first one arrived three weeks after Alessandro left.

Marco's hands trembled as he broke the seal. The letter was short—painfully short—and written in Alessandro's careful, elegant hand.

Marco—

The journey was long but uneventful. My father's condition is unchanged. We wait, as all of Florence waits, to see what the coming months will bring.

I trust you are working hard and making progress with your studies. The maestro speaks highly of your dedication. This does not surprise me. I always knew you had the talent; you needed only the opportunity to let it flourish.

Continue to practice your perspective drawings. Remember what I told you about the vanishing point—how all lines must converge toward a single, fixed horizon. This is true in art as in life. Keep your eyes on the horizon, Marco. Do not let the chaos of the present obscure your view of what lies ahead.

I remain, as always, your friend and teacher—

Alessandro

Marco read the letter three times. Then a fourth. Then a fifth.

On the surface, it was nothing. Polite. Distant. The kind of letter a mentor might send to a former student. Anyone who intercepted it would find nothing suspicious—just art instruction and vague pleasantries.

But Marco knew better.

Keep your eyes on the horizon. Do not let the chaos of the present obscure your view of what lies ahead.

It wasn't about perspective drawings. It was about them. About hope. About holding on even when everything seemed uncertain.

Alessandro couldn't say *I love you* or *I miss you* or *wait for me*. But he could say this.

Marco pressed the letter to his chest and closed his eyes.

I understand, he thought. *I'll find you there.*

The letters continued, arriving every few weeks—sometimes more frequently, sometimes with long gaps that made Marco sick with worry. Each one followed the same pattern: news of Alessandro's family (carefully vague), inquiries about Marco's progress (warmly encouraging), and instructions about art (loaded with hidden meaning).

Pay attention to the way light falls through a window in late afternoon, Alessandro wrote in February.

> *There is a quality to it—golden, almost warm—that cannot be replicated at any other hour. I find myself watching for it each day, even here, so far from our studios. It reminds me of better times.*

Our studios. Not *my* studios. *Our.*

Marco watched the light every afternoon after that. Let it fall across his face the way Alessandro must be letting it fall across his. It was the closest they could come to touching.

In March, the political situation worsened. Piero de' Medici's grip on the city was failing. Savonarola's influence grew stronger by the day. The letters began arriving less frequently, and when they did, they were shorter. More cautious.

The situation here remains uncertain, Alessandro wrote in early April

> *My father speaks of leaving Florence altogether—perhaps for Rome, perhaps further still. Nothing is decided. I am told to be patient, but patience has never been my strength.*
>
> *Continue your work, Marco. Let the brush be your voice*

when words fail you. Let the canvas hold what cannot be spoken aloud. Art endures when all else falls away. Remember this.

Marco did remember. He painted like a man possessed—canvas after canvas, each one better than the last. The maestro praised him. The other students whispered about his talent. Collectors began to take notice.

But none of it mattered. Not really. Because every night, Marco returned to the empty apartments, sat in Alessandro's chair, and read the letters by candlelight. Searching for meaning. Searching for hope. Searching for any sign that this separation would not last forever.

The last letter arrived in late May.

It was different from the others. Longer. More reckless. Marco could sense the desperation in every line, the way Alessandro's careful control was finally slipping.

Marco—

I write this knowing it may be my last letter for some time. My father has made his decision. We leave for Rome within the week. The roads are dangerous; travel will be slow. I do not know when I will be able to write again, or if letters will even reach you from such a distance.

I have thought often, these past months, about what I might say to you if I could speak freely. If there were no eyes watching, no ears listening, no danger in the truth. I have composed a thousand letters in my mind—letters I will never send, letters that exist only in the space between what I feel and what I am permitted to say.

But I will say this, and trust that you will understand:

Do you remember the evening we walked along the Arno, just before sunset? The way the light turned the water to gold, and the bridges seemed to float above their own reflections? You said it looked like a painting. I said the painting could never capture it—could never capture the way the air smelled, or the sound of the bells from Santo Spirito, or the feeling of walking beside you with nowhere else I needed to be.

That evening lives in me still. It is the horizon I look toward when the present grows too dark. It is the vanishing point where all my hopes converge.

You asked me once if I believed we would see each other again. I did not answer, because I did not know. I still do not know. The future is uncertain, and I have learned not to make promises I cannot keep.

But I will tell you what I do believe:

I believe that some things are stronger than distance. Stronger than time. Stronger than the chaos of politics and the cruelty of fate. I believe that what we found in each other was rare and true, and that such things do not simply disappear because circumstances demand it.

So I ask you this: remain hopeful. Not blindly—I know you are too wise for that—but deliberately. Consciously. As an act of will, even when the evidence suggests otherwise. Hope is a choice, Marco. It is perhaps the only choice that matters.

Permission to remain hopeful. I grant it to you. I grant it to myself.

Until we meet again—and I must believe we will—

Yours, Alessandro

Marco read the letter until he had memorized every word. Until the paper grew soft from handling. Until the ink began to blur from the tears he couldn't stop.

Permission to remain hopeful.

It wasn't a promise. Alessandro was too honest for false promises. But it was something better: a declaration. A commitment. A refusal to let go, even when letting go would be easier.

Marco folded the letter carefully and placed it with the others—a stack of pages that had become his most precious possession. Then he walked to the window and looked out over the rooftops of the Oltrarno, toward the river he could not see but knew was there.

Somewhere beyond the horizon, Alessandro was preparing to leave. Packing his life into trunks. Saying goodbye to the only city he'd ever known.

But he was not saying goodbye to Marco. Not really. Not in any way that mattered.

Permission to remain hopeful.

Marco pressed his hand to the glass. The sun was setting, and the light on the rooftops had turned the color of the ochre he mixed every morning in the studio. Somewhere out there, Alessandro might be watching the same sunset. Thinking the same thoughts. Holding onto the same fragile, stubborn hope.

"I'll wait," Marco whispered to no one. To everyone. To the boy who was too far away to hear. "However long it takes. I'll wait."

The light faded. The stars emerged. And Marco remained at the window, watching the horizon, refusing to look away.

Chapter Nineteen

TWO WEEKS FELT like two months.

Michael stared at his phone, rereading the last few messages for the third time that hour. He'd been doing this constantly — scrolling back, analyzing every word, every response time, every emoji or lack thereof, looking for some sign that things were different. That he'd broken something.

Because he'd told Levi. He'd actually said it — out loud, in a Dairy Queen, while crying into his hands like a child. And Levi had held his hand and brushed the hair out of his eyes and said *you don't have to be sorry.* And then... they'd driven home. And Michael had packed. And the next morning, Graham had driven him to the airport in the dark, and that was it.

They hadn't talked about it.

Not really. Not the thing itself. The first text came from Levi, that Sunday afternoon, while Michael was still in the air.

> Hope the flight's okay. Text me when you land.

And Michael had, and they'd talked that night — about the flight, about Nashville, about nothing — and the conversation had felt almost normal except for the places where it wasn't. The slight pauses before Levi responded. The way Michael kept starting sentences and deleting them. The careful, deliberate way they both avoided the word *gay* or *Dairy Queen* or *are we okay* or any of the hundred things that sat between every line.

They texted every day. Sometimes a lot. Sometimes just a few messages before one of them trailed off. It followed a pattern Michael had come to recognize: easy in the morning, when the day was ahead of them and there was stuff to talk about — school, Eli, the weather, whatever. Harder at night, when the distractions fell away and the quiet crept in and Michael lay on his bed staring at the ceiling, wanting to type things he couldn't figure out how to say.

How was your day?

Good. Yours?

Fine.

Fine. He hated that word. It was the door they both kept closing.

One night — a Tuesday, maybe, or a Wednesday, the days had started blurring together — Michael gave up pretending.

I miss you

He stared at it after he sent it. Three words. Not the three words trapped in his chest, but close enough to make his heart pound.

The dots appeared. Disappeared. Appeared again.

I miss you too

Michael waited for more. There wasn't more.

But Levi had typed it fast. Almost immediately. Like he'd been waiting for permission to say it.

Michael set the phone on his chest and stared at the ceiling. The house was quiet — his parents asleep down the hall, the familiar hum of the refrigerator, the occasional car passing on the street outside. All the sounds of home that didn't feel like home anymore.

He picked the phone up. Put it down. Picked it up again. His thumbs hovered over the keyboard, trying to find the next sentence — the one that would crack open the door they'd been carefully keeping shut for two weeks.

He didn't find it.

Talk tomorrow?

Yeah. Talk tomorrow.

Night Levi.

Night Michael.

He set the phone on the nightstand and rolled onto his side. Pulled the blanket up. Closed his eyes.

The words were right there. Every night, they were right there.

A thousand miles away, Levi set his phone face-down on the mattress beside him and stared at the dark ceiling.

I miss you too.

He'd typed it without thinking. The truest thing he'd said all day, and it had taken no effort at all. It was everything after that was impossible.

He'd wanted to say more. Had started to, twice — thumbs moving, then stopping, then deleting. What was he supposed to write? *I think about you constantly? I replay the Dairy Queen every night? When you told me you were gay, something inside me broke open and I still don't know what to do with it?*

He couldn't say any of that. Not through a phone. Not in words that could be screenshotted and saved and reread out of context. Some things needed a face. Needed breath. Needed the other person *there.*

He rolled over and stared at the wall. The room was dark. The house was quiet. His mom and Lucy were asleep in the next room.

He grabbed his phone.

The screen lit up, too bright, and he squinted at it. Their conversation stared back at him. *Night Michael. Night Levi.* Finished. Done. The door closed again, the way it closed every night.

But tonight he didn't want it closed.

He didn't type a word. Didn't trust himself with words. He just sent a single hug emoji and set the phone face-down on the mattress. Turned off the lamp.

There. It was out there.

His heart was hammering like he'd just sprinted a mile, which was stupid. It was an emoji. People sent them all the time. It didn't have to mean anything.

Except it did.

Michael heard the buzz in the dark.

He'd almost been asleep — that hazy edge where thoughts start dissolving into nothing — but his hand found the phone before his brain caught up. He blinked against the bright screen, eyes adjusting.

A hug emoji. That was all. Just the small, simple image of two arms holding on.

Something flickered in his chest. Warm. Quiet. The smallest spark of a thing he'd been afraid had gone out.

He couldn't help it. He smiled.

He sent one back. Set the phone down. Rolled over and pulled the blanket up.

Sleep finally came easy.

He lay there for a long time.

Sleep didn't come. He hadn't expected it to. His body was tired — school had started, and the newness of it was exhausting in ways he hadn't anticipated. New hallways, new faces, new routines. A locker with a combination he kept forgetting. Teachers who didn't know his name yet. Kids who looked at him and saw the new kid, the quiet one, the one who ate lunch alone and didn't seem to mind.

He did mind. He just didn't know how to say so.

But the tiredness in his body and the noise in his head were two different things, and right now his head was winning.

He rolled onto his side. Reached for the pillow — the extra one, the one he kept against the wall. He pulled it close without thinking, the way he'd been doing for weeks. Months, maybe. Since before the barn house, before Portland, before any of this.

It had started in the car.

Those nights when his mom drove until she couldn't drive anymore, then pulled over in some parking lot or rest stop and told them to sleep. Lucy would curl up in the backseat with her stuffed rabbit, out in minutes. His mom would lean her seat back and close her eyes, though Levi knew she wasn't really sleeping — just lying still, trying to hold herself together until morning.

And Levi would sit there, cramped and cold, his jacket wadded up against the window, reaching for something that wasn't there. His arms would close around nothing and he'd pull it toward his chest anyway — the emptiness, the absence of comfort — because the motion itself was all he had. The act of holding on, even when there was nothing to hold.

At the shelters, it was a blanket. Rolled up tight, pressed against his chest. At the barn house, it became a pillow. And somewhere along the way — he couldn't pinpoint exactly when — the pillow became Michael.

Not consciously. Not at first. It just happened. He'd be falling asleep, that hazy space where his guard dropped and his mind went soft, and he'd pull the pillow close and something in his chest would ease. And he'd realize he was imagining Michael's warmth. Michael's shoulder. The way Michael smelled — laundry detergent and something else, something clean and specific that Levi couldn't name but would recognize anywhere.

He didn't have a shirt. Didn't have a hoodie or a scarf or anything that actually carried Michael's scent. He had nothing except memory. So every night he rebuilt Michael from scratch — the weight of him, the warmth, the solid steady *realness* — and held on until sleep finally came.

It was embarrassing. Childish, probably. A nearly sixteen-year-old boy clutching a pillow in the dark, pretending it was someone else.

But he couldn't stop.

The pretending felt different. Heavier. Complex.

Because Michael had told him.

I'm gay.

Two words. Sitting in a Dairy Queen with melted ice cream and cold fries between them, tears running down his face, voice breaking, apologizing for it like it was something that needed forgiving. And Levi had held his hand and wiped his cheek and brushed the hair out of his eyes and said *you don't have to be sorry.*

But he hadn't said anything else.

He hadn't said: *Me too.*

Or: *I think I might be.*

Or: *When you said that, something inside me wanted to tell you as well.*

He'd just... been there. Held Michael's hand. Let him cry. And then they'd driven home and said goodbye and Michael had gotten on a plane and now they were a thousand miles apart, texting *fine* and *miss you* and hug emojis like that was enough.

It wasn't enough.

Levi pressed his face into the pillow and tried to think clearly. Tried to separate the tangle of feelings into something he could understand.

Michael was gay. That was a fact now. Not a guess, not a hope, not a maybe. Michael had said it out loud, to him, and it had cost him everything.

And Levi had felt — what? Relief? Recognition? The terrifying thrill of a door swinging open that he'd assumed was locked?

All of it. None of it. He didn't know.

He knew what he felt when he held the pillow. He knew what he felt when Michael's name lit up his phone. He knew what he'd felt at midnight on New Year's Eve when Michael kissed his cheek — the shock of it, the heat, the way his whole body had gone still like the world had paused to let that moment happen.

He knew what he'd felt in the Dairy Queen, watching Michael fall apart. Not pity. Not discomfort. Something fiercer than that. Something protective and tender and desperate all at once. Something that made him reach across the table and take Michael's hand like it was the most obvious thing in the world.

He'd never touched anyone like that before. Never wanted to.

So what did that make him?

He didn't have a word for it. Michael had found his — had wrestled it to the ground in a Dairy Queen booth and said it out loud through tears. But Levi wasn't there yet. The word existed somewhere inside him, but it was buried deep, under years of survival, under all the things he'd pushed down to make room for the things that mattered more — food, shelter, Lucy, his mom.

He'd spent so long not wanting anything. Not letting himself want. Because wanting led to disappointment, and disappointment led to pain, and pain was a luxury he couldn't afford when there were real problems — actual, life-or-death problems — that needed his attention.

But Michael had changed that. Michael had gotten around every wall, every defense, every carefully constructed barrier Levi had built to keep himself from wanting things he couldn't have. And he'd done it without trying. Without pushing. He just showed up. Kept showing up. Saw Levi — really saw him — and stayed.

And now Levi wanted. God, he wanted.

He wanted Michael here. Not a pillow, not a memory, not a hug emoji on a screen. The actual person. Breathing beside him in the dark. Close enough to touch.

He thought about Eli. The way Eli moved through the world like the world could take it or leave it. The way Eli had kissed Niles at midnight without hesitation, without apology. Eli didn't agonize. Eli didn't run cost-benefit analyses on his own feelings. Eli just *did*.

But Eli hadn't slept in a car for four months. Eli hadn't rationed cereal for his little sister while his stomach cramped. Eli hadn't learned, bone-deep, that the safest thing you could do was need nothing and no one.

Michael had cracked himself open in that booth. Had given Levi the most vulnerable, terrifying thing he had. And what had Levi given back?

Comfort. Presence. A hand. A touch.

But not the truth. Not *his* truth.

He owed Michael that. He knew he did. But he wasn't brave enough yet. Not through a phone. Not from a thousand miles away.

He needed to be in the same room. Needed to see Michael's face. Needed to know that when he said whatever he was going to say, Michael would be *there* — not a voice on a screen, not dots appearing and disappearing, but real and solid and close enough to reach.

Levi pulled the pillow tighter against his chest. Buried his face in it. Tried to find Michael there — in the fabric, in the warmth, in the dark.

It wasn't enough. It was never enough.

But it was all he had. So he held on.

A few days later, Michael's phone buzzed. He grabbed it, hoping—

But it was Eli.

How you holding up buttercup?

Michael almost smiled. Almost.

Fine

Liar

How do you know?

Because I know things. Also you just said "fine" which is code for "not fine at all"

I'm okay. Just... adjusting.

Mmmhmm. And how's our boy?

Michael stared at the screen. *Our boy*. Something about the way Eli said things sometimes — casual, throwaway, except nothing Eli said was ever really throwaway. Michael's stomach tightened. He wondered, not for the first time, how much Eli could see. How much he'd always been able to see.

He says he's fine too

Two liars in a pod. Adorable.

Shut up

Never. Listen - Niles and I are going to take Levi out this weekend. Get him out of his head a little.

Something loosened in Michael's chest. Not all the way — but enough to breathe.

Really?

Really. Science center. Niles is VERY excited about the space exhibit. I'm pretending to understand what he's talking about.

That would be really good. I think he's lonely.

I know he is. Takes one to know one.

You're not lonely. You have Niles.

I meant Niles, dummy. He knows what it's like to live in your own head. Figured he and Levi might have that in common.

Michael thought about that. About Levi alone in his house. About how easy it would be for him to just... disappear into himself. Go quiet. Stop reaching out.

Anyway. I'll send you pictures. Make you jealous.

Thanks Eli. Seriously.

Don't mention it. Now go do your homework or whatever it is teenagers do.

I'm 17, not 12

Same difference. Bye babe 💋

Michael laughed—actually laughed.

Eli set his phone down and looked over at Niles, who was curled up on the other end of the couch, laptop balanced on his knees, deep in research about something Eli couldn't begin to understand.

"Hey," Eli said.

Niles didn't look up. Eli reached over and tapped his knee.

Niles startled slightly, then looked up, remembering to angle his face toward Eli. "Sorry. What?"

"I was just texting Michael."

"Oh." Niles paused. "How is he?"

"He says he's fine."

"He's not fine."

Eli raised an eyebrow. "How do you know?"

Niles shrugged, looking back at his laptop. "He's not with Levi. Why would he be fine?"

Anyone else would have said it with a smirk, or a knowing look, or some kind of romantic inflection. Niles said it the way you'd say the sky is blue. Not a guess. Not an interpretation. Just what was obviously true, stated plainly, because why would you complicate it?

"What about Levi?" Eli asked. "You think he's okay?"

Niles was quiet for a moment. His fingers hovered over the keyboard, not typing.

"No," he said finally. "I don't think so."

"Why not?"

Another pause. Niles closed his laptop slowly, set it aside. He pulled his knees up to his chest—a posture Eli had come to recognize as *I'm about to say something that feels vulnerable.*

"At the party," Niles said quietly. "New Year's Eve. Levi came and found me. On the patio."

Eli remembered. He'd seen them through the window—two figures standing in the cold, breath fogging, not really talking but somehow communicating anyway.

"He didn't say much," Niles continued. "But he didn't have to. I could tell he just... needed to be somewhere quiet. With someone who wasn't going to ask him a lot of questions."

"And you were that someone."

Niles nodded slowly. "I know what that's like. Needing a place to just... exist. Without having to perform."

Eli reached over and took Niles's hand. Niles let him.

"I was thinking," Eli said carefully, "that maybe we could take him out this weekend. The three of us. Get him out of the house."

Niles's face did something complicated. "I don't... I'm not good at that. Planning things. Talking to people."

"You don't have to plan anything. I'll handle the logistics. And you don't have to talk—just be there."

"But what would we even do?"

Eli had been waiting for this. "The science center has that new space exhibit. The one you've been talking about for three weeks."

Niles's eyes lit up. Just for a second—but Eli caught it.

"The James Webb display?"

"That's the one."

"They have a replica of the mirror array. And a whole section on exoplanet detection methods. And—" Niles stopped himself, the enthusiasm draining from his face. "But Levi probably wouldn't want to do that. It's boring. For most people."

"I don't think Levi is most people."

Niles looked uncertain. "You should probably just take him yourself. You're better at... people."

"Maybe." Eli squeezed his hand. "But I think Levi might actually enjoy your company more than mine."

"That doesn't make sense."

"Doesn't it?" Eli shifted closer. "You said it yourself—he needed somewhere quiet. Someone who wasn't going to ask a lot of questions. Someone who understands what it's like to live inside your own head." He paused. "That's you, Niles. Not me."

Niles was quiet for a long moment. Processing.

"You really think he'd want me there?"

"I really do."

"What if I say something wrong? What if I talk too much about space and he gets bored and—"

"Then he gets bored. And that's okay. But I don't think he will." Eli smiled. "I think you might actually have more in common than you realize."

Niles considered this. His free hand was fidgeting with the hem of his sweater—a tell Eli had learned meant he was anxious but interested.

"Okay," he said finally. "But you have to text him. I can't—I don't know what to say."

"Already planned on it."

"And we're getting lunch there? At the museum?"

"If you want."

"They have a café. I looked it up once. The menu looked okay."

Eli bit back a smile. Of course Niles had already researched the café menu. Of course he had.

"Then that's what we'll do."

Niles nodded slowly. Then, almost to himself: "The James Webb exhibit closes in March. I've been wanting to see it."

"Now you will. And you'll have someone to share it with."

Something softened in Niles's expression. He didn't say anything—but he shifted closer to Eli on the couch, close enough that their shoulders touched.

Eli pulled out his phone and started typing.

Levi was in his room when his phone buzzed.

He'd been lying on his bed, staring at nothing, which was becoming a habit. The quiet here still felt strange — good strange, safe strange, but strange nonetheless. No car engine idling. No Lucy asking when they'd find somewhere to stop. Just stillness, and the distant sound of wind through the trees outside his window.

Most days, the quiet helped. Today it didn't. Today it just left room for his mind to circle back to the same place it always circled back to — a booth by a window, cold fries on a tray, and Michael's voice breaking on a word he'd been carrying alone for too long.

The phone buzzed again. Eli.

Hey stranger. Got plans this Saturday?

Not really. Why?

Niles and I are going to the science center this Saturday. The space exhibit. Want to come?

He'd never been to the science center—had only seen it from the outside, the big building near the waterfront that always looked interesting. He'd wondered what was inside but never had the chance to find out.

Me?

No, the other Levi. Yes you.

I don't want to be a third wheel or anything

You won't be. Niles specifically asked if you could come.

That surprised him. Niles had seemed nice at the party—quiet, a little awkward, but genuine. They'd stood on the patio together and watched the moon, not really talking, and it had been... comfortable. The kind Levi didn't find with most people.

He did?

He did. Something about wanting someone else to appreciate the "James Webb mirror array replica blah blah blah" with him. I have no idea what that means but he's very excited.

Levi almost smiled.

I don't know much about space stuff

Neither do I. That's what Niles is for. He'll explain everything. Probably twice.

Are you sure I won't be bothering you guys?

Levi. I'm inviting you. That means I want you there. Niles wants you there. You're not bothering anyone.

Levi stared at the message. His instinct was to say no—to stay in his room, to keep to himself, to not risk being a burden on anyone. That instinct had kept him safe for a long time.

But Michael was gone. And the walls of this small room were starting to feel like they were closing in.

Okay. Yeah. That sounds fun.

We'll pick you up Saturday at 11. Lunch at the museum. Wear something warm, the parking lot is brutal.

Thanks Eli

Don't mention it. See you Saturday.

Levi set the phone down and looked at the ceiling again. But this time, he was smiling.

His phone buzzed once more. Michael.

Hey. What are you up to?

Not much. Eli just invited me to go to the science center with him and Niles this weekend.

Oh that's awesome! Niles will love that. He's obsessed with space.

Yeah Eli mentioned something about a mirror array?

The James Webb thing. Niles talked about it for like 20 minutes at the New Year's party. I understood about 10% of it.

Lol. Should be interesting then.

Take pictures for me?

Of space stuff?

Of everything. I want to see.

Something warm spread through Levi's chest. He almost typed *I wish you were coming*. Almost.

Okay. I will.

Cool.

A pause. Then:

Hey so... I started reading uncle Graham's book. The first Oltrarno one.

Levi sat up so fast he nearly dropped his phone.

You're actually reading it??

Yeah. Figured I should see what all the hype is about. You made it sound pretty good when you told me about it.

"Pretty good" is an understatement. How far are you?

Just started. Marco just got to Florence. Met the guy at the gate.

Keep reading. It's so much better experiencing it than just hearing the summary.

That's what I'm hoping. I want to see what you see in it.

I want to see what you see in it.

Levi stared at the message until the screen dimmed.

Before Michael had trusted him — before the Dairy Queen, before the tears, before *I'm gay* came out broken and terrified across a table — Levi had never let himself think about it directly. Not really. The hope was always there of course, buried under everything else, but he'd kept it formless on purpose. Because if he never named it, it couldn't hurt him.

But Michael had said it. Out loud. To Levi.

And somewhere in the weeks since, the question Levi had been afraid to ask himself had begun to change. It wasn't *could Michael ever feel that way about a boy.* That was answered.

It was *could Michael ever feel that way about me.*

And now Michael was reading a story about two men in Renaissance Florence who couldn't say what they felt. Who wrote letters in code. Who held each other's faces in their hands and still couldn't find the words.

Michael wasn't just reading a book. He was reading *their* book. And Levi didn't know if Michael realized that yet, but Levi certainly did.

Text me when you get to the bath scene.

The WHAT?

You'll know. Trust me.

Now I'm scared.

Don't be. It's beautiful. You'll understand when you get there.

Okay okay. I'll keep reading. Talk tomorrow?

Yeah. Talk tomorrow.

Night Levi.

Night Michael.

Levi set the phone on his chest and stared at the ceiling again. But now there were two things to look forward to: Saturday with Eli and Niles. And Michael, making his way through the pages of a story that Levi had loved long before he understood why.

He understood now.

He wondered what Michael would think when he got to the parts about Marco and Alessandro. When he understood what the story was really about.

He wondered when Michael would.

Chapter Twenty

SATURDAY ARRIVED COLD AND BRIGHT.

Eli pulled up to the barn house at exactly 11:00, Niles in the passenger seat looking simultaneously nervous and relieved. They'd taken Donna's car—Niles's usual—but Eli was behind the wheel. Niles had been spiraling that morning at the thought of driving downtown, navigating traffic, finding parking. Eli had taken the keys without argument. Easy peasy.

Levi was already waiting on the porch, bundled in his new coat—the one from Christmas—and waved as they approached.

"He's punctual," Niles observed. "That's good."

"You sound like you're evaluating a job candidate."

"I'm just saying. Punctuality is underrated."

Eli bit back a smile and honked once. Levi jogged over and climbed into the back seat, bringing a rush of cold air with him.

"Hey," he said, slightly breathless. "Thanks for picking me up."

"Thanks for coming," Eli said, catching his eye in the rearview mirror. "Niles has been vibrating with excitement all morning."

"I have not been vibrating."

"You reorganized your wallet twice."

"That's not vibrating. That's preparation."

Levi laughed — short, almost startled, like he'd forgotten he could. Eli noticed Niles glance back at him, something curious in his expression.

"So," Levi said as they pulled onto the main road. "The James Webb exhibit?"

Niles turned in his seat, suddenly animated. "It's a replica of the primary mirror array. Eighteen hexagonal segments coated in gold. The actual telescope is at L2—that's the second Lagrange point, about a million miles from Earth—but this replica is to scale, so you can actually see how massive it is. The real mirror is 6.5 meters across."

Levi blinked. "That's... really big."

"It has to be. Infrared wavelengths require a larger collecting area to achieve the same resolution as shorter wavelengths. The bigger the mirror, the more light you can gather, which means you can see fainter and more distant objects."

Eli kept his eyes on the road, only catching fragments of what Niles was saying. It didn't matter—he probably wouldn't have understood most of it anyway. But he could see Levi's face in the rearview mirror: genuine interest, maybe even wonder. His boyfriend was in his element, talking about something he loved, and someone was actually listening.

That was all that mattered.

"Wait," Levi said. "So we're literally looking back in time?"

"Exactly. Light takes time to travel. When you look at something a billion light-years away, you're seeing it as it was a billion years ago. Webb can see light from over 13 billion years ago. Almost to the beginning."

Levi was quiet for a moment. "That's... kind of incredible."

Niles smiled — unguarded, lit up. "It really is."

Eli glanced in the mirror again. Levi was leaning forward slightly, engaged in a way Eli hadn't seen before. These two did have something in common.

The science center parking lot was, as Eli had warned, brutal.

Wind whipped off the water, cutting through coats and scarves like they weren't there. The three of them hurried toward the entrance, Niles walking slightly ahead, practically pulled by his own excitement.

"Wait," Eli said, grabbing Levi's arm just before they reached the doors. "Picture first."

"What? It's freezing."

"Exactly. Michael needs to see us suffering for his entertainment." Eli looked around, spotted a woman heading toward the entrance. "Excuse me—would you mind taking a photo of us?"

The woman turned, confused. "Sorry?"

Eli repeated himself, but she still looked uncertain, struggling to parse his voice. Levi stepped in quickly.

"He's asking if you could take our picture," Levi said, holding up Eli's phone. "Just one shot. We'll be fast."

He felt awkward doing it—stepping in like Eli couldn't handle himself—but it was freezing and he didn't want to stand here debating. He didn't give a shit who asked the woman, as long as she hurried up and took the damn picture.

"Oh! Of course." The woman took the phone, and the three of them huddled together in front of the science center sign, breath fogging, noses red, grinning despite the cold. Niles stood stiffly at first, but Eli threw an arm around his shoulders and pulled him close, and after a moment, Niles relaxed into it.

"Perfect," the woman said, handing Eli's phone back. "You boys have fun."

Inside, the warmth hit them like a wave. Levi pulled out his phone and looked at the picture Eli had just sent to their group chat.

Greetings from the frozen north 🥶

MICHAEL

I'm so jealous. It's like 60 degrees here.

LEVI

We're suffering for you

MICHAEL

I appreciate your sacrifice. Now go learn about space!

Levi hesitated for just a second, then typed:

Miss you

It was easier now. Not easy — but easier. Like a door they'd opened together that neither of them wanted to close again.

The response came almost immediately.

Miss you too. Take lots of pictures for me?

I will

Promise?

Promise

"Come on," Niles said, already moving toward the exhibit hall. "The Webb display is on the second floor."

Levi pocketed his phone and followed.

Niles came alive in the exhibit.

This was the Niles that existed underneath everything else — the anxiety, the rehearsed conversations, the constant performance of normalcy.

Here, surrounded by things he understood, he didn't have to perform. He just *was*.

"See these?" Niles pointed to a diagram of hexagonal shapes. "Each segment has actuators behind it that can adjust its position to within nanometers. That's how they align the whole array—tiny adjustments until all eighteen segments act like a single mirror."

"How do they even measure something that small?" Levi asked.

"Interferometry. They use the light itself to check alignment. If the segments are off, the light waves interfere destructively. When they're aligned, the waves add up constructively. It's actually really elegant."

Eli hung back, watching. He couldn't follow everything Niles was saying—partly because of the noise in the exhibit hall making lipreading difficult, partly because the concepts themselves were beyond him—but he didn't mind. Seeing Niles like this was worth any confusion.

Levi, to his credit, was keeping up. Asking questions. Taking photos of displays and short videos of some of the interactive exhibits. At one point, he recorded Niles explaining the infrared spectrum, capturing his animated hand gestures and the way his eyes lit up when he talked about wavelengths.

"Who's that for?" Eli asked quietly.

"Michael," Levi said, a little embarrassed. "He said he wanted to see everything."

"That's sweet."

Levi shrugged, but his ears had gone pink.

They spent nearly two hours in the space exhibit alone. Niles showed them the Webb replica—massive, gleaming, the gold-coated mirrors catching the light—and explained how the sunshield worked, and why the telescope had to be kept so cold, and what kinds of discoveries it had already made.

"There's a planet," Niles said, standing in front of a display about exoplanets, "called K2-18b. Webb detected signs of dimethyl sulfide in its atmosphere."

"What's that?" Levi asked.

"On Earth, it's only produced by living things. Mostly phytoplankton." Niles paused, letting that sink in. "It's not proof of life. But it's... suggestive."

Levi stared at the display. "So there might actually be life out there."

"There might be life everywhere. We just couldn't see the evidence before." Niles looked at him. "That's what Webb is for. Looking at things we couldn't see before."

Something about the way he said it made Levi go quiet.

He took another picture and sent it to Michael.

. . .

Lunch was late—nearly 1:30 by the time they made it to the museum café. They'd lost track of time in the space wing, which none of them minded. The crowds had already thinned, and they found a table tucked in a corner, away from the remaining families and their restless children. Niles visibly relaxed once they sat down.

"This is good," he said quietly, looking around at the relative calm. "I was worried it would be packed."

"Lucky timing," Eli said.

They ordered sandwiches and soup—nothing fancy, but warm and filling. Niles was still going, explaining something about gravitational lensing to Levi while they waited for their food.

Eli watched them, struggling to follow the conversation. The café still had enough ambient noise—clattering dishes, the hum of the kitchen, scattered conversations—that his hearing aids picked up everything, which meant they picked up nothing useful.

Levi noticed. Mid-sentence, he stopped and repeated what Niles had just said, angling his body so Eli could see his lips clearly.

"He's talking about how gravity bends light," Levi said. "So massive objects like galaxies can act like magnifying glasses for things behind them."

"Thanks," Eli said. The word wasn't big enough, but Levi had already moved on, like it was nothing.

"No problem." Levi said it casually, like it was nothing. Like it was obvious.

Niles had stopped talking, watching the exchange with a slight furrow in his brow. Then something clicked behind his eyes—understanding, maybe, or recognition.

"I should face you more," Niles said to Eli. "When I talk. I forget."

"It's okay. You get excited."

"But I should remember." Niles looked down at his soup, struggling with the words. "I know what it's like. When people forget... how to talk to you."

Eli reached under the table and took Niles's hand. Niles let him.

"You do fine," Eli said. "We're figuring it out together."

Niles didn't say anything. But his fingers tightened around Eli's, and he didn't let go for the rest of the meal.

After lunch, they explored the rest of the museum—the ocean exhibit, the dinosaur fossils, the hands-on physics demonstrations. Niles remained engaged, though quieter now, the morning's burst of energy settling into something steadier.

At one point, Levi stopped them in front of a display about bioluminescence.

"Okay," he said. "You two. Stand there."

"What?" Eli asked.

"I'm taking your picture. Michael wants to see everything, and that includes you two being disgustingly cute."

"We're not—" Niles started.

"You're holding hands," Levi pointed out. "You've been holding hands for like an hour."

Niles looked down at their joined hands as if noticing for the first time. His ears went red.

"Just stand there," Levi said, raising his phone. "Pretend you like each other."

Eli laughed and pulled Niles closer, throwing an arm around his shoulders. Niles was stiff for a moment, then relaxed, allowing himself to lean into Eli's side.

Levi took the picture. Looked at it. Smiled.

"Perfect," he said, and typed something before sending it.

Eli's phone buzzed a moment later. He looked at the group chat.

The photo was there—him and Niles, standing close, Eli grinning, Niles almost smiling. And underneath, Levi's caption:

LEVI

boyfriends

Eli glanced at Niles, whose face had gone from red to scarlet.

"Is that okay?" Levi asked, suddenly uncertain. "I can delete it if—"

"It's fine," Niles said quietly. Then, even quieter: "It's true."

Eli looked at him. Niles had never said that out loud before. Not to anyone.

Michael's response came a few seconds later:

MICHAEL

Levi stared at the heart for a long moment. His chest did something he couldn't control — a quick, involuntary tightening that had nothing to do with Eli and Niles and everything to do with a single red shape on a screen.

Eli watched him. Said nothing. But the smallest smile crossed his face — the kind he wore when he knew something someone else hadn't figured out yet.

They ended up at a fast food place for dinner—not planned, but Niles was still buzzing from the museum, talking about things he wanted to look up when he got home, and no one wanted to interrupt the momentum.

The restaurant was loud. Fluorescent lights. Families with screaming children. Everything Niles usually hated.

But he didn't seem to notice. He was still talking—about the Webb telescope, about exoplanets, about the expansion of the universe—and Levi was still listening, asking questions, genuinely engaged.

Eli sat across from them, eating his fries, half-following the conversation. The noise made it hard, but he'd stopped minding. Watching Niles like this—open, animated, *happy*—was worth any amount of frustration.

At some point, Niles's hand found Eli's under the table. Not holding it this time—just resting on his leg. Casual. Comfortable. Like it belonged there.

Eli's throat went tight. He blinked rapidly, looking down at his fries, suddenly overwhelmed by something he couldn't name.

This was new. All of it. The touching, the closeness, the way Niles was slowly—so slowly—letting him in. They'd kissed a few times. Nothing more. Eli wanted more, but he knew the package deal. Knew that pushing too hard would only make Niles retreat.

So he let Niles set the pace. Celebrated every small victory. Every hand-hold. Every moment of voluntary closeness.

And now this. Niles's hand on his leg, in public, without prompting. Without even seeming to realize he'd done it.

If all it takes is a science museum, Eli thought, *I'm buying an annual pass.*

He'd have to tell Graham that one later.

It was dark by the time they dropped Levi off at the barn house.

"Thanks," Levi said, climbing out of the car. "Today was... really good. I needed this."

"Anytime," Eli said. "Seriously. We should do it again."

Niles nodded. "The aquarium has a new jellyfish exhibit. If you wanted."

Levi smiled — a real one, unguarded. "Yeah. I'd like that."

He waved and headed inside. Eli and Niles watched until the door closed behind him.

The drive back was quiet at first. Eli kept his eyes on the road, navigating the dark streets, headlights cutting through the January night. Beside him, Niles was looking out the window, lost in thought.

"I don't think I could do it," Niles said softly.

Eli glanced over, but Niles was still facing the window. He couldn't make out the words.

He reached over and rested his hand on Niles's thigh—gently, just enough to get his attention.

Niles startled slightly, turning to look at Eli. Then he remembered—the darkness, the driving, the need to face him so Eli could catch his words in quick glances.

"Sorry," Niles said, angling toward him. "I said I don't think I could do it. Be with someone who wasn't... here."

Eli nodded, eyes flicking between the road and Niles's face. "Good thing I'm not going anywhere, then."

Niles didn't respond right away. But Eli felt the tension shift in Niles's leg beneath his hand. Not pulling away. Leaning in.

Eli kept driving, but he was acutely aware of the warmth under his palm. The way Niles hadn't moved his hand away. The way he seemed to be holding his breath.

It was a feeling Niles recognized—the excitement—but it had always been private before. By himself. Now it was Eli's hand. His boyfriend's hand. And that was new. More exciting. Terrifying and thrilling in equal measure.

He looked over at Eli, watching him drive. The profile of his face in the dim light. The easy way he handled the car.

Eli smiled slightly and shifted his hand—just a little, just an inch higher on Niles's thigh—before settling it again.

Niles gulped.

Eli kept driving.

After they got back to Eli's apartment, he turned on the TV—some nature documentary about deep sea creatures—but neither of them was really watching. Niles was pressed against Eli's side, closer than usual. After a while, Eli lifted his arm, and Niles tucked himself against his chest, head resting just below his shoulder.

It was the closest they'd ever been.

Eli wrapped his arms around him carefully, half-expecting Niles to pull away. He didn't.

"Is this okay?" Eli asked softly.

"Yes." Niles's voice was muffled against Eli's shirt. "This is good."

They stayed like that for a long time. The documentary played on, narrating the lives of creatures that lived in darkness, miles below the surface. Eli's arms grew tired, but he didn't move. Didn't want to break whatever spell had settled over them.

Niles was quiet for a while. Eli could feel him thinking — the slight tension in his body, the way his breathing changed when his mind was working through something.

Levi. Michael. The way Levi had taken all those pictures, sent all those texts. *Michael would love this. I have to show Michael.* Even the photo of him and Eli — sent to Michael with the caption *boyfriends.* And Michael's response: a single heart emoji.

Was that heart for them? For the picture? Or for Levi?

Niles didn't know. But he thought maybe it was all three. Maybe hearts could be for more than one thing at once.

He shifted, lifting his head to look at Eli.

Eli looked back, surprised by the sudden movement. Niles's face was right there—inches away, tilted up, finally visible.

"Hi," Eli said softly.

"Hi."

Niles didn't say anything else. He just stayed there, looking at Eli, his heart doing something strange in his chest.

Eli understood. He leaned down and kissed him.

It was soft at first—careful, gentle, the way their kisses had always been. But this time, Niles didn't pull back after a moment. He stayed. Let it linger. Let himself feel it.

When they finally broke apart, Niles's breathing was uneven. His cheeks were flushed. But he didn't look away.

Eli's hand found its way back to Niles's thigh—resting there, waiting, not pushing.

Niles looked down at it. Then, slowly, deliberately, he covered Eli's hand with his own.

And moved it higher.

Eli's breath caught. His eyes searched Niles's face, making sure.

Niles nodded. Just barely. But enough.

The TV murmured on. The apartment was warm. And somewhere between one heartbeat and the next, something new began.

Chapter Twenty-One

THE LAST SATURDAY before February arrived gray and cold, the kind of day that made Eli want to stay in bed with Niles and never leave.

But he had lunch plans with Donna. And canceling on Donna was not an option.

"You could come," Eli said, pulling on his sweater while Niles sat cross-legged on the bed, the sheet barely covering anything. In the few weeks since they'd really crossed into this "couple" territory, Eli still couldn't believe how far Niles had let him in. Sitting here now, naked under a sheet, talking like it was nothing—Eli couldn't have imagined this when they first met. He didn't want to call attention to it, though. The last thing he needed was for Niles to shrink back into self-consciousness. Besides, Niles had a good body. Eli felt privileged to be able to see it.

"I know." Niles picked at a thread on the comforter. "But if I don't go, she'll just focus on you. If I'm there, she'll... hover."

"She's your mom. That's what moms do."

"I know. But I'd rather she hover over you than me." A pause. "I think I'll just stay here. If that's okay."

Eli paused, sweater halfway over his head. Niles wanted to stay at Eli's apartment. Alone. Without Eli there. A month ago, that would have been unthinkable—Niles in someone else's space, without that person present, surrounded by unfamiliar things. But here he was, cross-legged on Eli's bed, asking to stay.

Meanwhile, Eli was about to have lunch with Niles's mother. The two of them crossing into each other's worlds, comfortable enough now to do it separately.

"Of course it's okay," Eli said, tugging the sweater down. "Make yourself at home. There's leftover pasta in the fridge."

Niles nodded. "Tell her I said hi."

"I'll tell her you're madly in love with me and we're eloping next week."

Niles's ears went red. "Don't you dare."

Eli grinned and grabbed his coat.

He was halfway to the bus stop when his phone buzzed. Graham.

Lunch today?

Can't. Already committed.

Hot date?

The hottest. Donna.

Ah. The mother-in-law.

Don't start.

She picking you up?

Bus.

It's freezing out.

Yeah? And?

I'll give you a lift.

You don't have to play chauffeur.

I'm not playing anything. It's 20 degrees and you're standing at a bus stop like a popsicle.

Who says I'm at the bus stop?

Are you?

...Maybe.

That's what I thought.

Fine. Fine. But hurry up. It's fucking freezing.

On my way.

Eli shoved his phone in his pocket and waited. And waited. The wind cut through his coat like it wasn't there. He bounced on his heels. Shifted his weight. Finally gave up on dignity entirely and started jumping in place, arms wrapped around himself, trying to generate any warmth he could.

He was mid-jump when Graham's BMW pulled up to the curb. The window rolled down, and Graham peered out at him.

"Training for pole vault?"

"What I do with poles is between me and Niles, thank you very much."

Graham choked on nothing, his face going red.

"Drive," Eli said, yanking open the passenger door and throwing himself inside. "Before I freeze to death and you have to explain to Donna why her future son-in-law is a popsicle."

Graham was still coughing as he pulled away from the curb.

"You're terrible," he managed.

"You love it."

Graham didn't deny it.

The restaurant was one of Donna's favorites—a quiet bistro near the waterfront with good lighting and manageable noise levels. Eli had suggested it months ago, and Donna had latched onto it immediately. *Our place,* she called it now, as if they'd been coming here for years.

When they walked in together, Donna was already seated at their usual corner table. Her face lit up when she saw Graham.

"Well, well," she said, rising to kiss Eli's cheek before turning to Graham. "Look what the cat dragged in. Graham Tierney, gracing us with his presence."

"I was just the driver," Graham said.

"Nonsense. Sit. Stay. Have lunch with us." She was already flagging down the server for another menu. "I insist."

Graham glanced at Eli, who shrugged. *You're trapped now,* the shrug said. *Might as well accept your fate.*

"I suppose I could eat," Graham conceded.

Donna beamed. "Wonderful. Now we can have a real conversation. Eli never tells me anything interesting."

"That's because you never stop talking long enough for me to get a word in," Eli said.

"Slander. Absolute slander." But she was smiling.

They ordered—salads for Donna and Eli, a bowl of soup for Graham—and

Donna launched immediately into the kind of conversation she loved best: gossip.

"So," she said, leaning forward conspiratorially. "I hear you're working on a new book."

Graham nearly choked on his water. "Where did you hear that?"

"I have my sources."

"Eli."

"I didn't say anything!" Eli held up his hands. "I swear."

"Angie, actually," Donna said, waving her hand dismissively. "She mentioned you've been holed up in your office more than usual. Typing sounds at all hours." She raised an eyebrow. "So? Is it true? A new Oltrarno?"

Graham shifted in his seat. "I'm... exploring some ideas. Nothing concrete."

"That's not a no."

"It's not a yes either."

"You're impossible." Donna turned to Eli. "He's impossible."

"I know. I feel like I've been telling him that for years."

"Speaking of impossible," Donna continued, her eyes glittering, "have you noticed anything strange going on at the Hendersons'? Across from you?"

Graham frowned. "Strange how?"

"Oh, I don't know. Late night visitors. A certain someone's car parked in the driveway well past midnight. Multiple times."

Eli leaned in, delighted. "Who?"

"I couldn't possibly say." Donna took a theatrical sip of wine. "But let's just say Mr. Henderson has been traveling for work quite a bit lately. And Mrs. Henderson has been... entertaining."

Graham's eyebrows shot up. "You can't be serious."

"As a heart attack. My friend Linda lives two doors down. She sees everything."

"That's called spying, Donna."

"It's called being observant." She set down her glass. "Anyway, Linda says the car belongs to someone from that new gym on Forest Avenue. Personal trainer, apparently."

"It's probably nothing," Graham said. "Maybe she's getting... trained."

Eli snorted. "At midnight?"

"Cardio is very important."

Donna nearly spit out her wine. "Graham Tierney, did you just make a joke?"

"I've been known to, on occasion."

"Mark the calendar," Eli said. "This is historic."

Graham sighed heavily, but the corners of his mouth were twitching. "Can we please talk about something else?"

"Fine, fine." Donna waved her hand. "But don't think I've forgotten about the book. I expect a signed first edition."

"There's no book yet."

"Yet. I heard that. I'm holding you to it."

Eli grinned. He loved this—watching Donna dig for information, watching Graham squirm. It was better than television.

"Speaking of which—how is that darling nephew of yours?" Donna asked, turning back to Graham.

Graham took a moment before answering. "He's... adjusting. Being back in Nashville."

"I imagine it's hard," Donna said. "After such a lovely visit."

"It is." Graham stirred his soup, not really eating it. "I think he misses it here more than he expected to."

"We actually took Levi out last weekend," Eli said, changing the subject slightly. "To the science center. Niles wanted to see the James Webb exhibit."

"Levi?" Donna's brow furrowed for a moment, then cleared. "Oh—the boy from the New Year's party? Quiet, striking eyes?"

"That's him," Eli said.

"He was with Michael most of the night, wasn't he?" Donna looked at Graham. "Your nephew. They seemed... close."

Graham nodded slowly. "They are."

"But Michael's in Tennessee now." Donna's expression shifted to sympathy. "That must be difficult for them. Being so far apart."

Eli glanced at Graham. Graham glanced back. Neither of them said anything for a beat too long.

"It's... complicated," Graham said.

Donna's eyes lit up. She leaned forward, wine glass forgotten. "Complicated how? Tell me everything."

Eli bit back a smile. Of course Donna would want the full story. The woman lived for complicated.

"They haven't actually talked about it," Eli said. "About what they are to each other. They spent the whole holiday dancing around it, and then Michael left, and now they're both miserable but neither one will say anything."

"They're seventeen," Graham added. "And scared. Neither of them has done this before."

"Done what? Fallen in love?"

"Admitted it. To themselves or each other."

Donna shook her head slowly. "That poor boy. Both of them, really." She looked at Eli. "And Niles picked up on all this?"

"He said he was worried about them. That he could tell they were struggling."

"My Niles said that?"

"He doesn't always show it," Eli said, "but he pays attention. He sees things."

"He always has," Donna said softly. "Even as a little boy. He'd notice things no one else did. The way people looked at each other. The things they didn't say." She paused, her eyes going distant for a moment — somewhere in the past, watching a younger Niles. "I used to think it was a burden for him. Seeing so much. But maybe it's a gift too."

"It is," Eli said. "I was the one who suggested we take Levi out, but Niles was hesitant at first. Thought I'd be better at the 'people' stuff. But I told him he and Levi might have more in common than he realized—that Levi might need someone who understood what it was like to live inside your own head. And I was right. They really connected."

Donna's eyes went bright. She blinked rapidly, reaching for her napkin.

"Well," she said, dabbing at her eyes with the back of her hand. "I'm glad he has someone who sees him so clearly."

"I do. Very much."

The conversation drifted, as conversations do. Donna told a long story about her neighbor's cat and a very unfortunate incident involving a bird feeder. Graham shared an update on Anthony and his latest Santa-related activities. Eli contributed a few observations about work, though accounting stories rarely made for exciting lunch conversation.

Then Donna set down her wine glass with a deliberate clink.

"So," she said, her tone shifting. "Niles has been spending quite a bit of time at your place lately."

Eli kept his expression neutral. "He has."

"More time there than at home, it seems."

"I suppose so."

Donna studied him. Underneath all the drama, she was sharper than people gave her credit for. "That science museum trip you mentioned—that was about two weeks ago, yes?"

"About that."

"And he hasn't slept at home since." It wasn't a question. She'd pieced it together from what Eli had shared, connected the dots the way only a mother could. "That's when things changed."

"That's true."

She was quiet for a moment, and Eli could see the war playing out behind her eyes. The mother who wanted to ask a thousand questions. The mother who knew her son was an adult—almost a college graduate—

and deserved his privacy. The mother who, despite everything, still worried about her boy, even if he was an adult and would insist he was fine.

"I'm glad he trusts you," she said finally. "Enough to... stay. That's not easy for him."

"I know."

"But I'm still his mother." She picked up her wine glass, then set it down again without drinking. "And I need to know that he's... that you're..."

She trailed off, clearly unable to bring herself to ask what she actually wanted to ask.

Eli took pity on her. Or maybe he just couldn't resist.

"You want to know if we're having sex."

Donna's face went pink. Graham suddenly became very interested in his soup.

"Not that it's anyone's business," Eli continued, matter-of-fact. "But yes. We are. And we're doing quite well in that department, thank you for asking."

"I wasn't—I didn't—" Donna fumbled for her wine glass. "That's not what I—"

"It's okay. I'd want to know too, if I were you." Eli softened his tone. "And for what it's worth—Niles is... he's a gentle soul. A complete gentle soul. He's not rushing into anything. We're taking our time. Learning each other."

Donna took a long sip of wine. "I trust you, Eli. I do. I know you're not... taking advantage."

"I would never."

"I know. It's just—" She shook her head. "He's my baby. He'll always be my baby. Even when he's thirty and married and has babies of his own."

"Well," Eli said, "no matter how hard we try, I'm pretty sure Niles won't be getting pregnant."

Graham choked on his soup, grabbing his napkin just in time to catch the spray.

Donna didn't even flinch. She was too busy watching Graham sputter, a delighted gleam in her eye. She caught Eli's gaze — a slight nod, a raised eyebrow, a smirk that said *well played*.

He was a member of her club now, after all.

Graham was still dabbing at his chin. "You two are going to be the death of me."

"But what a way to go," Donna said, patting his arm.

Eli would normally keep poking—it was his nature—but something shifted in him. He turned serious, redirecting Donna's attention back to where it belonged.

He reached across the table and gently pulled her wine glass away. She looked up, startled, as he took her hand in his.

"I will never break your son's heart," he said.

He said it slowly, carefully, pushing his voice to be as clear as he could make it. The words came out jumbled, the way they always did—the vowels too flat, the consonants blurred—but he didn't care. He needed her to hear this. To understand.

Donna's eyes filled with tears.

Graham, one of the last men in the world who still carried a handkerchief, reached into his jacket pocket and produced one. He handed it to her without a word.

"Oh, for heaven's sake," Donna said, dabbing at her eyes. "Look at me. Crying in the middle of a restaurant."

"It's a nice restaurant," Graham offered. "If you're going to cry somewhere, this is a good choice."

She laughed through the tears — loud, helpless, the kind of laugh that turned heads at nearby tables. She squeezed Eli's hand.

"You're a good man, Eli Pelletier," she said. "My son is lucky to have you."

"I'm the lucky one." Eli squeezed her hand once more, then released it. "Besides, can you imagine her as my mother-in-law?" He jerked his thumb toward Donna. "She'd cut my balls off if I did anything to hurt Niles."

Donna would, too. And her smile as she reached for her wine glass proved it.

Dessert arrived—a shared tiramisu that Donna insisted on ordering—and the conversation turned back to Graham.

"So," Eli said, pointing his fork at him. "The book. Tell us more."

Graham sighed. "There's nothing to tell. I've started down half a dozen different paths. None of them feel right. I get twenty pages in and realize I'm telling the wrong story."

"What's the right story?"

"I don't know yet. That's the problem."

"But you have something?" Eli pressed. "Something brewing?"

Graham was quiet for a moment. "Maybe. There's an idea. I'm not ready to talk about it yet."

"When you are, I want first dibs at reading."

"You'll have to wait until it's published like everyone else."

"That's not fair. I'm practically family now."

"Which is exactly why you'll wait. You'd read it in one sitting and then pester me with questions for months."

"That's called being an engaged reader. You should be flattered."

"I saw you and Levi going on about the first book over Christmas—poor Michael couldn't get a word in. I know what I'd be in for."

Eli grinned. "We were just enthusiastic."

"You were relentless."

Donna laughed. "He has a point, Eli."

"Whose side are you on?" Eli protested. "I want to be there from the beginning this time. Watch it come together."

Graham shook his head, but there was warmth in his expression. "We'll see."

But Graham was smiling, and Eli recognized what he was seeing. Graham was writing again — or trying to. After everything he'd been through, after losing Simon, he was still reaching for the work. Still trying to tell stories.

That meant something. Eli wasn't sure what, exactly, but it meant something.

They lingered over coffee — tea for Graham — until the lunch crowd thinned and the servers started giving them pointed looks.

"I should get back," Donna said finally, gathering her things. "Brett's attempting to fix the garbage disposal, and I don't trust him not to flood the kitchen."

"Niles gets his mechanical skills from somewhere," Eli said.

"Not from Brett, I assure you." She kissed Eli's cheek, then Graham's. "This was lovely. We should do it again."

"Anytime," Graham said.

"I'll hold you to that." She pointed at Eli. "And you — tell my son I love him. Even if he won't answer my texts."

"I'll pass it along."

She swept out of the restaurant, leaving a trail of perfume and energy in her wake.

Graham and Eli sat for a moment in the sudden quiet.

"She's a lot," Graham said.

"She's wonderful."

"She is." Graham smiled. "And she adores you."

"The feeling's mutual."

They gathered their things and headed for the door. Outside, the afternoon had turned colder, the sky low and heavy with the threat of snow.

"Thanks for the ride," Eli said. "And for staying."

"Thanks for letting me crash your lunch."

"Donna loved it. She never gets you to herself."

Graham was quiet for a moment. He looked out across the parking lot, his breath fogging in the cold air. "I'm not very good at..." He trailed off. Shook his head slightly. "I've gotten used to being alone. It's easier, in some ways. But it's not..." He searched for the word and didn't find it.

Eli watched him. He knew this Graham — the one who stood at the edge of something true and then backed away from it. He'd seen it a dozen times. The instinct to retreat into the house, into the office, into the quiet rooms where grief was the only company and at least grief didn't ask anything of you.

But today Graham had sat in a restaurant for two hours. He'd laughed. He'd made a dirty joke about cardio. He'd handed Donna a handkerchief and let Eli make him blush and been *present* in a way that Eli hadn't seen before.

Simon would have loved today. Eli was sure of that. Simon would have been the one making Graham stay, ordering another round of coffee, pulling stories out of Donna just to watch her light up. Simon would have kicked Graham under the table every time he started to withdraw. Simon would have been *on Eli's side*.

"You know what I think?" Eli said.

Graham looked at him.

"I think Simon would've liked today. I think he would've ordered dessert before anyone else and talked Donna into a second bottle of wine and made you stay until the restaurant kicked us out."

Graham's jaw tightened. But he didn't look away.

"I think he'd be pretty annoyed with the hermit version of you," Eli continued, keeping his voice light. Not pushing too hard. "I think he'd prefer the guy who just made a cardio joke in front of Donna."

Graham huffed — not quite a laugh, but close. "He would have made a worse one."

"See? He's on my side."

Graham looked at him for a long moment. Something moved behind his eyes — not grief, exactly. Something quieter. Like hearing a voice you'd been straining to remember.

"Come on," Graham said, pulling out his keys. "I'll drive you home."

"I can take the bus —"

"You're not taking the bus."

"Graham, it's fine. I'm a grown man. I can handle public transit."

"It's twenty degrees."

"I've survived worse."

"Eli." Graham held up the keys. "Get in the car."

"You know, this knight-in-shining-armor thing is getting old."

"Get. In. The. Car."

"Fine. But I'm picking the music."

"I'll regret this immediately."

"You will. And you'll love it."

• • •

Eli had his phone plugged into the aux cable and was three songs into what he called "the education of Graham Tierney" when he noticed they'd passed the turn for his street.

"You missed it," Eli said.

"Missed what?"

"My street. Back there." Eli pointed over his shoulder. "You literally just drove past it."

"I know. I need to make a quick stop first."

"A stop where?"

"My place. I need to grab something."

"What kind of something?"

"The kind that requires you to stop asking questions."

"That's not how I work and you know it."

"I'm aware. And yet I'm asking anyway."

Eli narrowed his eyes. "You're being weird."

"I'm being efficient."

"Those are not the same thing."

Graham didn't respond, just kept driving. Eli watched him — the set of his jaw, the way his hands sat on the wheel. Something was different. Not tense, exactly. More like... deliberate. Like Graham had made a decision about something and was holding onto it carefully, the way you carry something fragile.

They pulled into Graham's driveway. Graham hit the garage opener clipped to the visor, and the door rumbled upward, revealing the dim interior. Simon's white Volvo sat exactly where Eli had parked it the last time he'd driven it — gleaming, untouched, as if it had been waiting.

Eli barely glanced at it as he climbed out and followed Graham inside.

"So what's this important errand?" Eli asked, kicking off his shoes in the mudroom. "If you're about to ask me to help you move furniture, I charge by the hour."

"I wouldn't trust you with my furniture."

"Rude. I'm very strong."

"You're very mouthy. There's a difference." Graham was already heading down the hall toward his office. "Give me a minute."

Eli trailed after him, because Eli never gave anyone a minute. He leaned against the doorframe as Graham opened a filing cabinet and began rifling through folders — quickly, like he knew exactly what he was looking for.

The office was warm. Late afternoon light came through the glass wall, falling across the desk, the bookshelves, the cluttered corkboard above the drafting table pinned with index cards and scribbled notes. Eli's eyes drifted to a folder on the desk — thick, worn at the edges, held together with a rubber band. He recognized the handwriting on the tab. Graham's.

He picked it up before he could stop himself.

"What are you —" Graham started, looking up from the filing cabinet.

But Eli had already slipped off the rubber band and opened it. Inside were pages — typed, heavily annotated, covered in Graham's cramped handwriting. Margin notes, crossed-out paragraphs, entire sections circled with arrows pointing to new locations. It was the original manuscript. *The* manuscript. The first Oltrarno.

Eli went quiet.

He turned pages carefully, slowly, aware that Graham was watching him but not stopping him. The title page was different from the published version. A different title — one Eli didn't recognize.

"I didn't know you had a different title," Eli said, without looking up.

Graham was quiet for a moment. "Simon changed it. He read the first draft and said the original title was too academic. Too distant." A pause. "'Across the Arno' was his. He said the story wasn't about Florence — it was about crossing. Getting from one side to the other."

Eli turned another page. His fingers moved gently, the way you'd handle something borrowed from a museum.

Graham found what he was looking for in the filing cabinet. He pulled out a thin folder, sat down at the desk, and opened it. Inside was a single document — official, printed, with blank lines and a state seal. He pulled a pen from the cup on his desk and began writing, slowly and carefully.

Eli was too absorbed in the manuscript to notice. He'd found a section near the middle — Marco arriving at the Academy for the first time — and was reading with the kind of attention he usually reserved for things that mattered deeply. He traced a margin note with his finger. Graham had written: *More heat here. He's terrified but won't show it.*

"Eli," Graham said.

"Hmm?"

"Come sit here."

Eli looked up. Graham had stood and was gesturing to the desk chair.

"Why?"

"Because I'm asking you to."

"That's not a reason."

"It's the only one you're getting. Sit."

Eli closed the manuscript folder carefully, replaced the rubber band, and set it back on the desk. He crossed the room and sat in Graham's chair, feeling slightly ridiculous. "Okay. I'm sitting. Now what?"

Graham didn't answer immediately. Instead, he knelt — slowly, deliberately — so that he was eye-level with Eli. His knees cracked on the way down, and under any other circumstances Eli would have made a joke. But something in Graham's face stopped him.

This wasn't banter anymore.

Eli straightened. "What's happening?"

Graham's hands were in his lap. They were shaking slightly. He looked up — not at Eli, but past him, toward the window, toward something Eli couldn't see. His lips moved, just barely, like he was having a conversation with someone who wasn't in the room.

Then he came back. Looked directly at Eli, positioning himself so there would be no mistaking a single word.

"I want you to do something for me," Graham said. "And if Simon were here —"

His voice caught. He looked up again, blinking hard, jaw working. His hands gripped his knees.

"If Simon were here," he tried again, steadier now, his eyes coming back to Eli's, "he'd want this. And I —" A breath. "I want this. So I need you to do this for me. If not for you, then for me. Do you understand?"

Eli didn't understand. Not yet. But he'd never seen Graham like this — this focused, this unguarded, this close to breaking. This wasn't a request. It wasn't a favor. It was something Graham had already decided, something that had been building in him maybe for weeks, maybe longer, and was only now finding its way out.

Eli nodded.

Graham stood. Placed one hand on the desk, the other on the back of the chair. Gently, he turned the chair so Eli faced the desk.

The folder was open. Inside lay the completed and signed title to a 2023 White Volvo XC60. Graham's signature was on the seller's line, the ink still fresh. Below it, on the buyer's line, Graham had written in careful block letters: **ELI PELLETIER**.

A pen lay beside it.

Graham picked it up and placed it in Eli's hand.

"I want you to sign your name there," Graham said.

Eli stared at the paper. The words swam for a moment — legal language, dates, VIN numbers — before the meaning of it settled over him like something heavy and warm.

He started to turn. "Graham, I can't —"

But Graham's hand was on the chair, holding it steady, and his other hand was on the desk, and Eli realized he'd been positioned exactly so that he couldn't turn around. Couldn't face Graham. Couldn't argue face-to-face, because Graham knew — knew Eli's stubbornness, knew his pride, knew that if they locked eyes right now, Eli would fight him on this until one of them gave out.

"The insurance," Eli started. "And maintenance, and —"

"Handled."

"It's too much. This is Simon's car. I can't just —"

"Eli." Graham's voice was quiet. Close. Right behind him. "Simon is giving you his car. I'm simply signing my name on his behalf."

Eli bit his lip. Hard. His vision blurred and he blinked rapidly, staring at the title, at his own name written in someone else's hand.

How do you say no to a ghost?

He picked up the pen. His hand was unsteady, and his signature came out messy — worse than usual — but it was there. He capped the pen and set it down.

Graham's hand lifted from the chair. Eli heard him take a breath — a long, slow one, the kind that comes after you've been holding something for a very long time. Then his footsteps moved down the hall, and Eli heard the kitchen faucet run, and then silence.

Eli sat in Graham's chair.

He looked at the desk. The manuscript folder, held together with a rubber band. The title document with two signatures drying. The pen.

He looked up at the glass wall. The snow had started — light, scattered flakes drifting past the window, catching the last of the afternoon light. Beyond the glass, the yard sloped down toward the trees, and beyond the trees, somewhere, the ocean he couldn't see but knew was there.

He was sitting in the desk of the author he'd spent years admiring from a distance. The writer whose books had found him when he was young and lonely and desperate for stories where people like him existed. The manuscript was right there — the original pages, covered in notes, carrying the fingerprints of every draft, every revision, every moment Graham had poured into building a world where two men could love each other across centuries.

And on the cork board above the drafting table — index cards, scribbled notes, a rough outline for what looked like another Oltrarno novel. The next one. The one Graham kept saying didn't exist yet.

Eli looked at all of it. The office, the snow, the manuscript, the cork board, the title with his name on it.

Graham hadn't just given him a car. He'd given him custody of something — a memory, a piece of Simon that still moved through the world, that would carry Eli to work and to Niles and to the science center and to all the ordinary places a life is built from. Simon's car would become Eli's car, and the seats would eventually forget one shape and learn another, and that was okay. That was the point.

It was trust. It was a passing of something precious from one set of hands to another. And Eli understood — quietly, completely — that he would carry it carefully for the rest of his life.

He wiped his eyes with the back of his hand. Sniffed once. Looked at the manuscript folder one more time.

Then he stood and went to find Graham.

Chapter Twenty-Two

THE PHONE RANG at seven o'clock on a Tuesday evening.

Graham glanced at the screen. Becca.

"Hey, little sister."

"Hey yourself." Her voice had that distracted quality—half-present, half-somewhere else. "You got a minute?"

"For you? Always."

He heard her moving around—a door closing, the creak of what was probably the porch swing. Finding somewhere the kids wouldn't hear.

"It's Michael," she said.

Graham's chest tightened. "What about him?"

"He's fine. Nothing's wrong. Not like that." A pause. "He's just been... off. Since he got back."

"Off how?"

"I don't know how to explain it. Moody, but not the usual kind. He's somewhere else. In his head all the time. And he keeps mentioning that boy—Levi. The one staying at your neighbor's place."

"He mentions him?"

"Constantly. Everything reminds him of Levi. Everything he sees, he wants to show Levi. I swear, Graham, I've heard that name more in the last month than I've heard his own friends' names in a year." She exhaled. "What happened up there? Between them?"

Graham weighed his words. "They got close."

"How close?"

"Close."

"Graham."

"What do you want me to say, Becca?"

Silence. Then, quieter: "I want you to tell me what's going on with my son."

"I think you already know."

More silence. He could hear the porch swing creaking—she was moving, restless.

"I'm worried," she said finally.

"About what?"

"About him. About how hard things could be for him. You know what the world is like."

"I do."

"People are cruel. They say they've changed, but they haven't. Not really. Not all of them." Her voice was tight. "I just don't want him to have to go through that."

Graham let that sit for a moment. Then: "Becca, can I ask you something?"

"What?"

"Are you worried about what the world will do to Michael? Or are you worried about something else?"

"What's that supposed to mean?"

"It means what it means."

"I don't have a problem with it, Graham. If that's what you're implying." Her tone sharpened—defensive, the way she always got when she felt cornered. "I never have. You're my brother. I love you."

"I know you do."

"Then why are you making this into something it's not?"

"I'm not making it into anything. I'm just asking."

"And I'm telling you. I don't have a problem."

Graham was quiet. The silence stretched between them, heavy with years of things unsaid.

"You were never warm with Simon," he said finally. "Polite. Decent. But never warm."

"That's—" She stopped. Started again. "That's not true."

"It is true. And you know it."

"I was perfectly nice to Simon. I was at your wedding. I sent birthday cards. I—"

"You kept him at arm's length, Becca. For thirty years."

"I did not."

But her voice had gone thin. Brittle. The defensiveness that proved the very thing she was denying.

Graham softened his tone. "I'm not trying to attack you. I'm trying to understand. Because Michael is going to need you. Really need you. And I need to know you can be there for him."

"Of course I can be there for him. He's my son."

"Then be there. All the way. Not polite. Not decent. *There.*"

She was crying now—he could hear it. Quick breaths, the wet sound of tears she was trying to hide.

"I don't know what you want from me," she whispered.

"I want you to figure out what's been in the way. Between us. Between you and Simon. Whatever it is that makes you hold back." He paused. "Not for me. For Michael."

She didn't answer. Just the creak of the porch swing, the sound of her breathing.

"I have to go," she said finally.

"Becca—"

"I'll talk to you later, Graham."

The line went dead.

That night, Becca lay in bed staring at the ceiling while David scrolled through his phone beside her.

"You're thinking loud," he said without looking up.

"Sorry."

"Don't be sorry. Just tell me."

She rolled onto her side. He set his phone down and looked at her—really looked, the way he did when he knew something was wrong.

"I talked to Graham tonight."

"About Michael?"

"How did you know?"

David gave her a look. "Becca. Come on."

"What?"

"Our son has been moping around like someone stole his dog. He checks his phone every five seconds. He talks about this Levi kid nonstop." David shrugged. "I'm not blind."

"You think he's..." She couldn't finish the sentence.

"I think he's in love. Whether he knows it or not." David paused. "And I think he's scared to talk about it."

"Scared of what?"

"Of what we'll say."

The words landed hard. Becca looked away.

"Graham said something," she said quietly. "About Simon. About how I was never warm with him."

David didn't respond right away. That was answer enough.

"You noticed too," she said. It wasn't a question.

"Yeah. I noticed."

"Why didn't you ever say anything?"

"Wasn't my place." He shifted, propping himself up. "I never understood it, though. I didn't have a problem with Graham being gay. Took him and Simon fishing that time, remember? You stayed home."

"I remember."

"You could have come."

"I didn't feel like it."

"Didn't feel like it. Or didn't want to."

Becca's jaw tightened. "What's the difference?"

"You tell me."

She sat up, suddenly needing to move. "I don't know why everyone's acting like I'm some kind of bigot. I'm not. I've never said one hateful thing about Graham or Simon or anyone—"

"No one's calling you a bigot, Becca."

"Then what are you calling me?"

"I'm not calling you anything. I'm asking you to think about it."

"Think about what?"

"About why you always kept a distance. About what's really going on." His voice was gentle but firm. "Because whatever it is, Michael can feel it. Kids always can. And if he thinks—even for a second—that his parents won't be okay with who he is..."

"I would never reject my son."

"I know you wouldn't. But does he know that?"

Becca opened her mouth to argue. Closed it. She didn't have an answer.

David reached over and took her hand. "Figure it out, Bec. Whatever's been in the way—figure out what it is. Because our kid is going to need us to be solid. Both of us. And you can't be solid if you don't know where you stand."

He squeezed her hand, then turned off his lamp. Within minutes, his breathing slowed into sleep.

Becca stayed awake.

She knew. That was the thing she couldn't say—to Graham, to David, to anyone. She knew exactly what had been in the way all these years. She just felt stupid admitting it. Childish. Like a grown woman shouldn't still be carrying around a wound from when she was a kid.

But there it was. The truth she'd buried so deep she'd almost convinced herself it didn't exist.

Grammy.

That's what she'd called him when they were little. Her big brother. Her protector. The one who let her follow him around, who read her stories, who made her feel like the most important person in the world.

And then he'd hit high school and everything changed. He pulled away. Stopped wanting her around. Started calling himself Graham instead of Grammy, like he was shedding the person he used to be. The person who belonged to her. She was only eight or nine, too young to understand that teenagers naturally pulled away from their kid sisters. All she knew was that Grammy was gone, replaced by this distant, distracted stranger who barely looked at her anymore.

Then he left for Columbia. And then he met Simon. And he never really came back—not the way she'd hoped. He had a new life, a new love, a new world that didn't include her.

Simon hadn't stolen her brother. She knew that. Intellectually, she'd always known that. Graham had already been pulling away long before Simon came into the picture. But her eight-year-old heart had needed someone to blame. And Simon was easy. Simon was there. Simon was the reason Grammy never came home to be her brother again.

It wasn't about Graham being gay. It had never been about that. It was about losing him. And she'd been so ashamed of that childish, petty feeling that she'd never admitted it—not to Graham, not to David, not even to herself.

But Michael didn't know any of that. All Michael saw was his mother keeping a distance from his uncle's husband. All Michael felt was some invisible wall that told him maybe—just maybe—his mom wasn't as okay with things as she claimed to be.

And now her son was in love with a boy. And he was scared to tell her. Because of something that had nothing to do with him and everything to do with a hurt she should have let go of decades ago.

Becca pressed her palms against her eyes.

She was forty-three years old. A mother of three. And she was still carrying around the grief of a little girl who missed her big brother.

MICHAEL WAS in a mood when he got in the car.

Becca could tell immediately — the way he threw his backpack into the backseat, the way he slumped against the door instead of sitting up straight, the way he stared out the window like he'd rather be somewhere else. She had a pretty good idea where, too.

"Good day?" she asked, pulling away from the school.

"Fine."

"Just fine?"

"Yep."

She let it go. Seventeen-year-old boys weren't known for their conversational skills, especially after a full day of classes. She'd learned to pick her battles.

They drove in silence for a few minutes. Becca kept glancing at him — the set of his jaw, the tension in his shoulders. Something was eating at him. Had been for weeks, really, ever since he came back from Maine.

She thought about her conversation with Graham. With David. The things she'd been turning over in her mind for days now, trying to find the right words.

"I talked to your uncle the other day," she said.

Michael's head snapped toward her. "About what?"

"Just catching up. Seeing how he's doing."

"He's fine."

"I know he's fine. I was just —"

"Why are you asking about him?" Michael's voice had an edge now. Sharp. Protective. "You never call him."

That stung. Mostly because it was true.

"I call him."

"Like twice a year. On his birthday and Christmas."

Becca gripped the steering wheel a little tighter. "I've been trying to do better."

"Why now?"

"What do you mean, why now?"

"I mean why now. Why are you suddenly so interested in Uncle Graham?" Michael turned in his seat to face her fully, his voice rising. "Is this about me? Are you checking up on me through him?"

"Michael —"

"Because I'm fine. I don't need you calling him to find out what's going on with me. If you want to know something, just ask me."

Becca was taken aback. Michael had never spoken to her like this. Not once. He'd always been her easy child — the one who kept the peace, who didn't make waves. This anger, this intensity — it was like looking at a stranger.

Or not a stranger. Like looking at Graham, all those years ago, when he'd started pulling away.

"I wasn't checking up on you," she said carefully. "I was just —"

"Then what? What were you talking about?"

"I was thinking about him. About how I haven't been as close to him as I should have been. Over the years."

"Because he's gay?"

She flinched.

"No. That's not —"

"Because I didn't think you had a problem with that. That's what you always said. 'I don't have a problem with it.'" Michael was practically spitting the words now. "But you never go visit him. You barely came to the wedding. You —"

"I was at the wedding."

"For like five minutes. You flew in and flew out the same day. You didn't even stay for the reception."

The light turned red. Becca braked harder than she needed to, her hands shaking on the wheel.

"It's complicated, Michael."

"What's complicated about it? Either you're okay with your brother being gay or you're not. It's pretty simple."

"It's not that simple."

"Then explain it to me. Because from where I'm sitting, it looks like you say one thing and do another. And I'm tired of —" He stopped. Looked away. His jaw was working, like he was fighting to keep something down.

"Tired of what?" Becca asked quietly.

Michael didn't answer. But his hands were balled into fists on his thighs, and Becca could see something in his face she hadn't seen before — not just anger. Fear. The specific fear of someone standing at the edge of something and looking down.

The light turned green. Becca accelerated slowly, her mind racing. This wasn't just about Graham. This was about something else. Something Michael was carrying that he couldn't put down.

"Your uncle and I..." she started. Her voice came out smaller than she intended. "When we were kids, he was everything to me. Did you know that?"

Michael shook his head, still not looking at her.

"I used to call him Grammy. Because I couldn't say Graham when I was little." She tried to smile at the memory, but it wouldn't come. "He was ten years older than me. He'd carry me on his shoulders. Read me stories. Let me follow him everywhere. He was my whole world."

Michael was quiet now. Listening, despite himself.

"And then he got older. Hit high school. And suddenly he didn't want his kid sister around anymore. He started going by Graham instead of Grammy. Started spending all his time with his friends. With his own life." Becca's throat was tight. "I was eight. I didn't understand any of it. I just knew my brother didn't want me anymore."

"Mom —"

"And then he was gone. Not just pulling away — *gone*. He went to live with Aunt Margery. I was eight, Michael. Nobody explained anything to me. One day Grammy was there and the next he wasn't, and nobody would tell me why."

"Why didn't you ask?"

"I did. I asked Mom. She said he needed some time and that everything was fine." Becca's jaw tightened. "And I was eight. When your mother tells you everything is fine, you believe her."

"But later. When you were older. You could've called him."

Becca was quiet for a long time. Long enough that Michael thought she wasn't going to answer.

"By the time I was old enough to pick up the phone," she said, "I'd already decided I knew the answer. He left because he didn't want us. Didn't want *me*. And I was so afraid of hearing him say that out loud that I never asked." She shook her head. "It's easier to live with the story you've made up than to risk finding out the real one is worse."

Michael stared at her.

"I know," she said. "I know how that sounds."

She didn't say anything else for a moment. Just drove.

"Then why did you let me go up there each summer?"

"Your father."

"Dad?"

"He's always been a big fan of your uncle. Wanted you to have the experience — the fishing, the woods, that stuff." She almost smiled. "You always came back a different kid. Taller. Calmer. He saw that."

They were on their street now. Becca slowed the car, not ready for this to end.

"It was never about Graham being gay," she said. "It was about losing my brother. And I was so ashamed of feeling that way — so embarrassed that I was still carrying around this stupid childhood hurt — that I never talked about it. I just kept my distance. I let Simon think I didn't like him even though I knew that wasn't true." She glanced at Michael. "And I think maybe you picked up on that. Even if you didn't know what it was."

Michael was staring at her. His anger had drained away, replaced by something she couldn't read.

"Why are you telling me this?" he asked.

Becca pulled into the driveway and put the car in park.

She hadn't planned this. None of it — not the Grammy story, not the confession about Simon, not any of the things that had just come tumbling out of her in the space of a ten-minute drive. She'd planned to ask about his day. Maybe mention Graham casually. Feel him out.

But Michael had pushed, and she'd answered, and now they were sitting in the driveway with the engine running and something open between them that had never been open before. And the question she'd been carrying around for weeks — the one she'd rehearsed in the bathroom mirror, the one she'd tried to ask David about and couldn't finish, the one that sat in her chest every time Michael said Levi's name — was right there. Right at the surface.

She looked at her son. Her little Mikie, like she used to call him, was now Michael — almost an adult, asking her questions like one. The confidence she'd seen building in him since he came back from his uncle's was right there in his face, even through the anger. He was growing up. And this was the first time they'd ever spoken to each other this way.

So she just said it.

"Is Levi your boyfriend?"

It came out gentler than she expected. Not an accusation. Not even really a question. More like a door she was holding open, letting him decide whether to walk through it.

Michael looked like he'd been hit. His mouth opened. Nothing came out.

"I don't — we're not —" He shook his head, his voice cracking. "I don't know what we are."

"But you want him to be."

Michael's eyes filled with tears. He turned away sharply, jaw clenched, fighting to hold himself together.

"Honey." Becca reached across the console and took his hand. "Talk to me."

And Michael — who had said the word in that Dairy Queen booth back in Portland with tears running down his face, who had carried it quietly inside himself for weeks, who had stopped questioning and started settling into the truth of it — looked at his mother. And what he saw wasn't distance. Wasn't polite tolerance. Wasn't the careful, measured warmth she'd always given Graham.

She was *there*. Actually there. Leaning toward him across the console with her hand on his, waiting.

"I'm gay," he said.

Not *I think*. Not *maybe*. Just the word, steady and clear, the way it sounded now that he'd lived inside it long enough for it to fit.

Becca squeezed his hand. "Okay."

"Okay?" He searched her face — not for acceptance, but for distance. For the first sign of that invisible wall going up.

It didn't.

"Okay." She unbuckled her seatbelt and leaned across the console, wrapping her arms around him as best she could with the gearshift between them. It was awkward — he was too tall, the angle was wrong — but she held on anyway. "I love you. That doesn't change. Nothing changes."

Michael grabbed onto her. Not because he was drowning — but because she was *there*, and he needed to feel it, needed to know it was real and not performance.

"I was so scared," he said into her shoulder. "That you'd... pull back. Like with Uncle Graham."

Becca's breath caught. She held him tighter.

"That's on me," she said. "I gave you reasons to think that. But I'm telling you now — I'm not going anywhere. Not an inch. Do you hear me?"

They stayed like that until Michael's breathing steadied. Until he pulled back, wiping his face with his sleeve, embarrassed and relieved and exhausted all at once.

"What about Dad?" he asked quietly.

Becca smiled. "What about him?"

"Does he... would he..."

"Michael." She reached out and smoothed his hair back from his forehead, the way she used to when he was small. "Your father knew before I did."

"What?"

"He's not blind. He sees how you light up when you talk about Levi. How miserable you've been since you came home." She paused. "He's been waiting for you to tell him. Whenever you were ready."

Michael stared at her. "Wait. How did you know?"

Becca just looked at him.

"You're my kid, Michael. I know your face."

Michael nodded slowly, taking it in. Then, quieter: "I still haven't told Levi. How I feel about him."

"Why not?"

"I told him I'm gay before I came home. But I didn't tell him that I ..." He trailed off. "I don't know if he feels the same way about me."

Becca considered this. "Do you really think Levi would be this close to you if he didn't feel the same way?"

Michael didn't answer.

"I can't tell you what to do," she said. "But maybe you should talk to your uncle. He's been where you are. He might have some perspective."

"Yeah." Michael exhaled. "Yeah, maybe I will."

That night, over reheated lasagna and a hastily assembled salad, the family gathered around the dining room table.

Becca had always insisted on this — sitting down together, no phones, pretending to be a normal family for at least one meal a day. The kids complained, but they showed up. That was what mattered.

Michael's sister, Maddie, was fifteen and had opinions about everything, most of them delivered at volume. His brother, Jack, was ten and still young enough to think arguing with Maddie was a sport he could win. Tonight it was about who'd finished the Frosted Flakes — a crime Maddie was prosecuting with the intensity of a courtroom drama while Jack mounted an increasingly flimsy defense. David was refereeing half-heartedly while loading his plate with seconds.

Becca watched Michael across the table. Saw him push his food around. Saw him glance at his dad. Then at her. Then back at his plate.

She knew what was coming. She gave him the smallest nod.

He set down his fork.

"Dad?"

David looked up. "Yeah, bud?"

Michael had said the word twice now. To Levi. To his mom. Each time it had gotten a little easier — not easy, but easier. Like a muscle he was learning to use.

But this was different. This was the whole table. Maddie and Jack right there, forks frozen mid-bite, already sensing something was off. This was saying it to his family — all of them, at once — and letting it be real in a way it hadn't been yet.

He looked at his dad. David was watching him with that steady, patient expression he always had — the one that said *take your time, I'm not going anywhere.*

"I'm gay."

He said it clearly. Not loud, but not a whisper either. Not to his plate. To his father's face.

The table went quiet. Maddie and Jack looked from Michael to their parents and back again.

David set down his fork.

"Thanks for telling me, Michael."

Michael held his gaze, waiting. Not for rejection — he'd stopped bracing for that somewhere between the car and the dinner table. He was waiting to see his father's face. To see if it changed.

It didn't.

David pushed back from the table and walked around to Michael's chair.

"Come here," he said.

Michael looked up, confused. David pulled him to his feet and wrapped his arms around him — a real hug, the kind he used to give when Michael was little and had scraped his knee or had a nightmare. Strong and warm and certain.

Michael grabbed on. Held tight. Buried his face in his father's shoulder. Not because he was afraid anymore. Because it felt good to be held by someone who already knew and had been waiting for him to get here.

David held him there, one hand on the back of his son's head. "I love you," he said quietly. "I'm proud of you. And nothing about this changes anything. You hear me?"

Michael nodded against his shoulder, unable to speak.

Becca looked down at her plate, blinking hard. All her worries, all the battles she'd been fighting inside herself — they shrank to nothing watching her husband hold their son.

Maddie and Jack sat frozen, wide-eyed.

"But —" Maddie started.

"Not now," Becca said firmly.

David released Michael with a final squeeze to his shoulder, and they both returned to their seats. Michael wiped his eyes with the back of his hand, not quite looking at anyone.

Maddie leaned toward him, close enough that only he could hear. "I already knew, dummy."

Michael almost laughed.

Jack, who had been watching all of this with the wide-eyed concentration of a boy trying very hard to keep up, looked around the table.

"Does Michael have a boyfriend?"

Michael's face went red. Becca stepped in before he had to answer.

"Alright. Everyone save room. I picked up a fudge-topped brownie at the store." She was already on her feet, heading for the kitchen. "And I think there's ice cream in the freezer."

"Chocolate?" Jack asked, the boyfriend question already forgotten.

"Chocolate."

Jack was out of his chair before she finished the word.

But when Michael glanced at his dad — really looked at him — David met his gaze. Steady. Sure.

Michael had carried this for awhile. And now his family knew. The world hadn't ended. His dad was eating lasagna like nothing had changed.

Because nothing had.

Chapter Twenty-Four

MICHAEL WAITED until his siblings were asleep before he called.

He sat on his bed, phone in hand, staring at Uncle Graham's contact for a full five minutes before he finally pressed the button. It rang twice.

"Michael." Graham's voice was warm. Unsurprised. "I was wondering when you'd call."

"You knew?"

"Your mother called me. After your conversation in the car."

Michael groaned. "Of course she did."

"She was happy, Michael. Relieved. She wanted me to know you were okay."

"I'm okay." He paused. "I think. I don't know."

"Tell me."

So Michael did. He told him about the car ride, about dinner, about his dad hugging him like he was six years old again. About how Maddie had whispered that she already knew. About how his mom had cried after dessert, when she thought no one was looking.

"She told me about Grammy," Michael said. "About when you were kids."

Graham went quiet. Not just a pause — a stillness, like the word had uncovered something.

"She told you that?" His voice was different now. Softer.

"Yeah. About how she felt like she lost you. How she blamed Simon, even though she knew it wasn't really about him."

"I didn't know she remembered that name." Graham exhaled slowly. "Grammy. I haven't thought about that in... God. Decades."

"She remembers everything, I think. She just never talked about it."

Silence stretched between them. Michael could hear his uncle breathing — slow, uneven, like he was working through this.

"How are you feeling?" Graham finally asked. "Really?"

"Better. Than I expected, I mean. Saying it to Mom and Dad was..." He searched for the word. "It wasn't as hard as I thought it would be. The word isn't the scary part anymore."

"What is?"

Michael bit at his thumbnail. "Levi."

"Ah."

"I told him. Before I left Maine. That I'm gay."

Graham was quiet for a moment. "How did he respond?"

"He held my hand." Michael's voice went small. "He was... really good about it. Like it didn't change anything."

"But?"

"But I didn't tell him the rest. I didn't tell him how I feel about him. And now we text every day and it's great, but it's all just... usual bullshit. I mean, I like it. But, I don't know how to get past that."

"What do you want to say to him?"

Michael was quiet for a long time. "That I think about him constantly. That I miss him so much it actually hurts. That when he sends me a picture of something stupid — like his breakfast, or the sky, or whatever — my whole day gets better." He exhaled. "That I think I'm in love with him. And that scares the shit out of me."

"Why does it scare you?"

"Because what if he doesn't feel the same way? What if I say all of that and he just... likes me as a friend? Or what if he did feel something but I waited too long and he moved on? I'm a thousand miles away. I can't even —" Michael caught himself. Took a breath. "Sorry. I'm spiraling."

"You're not spiraling. You're thinking out loud. There's a difference." Graham paused. "Can I ask you something?"

"Yeah."

"When Levi held your hand that night. Did that feel like friendship to you?"

Michael didn't answer right away. He was back in that booth — Levi's thumb brushing across his knuckles, Levi's eyes steady on his, Levi brushing the hair off his forehead like it was the most natural thing in the world.

"No," he said quietly. "It didn't."

"Then trust that."

"But what if I'm reading it wrong?"

"You might be. That's always a risk. But Michael — I watched you two together over Christmas. The way he looked at you. The way he lit up when you walked into a room." Graham's voice warmed. "That wasn't friendship."

Michael felt his throat tighten. "I want to tell him. I just don't know if I can do it over text. Or even on the phone. It feels like something I need to say to his face."

"Then say it to his face."

"He's in Maine. I'm here."

Graham didn't respond right away. The silence stretched long enough that Michael checked his phone to make sure the call hadn't dropped.

"Uncle Graham? You still there?"

"I'm here." Graham's voice was distant, distracted. "Just thinking."

Michael waited.

On the other end of the line, Graham was turning something over in his mind. Grammy. Becca as a little girl, following him everywhere. The distance that had grown between them — not because of Simon, not really, but because he'd let it. Because it was easier to stay away than to bridge the gap.

He'd told her to figure out what was in the way. But maybe that wasn't fair. Maybe he needed to meet her halfway. Show up. Be present. Be her brother again, the way he hadn't been in thirty years.

If he wanted her to be honest with herself, maybe he ought to help with the heavy lift. He hadn't realized this was what her struggles had been about all along. And now — sitting with it — he couldn't bring himself to care whose fault was whose. If there even was such a thing.

He loved his sister. He'd always loved her. And maybe it would be easier to do this on her turf. Show her he wanted to be there. See her and David and the kids.

He only wished Simon were around to talk to her himself. To finally clear the air that had been clouded for so long.

And Michael — scared and hopeful and trying so hard to be brave. Best to be there in person, Graham thought. For some things, a phone call won't do.

"What if I came out there?" Graham said suddenly.

"What?"

"To Nashville. To visit your mom. And then..." The idea was forming as he spoke, pieces clicking into place. "Then you and I could fly back to Maine together. For spring break."

Michael sat up so fast he nearly dropped the phone. "Wait — seriously?"

"I've been meaning to visit. Really visit, not just passing through. And your mother would feel better knowing you're traveling with me." Graham paused. "Plus, it would give you the chance to tell Levi in person. The way you want to."

"Uncle Graham. Are you serious right now?"

"I'm serious."

"Yes. Yes. Oh my God, yes." Michael was already on his feet, pacing the room. "When? How long? Can I FaceTime Levi right now and tell him? I need to tell him. He's going to freak out."

Graham laughed — warm and surprised. "I don't have the details yet. I need to work things out with your mom. But yes... call Levi. Tell him you're coming."

"Thank you. Thank you so much."

"Don't thank me yet. You still have to actually talk to him when you get here."

"I know. I will. I promise."

"Good." A pause. "Now go call your boy."

Michael immediately pulled up Levi's contact. His thumb hovered over the FaceTime button. His heart was pounding.

Feel the fear and do it anyway.

He pressed the button.

Levi answered on the third ring, his face appearing on the screen lit by the dim glow of his bedside lamp.

"Michael? Hey—is everything okay?"

"Everything's great. Better than great." Michael was grinning so wide his face hurt. "I have news."

Levi shifted, propping himself up against his pillow. "What kind of news?"

"Spring break. I'm coming back to Maine."

Levi's eyes went wide. "Wait—what? Seriously?"

"Seriously. Uncle Graham is flying out here first to visit my mom, and then we're flying back together. I'll be there the whole week."

"Michael." Levi's voice cracked on the name. "Michael, are you serious right now?"

"I'm serious. I promise."

"Oh my God." Levi was laughing now, disbelieving, his whole face transformed. "I can't—I didn't think—when you said spring break before, I didn't know if you meant it. People say things, you know? But you actually—you're really coming?"

"I'm really coming."

"I can't believe it." Levi ran a hand through his hair, still laughing. "This is the best news I've gotten in... I don't know. Forever."

Michael's chest ached with everything he wanted to say. *I told my parents. My dad hugged me. I think I'm in love with you.* The words were right there, pressing against his teeth, desperate to escape.

But Levi looked so happy. And it was late—nearly midnight in Maine—and Michael could see the tiredness around Levi's eyes even as he smiled. And there was so much to say, too much, and Michael didn't know how to start.

"I missed you," he said instead. The safest true thing.

Levi's smile softened. "I missed you too. So much."

"It's only like a month away now. We can count down."

"I'm literally going to mark it on my calendar." Levi laughed again. "Actually, I'm going to mark it on every calendar. Mom's calendar. Lucy's calendar. Graham's calendar if I can find it."

"You're ridiculous."

"You love it."

Michael's heart stuttered. *Yes. I do. I love you.*

"I should probably let you sleep," he said, even though he wanted to stay on the call forever. "It's late there."

"Yeah, probably." Levi didn't look like he wanted to hang up either. "But text me tomorrow? And the day after that? And every day until you get here?"

"Obviously."

"Promise?"

"Promise."

They lingered for another moment, neither wanting to be the one to end the call. Finally, Levi said, "Goodnight, Michael."

"Goodnight, Levi."

The screen went dark.

Michael sat there, staring at his phone, his heart still racing. He'd chickened out. He'd had the perfect opportunity to say something real, and he'd chickened out.

But Levi was happy. And spring break was coming. And maybe some things were better said in person anyway.

He needed to tell someone. Not his parents — they'd been amazing, but this was different. Not Uncle Graham — they'd just talked. He needed Eli.

Now the Eli text exchange. This is the big tonal shift. Michael isn't confessing to Eli — he's bringing Eli into the club. And he should tease back. Let me draft the revision:

You awake?

Always. What's up buttercup?

I just FaceTimed Levi. Told him I'm coming for spring break

AND???

He was really happy Like REALLY happy

Obviously. That boy has been pining like a Victorian widow. I'm surprised he didn't propose on the spot.

lol shut up

I will not. So? Did you tell him anything else?

Michael stared at the screen. His knee was bouncing. But this didn't feel like the car, or the dinner table. This felt easy. Like telling someone something they already knew.

No. But I have something to tell YOU

Oh?

I'm gay

...

That's it? That's your reaction?

I'm sorry, was I supposed to be SURPRISED?

You could at least pretend

Sweetie. I knew before YOU knew.

How??

You looked at Levi like he was the last slice of pizza at a party

I did NOT

You absolutely did. Graham saw it. I saw it. The FURNITURE saw it.

Oh my god

Welcome to the club though. Officially. How does it feel?

Honestly?

Yeah

Kind of amazing

Michael grinned at his phone. He hadn't expected that to be the answer. But it was true. Saying it to Eli — after Levi, after his mom, after the dinner table — didn't feel like a confession. It felt like arriving somewhere.

THAT'S what I wanted to hear. Now. Tell me everything. How did it go with your parents?

So Michael did. He told Eli about the car ride with his mom, about the dinner table, about his dad's hug. About calling Graham. About the plan for spring break.

I can't even with you right now. This is the best story I've heard all week.

Better than the science museum?

WAY better. Although Niles did touch my leg at dinner so that was also a highlight

ELI

What?? I'm allowed to be happy too!

You two are disgusting and I love it

Aww look at you. Baby gay already shipping.

Is that what that means?

Oh honey. We have so much to teach you.

Michael laughed. Something had shifted — not just in him, but between them. Eli wasn't talking down to him anymore. Or maybe he'd never been. Maybe Michael just hadn't been ready to hear it as anything other than an adult humoring a kid.

Speaking of which — Niles and I have been batting around an idea.

What kind of idea?

We were thinking about coming to Nashville.

Wait WHAT??

For spring break. His is two weeks before yours. We've never been. Thought we'd surprise your sorry ass.

Seriously??

Seriously. You can show us the sights!

I mean yeah there's tons of stuff Niles would love the science museum and there's this full size replica of the Parthenon

Sights AND hot men 👀

ELI

What?? You're gay now! Officially! You're allowed to LOOK.

I'm not looking at cowboys

Who said anything about cowboys?

...

YOU'RE BLUSHING I CAN TELL THROUGH THE PHONE

I hate you

You love me. So? Can we come?

Yes Obviously yes You could stay with us or at a hotel if that's less weird

Hotel probably. Niles needs his space to decompress. But we'd definitely hang out every day.

This is going to be amazing

It's going to be FABULOUS. Get used to saying that word.

Michael typed it before he could overthink it.

Fabulous

Eli's response was immediate.

I'M SCREENSHOTTING THIS. THIS IS GOING IN THE ARCHIVE. BABY GAY'S FIRST FABULOUS.

You're the worst

I'm the BEST and you know it

Yeah You kind of are

Michael set his phone down for a moment. Picked it up again. Put it down. The Nashville thing was exciting, the coming out was done, and Eli was being Eli — loud and warm and impossible. But there was something else. The thing underneath all of it. The thing he hadn't said to anyone yet.

He picked the phone back up.

Can I ask you something?

Always.

How did you tell Niles you liked him? Like... more than liked him.

I asked him to get coffee. Then I panicked for three hours before the date.

That doesn't sound like you

Babe, everyone panics. The trick is doing it anyway.

I think I'm in love with Levi

Michael stared at the words on his screen. He'd never typed them before. Never even let himself think them that clearly. But there they were.

Eli didn't respond right away. Three dots appeared. Disappeared. Appeared again.

STOP THE PRESSES. ALERT THE MEDIA. SOMEONE CALL ANDERSON COOPER.

ELI

Sorry sorry. But also: DUH.

Is it that obvious?

Babe. You named your WIFI password after him.

I DID NOT

You would though. Don't lie.

Michael laughed. His eyes were burning.

Is that bad?

That's the gayest thing you've done so far and I'm INCLUDING the coming out. I'm so proud.

Shut up

No but seriously. When you see him. Just say it. You don't need a speech. You don't need a plan. Just look at him and say it.

What if I throw up

Then you throw up and say it anyway. Romance isn't always pretty.

There's that gay wisdom again

You're learning.

Thanks Eli For real Like you're easy to talk to

That's me. Easy Eli. Wait no that sounds wrong.

LMAO

Forget I said that. Point is — you're doing great. And when you get to Maine, just tell him. He's not going to run.

How do you know?

Because that boy PINES, Michael. He pines like it's a competitive sport.

Okay Okay I'll tell him

Good. Now go to sleep. It's late.

Yeah mom

Excuse me? I am a COOL mom.

Goodnight COOL mom

Night, fabulous son. 💕

. . .

The next day, Eli was sprawled on the couch at his apartment, Niles tucked against his side, when his phone buzzed.

Lunch tomorrow? My treat.

Magic words. Where and when?

That place by the water. Noon.

Done.

He set the phone down and looked at Niles, who was deep in his laptop, researching something intently.

"What are you looking at?" Eli asked.

"Nashville restaurants. I'm trying to find places that aren't too loud."

"We haven't even bought plane tickets yet."

"I know. But I want to be prepared." Niles didn't look up. "There's a science museum. And something called the Parthenon, which is a full-scale replica of the one in Greece. I don't understand why it's there, but I want to see it."

Eli smiled. He'd suggested the trip half-expecting Niles to panic, but giving him the reins—letting him plan and research—had worked perfectly. This was how Niles processed new things: by knowing everything about them in advance.

Funny, too, how Michael had suggested nearly the same things.

"Whatever you want," Eli said. "You're the tour guide."

"We'll need at least three days. Maybe four. There's a lot to see."

"Then we'll do four."

Niles finally looked up. "You're sure this is a good idea?"

"Traveling together?"

"Yes. What if I get overwhelmed and ruin it?"

Eli reached over and took his hand. "Then you get overwhelmed and we figure it out. That's what we do."

Niles considered this. "Okay."

"Okay?"

"Okay." He went back to his laptop, but his fingers found Eli's and held on.

Lunch with Graham the next day was at their usual spot—quiet, good light, manageable noise. Graham was already there when Eli arrived, nursing a cup of tea.

"No Niles?" Graham asked as Eli sat down.

"He's at class. Besides, I think he's researched Nashville enough for one lifetime. I needed a break from hearing about honky-tonks and hot chicken."

Graham smiled. "You're really going?"

"We're really going. His spring break is two weeks before Michael's. Trial run."

"Trial run?"

"Of traveling together. Any relationship that can survive a trip is marriage material." Eli picked up the menu. "At least, that's my theory."

"Simon and I went to Italy three months after we started dating. Nearly killed each other." Graham's eyes softened at the memory. "But we figured it out."

"See? Proof."

They ordered—salads again, soup for Graham—and settled into conversation.

"So," Eli said. "Nashville. You're going too?"

"Before Michael's break. Spending a week with Becca." Graham stirred his tea slowly, eyes on the spoon. "It's overdue. I haven't been the brother she needed. Not for a long time."

"From what I hear, she had her own stuff to work through."

"She did. But that doesn't let me off the hook." He set down his spoon. "I don't know exactly what I'm going to do when I get there. What I'm going to say. I just feel like I need to go."

"Then go," Eli said. "Sometimes you don't need to overthink it."

Graham raised an eyebrow. "Sometimes?"

"By 'sometimes' I mean all the time. You overthink everything. Just show up. Be there. The rest will figure itself out."

Graham was quiet for a moment. Then, softly: "You sound like Simon."

"I'll take that as a compliment."

"It was."

Eli nodded. "Michael said you're flying back with him?"

"That's the plan. He wanted to tell Levi in person. About everything."

"Yeah, he told me." Eli leaned back in his chair. "Those two, I swear. They're going to give me gray hairs."

"You could always stay out of it."

"Ha." Eli pointed his fork at Graham. "Too late for that."

"That's what I was afraid of." But Graham was smiling. "Just don't push too hard. They need to figure this out themselves."

"I know, I know. I'll be good." Eli paused. "Mostly good."

"Eli."

"Fine. I'll be an angel. A perfect, patient, non-meddling angel."

Graham just looked at him.

"Okay, maybe not an angel. But I'll keep my mouth shut until at least June."

"That's all I ask."

Chapter Twenty-Five

THE FLIGHT WAS UNEVENTFUL, which was exactly what Niles needed.

He'd prepared for every contingency—noise-canceling headphones, a window seat so no one would need to climb over him, a precisely timed arrival at the airport so they wouldn't have to wait too long at the gate. Eli had watched him orchestrate the whole thing with a mix of amusement and admiration.

"You know," Eli said as they touched down, "most people just wing it."

"Most people are wrong."

Eli laughed and squeezed his hand.

Michael was waiting for them at baggage claim, bouncing on his heels like a golden retriever who'd heard the word "walk." When he spotted them, his whole face lit up.

"You're here! You're actually here!"

"In the flesh," Eli said, pulling him into a hug. "Miss me?"

"Obviously." Michael turned to Niles, hesitated for just a moment, then offered a slightly awkward wave. "Hey, Niles."

"Hello." Niles gave a small nod. "Thank you for the restaurant recommendations. I cross-referenced them with noise level reviews on Google. The Italian place on Saturday should be acceptable."

Michael blinked. "I... didn't send restaurant recommendations?"

"Eli forwarded your texts. I appreciated the data."

Michael looked at Eli, who shrugged. "He likes to be prepared."

"I'm getting that."

They collected their bags—one sensible carry-on each, because Niles had calculated the optimal packing strategy for a four-day trip—and headed for Michael's car.

"Mom wanted me to invite you for dinner tonight," Michael said as they loaded the trunk. "But I told her you'd probably want to settle in first."

"Smart boy," Eli said. "We'll do dinner tomorrow. Tonight is decompression time."

"Decompression is essential after air travel," Niles added. "The pressurized cabin environment causes—"

"Babe. He gets it."

"I was just explaining."

"I know. And I love you for it." Eli kissed his cheek. "Now let's go see this hotel you picked."

The hotel was perfect—quiet, clean, exactly the right distance from downtown. Niles had spent three weeks researching options, reading reviews, cross-referencing locations with traffic patterns and noise ordinances. The result was a room on a high floor facing away from the street, with blackout curtains and a white noise machine Niles had packed in his carry-on.

"This is nice," Eli said, flopping onto the bed. "Good job."

Niles was already checking the thermostat. "The temperature is two degrees higher than optimal. I'll adjust it."

"You do that." Eli stretched out, watching him move around the room with quiet efficiency. This was Niles in his element—controlling variables, creating order out of chaos. Travel could be overwhelming for him, but planning travel? That was a puzzle, and Niles loved puzzles.

"Are you tired?" Niles asked, not looking up from the thermostat.

"A little. You?"

"Yes. But I don't want to sleep yet. My circadian rhythm will be disrupted."

"We could just lie here for a while. Watch something mindless."

Niles considered this. "That would be acceptable."

He climbed onto the bed next to Eli, maintaining a careful few inches of space between them. Eli reached over and pulled him closer.

"Come here. I didn't fly a thousand miles to not cuddle."

"One thousand and ten point three, by air. One thousand one hundred and eighty-nine point five if you drive."

"Close enough."

Niles settled against his chest. They'd made it. First flight together, first hotel together, first trip together. And so far, nothing had gone wrong.

"This is nice," Niles said quietly.

"Yeah?"

"Yes. I was worried I would ruin it."

"You haven't ruined anything."

"The trip just started."

Eli laughed and kissed the top of his head. "You're not going to ruin it. And even if something goes wrong, we'll figure it out."

Niles was quiet for a moment. Then: "I like that you say that. 'We'll figure it out.' It makes things feel less... overwhelming."

"That's because we're a team. Teams figure things out together."

"I've never been good at teams."

"You're good at this one."

Niles tilted his head up to look at him. "I am?"

"You are."

He kissed him—slow, gentle, unhurried. When they pulled apart, Niles was smiling.

"Okay," he said. "Let's watch something mindless."

The next morning, Michael picked them up for what Niles had officially titled "Day One: Cultural and Scientific Exploration."

"He made an itinerary," Eli explained as they climbed into the car. "With time blocks."

"I like itineraries," Michael said. "Where are we going first?"

Niles pulled out his phone and consulted his notes. "The Parthenon. It opens at nine. If we arrive by nine-fifteen, we'll avoid the initial rush but still have adequate time before the lunch crowds."

"The Parthenon it is."

They drove through Nashville's streets, Eli in the passenger seat watching the city go by while Niles studied his phone in the back. Michael pointed out landmarks as they passed—the Ryman, the honky-tonks on Broadway, the Batman Building (which Niles immediately researched and informed them was actually called the AT&T Building, but he understood why people called it that because the resemblance was statistically significant).

"You really do your homework," Michael said.

"Knowledge reduces anxiety."

"I get that." Michael glanced at him in the rearview mirror. "I'm the same way. I like to know things before I have to deal with them."

"That's logical."

"It drives my sister crazy. She just wants to figure things out as she goes."

"That sounds chaotic."

"It is. But she makes it work somehow."

They pulled into the parking lot at Centennial Park, and Niles got his first look at the Parthenon—a full-scale replica of the ancient Greek temple, sitting incongruously in the middle of a Nashville park.

"I still don't understand why it's here," he said.

"Tennessee centennial exposition," Michael offered. "1897. They built it as a temporary exhibit and then just... never took it down."

"That seems inefficient."

"Maybe. But it's kind of cool, right? Having a piece of ancient Greece in the middle of Nashville?"

Niles considered the building for a long moment. "Yes," he admitted finally. "It is kind of cool."

They spent an hour inside, Niles absorbing every plaque and information panel while Eli and Michael trailed behind, exchanging amused glances. The statue of Athena—forty-two feet tall, gilded and imposing—held Niles's attention for a solid fifteen minutes.

"She's impressive," Eli said, coming to stand beside him.

"The original was made of ivory and gold. This one is a replica, but the proportions are accurate." Niles tilted his head. "I like her."

"Yeah?"

"She's the goddess of wisdom and strategic warfare. Those are good things to be the goddess of."

"Better than being the goddess of, what, chaos?"

"That would be Eris. She's less popular."

"I can see why."

Michael appeared at Eli's elbow. "Science museum next?"

Niles's eyes lit up. "Yes. The planetarium show starts at one-thirty. We should leave here by twelve-fifteen to account for traffic and lunch."

"Lunch is part of the itinerary?"

"Of course. I identified three restaurants within a six-minute drive of the museum. I've ranked them by noise level and menu variety."

Michael looked at Eli. "He's amazing."

"I know." Eli slipped his arm through Niles's. "Come on, genius. Let's go get you some lunch."

The science museum was everything Niles had hoped for.

They spent three hours wandering through exhibits—space exploration, human biology, natural disasters, technology. Niles absorbed it all with quiet intensity, occasionally pulling out his phone to take notes or look up additional information. Eli stayed close, letting him set the pace, stepping in when crowds got too thick or noise levels got too high.

Michael, to his credit, kept up admirably. He asked questions—real questions, not just polite ones—and listened when Niles explained the physics of black holes or the peculiarities of quantum entanglement. By the time they reached the planetarium, the three of them had learned how to navigate around and with each other—having fun instead of treating Niles's intensity as an obstacle. Michael was impressed. Eli was impressed Michael understood half of what Niles was saying.

"This is nice," Michael said as they settled into their reclining seats, the pre-show lights dimming around them.

"What is?" Eli asked, though he was already losing the thread. The theater was going dark, and dark meant he couldn't see lips, couldn't read faces. He'd catch what he could and let the rest go.

"This. Hanging out." Michael's voice came from somewhere to his left. "I don't have a lot of friends who get it. The liking-guys thing."

Eli turned toward the sound, catching the shape of Michael's profile against the faint glow of the ceiling. "Have you thought about telling them? Your friends here?"

"Some of them. Eventually. But it's different here. Everyone knows everyone's business."

The ceiling above them began to transform into a field of stars, and Michael fell silent. Eli felt Niles's hand find his in the darkness—a small anchor. He squeezed back and let the show wash over him, catching fragments of the narration when the volume peaked, losing it when it dipped into softer registers.

Afterward, blinking in the bright lobby light, Michael picked up where he'd left off.

"It's weird here. Being out. My parents know, Maddie knows, but at school it's like I'm living a double life. Up in Maine it felt... I don't know. Easier. Like it didn't matter as much."

"That's because you were around people who already got it," Eli said, relieved to be back in a world he could navigate. "Here you're starting from scratch."

"Yeah." Michael was quiet for a moment. "I keep thinking about spring break. Being back up there. Being around you guys again."

"Few more weeks. You'll survive."

"Barely."

Dinner with the family was... a lot.

Michael's mom was warm and welcoming, hugging Eli like they'd known each other for years. His dad shook hands firmly, asked polite questions about their flight. His younger siblings stared openly at Eli—specifically at his hearing aids—until Michael hissed at them to stop.

"It's fine," Eli said. "You want to ask something?"

Jack—the one who'd been staring most openly—nodded eagerly. "What are those things in your ears?"

"Hearing aids. They help me hear better."

"Can you hear me right now?"

"Mostly. It helps when I can see your face."

"That's cool." He seemed satisfied with this answer and returned to his mashed potatoes.

Niles sat quietly through most of the meal, answering questions when asked but otherwise observing. Eli could see him cataloging information— the family dynamics, the conversational patterns, the way Michael's parents looked at each other when they thought no one was watching.

After dinner, while the adults lingered over coffee, Michael pulled Eli onto the back porch. Through the window, Eli could see Niles still at the table, listening intently as Michael's dad explained something about the house's electrical system. Niles looked genuinely interested. Of course he did.

"So?" Michael asked. "What do you think?"

"Of your family?"

"Yeah."

"I think they're good people." Eli leaned against the railing. "Your mom's funny. I like her."

"She likes you. She kept asking about your hearing aids after you left last night. Not in a weird way — she just wanted to make sure she was facing you when she talked."

"That's sweet."

"Yeah. She's like that." Michael was quiet for a moment. "My dad took me to a car show last weekend. Just the two of us."

"Fun?"

"Really fun, actually. We never used to do stuff like that. Just us. But since I told them, it's like..." He searched for the word. "Like he wants me to know nothing's different."

"Is it? Different?"

"No. That's the thing. It's not. He's just... Dad." Michael leaned against the railing. "My dad asked about Levi the other day."

Eli's eyebrows rose. "What did you say?"

"What am I supposed to say? He already knows. Mom already told me he knows. It's like —" Michael exhaled. "Everyone in my life knows I'm in love with this boy except the actual boy."

"That is... objectively hilarious."

"It's not funny."

"It's a little funny."

Michael tried to glare at him. Failed. "Okay. It's a little funny."

"It's just — I already did the hard part. I said I'm gay. But now it's like there's all these smaller conversations I didn't know I'd have to have."

"Welcome to the rest of your life." Eli bumped his shoulder. "It gets easier. I promise."

"How much easier?"

"Enough that eventually you stop thinking about it."

Michael seemed to sit with that for a moment. Then he straightened up, affecting an exaggerated pose. "So? How am I doing? On a scale of one to fabulous?"

"Oh my God."

"What? You said I needed to practice."

"I said you needed to get comfortable. There's a difference." Eli squared his shoulders, tossed his head, and let one hand drift to his hip. "*That's* fabulous. What you just did was community theater."

"Excuse me?"

"Darling, you can't just *say* the word. You have to *embody* it." Eli struck another pose. "See? Commitment."

"You look ridiculous."

"I look *iconic*. There's a difference. Now try again."

Michael laughed, shook his head, and tried again — scarf flip, hip cock, the whole thing. It was terrible. Eli loved it.

"Better. We'll work on it."

"I'm going to be so annoying when I get good at this."

"Oh, honey. I'm counting on it."

They stood there for a while longer, watching the Nashville skyline glitter in the distance, before heading back inside to rescue Niles from small talk.

On their last night, Eli and Niles lay in the hotel bed, the white noise machine humming softly in the corner.

"That was good," Niles said. "The trip."

"Yeah?"

"Yes. I didn't ruin it."

Eli smiled in the darkness. "No, you didn't."

"Michael is nice. I like him."

"I like him too."

"He's scared about Levi."

"I know. But he'll figure it out."

Niles was quiet for a moment. Then: "I was scared about you."

Eli turned onto his side. "What do you mean?"

"When we first started... this. I was scared I would do something wrong. Say the wrong thing. Be too much, or not enough." Niles's voice was quiet, careful — like he was handling something fragile. "I was scared you would realize I wasn't worth the effort."

"Niles—"

"But you stayed. And you kept staying. Even when I was difficult. Even when I didn't know how to..." He trailed off. "I don't know why you stayed. But I'm glad you did."

Eli reached over and pulled him close. "I stayed because I wanted to.

Because you're worth it. Because being with you is the easiest thing I've ever done."

"That doesn't make sense. I'm not easy."

"You're not. But loving you is." He kissed Niles's forehead. "And for what it's worth? I was scared too."

"You were?"

"Of course. Everyone's scared when they fall in love. The trick is doing it anyway."

Niles was quiet for a long moment. Then, very softly: "I love you."

They'd said it before—casually, in passing—but this felt different. This felt like Niles choosing the words carefully, deliberately, meaning every syllable.

"I love you too," Eli said. "Now go to sleep. We have an early flight."

"The flight is at eleven. That's not early."

"Early for me."

Niles huffed something that might have been a laugh. Eli reached over and turned off the lamp, plunging the room into darkness.

In the dark, Eli couldn't hear much. Couldn't see Niles beside him. But he could feel him—the warmth of his body, the shift of weight on the mattress. And then Niles's hand, sliding across his chest. Not settling. Moving.

Eli smiled into the darkness. Niles wasn't quite ready for sleep, it seemed. In fact, he was quite ready for something more interesting.

Eli liked this side of Niles. The confidence that emerged when no one else was watching. The way he knew what he wanted and reached for it. Sometimes, Niles surprised him.

He'd always welcome these sorts of surprises.

Chapter Twenty-Six

AMERICAN AIRLINES 5069 from DC landed just before three.

Graham might've caught an earlier flight on Southwest out of Portland, but nothing flew direct to Nashville. Besides, he had too many miles with American. Well—Simon did, really. But if he had to transfer anyway, might as well travel in comfort. First class meant more legroom, fewer elbows, and a glass of wine that almost made the layover worthwhile.

Simon would've laughed at him. *"You and your creature comforts."* But Simon had been the one to rack up all those miles in the first place, flying back and forth to conferences and client meetings. It seemed fitting to use them now.

The flight had given Graham too much time to think. He'd spent the hours watching clouds drift past while his mind churned through everything he wanted to say. Everything he should have said years ago.

Grammy.

He still couldn't quite believe Becca remembered that. Couldn't believe she'd carried it with her all this time, that childhood nickname wrapped around a childhood wound. He'd been so busy growing up, becoming himself, that he'd never stopped to consider what he might be leaving behind.

Or who.

The last time he'd been to Nashville was—what, six years ago now? Seven? Simon had been on one of his European conference trips, and Graham had stopped through on his way out west for a book event. A quick visit. Dinner with David and Becca, a night in the guest room, gone by morning. He'd seen them at Simon's funeral, of course, but that was different. He hadn't really been paying attention to anyone or anything that day. He'd barely been present in his own body.

Graham collected his single bag—he'd learned to pack light over the years—and made his way through the terminal.

Becca was waiting at arrivals.

She looked older than he remembered, which was stupid because of course she did. They both did. But something about seeing her in person —not on a screen, not in a photograph—made the years between them suddenly, painfully real.

"Hey," she said.

"Hey yourself."

They stood there for a moment, awkward in a way they'd never been as children. Then Becca stepped forward and hugged him—really hugged him, not the quick, perfunctory embrace they'd exchanged at holidays and... well. Simon's funeral.

"I'm glad you came," she said into his shoulder.

"Me too."

She pulled back, wiping at her eyes with a shaky laugh. "God, look at me. You just got here and I'm already crying."

"I have that effect on people."

She swatted his arm, still laughing, still crying a little. "Come on. David's got lunch waiting. The kids are at school, so we have a few hours before chaos descends."

"Chaos?"

"You'll see."

The house was exactly as Graham remembered it—warm, lived-in, slightly cluttered in a way that spoke of a family actually using the space rather than just occupying it. David met them at the door with a firm handshake and a genuine smile.

"Good to see you, Graham. It's been too long."

"It has. That's on me."

"It's on all of us." David clapped him on the shoulder. "Come on. I made sandwiches. Nothing fancy."

They ate at the kitchen table—turkey clubs, chips, iced tea—while making small talk about the flight, the weather, Michael's college applications. Safe topics. Surface-level.

Graham appreciated it. He wasn't ready for the real conversation yet. He needed to ease into it.

After lunch, David excused himself to run errands—transparently giving them space—and Graham found himself alone with his sister for the first time in years.

"So," Becca said, refilling their glasses. "Here we are."

"Here we are."

She sat down across from him, her hands wrapped around her tea like she needed something to hold onto. "I don't really know how to do this, Graham. The talking thing. I've been thinking about what to say ever since you called, and I still don't..." She shook her head. "I don't know where to start."

"That makes two of us."

"Great. So we're both hopeless."

"Apparently."

She tried to smile, but it flickered and died. "Michael told you. What I said to him. About... Grammy."

The name hung between them.

"He did," Graham said.

"I didn't plan to tell him. It just came out. He was so upset, and I was trying to explain why I'd been distant with Simon, and suddenly I was talking about things I hadn't thought about in thirty years." She pressed her palms against the table. "I didn't even know I was still carrying it around. I thought I'd dealt with it. Moved on. But apparently I just... shoved it down somewhere and pretended it wasn't there."

"Some things don't move past. They just move deeper."

Becca looked at him—really looked, in that searching way she'd had even as a child. "You didn't know, did you? How much it affected me. When you pulled away."

Graham set down his glass. His chest felt tight. "No. I didn't. I was so... Becca, I was so wrapped up in my own stuff. Trying to figure out who I was. What I was." He stopped. Started again. "High school was... I knew, okay? I knew I was different. Knew I liked guys. But I couldn't say it. Couldn't even think it most days. I just kept my head down and counted the days until I could get out."

Becca was quiet, watching him.

"And you were—God, you were eight. Nine. This little kid who wanted to follow me everywhere, and I just..." He rubbed his face. "I pushed you away. I pushed everyone away. Because I couldn't let anyone get too close. Couldn't risk them seeing what I was trying so hard to hide."

"Graham—"

"No, let me—I need to say this." He took a breath. "I didn't mean to hurt you. I wasn't even thinking about you, which is almost worse, right? I was so focused on surviving. On getting through each day without anyone figuring out my secret. And then I got to Columbia and I met Simon, and suddenly I could breathe. For the first time in my life, I could actually breathe. And I just... I never looked back. I never thought about what I'd left behind."

His voice cracked on the last word. He hadn't expected that.

"You were eighteen," Becca said softly. "You were supposed to leave."

"Leaving isn't the same as disappearing. I could have called more. Come home more. But every time I thought about going back, I just..." He stopped. This was the edge of it. The thing he'd never told her. The thing he'd spent thirty-five years burying.

Becca was quiet for a moment. When she spoke, her voice was thick. "I blamed Simon. For years. I told myself I didn't have a problem with you being gay, and I didn't—I really didn't—but I couldn't separate him from losing you. Every time I saw him, I saw the person who took my brother away. And I know that's not fair. I know he didn't take you anywhere. You left on your own, long before you ever met him. But I was eight, Graham. I didn't understand any of that. I just knew that Grammy was gone, and then you were gone, and then there was this man who got to have you when I didn't."

"Becca..."

"And I was so ashamed of feeling that way." Her voice broke. "Because it's petty. It's so petty. I'm a grown woman carrying around a grudge from when I was in third grade. But I didn't know how to let it go. I didn't even know I was still holding onto it until Michael—" She stopped, pressed her hand to her mouth.

Graham reached across the table and took her other hand. He was trembling, and he didn't know if it was from the weight of what she'd just said or from what he was about to.

"Becca. I need to tell you something."

She looked at him, startled by the shift in his voice. The rawness of it.

"I didn't just leave."

"What do you mean?"

Graham opened his mouth. Closed it. His hand went to his cheek — that old gesture, the one he didn't even know he did. He'd spent thirty-five years keeping this contained. Keeping it neat. Keeping it away from everyone except Simon, and even Simon had only gotten the measured version, the one Graham could control.

But he couldn't control it now. Becca was sitting across from him with mascara streaking down her face, telling him she'd spent her whole life blaming the wrong person, and he couldn't let her carry that anymore.

"Dad caught me with a boy." His voice broke on the word. "Senior year. In my room. We weren't even — we hadn't even kissed yet, Bec, we were just—" He pressed his fist against his mouth. "And Dad beat the shit out of me."

The kitchen went silent.

"He hit me so hard I went down. I hit my head. And I—" Graham's breath shuddered. "I don't know what happened after that, Bec. I woke up in the hospital. Mom never really told me the details. I had to drag bits and pieces out of her over the years, and even then she'd change the subject or say she couldn't remember." He shook his head. "All I know is I was on my bedroom floor and the next thing I remember is a hospital room."

Becca's face had drained of color. She was shaking her head, not in denial but in the slow, horrified way of someone watching the ground shift beneath a lifetime of assumptions.

"I don't even know where you were. Asleep, I guess. You must have been—"

"The sirens," Becca whispered.

Graham stopped.

Becca's eyes had gone distant, focused on something far away. Something buried so deep she hadn't known it was there.

"I remember sirens," she said slowly. "I woke up. It was dark. And there were lights — red and blue, through my curtains. And Mom came in and told me to go back to bed. That everything was fine."

"She said everything was fine, Graham." The last word broke apart in her mouth.

The air between them was unbearable.

"And in the morning..." Becca's hand was trembling against the table. "Aunt Margery was there. And you weren't. And Mom said you'd gone to stay with Aunt Margery for a while." She looked at him, her face crumpling. "And then you never came back."

Graham couldn't speak. He hadn't known she'd heard the sirens. Hadn't known she'd woken up. All these years, he'd imagined her sleeping through it — oblivious, protected. But she'd been awake in her room, watching red and blue lights move across her ceiling, and their mother had told her to go back to sleep.

"Why didn't you tell me?" Becca's voice cracked wide open. "All these years, Graham — I thought... I didn't know why you left. I thought you just didn't want us anymore."

"You were eight, Bec."

"But later! When I was old enough—"

"It didn't matter."

"How can you say that?"

"Because I couldn't—" His voice gave out. He pressed his hand over his eyes. "I couldn't think about any of it, Becca. That house. That life. Everything about going back there reminded me of—" He shook his head. "I just needed it gone. All of it. And by the time I got to Columbia and met Simon, I finally had something that didn't hurt. Something that was mine. And I held onto that and I never looked back."

He didn't say the rest. Didn't say that "all of it" had included her. That the eight-year-old girl down the hall had been wrapped up in everything he was running from — not because of anything she'd done, but because she belonged to the world that had broken him.

He didn't say it. But Becca's face told him she understood.

"I didn't think you hated me," she managed. "I just... didn't know why you left."

They sat with that. The truth of it. How close those two things had always been — not knowing why, and filling the silence with the worst explanation you could find.

Becca wiped her face with the heel of her hand. She stared at the table for a long time, her jaw working, and Graham could see it happening — the grief giving way to something harder. The questions forming. The math she was doing, adding up all the things that should have told her, all the people who could have.

"Mom knew," she said finally. Not a question.

Graham didn't answer.

"She was there. She told me to go back to bed. She—" Becca's voice was rising now, anger threading through the grief. "She should have fought for you, Graham. She should have done something—"

"She did what she could. She got me out of the house. Got me to Aunt Margery's."

"That's not enough!" Becca's palm hit the table. "Her son was beaten unconscious and she just — shipped him off and never talked about it? Never held Dad accountable? Never told me the truth?"

"It was a different time, Becca. And she was scared. And what was done was done." Graham's voice was gentle but firm. "I didn't want her carrying that guilt for the rest of her life. I still don't. It's ancient history."

"It's not ancient history. It's the reason for everything." Becca pressed both hands over her face, her shoulders shaking. "It's why you left. It's why you never came home. It's why you didn't come to Dad's funeral—"

"Yes."

"—and I thought that was because you didn't care. I thought you just... moved on. Found Simon and forgot about us. And the whole time—" She couldn't finish.

Graham stood and walked around the table. He pulled a chair next to hers and sat down, wrapping his arm around her shoulders. She turned into him the way she used to as a little girl — face against his chest, hands fisted in his shirt.

"I never forgot about you," he said quietly. "I just didn't know how to come back. And I didn't want to bring all that poison with me."

Becca cried for a while. Graham held her and let her.

When she finally pulled back, her face was blotchy and swollen. She looked wrecked — but also somehow lighter.

"I'm so sorry," she said. "For all of it. For blaming Simon. For being cold to him all those years when he didn't deserve it. For making you feel like you couldn't come home." She wiped her face roughly with her sleeve. "God, Graham. He was the best thing that ever happened to you, wasn't he?"

"He was." Graham's eyes were bright. "He wanted to hop a train to Maine and beat the shit out of Dad when I finally told him. Between freshman and sophomore year."

Becca let out a broken laugh. "I would have helped him."

"I know you would have." He squeezed her shoulder. "But that was a long time ago. And... well. Here we are."

"Here we are," Becca whispered. Then, after a moment: "Have you and Mom ever talked about it?"

"I don't think any of us have ever talked about it directly. That's how our family works, Bec. We bury things."

"Not anymore," Becca said fiercely. "I'm done burying things."

Graham looked at her — his baby sister, forty-three years old, red-eyed and defiant and done pretending — and felt something in him give way.

"Good," he said. "So am I."

She tried to smile, but it flickered and died. "So what happens now?"

Graham thought about it. "I don't know. But I know I want to be around more. Especially for the kids." He paused. "Especially for Michael."

Becca nodded slowly. "He's going through a lot right now."

"He's going through what I went through back when I was his age." Graham looked at her. "And I know you and David have been great — he told me, and I can see it. But there are things he can't talk to you about. Things that are easier to say to someone who's—"

"Who's been there," Becca finished. "I know."

Graham nodded. "I didn't have that. I had no one I could ask, no one who understood. And I don't want that for him."

Becca was quiet for a moment. "You need to be there for him, Graham. I'm his mom, but I can only talk to him so much about this... stuff."

"Stuff?" Graham made air quotes. "What 'stuff' are you referring to, exactly?"

Her face went pink. "You know. The... stuff."

"I really don't. You'll have to be more specific."

"Graham."

"Is it the dating stuff? The kissing stuff? The—"

"Oh my God, stop." She was laughing now, swatting at him. "You're terrible."

"Just trying to clarify."

"You know exactly what I mean." She made her own air quotes. "Besides, he's not going to talk about that 'stuff' with mom and dad. We're 'old' and we 'don't know what it's like.'"

"Well. He has a point."

"Excuse me?"

"I mean—when's the last time you thought another guy looked hot?"

Becca's jaw dropped.

"Scratch that. Bad example." Graham held up his hands. "I mean—"

She burst out laughing. Really laughing, the kind that made her double over. "Oh my God. Your face."

"You know what I meant."

"I really don't. You'll have to be more specific."

"Okay, okay. Point taken." He was laughing too now. "Point being—Michael looks up to me. At least, I think he does."

"He does." Becca sobered. "He really does. He adores coming to your place in the summer. It nearly killed him that he wasn't able to last year."

The words landed heavier than she'd probably intended. Graham looked at her. "Speaking of. Why didn't you let him come?"

Becca went quiet. She studied her hands for a moment, searching for the words. "I... I don't really know. Honestly."

Graham gave her a look—the look, the one she remembered from when they were kids. The one that said *try again*.

"Fine." She sighed. "I thought he'd get in your hair. Especially when you were dealing with Simon..." She didn't finish the sentence, but she didn't need to.

"You might have been right," Graham admitted. "At the time, I probably would have thought the same thing. I wasn't really... thinking. About much of anything."

"But looking back?"

"Looking back, maybe he should have come. It might have helped. Both of us."

Becca nodded slowly. "I'm glad he convinced me to let him come for Christmas."

"Why did you? Let him, I mean."

"He pleaded." She smiled faintly. "But... he's my kid, Graham. I couldn't imagine him not being here for Christmas, you know?" She paused, something shifting in her expression. "But..."

"But what?"

"It's nothing."

"No, Becca. What?"

She took a breath. "He said you were going to be sitting up there in your dark house all alone. No one there to keep you company." Her voice wavered. "And I couldn't bear that thought, Graham. I know Simon was everything to you. And I'm sorry I never let myself get close to him. I'm sorry I kept that distance all those years. But—" Her eyes filled with tears again. "I couldn't let you be alone. On your first Christmas without him..."

"Gone," Graham finished quietly. "You can say it."

They sat in silence for a moment, both of them looking out into nothing. Remembering Simon.

Graham finally took a breath. He hadn't talked about Simon like this in front of Becca. Not ever.

"I'm glad you sent him," he said finally. "He... well. He helped. Is helping."

Becca nodded.

"Besides," Graham said, trying to pep himself up, "he got to meet Levi. And... well. The rest, they say, is..."

"Speaking of." Becca leaned forward. "Do you think they've talked? I encouraged him to just talk to the boy, but..."

"I don't think so. When I spoke with him, he felt like he should do it in person. It's why I suggested he come back with me next week while he's off."

Becca nodded, relief flickering across her face. "I'm grateful you're flying back with him. I know he did fine on his own before, but... he's still my baby."

Graham nudged her gently. "He's growing up, Becca. And your relationship is going to change. I know what that's like."

She did too now. Especially after today.

"He'll still be my baby," she said firmly.

"Perhaps. But don't treat him like one."

The kids came home in a thunderous cascade of backpacks and complaints and questions about snacks. Graham watched Becca transform into mom-mode—fielding requests, arbitrating disputes, somehow keeping track of three different conversations at once—and felt a pang of something like admiration.

She'd built a good life. A full life. He'd missed so much of it.

Michael arrived last, fresh from school, and his face lit up when he saw Graham.

"Uncle Graham!" He crossed the kitchen in three strides and hugged him. "You're here!"

"I'm here."

"How was the flight? Did Mom cry yet?"

"Michael!" Becca protested.

"What? It's a valid question."

"The flight was fine, and yes, she cried," Graham said. "Twice, actually."

"Only twice? She's slipping."

"I'm standing right here," Becca said.

"We know." Michael grinned at her, then turned back to Graham. "So where are you staying? The Marriott?"

"Actually, I was hoping I could stay here. With you all. For the week."

Michael's eyebrows shot up. "Wait—the whole week? Here?"

"If that's okay."

Becca blinked. She'd assumed—well, she'd assumed she'd be dropping him at a hotel after they'd spent some time together. That's what he always did.

"Of course it's okay," she said, already moving toward the hallway. "The guest room is—Michael, go get my craft stuff off the bed in there."

"Becca, I can move things myself—"

"Michael." She ignored Graham entirely. "I want to make sure his room is up to standard."

"Oh, well, in that case," Graham said, straightening up. "Michael, please ensure I have fresh linens and towels. And draw a bath with rose petals floating on top. Water temperature precisely at ninety-eight point six degrees—"

Becca's fist connected with his arm.

"Ow!"

"I may be your little sister," she said, squaring up to him, "but I run this house..." She poked his chest. "Grammy."

The younger kids giggled. Michael too. Graham rubbed his arm, grinning.

He turned to Michael. "Don't mess with her."

"Tell me about it," Michael said, and disappeared down the hall before Becca could get him too.

The week passed faster than Graham expected.

He helped David with a project in the garage—building shelves, mostly handing tools and staying out of the way. He had dinner with the family every night, learning the rhythms of their household, the inside jokes he'd never been part of. He took long walks through the neighborhood, thinking about Simon, about Becca, about all the ways life could surprise you if you let it.

And he talked. With Becca, late at night after the kids were in bed. With David, over morning tea—well, tea for Graham, coffee for David—while everyone else slept. With Michael, in stolen moments when they could speak without siblings eavesdropping.

"You nervous?" Graham asked him one afternoon. They were sitting on the back porch, watching the clouds roll in. "About spring break?"

Michael's leg started bouncing. "A little. A lot, actually."

"About Levi?"

"About everything." He chewed at his thumbnail. "What if I get there and I can't say it? What if I freeze again?"

"Then you freeze. And you try again."

"What if he doesn't feel the same way?"

"Then you'll survive. And you'll know. Either way, you won't be stuck wondering anymore."

Michael was quiet for a moment. "What if he does feel the same way?"

Graham smiled. "Then you'll figure out what comes next. Together."

"That sounds terrifying."

"It is. It's also wonderful." He looked at his nephew—this brave, scared kid on the edge of something new—and felt a rush of affection. "You know, when I met Simon, I was just as scared as you are now. Maybe more. I spent months convincing myself it could never work, that I was imagining things, that I was better off not saying anything."

"What changed?"

"I got tired of being scared. And I realized that not knowing was worse than any answer he could give me." Graham paused. "So I told him. Badly. Stumbling over every word. And he just looked at me and said—"

"'I know. I was waiting for you to figure it out.'" Michael smiled. "You told me that already."

"Did I? I'm getting old."

"You're not that old."

"Old enough." Graham reached over and ruffled his hair. "You're going to be fine, Michael. Whatever happens. I promise."

Michael didn't look entirely convinced, but he nodded. "Okay. I'll try to believe you."

"That's all I ask."

The night before they left, Becca found Graham on the back porch, staring up at the stars.

"Can't sleep?" she asked, settling into the chair beside him.

"Too much thinking."

"About what?"

"Simon. You. Michael." He shrugged. "Everything."

She was quiet for a moment. "I'm glad you came, Graham. Really glad."

"So am I."

"I know this week wasn't... I mean, we didn't solve everything. There's still a lot of history between us."

"There is. But we made a start."

"Yeah." She pulled her sweater tighter around herself. "I want to keep going. After you leave. I want to actually be your sister again. Not just someone you see at holidays."

"I want that too."

"So we'll call each other. Regularly. Not just birthdays and Christmas."

"Deal."

"And you'll come back. For Thanksgiving, maybe. Or Christmas. Bring your whole... whatever it is. Eli and Niles and whoever else."

Graham laughed. "My 'whatever it is'?"

"You know what I mean. Your people. Your found family or whatever they call it."

"I'll ask them. I think they'd like that."

Becca reached over and took his hand. "Thank you, Grammy."

The name hit him like a wave—grief and love and memory all tangled together. He squeezed her hand.

"Thank you, little sister."

They sat there together, watching the stars, until the cold drove them back inside.

The next morning was chaos—bags to pack, flights to catch, last-minute hugs and reminders and promises to call. Michael vibrated with barely contained energy, checking his phone every thirty seconds like Levi might somehow sense he was coming.

"Ready?" Graham asked him at the airport, bags checked, boarding passes in hand.

Michael took a deep breath. "Ready."

"You don't look ready. You look like you're about to throw up."

"Thanks. That's helpful."

"Just being honest." Graham smiled. "Come on. Let's go get you your boy."

Michael's ears went red, but he was grinning as they headed for the gate.

Chapter Twenty-Seven

THE CLOUDS below looked like cotton stretched thin over gray. Michael stared out the window as Portland came into view—tiny houses, snow-dusted trees, the sprawl of the coast disappearing into winter haze. His stomach tightened.

"You're quiet," Graham said.

"Just thinking."

"About?"

Michael didn't answer. He was thinking about Levi. About what he was going to say. About what it would mean if he actually said it.

He'd never wanted something so much in his life. And he'd never been so terrified of getting it.

Even if Levi felt the same way — and Michael was pretty sure he did, had been pretty sure since Christmas, maybe before — what then? They lived a thousand miles apart. How would that work? Would they text every day? FaceTime every night? And what happened in the fall when Michael started college — would he pick somewhere close to Maine? Was that insane? Was he planning his entire future around a boy he'd kissed exactly zero times?

And Susan. Would she be okay with this? Her son, her situation — everything she was already carrying. Michael showing up with feelings on top of all that.

His brain was going to explode.

"Michael."

Graham's voice cut through the spiral. Michael blinked, realizing he'd been gripping the armrest so hard his knuckles were white.

"Sorry. I'm just..."

"I know." Graham's voice was gentle. "Can I offer some advice?"

"Do I have a choice?"

"Not really." Graham shifted in his seat to face him. "Try not to see all of this as obstacles. See them as steps. Toward something potentially really good."

"But what if they're not good? What if I mess it up?"

"Then even those help you learn to see better. For the next time."

"That's very philosophical."

"I'm old. I'm allowed to be philosophical." Graham paused. "But you can't live without taking a moment to breathe, right? So breathe. Whatever happens when we land—it's just a step. Not the whole staircase."

Michael took a breath. Then another.

"Okay," he said. "Okay."

The plane began its descent.

Portland International Jetport was small—nothing like Nashville or the chaos of the DC layover. Michael followed Graham through the terminal, backpack slung over his shoulder. They hadn't bothered checking anything, so they walked straight out of the security area and into the main lobby.

Eli was standing near the exit, staring at his phone, looking profoundly bored.

Graham and Michael walked toward him. Graham nudged Eli's arm as they approached.

"Jesus!" Eli jumped, hand flying to his chest. "You scared me."

Michael managed a half-smile, but it didn't reach his eyes. He was still a bundle of nerves, his mind already racing ahead to whenever he'd see Levi.

Eli caught the mood immediately. "Oh good, you brought your anxiety. I was worried you'd left it in Nashville."

Graham rolled his eyes. "He's just thinking."

"Thinking. Sure." Eli pulled Michael into a hug, squeezing an extra moment to whisper in his ear: "It'll be okay."

Michael nodded against his shoulder, not trusting his voice.

When they separated, Graham asked, "You took care of the car, right?"

"Oh, sure. Niles and I challenged some bros racing the other night. You might need new tires, but no major dents."

"What?" Michael looked between them, confused.

"The asshole here—" Graham pointed at Eli.

"That's *Ms.* Asshole, thank you."

"—took my car while I was in Nashville. So who knows what state it's in."

"*Perfect* state, thank you!" Eli grinned. "Pristine. Immaculate. You're welcome."

Michael finally smiled, felt a small laugh escape. Eli had that effect.

"There he is!" Eli said.

Michael thought he meant the laugh—but Eli was looking past him. Michael turned to follow his gaze.

And there was Levi.

He'd just come from the restroom, apparently, and had walked up behind them while they were talking. He was wearing that green jacket again—the one from New Year's Eve—and his hair was longer than Michael remembered, curling slightly at the ends.

Time stopped.

Then Levi crossed the distance between them and slammed into Michael with the ferocity of a charging elephant, arms wrapping around him, holding tight.

"I missed you," Levi said into his shoulder. "God, I missed you so much."

Michael couldn't speak. He just held on.

Behind them, Eli murmured to Graham: "He texted earlier. Wanted to come. No plan or anything—just wanted to be here."

Graham nodded, watching the two boys. Wondering if maybe—finally—they might actually *talk*.

Michael was near tears. All his tension, all his fear, still right there under the surface. But then they both became aware of Graham and Eli staring a hole through them. And the other travelers scurrying around them, trying to get to the exit. And suddenly the moment felt too big, too public.

Fear overtook them both, and they released each other. Neither of them spoke.

Graham let out a sigh. He was tired—traveling always did that to him. Simon had loved it. Could hop from one plane to the next, hotel to airport, loved every minute. But Graham? It was exhausting, all that waiting and sitting and waiting again.

"Let's go," he said. "Levi, good to see you. You coming with us to dinner?"

Levi blinked. "Dinner?" He hadn't thought through anything when he'd texted Eli. "Uh... sure."

Eli stepped between the boys, draping an arm around each of their shoulders. "This dinner you speak of," he said to Graham. "Where would this be at?"

Graham exhaled a half-laugh. "Fine. My treat. Your choice."

"Good answer." Eli released them and headed for the exit. "Follow me."

Graham fell into step behind him, the boys bringing up the rear.

Michael's hand brushed against Levi's. He wanted to grab it, hold on, never let go.

But once again, they got in their own way.

In the parking garage, Eli literally bumped into Graham as they both reached for the driver's door.

Eli looked at him. "What?"

"I'm driving."

"You're still officially traveling."

"What? We're home."

"Not yet." Eli held up the keys. "You said I had the car while you were traveling. You're not home until you walk through your front door. So—" He waved his hand. "Get your ass over to the passenger side."

"Excuse me?"

"You're excused. Now go. I'm driving us to dinner."

"You're terrible, you know that?"

"I'm *everything*. Now get."

Michael and Levi watched the exchange with barely concealed amusement.

As Michael and Levi both reached for the same rear door behind Eli, they bumped into each other—then immediately started pretending to bicker the same way Graham and Eli had been.

Eli spun around once everyone was in the car. "Why don't you two just get on with it?"

Both boys froze. "Get on with what?"

"Married. You two already bicker like an old married couple."

Graham snickered from the passenger seat.

Michael's mouth dropped open. Levi started to laugh—then looked at Michael and stopped, his face going slightly red.

But he felt it inside. The truth of it.

Michael caught his eye and smiled.

Eli turned the radio on and began pulling out of the parking spot.

"Why'd you turn that on?" Graham asked. "You can't even hear it."

Eli didn't miss a beat. He reached over and cranked the volume so loud everyone clapped their hands over their ears.

Graham lunged for the knob, spinning it down. "What the hell?"

"What? You reminded me I needed to be able to hear the radio. Just following orders." Eli smirked.

"You're a bitch, you know that?"

Eli beamed. "Why, thank you, Graham! That's so sweet."

Levi laughed out loud at that. Michael tried to contain his own laughter but failed.

Graham shook his head, but he knew—he loved having Eli in his life. Loved having all of them here.

"Where's Niles?" Michael leaned forward between the seats.

Eli caught his lips in the rearview mirror. "School, then heading home. He says he'll see you both some other time. Welcome back, all that."

"When will you see him next? Maybe we can plan dinner with him or something."

"Oh, when I get home."

Michael didn't follow. "Didn't you just say Niles was heading home after school?"

"Yeah. Our home."

Levi's head snapped up. He hadn't heard this. Neither had Graham.

"What?"

"Oh—did I not mention?" Eli was enjoying every minute of this, drawing it out. "Niles officially moved in with me the other day. Donna is scared shitless, but he's practically been living with me for weeks anyway, so—"

From the back seat, Michael and Levi erupted with questions, talking over each other.

"Wait—what?"

"When did this happen?"

"Are you serious right now?"

"Really? Niles is living with you now?"

Eli didn't miss a beat. "Well, I hope so. We've been wearing each other's underwear for the past week, so..."

Graham would've done a spit take if he'd been drinking something. Levi let out a guffaw. Michael couldn't believe what he'd just heard—but then realized, yes. Yes, he could. It was Eli.

They pulled up to a fancy-looking restaurant on the way home. As they parked, Levi pulled out his phone to text his mom. Michael looked over his shoulder without thinking—then caught himself.

"Sorry. I didn't mean to—"

"I don't care." Levi glanced at him. "You're practically family."

Graham caught that. Filed it away.

Dinner was... something.

More of the Graham and Eli show, really. The food was good—Eli said it was "French Fusion," which Michael didn't understand until Eli asked how his foie gras tasted. Michael didn't know what it was, but it was delicious.

Graham decided it was best not to tell him.

Eli worked the table the way he always did — jokes, questions, pulling everyone in. But Michael noticed he kept steering things toward Levi. Drawing him out. Getting him to laugh, to relax, to look at Michael when he answered. Graham played along, setting up Eli's jokes and letting them land.

Michael noticed more than he used to. Somewhere in the last few months — the coming out, the conversations, the slow process of letting himself be who he was — something had shifted. Before, he could tell Levi was nice-looking. Now he gave himself permission to really see him. To think: *He's really cute.*

It still felt a little weird to say that, even in his own head. But it also felt right.

Levi *was* cute. Really cute. Especially when Eli had him laughing so hard he almost snorted water out of his nose. Or when Levi would look over at Michael and smile, sharing the enthusiasm of whatever story was being told.

God, he was so cute.

As the meal wound down, Eli announced that his time as chauffeur was almost at an end.

"I only had Dad's car until he officially came home," he said, nodding at Graham. "Per our agreement at the parking garage."

"I'll swing by and drop the boys off first," Graham said. "Then take you home. Give them some time to catch up."

Eli considered this. "Fine. But on one condition."

"What?"

"I still get to drive." He grinned. "You can have your snooty fancy-pants BMW once we get back to my apartment. It's been *such* a chore driving in such luxury, but I'll suffer through."

Graham shook his head. Whatever was he going to do with him?

They dropped the boys off first. Michael remembered the alarm code, punching it in as Levi stamped snow off his boots in the entryway. Eli backed out of the driveway, and he and Graham headed toward the apartment.

The car was quiet for a moment.

"I'm happy for you," Graham said finally. "For you and Niles."

Eli glanced at him. "You couldn't say that in front of the boys?"

"I could have. But I wanted you to hear it quietly. From me, directly. Because it's a serious moment." He paused. "And one I'm very happy about. For both of you."

Eli, normally snarky and quick with a comeback, went quiet. Thoughtful.

"I remember that first night I saw you," he said. "You drove up in this very car and looked at me like some creepy pervert while I was waiting for the bus."

"I was *not* a creepy pervert!"

"I know that *now*. But back then—"

"Okay, okay."

"But seriously." Eli's voice softened. "I can't believe how... I'm gonna say something real. Not joking. I mean this in a good way. Promise you won't laugh."

"I promise nothing."

"I hate you, you know that?"

"Yes. Ever since I stalked you as a creepy pervert at bus stops."

Eli laughed. Graham didn't usually get the last word—but this time, he'd won.

"Seriously though," Eli said, his voice quieter now. "I love you, Graham. You're sort of like my father. Or older brother. Or... something."

"I'm something, all right. But I refuse to be your dad. Besides, don't you already have one?"

"You know what I mean! Can't I at least give you a compliment sometimes?"

"Sure. Whenever you're ready."

"I'm going inside." Eli pulled into his parking spot and cut the engine. "Night, Graham."

They both got out. Graham came around to the driver's side as Eli headed for his building. But before Eli could disappear through the door, Graham caught his arm.

"Eli."

Eli turned.

"I love you too." Graham pulled him into a hug. Held on for a moment. Then added, just to break the tension: "...son."

Eli stepped back, fighting off a tear, and injected humor to deflect. "That's *daughter*, thank you!"

Graham laughed. "I'll text you tomorrow. I don't know what's going on with the boys."

"I want ALL the details!" Eli yelled as he disappeared through the door.

Graham saw Niles appear in the doorway, and he gave a small wave. It was nice, seeing those two together. They couldn't be more different, yet more compatible.

He drove home.

. . .

Meanwhile, Michael had dropped his backpack in "his room"—which hadn't changed since Christmas. The sheets and bed had clearly been washed, the room cleaned, but his clothes from last time were still hanging in the closet, still folded in the dresser.

It was, in every way, *his* room.

"You should get some posters or something," Levi said from the doorway. "Decorations. Make it feel like home."

Michael sat on the edge of the bed and took off his coat. Started untying his shoes. Levi stood there, still in his jacket and snow boots, holding his cap.

"Take your coat off," Michael said, patting the spot beside him. "Graham won't be home for a while."

Levi carefully placed his things on the desk chair, then sat down next to Michael. Close, but not too close.

"Your boots," Michael said.

Levi looked down. "Oh—sorry. I should have taken them off at the door." He bent to untie them.

Michael reached out and grabbed his hand.

Levi looked up. They were face to face now. Inches apart.

"Is everything okay?" Levi's voice was worried. "What's wrong?"

Michael felt tears pricking at his eyes. All the words he'd rehearsed, all the speeches he'd practiced — they were gone. His mind went blank. And what came out was:

"I... like you."

Levi went still.

"No—I mean—yes—I mean—" Michael was making a mess of this. "I *like* you, Levi. Like... *like* you."

Levi's face tensed. His whole body tensed.

Michael saw the reaction and his heart cracked. He'd fucked it up. He'd misread everything. Levi wasn't—he didn't—

The tears came. Michael couldn't stop them.

"I'm sorry," he managed. "I'm so sorry. I thought—I must have been wrong—I'm such an idiot—"

Levi started shaking his head. "No. No, you've got it wrong. You're wrong—"

Michael heard *you're wrong* and felt his chest cave in. Wrong about Levi. Wrong about everything. Levi wasn't gay, had never been interested, and Michael had just ruined the best friendship he'd ever—

"No—I like you too!"

Michael didn't hear it. He was spiraling, drowning in his own shame.

Levi grabbed Michael's face with both hands, forcing him to stop, to look, to *see*.

"I like you too," Levi said. His voice was trembling. "I like—"

He couldn't get past the word *like*.

Their eyes locked.

And Levi kissed him.

Michael's entire life stopped.

Then started again.

Levi didn't know what he was doing. But Michael hadn't pulled away. In fact, Michael was pushing in harder, kissing him back.

Michael's fears, his tears—all of it fell away. He grabbed Levi's jacket and pulled him closer, falling back onto the bed, bringing Levi down on top of him.

Levi's mind was racing, but somehow he let himself stop thinking. Just followed what was happening. Levi wrapped his arms tighter around him as Michael drew him down. Neither of them noticed Graham walk down the hall.

He'd pulled the car into the garage and come in quietly, still thinking about his conversation with Eli. He wasn't listening for the boys—wasn't thinking about them at all—until he walked past Michael's room and saw them.

Holding each other. Kissing.

Graham stood for a moment, witnessing something that looked like a scene from a film. Then he turned and moved down the hall to his office, shutting the door softly behind him. Not to hide. To give them their moment.

Graham sat at his desk and turned on the radio. Something baroque played softly—Vivaldi, maybe. He let his mind drift, trying to give the boys their space.

His eyes fell on the manuscript he'd been struggling with for months. The next Oltrarno. The one he couldn't figure out how to write.

Beside it sat the folder containing the original manuscript of *Across the Arno*—the first book. Levi had finished reading it after Michael left at Christmas, and Graham had left it sitting on his desk. For inspiration, he'd told himself. Though really, he'd just been too lazy to put it away.

Now he looked at it and thought of Michael and Levi down the hall. And he remembered.

The first book. Marco and Alessandro. He'd painted their story up to a point, then gotten stuck. He knew there was an ending—he could feel it—but he couldn't find the words.

It was Simon who'd found them for him.

They'd been young then. Living in that tiny apartment with the leaky radiator and the view of a brick wall. Graham had been sitting at his desk, staring at a blank page, when Simon came up behind him and started rubbing his shoulders. Kneading out a knot.

"Come to bed."

"I can't. I need to finish this."

"You need to take a break."

"I need to figure out the ending."

Simon had swung him around on his desk chair and sat down on his lap. Playful. Insistent. Graham had tried to shoo him away—*work to be done, struggling with the ending*—but Simon kept kissing him, distracting him, until finally Graham gave in and let himself be led to their bed.

Afterward, lying there in the dark, Simon's warm body pressed against his, Graham had looked up at the shadows on the ceiling and felt Simon's breath against his neck.

"I love you," Simon had whispered.

And Graham had known. That was how he wanted the book to end. Not with a grand declaration or a dramatic climax. Just two people, holding each other in the dark, with everything ahead of them still unknown.

That was the ending he'd written. Marco and Alessandro, together at last, the future uncertain but no longer frightening. Because they had each other.

Now, thirty years later, Graham sat in his office and listened to the baroque music playing softly. He thought of Michael and Levi down the hall—young and scared and finally, *finally* brave enough to reach for what they wanted.

He thought of Simon. Gone now. Like Marco was gone, in the world of the books.

But Alessandro remained. Older. Wiser. Carrying Marco's memory forward, passing the legacy to the next generation.

Graham looked at the blank page in front of him.

And he knew, at last, how he wanted to write the final Oltrarno.

Chapter Twenty-Eight

THE OLTRARNO

THE ROAD to Rome was long, and Marco walked most of it alone.

He had coin enough for a mule, but he preferred his feet. Preferred the rhythm of walking, the way it gave his mind time to settle. The countryside rolled past him in shades of brown and gold—autumn in full bloom, the harvest nearly done, the air carrying the sharp sweetness of overripe grapes and woodsmoke.

A year had passed since Florence burned.

Not literally, of course. The city still stood, its towers and domes unchanged against the Tuscan sky. But the Florence Marco had known—the one where he had learned to paint, where he had first touched Alessandro's hand in a darkened workshop, where he had discovered what it meant to love and be loved—that Florence was gone. Scattered to the winds like ash.

The Medici had fled. Lorenzo's enemies had risen, briefly, triumphantly, before being crushed in turn by forces larger than any of them. Alessandro's family had escaped to Rome, where his father still held influence with the papal court. Marco had stayed behind, painting, surviving, trying not to think about the boy with the golden hair who had seen something in him no one else had ever seen.

And now here he was. Walking toward Rome. Summoned by the Vatican itself.

It still didn't feel real.

• • •

The letter had arrived three weeks ago, carried by a messenger in papal livery. Marco had stared at the seal for a full minute before breaking it, certain there had been some mistake.

> *To the painter Marco di Benedetto, greetings.*
>
> *His Holiness requires artists of exceptional skill for a project of great importance. Your work has come to our attention.*
>
> *You are commanded to present yourself at the Vatican before the Feast of All Saints.*

Commanded. As if Marco were someone who could be commanded. As if he mattered enough to summon.

He had shown the letter to his master, the old painter who had taken him in after Alessandro left. The old man had read it twice, then looked at Marco with something like wonder.

"You're going," he said. It wasn't a question.

"I don't understand how they even know my name."

"Does it matter?" The old man pressed the letter back into Marco's hands. "Someone knows. Someone with influence. Don't waste time questioning gifts, boy. Just accept them."

So Marco had packed his small bag, said his goodbyes, and started walking.

Toward Rome. Toward whatever waited for him there.

Toward, perhaps, the only person who had ever truly believed in him.

The Vatican was overwhelming.

Marco had seen grand buildings before—the Duomo in Florence, the palaces of the wealthy merchants who had occasionally commissioned his work. But this was something else entirely. Stone and marble and gold, columns reaching toward heaven, paintings and sculptures in every corner. The weight of centuries pressed down on him as he walked through the corridors, following a silent clerk toward his audience with the cardinals.

He felt small. Insignificant. A country boy from nowhere, pretending to belong among giants.

The audience itself was a blur of crimson robes and pointed questions. Two cardinals, flanked by secretaries and assistants, examined his portfolio with expressions Marco couldn't read. They asked about his training, his techniques, his previous commissions. They spoke to each other in rapid Latin, only some of which Marco could follow.

He answered as best he could. Kept his voice steady. Tried not to let his hands shake.

When it was over, the senior cardinal gave a curt nod. "You will be informed of our decision. Quarters have been arranged for you in the adjoining apartments. You may wait there."

Wait. As if Marco had anywhere else to go.

His room was small but clean—a narrow bed, a desk, a window overlooking a courtyard. Marco set his bag on the floor and sat on the edge of the mattress, staring at nothing.

He should feel excited. Honored. Grateful. This was an opportunity most painters would kill for—a chance to work on a papal commission, to have his name associated with the greatest project of the age.

Instead, he felt hollow.

What was he doing here? He didn't belong among these people—the princes of the Church, the master artists, the men who shaped the world with their wealth and influence. He was Marco di Benedetto, a nobody from a small town, a boy who had learned to paint because it was the only thing that made sense to him.

A boy who had loved another boy, once. And lost him.

Marco lay back on the bed and closed his eyes. The ceiling was plain white plaster, unmarked by the elaborate frescoes that decorated the public halls. Tomorrow he would learn whether he had been accepted or rejected. Tomorrow his life would change, or it wouldn't.

Tonight, he was just tired.

The knock came late, when the candles had burned low and Marco was drifting somewhere between sleep and waking.

He sat up, heart pounding. Who would come to his door at this hour? Had he done something wrong? Had the cardinals changed their minds, decided to send him away?

He crossed to the door and opened it.

And there, in the flickering torchlight of the corridor, stood Alessandro.

Marco's breath stopped.

A year had changed him. His shoulders were broader now, his jaw more defined. He wore the fine clothes of a nobleman's son—velvet and silk, a gold chain around his neck. But his eyes were the same. That clear, steady gaze that had always seen straight through to Marco's soul.

"Hello, Marco," Alessandro said.

Marco couldn't speak. Couldn't move. Couldn't do anything but stare at the ghost who had suddenly become flesh.

"May I come in?"

Marco stepped aside, still mute, and Alessandro entered the small room. The door closed behind him. They stood facing each other in the candlelight, the silence stretching between them like a held breath.

"You're here," Marco finally managed.

"I'm here."

"How—I don't understand. The summons, the commission—"

"Me." Alessandro's voice was quiet. "I arranged it. My father still has influence with His Holiness. It took months—letters, favors, promises. But I finally secured enough support to bring you here."

Marco shook his head, trying to make sense of it. "But why go to such lengths? I'm nobody. I'm—"

"You're the most talented painter I've ever known." Alessandro took a step closer. "And I've missed you every day for the past year."

Marco felt something crack open in his chest. He felt his eyes burn — something he hadn't let happen in years — but something about seeing Alessandro again, about hearing those words spoken aloud, undid him completely.

"I thought I'd never see you again," Marco whispered. "After your last letter—when you said you had to flee—I waited. Months. Nothing."

"I know. I'm sorry." Alessandro's jaw tightened. "I couldn't risk writing once I started working on this plan. Too many eyes at the Vatican. Too many people who would have questioned why a Medici ally was so interested in some unknown painter from Florence. I had to be careful."

"I understand." And Marco did. He understood the danger, the secrecy, the impossible position they were both in. He had understood it from the very beginning.

But understanding didn't make the past year hurt any less.

"The project," Alessandro said, "is real. His Holiness wants a new chapel decorated—the finest artists in Italy, working together. I've been appointed to oversee it." A small smile crossed his face. "Which means I have some say in who participates."

"And you chose me."

"Of course I chose you." Alessandro reached out and took Marco's hand. "I've always chosen you. From the moment you walked into the academy with those drawings tucked under your arm, looking terrified and defiant all at once. I knew then."

"Knew what?"

"That you were the one I wanted. The only one." Alessandro's thumb traced circles on Marco's palm. "But I knew they would see what I see. What I've always seen."

"And what is that?"

"Light." Alessandro's voice was soft. "Do you remember what I wrote in my letters? About the light I see in you?"

Marco nodded. He had read those letters so many times the paper had grown soft and worn.

"It's still there," Alessandro said. "Brighter than ever. You just needed to give yourself permission to see it."

Marco looked at him—this boy, this man, who had changed his life so completely. Who had seen something in him before Marco could see it in himself. Who had reached across distance and danger to bring him here, to this moment.

"I was so afraid," Marco admitted. "Coming here. I didn't think I belonged. I thought they would see through me—see that I'm just a country boy, a nobody—"

"You are not a nobody." Alessandro's voice was fierce. "You are Marco di Benedetto. You are brilliant and talented and brave. And you are mine." He paused. "If you still want to be."

Marco answered by kissing him.

It was different from their kisses in Florence—those had been stolen, furtive, always shadowed by the fear of discovery. This kiss was slower. Deeper. They had time now. They had privacy. They had each other.

When they finally pulled apart, Marco was trembling.

"I've wanted this for so long," he said.

"So have I." Alessandro rested his forehead against Marco's. "May I stay with you tonight? Please."

Marco didn't answer with words. He simply took Alessandro's hand and led him to the narrow bed.

Later—much later—they lay tangled together in the dark.

The candles had burned out hours ago, but Marco was not asleep. He lay with his head on Alessandro's chest, listening to the steady rhythm of his heartbeat, feeling the warmth of his body, the gentle rise and fall of his breath.

Through the shuttered window, faint light filtered in from the courtyard torches. It played across the plain white ceiling, dancing and shifting, casting shadows that moved like living things.

Marco watched the patterns form and dissolve. Stories, he thought. The light was telling stories.

He thought about the journey that had brought him here. The workshop in Florence. The first time Alessandro had looked at him—really looked, as if seeing something no one else could see. The terror and the joy of realizing what he felt. The pain of separation. The long year of waiting, hoping, trying not to hope.

And now this. Alessandro's arms around him. Alessandro's breath warm against his hair. Alessandro's voice, murmuring something soft and sleepy that Marco couldn't quite hear.

It didn't matter. He didn't need to hear the words.

He already knew.

Marco had spent his entire life searching for something he couldn't name. A sense of belonging. A place to call his own. He had thought, for a long time, that it meant a physical place—a city, a workshop, a room to call his own.

But it wasn't that. It had never been that.

He remembered the day he first crossed the Arno. How young he'd been. How terrified. Just a country boy with a sheaf of drawings tucked under his arm, his mother's voice still in his ears—*Go. Your talents will find a home there. Let them.* He had stood on the bridge for what felt like hours, watching the water rush beneath him, almost turning back a dozen times.

He only knew of the academy. That was why he'd come—the only reason he'd come. A desperate hope that someone there might see something in his work, might give him a chance at a future beyond the insignificant life he'd been born into.

But he hadn't known about the rest. Hadn't known about Alessandro. Hadn't known that a boy with golden hair and steady eyes would look at his drawings and see not just talent, but *him*. Hadn't known what it meant to love, or to be loved.

He had simply walked forward into the unknown, trusting that the far bank held something worth reaching.

Now, lying in Alessandro's arms in a small room in Rome, Marco understood. The Arno had never been the destination. It was only ever the beginning. The river had carried him forward—not to a place, but to a person.

Home wasn't a place.

Home was this.

Alessandro's heartbeat beneath his ear. Alessandro's warmth against his skin. Alessandro's love, steady and certain, asking nothing in return but Marco's own heart.

Marco closed his eyes and let himself drift.

Outside, Rome waited. The cardinals and their grand plans. The chapel that would bear his brushstrokes.

But that was tomorrow.

Tonight, Marco was home.

The Oltrarno Passages

Across the Arno is the first book in **The Oltrarno Passages**, a series following the lives of Michael, Levi, Eli, Niles, Graham, and the family they've found in one another — set alongside the continuing tales of Marco and Alessandro that Graham and Simon first brought to life together.

Their stories are far from over.

About the Author

Michael Manosca first pursued a career in the arts, studying in Chicago, but storytelling has always been at the heart of his creative expression. His travels across the world have shaped his perspective, infusing his writing with the depth and nuance of the people and cultures he has encountered.

Michael writes in a deeply personal format, inspired by the relationships and experiences that shaped his upbringing. He explores the intricacies of friendship, the search for identity, and the quiet moments that define us. Through vivid characters and emotional depth, he hopes to craft stories that linger in readers' minds long after the final page.

When not writing, he can be found wandering the northern woods, exploring new cities, or enjoying a lively conversation in a tucked-away café. He currently resides along the western coast of the United States and is already working on his next story.

Also by Michael Manosca

Beyond Ties that Bind

Treffen

Bloodlines

Prism

Almost Always

Reflections at the Window

Flickering

A Language of Water

Static & Signals

The Oltrarno Passages: The Far Bank

www.ingramcontent.com/pod-product-compliance
Lightning Source LLC
LaVergne TN
LVHW010637110826
845149LV00014B/2865

* 9 7 8 1 9 6 9 9 1 5 1 3 0 *